Rejected and Loved

Rejected and Loved

From Ishmael to
Hope for the Middle East

Laurens de Wit

ISBN 9789083221908
NUR 342, 320

First edition

Rejected and Loved, translated from 'Afgewezen en Geliefd'

© Laurens de Wit, 2022
www.godlovesishmael.com

Publisher: TransConnect, the Netherlands

Cover design: Advanced Media, Veendam, the Netherlands
Translation: Jenneke Kaddis

All Scripture references are from the English Standard Version, unless otherwise marked.

Contents

After the railway crossing barriers were closed, Kerem used to tell me, 'Change the signal to green.' Following his instructions, I would reach up to the shiny handle, grab the safety catch and turn the heavy arm downward. The chain would rattle, and half a mile away the red signal arm would move into the 'safe' position. Thus, I spent many an afternoon in the railroad crossing operating room with our Turkish tenant. After living several months in our home, Kerem brought his wife and children from Turkey. Immediately, I befriended his eldest son, who was my age. I enjoyed the hospitality and warmth of this Islamic family and spent many happy hours in the house that the Dutch Railroad Company had assigned to its immigrant employee.

Years later, I moved to the Middle East and became immersed in the Arab culture. Initially I felt unsafe, but the more I became acquainted with neighbors and colleagues, the more I enjoyed their hospitality and community life. My experience, however, did not fit the image I had from the Bible. I was familiar with the story of Hagar's encounter with the Angel of the Lord in Genesis chapter 16, where the Angel had told her that the infant in her womb would be like a stubborn, wild donkey, and always quarreling with others. Didn't the Bible expositors take this to be a reference to the aggressive and wild Arab nomads in the Middle East?

One day, as I carefully re-read the story, I wondered how Hagar would have understood the message from God. To my surprise I found out that, from her perspective, God pronounced great blessings over Ishmael.

This prompted me to research the Bible regarding Ishmael and his descendants and as a result, I discovered some intriguing concepts. For instance, from a certain point the Ishmaelites are no longer mentioned, but instead Arabs appear on the scene.

An in-depth study confirmed that the term "Arabs" refers to the descendants of Ishmael, not only in the Bible, but also in other historical records. Over time, more and more peoples were grouped with them, so that today it is difficult to determine which Arabs are to be seen as true descendants of Ishmael and which are not.

While studying all the prophecies about the nations surrounding Israel, I began to see a pattern regarding the Arabs. As a result, some prophetic utterances in the Old Testament became much clearer to me. I noticed that several of these promises have not yet come true. Apparently, they are yet to be fulfilled!

I felt excited, yet hesitant, for I did not want to make arbitrary claims of things that no one had ever noticed before. Then some friends pointed me to others, such as the Lebanese scholar Tony Maalouf, who had discovered the same thing. In fact, already in 1847 a Jewish writer named Isaac Da Costa wrote a poem in which he looked forward to the fulfillment of these promises.

Would this not be an important message for the Arabs and for all who consider Ishmael's father Abraham to be their spiritual father? What would happen if the Christians were to realize that God loves the Muslims as much as He loves them? What if the Muslims discovered how important they are in God's eyes and that He still has a unique plan for them after they have put their trust in Jesus Christ? Imagine the Jews personally witnessing God's love and mercy, reaching out to the hearts of their neighbors with whom they often live in discord. Humanity might face a wonderful future. True peace could come to the Middle East. All may be able to see the loving-kindness of the all-wise God, even those who believe God doesn't care about the suffering in the world.

This led me to write down my discoveries and insights in a way that is easy to understand. I ended up with a textbook in story form, combining fact and fiction. Each chapter is marked with a balloon mentioning the Bible passage on which it is based. Thus, the reader can easily check what is Biblical and what is fictional. I also included genealogies and timelines to indicate the historical figures versus the fictitious ones. Finally, I have added some links to a website where many background articles and in-depth studies can be found on important or controversial topics.

I hope and pray that you will read this book with an open mind and encourage you to study the Bible passages as if you were reading them for the first time. Allow God to speak to you through his Word. The Holy Spirit will guide you concerning his plans for the descendants of Ishmael and the role He may have for you in the fulfillment of his plans.

I wholeheartedly agree with the words of Isaac Da Costa, who wrote, "'Will these things really be so?' you ask, and I answer, 'Maybe not exactly according to this interpretation, perhaps in a different order, maybe not separately, but simultaneously or soon after one another and flowing together. But it is also possible that many more glorious things are to be expected, than we find recorded here from the Scriptures.'"[1]

I look forward to the unfolding of God's plan with all those who claim Abraham as their patriarch through Ishmael, Arabs and Muslims alike, and how this will impact the Jews, his chosen people.

Let us love them all with God's love. May his name be glorified.

Laurens de Wit

Word of thanks

First of all, I thank God the Father in heaven for opening my eyes to his great love for the Arabs, as recorded in the Bible. He inspired me to write down all the stories in this book. When I was wondering if a textbook in story form was wise, He led me to the conclusion that I should follow his example. His book, the Bible, doesn't follow the rules of one particular literary style either.

I also want to thank all who have stood behind me in the two years that I've been working on this book. I especially thank my wife who has always encouraged me, as well as those who have been thinking along with me and sacrificed many hours of their free time proofreading and giving me feedback. I would also like to thank the Arab men and women who have patiently helped me to properly articulate the mindset of Muslims. Finally, this English edition would not have come into existence without the tireless efforts of the translator and of Bill Stowe, Alan Pashkevich, Helen Cook and other proofreaders.

I dedicate this book to all my Arab friends who have embraced me. They gave me a love and appreciation for the Arab world and culture.

I also want to dedicate this book to all those who consider themselves to be sons and daughters of Ishmael. God knows your silent pain and grief over the rejection that you experience in many ways, especially in and from the West. God has a message of hope for you: you are valuable and loved. God even has a very special plan for your life. Put your trust in the Messiah and let him use you to be a blessing for many.

Part 1

The Beginning of a Great People

About God's hand on the life of Ishmael,
the patriarch of twelve tribes
in the Middle East

"The LORD has listened to your affliction."
Genesis 16:11

Abraham's children and grandchildren

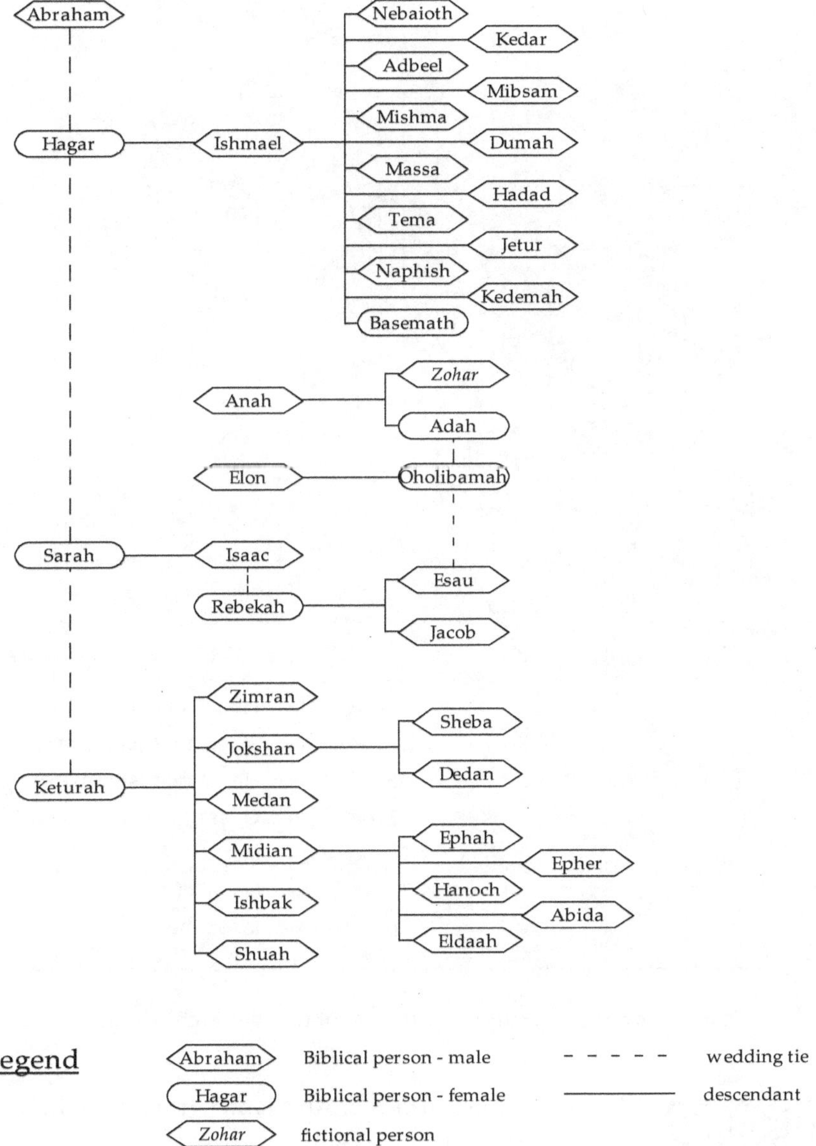

Family tree of Abraham's descendants

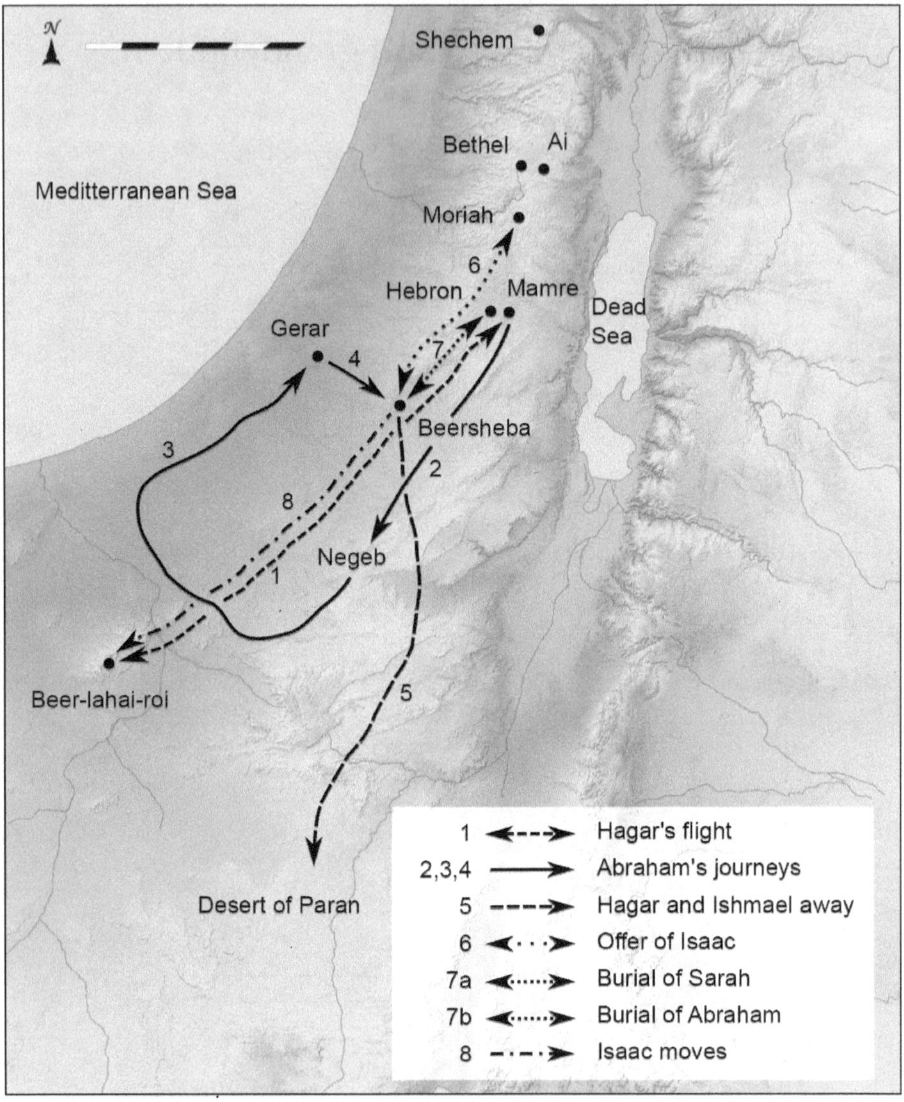

Several important locations in the life of the patriarch Abraham

For an animation clip of Abraham's travels, go to
www.godlovesishmael.com/journeys

One day, four thousand years ago...

1 The Word of God

Bare mountains rise up on every side from the desolate landscape. Their shapes are rugged, having been carved out by numerous sandstorms. Here and there, scattered bushes appear between the cracks. The valley is decorated with large boulders as well as several acacia trees. Desert dust has turned the leaves on the trees to a yellowish-brownish color, causing them to appear lifeless. Only after one of the rare rain showers do the leaves wash clean and then for a few days they look fresh and green. On days like that, rainwater gushes down the mountain slopes, quickly turning into a swirling flashflood, yet disappearing within a matter of hours. Two full moons ago, the rainy season ended and now the entire valley looks barren. The dry carcass of a gazelle emphasizes the ominous atmosphere.

Trails mark the winding road connecting Canaan to Egypt. It is tranquil. The only thing that can be heard is the soft whisper of the warm wind. High above, silhouetted against the deep blue sky, an eagle circles in search of prey. Other than that one eagle, there is no trace of life in this sweltering heat. With the sun at its zenith, both man and beast have withdrawn to the shades during this part of the day.

Yet, a solitary person appears, dressed entirely in black. The enormous shadows cast by the surrounding rock formations accentuate the woman's insignificance as she struggles through the *wadi*.* Her head bent down on her chest and her eyes downcast, she tries to protect herself from the fine dust by covering her face with her veil. She looks worn out.

Why would a woman be there, all by herself on this trade route, which is normally only frequented by men and their caravans of camels and donkeys? She's not carrying anything, not even a water skin. She has nothing but the clothes on her back. There is no one with her, no one protecting her. All alone, she plods through the barren land, on her way to…, where could she be going?

Feelings of relief compete with utter desperation in her heart. *At least I am free*, she reasons with herself; *never again will I be terrorized or beaten by my mistress. At home, my father and brothers will protect me.* Mentally she counts the days she has been walking, and she estimates it must be about four days.

---

* A *wadi* is a dry riverbed.

Besides, if my master had wanted me back, his servants would have overtaken me on their speedy camels by now.

Her stomach grumbles with hunger and she wonders whether she will be able to reach her home. Since she escaped her mistress she has hardly found anything to eat, and she still has many days to go. But at this very moment it is thirst that plagues her most; her tongue feels thick and dry. The last time she had a drink was shortly before sunrise. *I must be close to the well, but where can it be?*

One mountain resembles the next; she has been here only once before. That was years ago, when she and her master traveled from Egypt to Canaan. While she trudges on, memories from that journey overwhelm her.

What a joy that had been! Filled with a sense of wonder having been freed from the cruel master in Egypt who used to beat her and who sometimes used to withhold food from her as a punishment. She had wondered so often how she would be able to take abuse like her parents had suffered. But her new master, with his funny foreign accent, had been so different, so kind. He had never hit her; he was hardly ever angry with any of his servants. He even treated the sheep and donkeys with respect, as if they were precious to him.

In the beginning she had been homesick. She had longed for her parents and her older brothers, but soon her new master's servants came to consider her as their sister. Her master had strictly forbidden them to mistreat any of the girls. She had felt very safe there.

After many bends in the dusty road, the woman finally notices a cluster of palm trees in the distance. The luscious foliage betrays the presence of a large spring, a sanctuary in the desert where travelers stop to drink, rest, and sometimes spend the night.

Fortunately, everything is quiet. At the previous oasis where she had slept, the men had pestered her. She had been so frightened. Her master had been a kind man, but the inhabitants of this strange land are evil. She can't trust any of them. She has heard numerous stories about the dangers lurking on these roads. She is vulnerable, especially as a woman on her own. Screaming for help would have been of no use; no one knows her, and no one would have even cared. She was but an insignificant slave, a human being without value.

Suddenly she realizes something. At the last well, just as one of the men grabbed her arm, a lion appeared out of nowhere! So quickly as a flash the men left her, busying themselves protecting their donkeys against the predator. The lion saved her life!

Relief sweeps over her when she spots a basket next to the well. Even though the water is low this time of year, she is able to draw enough water to quench her thirst, as well as wash the dust off her face and hands. The cool water feels good on her hot skin. Only now does she realize how exhausted she is. Here, in the shade of the towering palms, is a good place to sit and rest a while. As she closes her eyes, she allows her thoughts to wander again.

Just a few months ago her life had been wonderful. She had been chosen to become the master's concubine. It had been the most beautiful day of her life. This was the best possible future for a slave girl like herself. If she were to have his child, and if that child were to be a son, he would inherit the master's wealth and she would cease to be a slave. Instead, she would be taken care of in her old age. Of course, she would have had to relinquish her son to her mistress, because Sarai was barren herself, but her master, the father of her son, would care for her every need. Even if her master were to die, her son would surely take care of her. What a wonderful future! Then she had become pregnant. She had been so excited that she had told everyone within hearing.

Unfortunately, along with the pregnancy, problems started. She was no longer a slave, but her mistress had thought quite differently about that. She put her to work doing the most mundane and humiliating tasks, just as if nothing had changed.

Well, she had decided that she wasn't going to take it any longer. There were plenty of other slaves to do her job; she refused to be treated like them. After all, she was now the master's wife, only second to Sarai. With this position came certain rights and she was determined to enjoy her life a bit more, just like her wealthy owners. At first, the master had defended her, but in his weakness for his first wife he had relented. "My wife Sarai is your mistress," he had stated. Since the master's word is law, Sarai could do whatever she wanted towards her.

From that day on her life was chaotic and then became out of control. So she had decided that she would return to her parents' house in Egypt. Anything was better than the daily pain of humiliation.

"Hagar," a quiet, firm voice speaks.

The woman looks up, alarmed; she had not heard anyone approach. *Who is this? How does he know my name? What does he want?* Facing her is a stranger. She doesn't recognize him; neither does she remember his voice. His dark brown eyes are friendly yet piercing. It is as if he knows exactly what she feels and thinks.

"Servant of Sarai, where have you come from?"[2]

How does he know this? Hagar is frightened and wants to run away from him, since strange men are usually not to be trusted. At the same time she is excited, as this man is different. He radiates a sense of peace, which reminds her of her master. She answers his question, and then, without hesitation, she tells him the whole story from beginning to end. She tells him about her promotion, and about the growing tension between her and Sarai. "Sarai yelled at me time and time again, 'you will do exactly as I say; you are my servant!' Every time those words hurt me deeper and deeper. I have always been a faithful servant. But now that I am expecting a baby, she still doesn't want to relieve me of the heavy household duties. And she continuously mistreats me."

As Hagar shares her painful experiences with the stranger, her muscles tense and her cheeks flush with renewed anger. "And then there was an accident," she continues, "I was tired, and the kettle was heavy; it slipped out of my hands. Boiling water splashed over the side and burned Sarai's foot."

Recounting the events of that day, Hagar realizes that it wasn't entirely by accident. Deep in her heart she had often hoped that something awful would happen to Sarai, and in her anger and frustration Hagar had handled the kettle rather roughly. "Sarai was furious! She ranted and raved, and then…"

Hagar points at her left cheek and neck. Her skin is scarlet and full of large blisters. She feels the pain of rejection again and bursts into tears. The stranger looks at her full of understanding and compassion. It is as if he bears her pain. Sobbing, Hagar blurts out, "Why did Sarai have to throw scalding water in my face? I didn't hurt her on purpose. I couldn't take it anymore, so I fled."

The man speaks again. He neither encourages her, nor passes judgment. Instead, he calmly asks her, "Where are you going, Hagar?"

"I am on my way to my parents' house in Egypt. They are the slaves of a wealthy businessman. I used to work for him as well. Perhaps he will take me back. And if not, I will find somewhere else to work."

The stranger listens attentively. When Hagar has finished speaking, he says to her, "Return to your mistress."[3]
What? Immediately, she feels disdain. *You can't be serious!* But he is serious.

"Submit to her," he continues. Just the thought of it fills her heart with terror. *Return to that horrible woman? Never!* With clenched fists and tightened lips, she endeavors to contain her rage and quickly turns her head away to avoid his confronting gaze. She would like to shout at him, "Are you out of your mind?" But his words have such authority, that she doesn't dare contradict him.

After she lets his words sink in a little, Hagar ventures a quick glance at his face. Looking into his eyes she senses an inexplicable peace, which melts the anger and bitterness in her heart. Could it be that this is the best way for her and her unborn child?

"I will surely multiply your offspring", the stranger continues, "so that they cannot be numbered for multitude."[4]

Hagar is visibly confused. *What does he mean? How can he do such a thing? Is he proposing to marry me?* Her face relaxes, but she represses a smile, not only because her burned face still hurts, but also because she doesn't want to laugh at him. *What a peculiar man*, she can't help thinking. To make sure that she is not dreaming she takes a deep breath. The fresh air, the smell of greenery and flowering plants surrounding the spring are enough to convince her. *This is not a dream! This is for real!*

Meanwhile, the man keeps talking with quiet confidence. "You are pregnant and shall bear a son."[5]

But… but how does he know that I will have a son. Wouldn't it be just as possible for me to have a daughter? Then joy overtakes her confusion. Wonderful, a son! To have a son is the greatest desire of every woman, and her firstborn will be a son! It is almost too good to be true. She would like to dance for joy. But at the same time doubt creeps into her heart. Can she trust the words of this stranger? *But he knew my name and even whose slave I was.* She continues to listen eagerly, for he isn't finished speaking yet.

"You shall name him Ishmael," he says, "because the Lord has listened to your affliction."[6]

Little by little, Hagar starts to remember the stories her master Abram used to tell; stories about his God and how He had instructed him to move to an unknown place, how he had listened, and how this God had taken care of him. She used to watch Abram build altars for this God. Back home, she had only known about the Egyptian gods. Since these were very powerful deities, she had remained faithful to them. But the words of this man sound so like the way Abram used to speak about God. This stranger speaks with the same convincing certainty and yet it all seems so impossible. After all, she is Hagar, only a worthless slave. As a child she had heard that all too often, and isn't that exactly what Sarai has been telling her lately?

Is the God of Abram interested in me then, a slave girl? Has he really heard about my suffering, about my difficulties with my mistress? This is what the stranger says. And such a beautiful name. Hagar can't imagine a more perfect name for her son. Ishmael – "God hears". Could it be possible that God has heard her silent pleas?

In the quiet of her heart she had often wished that she could meet Abram's God. Suddenly, it dawns on her. This is it! She is meeting Abram's God, face to face! At once she sees how easy it was for her to share her burdens with him. His gentle appearance exudes confidence and she feels completely safe.

The man hasn't finished yet. "He shall be a wild donkey of a man; his hand against everyone and everyone's hand against him, and he shall dwell over against all his kinsmen."[7]

In her mind Hagar pictures the wild donkeys near the water wells. She has seen them often, and even more often has she wished to be as free as they are. Abram was a wealthy man, with lots of donkeys, but they were not free to roam wherever they wanted. They had to obey their master. Hagar felt the same way, as if she was some kind of animal, who deserved a scolding or a beating when disobedient. She had tolerated more than enough of this and so had fled from the tyranny of Sarai.

This man promises that her son will be free. It would be a miracle indeed! She had hoped for just such a promise when she became Abram's concubine. But that dream had been shattered when she decided to flee, back to her parental home, where her parents were slaves, where her grandparents and all her other relatives were slaves. *A wild donkey*... freedom...* the words reverberate through her head.

As she turns to thank the man for his great encouragement, he is nowhere to be found. Hagar climbs a high rock and peers into the distance in every direction, but to no avail. He has disappeared without a trace, just like his appearance earlier, suddenly and silently.

Hagar then fully realizes who this stranger must have been. He couldn't have been a mere man. He was an appearance of God himself. Only God himself could have known who she was. Only He could have told her about her offspring. Only He could have known that she is expecting a boy.

How does God want me to respond to him? Hagar muses. Then she remembers Abram and how he communicates with God. He would often go for a walk during the twilight hours of the evening and talk out loud. It had almost looked funny to her, as if he were talking to himself, and yet it had been such a familiar sight that she had become quite used to it. Perhaps she should give it a try.

Slightly uncomfortable, yet deeply grateful she utters, "You are the God who sees me."

At that very moment, her heart overflows with gladness and the last trace of fear vanishes. The baby inside her womb stirs. Hurriedly she follows the same tracks of the dusty road she had trodden. She still can see the vague prints of her footsteps. What a change has come over her. God has seen her plight. Now all will be well.

---

* More information about the wild donkey can be found at
www.godlovesishmael.com/donkey.

2 God's Greatness Visible

The soft blue shimmer of the moon covers the mountains and changes the appearance of the brook down below into a thin silvery snake. Apart from the shrill squeaks of some bats, the only other familiar sound is the soothing crackling of nearby wood fires. Camels and sheep are sleeping peacefully near to darkly silhouetted Bedouin tents.

Only one person can't get to sleep. Abram has been tossing and turning all night, and he can't stop himself from thinking about the events of the previous day. It had started as an ordinary day. At the crack of dawn he got up from his bed for his morning stroll. When he returned for breakfast, the servants were anxiously running back and forth. He had ordered them to calm down and asked for an explanation for all the ruckus they were causing.

"Hagar is gone," they told him. "All her clothes are still in the tent, but we can't find her anywhere."

"Oh well, she will turn up sooner or later," he had responded confidently.

But when the sun was overhead and the scent of fresh baked bread for the midday meal wafted throughout the encampment, Hagar had still not returned. It wasn't until then that Abram started to worry, and he sent some of his menservants out to search the surroundings. They returned at sunset without Hagar. Sarai had then recounted in detail the incident of the day before. At that moment it dawned on Abram that Hagar must have run away and now he can't stop thinking about it.

Finally he gets up and without a sound, he goes out of the tent. He walks towards his favorite spot, a place where he can be at peace when there are too many distractions in the encampment. Trying not to disturb the silence of the early morning hours, he carefully avoids the loose rocks scattered on the way to the top of the hill. Thanks to the bright moonlight, he can see exactly where he is going and the climb is easy. As he reclines on a protruding rock, his trained eyes scan the valley below. *If only Hagar would come back. She is carrying the child of God's promise.*

While he meditates upon the time that God spoke so powerfully to him, Abram looks up and watches the twinkling stars in the cloudless sky. It had been many summers ago, but God's words have been engraved in his mind ever since. "Look up at the sky and count the stars — if indeed you can count them. So shall your offspring be."[8]

Abram had believed God. After all, hadn't God also taken him out of Ur, guided him to this foreign land, and provided for all his needs? Abram had greatly rejoiced when he found out that Hagar was with child. But now she is gone. Softly he prays, "Lord God, please bring Hagar back. I want to trust you to fulfill your promises."

Abram unwittingly begins to count the stars. As he lifts his eyes to the sky, slowly peace settles back in his heart. God is good. He will surely do as He promised; this Abram knows.

The next few days seem to drag. All kinds of thoughts take hold of Abram's mind. He should have never told Sarai that she could treat Hagar any way she pleased. Sarai might be his wife, but Hagar was carrying his child. He feels ashamed of giving in to the whims of his own wife. He, the leader of his clan, who is not afraid to fight against kings, had been afraid to displease Sarai.

It is now clear to him that Hagar has run away because of Sarai. Abram is consumed by negative thoughts. *Why would Hagar ever come back? She has been so mistreated by her mistress. The desert is a dangerous place. Perhaps some predator has killed her, or maybe one of the surrounding tribes has taken her hostage.*

Every time such thoughts enter his mind, Abram purposely focuses his attention on the God who made him that personal promise. *Hagar must come back, for He has promised that my offspring would be too numerous to count.*

In the evening, as the setting sun drapes the mountains in an orange-red hue, Abram enjoys the cool breeze, while he rests under a large tree. A young servant comes running toward him. He is yelling something, but Abram can't quite understand what it is about. It is impolite to shout at the master, also from far away, so the young man must have something of great importance to report. Slightly irritated at having to break up the conversation with some of the other men, Abram listens intently. Finally, he gets it. The boy cries that Hagar is coming!

Abram cannot quite believe it, but his heart is beating faster.

After a few minutes, a lone female figure appears around the bend. Immediately Abram gets up and walks as fast as he can to meet her. He warmly embraces her with both relief and love.

That same evening all the older servants are invited into the tent of meeting. As hot drinks are served in tiny earthenware cups, steam rises and becomes visible in the flickering light of the campfire in front of the tent. The buzz of dozens of voices is indicative of the general excitement over Hagar's return. The tent fills with people, and as soon as everyone has found a place on the ground to sit, Abram speaks. "Today is a day of celebration," he begins, "for the lost sheep has returned home."

Then he directs his attention to the woman next to him. "We are all glad that you have returned to us, Hagar."

Everyone nods with approval. "I will now give you an opportunity to share with us what has happened to you."

Hagar looks at Abram with gratitude as she gets ready to speak. Except for the rustling of some of the animals that are trying to get comfortable on the straw spread out for them, the entire place is hushed in anticipation of Hagar's story. She tells them all about her flight, how frightened she was traveling alone, about how some men had bothered her and how seemingly out of nowhere a lion had appeared to distract the villains. She continues by describing her wondrous meeting with the stranger who called her by name and who knew where she had come from.

When Abram hears her talk about the stranger, his heart skips a beat. *I remember someone who spoke just like that; where was that again? Who could that have been?*

"He told me that I would become the mother of a great nation," Hagar continues.

"Not true, I am that mother!" Sarai interrupts her sharply.

Abram glances at his wife. Calmly, yet resolutely he admonishes her to be quiet. It was her fault that Hagar had run away. Now Abram will make sure that that is not going to happen again. Sarai is clearly alarmed by her husband's reaction, and she knows that it is better to shut her mouth.

Because of Sarai's interruption, Abram has forgotten what he heard last. "Can you please say that again?" he asks Hagar.

"From this child a great nation will come," she repeats.

When Abram hears these words he realizes why this strange man had seemed so familiar to him. He talked to Hagar in the same way God had spoken to him soon after he arrived in Canaan. God had promised him just the same thing: that his offspring would become a great nation. Abram concludes that it was God himself who had spoken with Hagar as well. The Lord is going to be true to his promises after all. Almost instantaneously Abram exclaims, "Praise be to the Lord, the Lord God Almighty."

During the weeks that follow, life in the Bedouin camp returns to normal. Hagar has stopped boasting about her pregnancy. Whenever Sarai sets her to a task, she does it without complaining.

Hagar hasn't shared everything the stranger told her. If Sarai knew the whole truth, she would certainly take advantage of her. No, Sarai is not to know that the man has instructed her to obey her mistress. That part she keeps to herself.

Hagar does submit and complies obediently. In the beginning it had been so difficult. Sarai would mock her and send her on all sorts of useless and trivial errands. Hagar had to keep a stiff upper lip. But whenever she focused on those promises, she felt an inexplicable power in controlling her emotions.

Gradually, Sarai changes. Abram has reprimanded her, saying she ought to be thankful that Hagar is back and that she should be gentler. At first that was easier said than done, but Sarai tries. In time, she notices a change in Hagar. No longer does she brag about her pregnancy. As she starts to look forward to the birth of her son, Sarai decides that it is better to put the pain of the past behind her. Even if he didn't come from her own womb, this child will be her son. With his birth the stigma and shame of her barrenness will be erased.

A few months later, the birth pains announce the coming of the baby. Hagar is thrilled at the thought of holding her little one in her arms. On the one hand she is deeply convinced that it will be a boy. God had clearly said so. On the other hand, she can't help but wonder. *What if it is a girl after all? What will my master then say? Remarkable that one can be so doubtful, even after such an extraordinary encounter with God. Would others have doubts like that too?* Afraid he will label her an unbeliever, she doesn't dare tell Abram about her conflicting thoughts. Fortunately, she doesn't have to wait long for the answer.

When Abram cradles his baby boy in his arms, his face beams with joy and his eyes are filled with tears. God is so good. How many years has he been waiting for this moment? This is his first-born, his heir, and the one who will bear his name. This is the son through whom God will give many descendants. God has kept his promise. As Abram's heart overflows with gratitude, he decides to organize a grand feast to celebrate this special occasion. Besides his relatives and his servants, Abram also invites his friends in Canaan. He wants to let everyone know that God has removed the shame of being childless. While his brothers, Nahor and Haran, had had children years ago, he, Abram, servant of the Lord Most High, had remained childless. But God has reversed his fate and fulfilled his promise.

Indeed, this is not just any son. Abram remembers every detail of what Hagar had shared on the evening of her return to the camp. "He shall make me the mother of a great nation." Hagar had even come back with a name for the boy. Every word she spoke that night has been carved into his memory.

Especially what Hagar said about Ishmael's future affects Abram greatly. "Ishmael will be a wild donkey of a man."

It resonates beautifully with what God had told him, Abram, as well. "Know for certain that for four hundred years your descendants will be strangers in a country not their own and that they will be enslaved and mistreated there."[9] At that time these were disturbing words, evoking feelings of fear and sadness in Abram. His offspring will suffer immensely. Oh, he would do anything to prevent that. But God has providentially confirmed through Hagar that Ishmael will be a wild donkey of a man. Abram thinks about the herds he has seen on his journey from Ur to Canaan. Those wild beasts kept their distance from men. He had not even attempted to catch a few. It was a beautiful sight to see them roam around in freedom and some of his donkeys had become restless when they heard the wild ones' bray. Who knows, had they not been tied up so well, they might have run away to freedom too.

This is what God will give Ishmael: freedom. A time of slavery may be coming, but one day his descendants will be free.

One by one, Abram's neighbors and friends arrive at the camp to congratulate him on the birth of his son. Proudly he tells them about Hagar's meeting with the stranger. Some of them have heard the story before, but it continues to fascinate them, undoubtedly because the prediction of a son has come true.

"And then the man said to her, 'You shall name him Ishmael', so that is his name," Abram explains.

The company turns very quiet. Ishmael! What a splendid name! Abram certainly serves a peculiar god, so different from all the other gods they worship in Canaan. They bring them sacrifices, and when they ask their gods, the rains sometimes come. Sometimes the gods defeat their enemies, after the people perform rituals, but they never speak. They have never spoken at all. On the other hand, Abram's God has instructed him to come to this land. He has even told him what to name his son, a name with a beautiful meaning, "God hears."

They also remember how, with his small band of armed men, Abram had fought five powerful enemy kings to free his nephew Lot. When he had asked them to join him in battle, they had responded, "You are out of your mind, we cannot possibly fight that many armies."

Abram had responded confidently that God would be with him and give him success. In the end only three of his best friends had accompanied him, and they accomplished the impossible.

With only a few hundred men Abram defeated all five of the hostile kings and their mighty armies. What kind of god is Abram's God?

Ishmael is hardly ever sick and grows quickly. While crawling around in the tent, he finds all sorts of interesting things to put into his little mouth. His parents often laugh at his antics. It is just so cute when he has a mustache of dirt, sticking to the drool from his nose. During the first few years of his life,

Ishmael remains in Hagar's care. She nurses him and whenever needed she makes him new clothes. But as soon as Ishmael is weaned, he will sleep in Sarai's tent; after all he is legally her son. Sarai is Abram's spouse, while she, Hagar, is only a concubine.

All too soon Ishmael's third birthday arrives, which means he is ready to be weaned. Abram celebrates this first milestone in his little son's life with a feast for all his servants. Everyone is delighted to have an afternoon off, although the men in Abram's household are the ones who will enjoy the celebration party the most. The women are required to make drinks, prepare refreshments of fruit and nuts, and wash the dirty dishes afterwards.

When Ishmael turns six, playtime is over. The time has come to learn to carry responsibilities by doing his chores. Ishmael doesn't mind. On the contrary, he has looked forward to this day with great anticipation. Finally, he will be allowed to join Father when he goes to market to trade for goats or sheep. Father has even given him a few little lambs to care for. Ishmael savors his childhood. He turns out to be a healthy and studious boy, and everyone in the camp admires him.

One day, Ishmael discovers something curious about himself. "Mama, why is the color of my skin darker than yours or dad's," he asks.

"That's an amazing story, my son," Sarai answers. She has been expecting this question for some time already, and this is a good moment to talk to him about it. "You are my legitimate son, and yet I didn't bear you," she says.

As Ishmael looks at his mother with growing curiosity, she explains that Hagar gave birth to him. But before she can finish, Ishmael jumps up with a guileless "OK" and runs off to continue playing with his friends. He feels safe in Sarai's love and his curiosity has been satisfied. It is time for Ishmael and his peers to practice throwing pebbles. Every shepherd needs to be an expert stone thrower to keep the sheep from straying and, when he is older, he wants to be able to show the animals who is boss.

3 A Painful Surprise

"Ishmael!" a man calls out from a distance, his voice echoing against the mountainsides.

The tall youth turns towards the direction of the sound and shouts back, "What's going on?" Meanwhile his eyes survey the landscape for the owner of the voice.

"Your father needs you."

Now Ishmael recognizes the voice of Eliezer, his father's most trusted servant. *That's odd. Why would Father call me? We haven't been out with the sheep for very long, and it is not time for lunch yet! Did something bad happen?* Quickly, Ishmael pulls up his long tunic and tucks the pleats behind his belt. Then he runs over the rocks and loose stones to Eliezer. Breathing heavily Ishmael reaches him and asks, "What's the matter, Eliezer?"

Eliezer shrugs. "The master only said that he needs you."

Immediately, the boy runs off again. With his long, muscular legs, he jumps from rock to rock, skillfully avoiding all obstacles. As he races home, all kinds of thoughts enter his mind. *No special guests have arrived, and no accident has happened. Father said to me this morning, "See you tonight, my son." So, it is impossible that he forgot an appointment. Still, there is something serious, otherwise my father would have never sent for me. Even Eliezer doesn't know what's going on.*

A little while later Ishmael reaches the camp. Abram is waiting for him in his tent. His son removes his sandals, walks across the intricately woven rugs, and kisses his father on the forehead. "What has happened, Father?" Ishmael sounds worried. His father is ninety-nine years old; he looks pale. Something horrible must have occurred.

"Come and sit with me, my son," Abram says as he gestures invitingly. Ishmael squats next to the old man, all the while watching him carefully. When he is seated, Abram begins, "Do you remember how your mother met the Lord near the well?"

Ishmael nods heartily. He remembers it well; in fact, he knows the story by heart, every word, and every detail of it.

"You recall how I heard God's voice, while I was still living in the land of my birth?"

"Yes, of course, the Voice who told you to …"

Abram motions his son to silence. "Good", he continues, "this morning that same Voice spoke to me again."

"What did He say?" Ishmael asks expectantly. When that Voice speaks, usually something good follows; he knows that from his parents. But if it truly were that same Voice, why does Father seem so tense?

Abram clears his throat and goes on, "God has promised me once again that I will have numerous descendants."

"Father, that is wonderful. This is the third time that God has made you this promise. Surely, it will come true. Don't worry about me at all. The Lord will bless me and keep me."

Abram motions for the boy to be quiet. "The promise is different, my son." As he speaks, a tear rolls down his cheek and into his beard. Ishmael badly wants to comfort his father, but he knows he must listen first.

"God has told me that I shall be the father of more than one people. Again, He promised me that this land, where we now dwell, will belong to my descendants. Now, God wants to affirm his covenant with me in a unique way." Ishmael can't really understand his father. Why be so glum with such a glorious future? He almost voices his thoughts to Abram, but then controls himself and continues to listen.

Abram explains to him what God is asking from them to seal the covenant. Ishmael shivers when he hears about the circumcision.* As a young man he is very conscious about his manhood. He knows how sensitive that part of the body is. Not too long ago, he accidentally bruised himself right there, and he had hurt for hours.

"When will you do this, Father?" he asks. He hopes that it will be in a few days' time as tomorrow he is planning to have a camel jumping competition with some of his friends. It is a popular game, where several camels are placed next to one another. The one who can jump over the most camels is the winner. Ishmael is tall and agile. He stands a good chance of winning. It is a way for him to bring honor to his family. His father is a well-respected man in the community and he, Ishmael, wants to show that he truly is his father's son.

Once again, Abram admonishes Ishmael to be silent. "There is more; you are going to have a little brother."

"Oh, Father, that is just marvelous. I have often longed to have a brother."

Abram looks at his son and smiles. "You're a good boy; I am proud of you."

Then he becomes silent again, searching for the right words to say. He doesn't want to hurt his son, and yet he must tell him. "God has told me what to name your brother, just as He told your mother what to name you. His name will be Isaac."

---

* More information about the history can be found at
  www.godlovesishmael.com/circumcision.

Still Abram hasn't told Ishmael everything. Silently he prays, "Lord, I don't want to hurt my son. I don't want him to feel rejected. Please help me to find the right words."

Ishmael senses that his father is keeping something from him. Until now he has only told him good news. There is really nothing to be upset about. "Father, why are you distressed? Why don't you just tell me what's on your mind? I know that you love me and I love you."

Ishmael's kind words reassure Abram. "Yes, indeed, I love you very much my son. That is why it is difficult for me to share with you what God has told me. I asked him if there was any other way, but He said that it is his plan."

Ishmael eyes his father with compassion. He forces a tiny smile to show Abram that he is not worried.

"God said that Isaac … that he …" Abram hesitates. His throat is dry. He faces his son. Tears sting his big brown eyes. The lines in his forehead seem deeper than ever. Disheartened he utters, "God is making the covenant with Isaac, not with you."

Dismayed, Ishmael looks down at his feet. He had expected anything but this. This can't be true. His father must have misunderstood. He wants to scream and yell, but a young man may never raise his voice against his father. It would be shameful if he did so. Ishmael controls himself, but he is filled with worrying. *I am the firstborn; the covenant is mine. It is impossible for the covenant to be made with a younger brother. Didn't God promise my mother that I would become the father of a great nation?*

Ishmael is angry and voices his thoughts to his father. He reminds Abram of all that he remembers from his parents' previous meetings with God. Then he questions Abram, "Father, are you sure that this is from God?"

Abram feels torn inside. Hasn't he been wondering the same thing? He strives to trust God at his word. Ishmael is right. All the promises could just as easily refer to his life. Hadn't Abram prayed for the return of Hagar for just this reason? Everything had pointed to that. Yet, Abram feels a real peace; in the words that God spoke today he has recognized the voice of his Creator.

He thinks back to the time when he and Sarai had discussed the plan. "The Lord has caused me to be barren, and now that my monthly cycles have ceased, I shall never have a child," she had told him. All this time God could have given them a child. Abram had waited for a miracle for ten years, but God had not opened Sarai's womb. Apparently, God had a different plan in mind with regards to his promises.

When Sarai suggested that Abram take Hagar as a concubine to father children, it had seemed like a plausible and even a godly idea. Abram didn't need to think very long about it. He hadn't wasted any time to take Hagar as his wife. At the time it had seemed like a perfect plan. All the pieces had fitted together and God had blessed their union with a son. If this hadn't been God's intention, wouldn't He have prevented Hagar from getting pregnant? No, surely God had meant for Ishmael to be born!

Abram reaches for his son's hand and reaffirms his love for him. "Ishmael, you are and will always remain my firstborn. There is nothing in the world that can change that. I have asked God to bless you and He has promised me He will." Abram ponders whether he should tell Ishmael all that God has revealed to him. He notices his son's anxiousness for what might be coming next. He is such a fine young man; thirteen years old already. If he knows the whole story, he will probably be able to deal with this better, and hopefully not turn his back on God in his anger.

So Abram continues, "God will bless you richly. He will give you twelve sons, and each one of them will be a prince. You will become a great and mighty people."

While he speaks, he remembers the exact words the Lord spoke to him that morning. At the time he hadn't grasped the significance of those words, but now he can see it clearly. They were powerful words and a confirmation of God's love for Ishmael. "These are the words God spoke to me," Abram continues, "As for Ishmael, I have heard you; behold I have blessed him."[10]

Bewildered Ishmael looks at his father. What is he trying to say?

Abram sees the questioning in his eyes and explains what he himself has only just come to understand. "My son, do you remember what God told your mother after she had run away from home?"

Ishmael nods.

"God doesn't want to bless you just because I asked him to. Fourteen years ago He already decided to bless you." As soon as he has spoken these words, Abram is overwhelmed by a deep sense of gratitude. God deeply cares about the fate of his son. Suddenly another notion enters his mind. *The way in which God intervened when Hagar fled was not only the result of my prayers. He showed himself to Hagar as a man of flesh and blood. Never did anyone behold him so clearly. There must be a deeper meaning to all of this.* Abram can't imagine what it could possibly mean, but it spurs him on to encourage his son further. Fully convicted, Abram resumes, "God has a specific plan for your life, Ishmael, and I know He will accomplish it. I understand that you are disappointed now, but be assured that God will do as He promised. He loves you dearly."

"And what about the promise of the land?" Ishmael asks.

"I don't know, my son, but God will take care of you. He has cared for me and provided for all our needs during these twenty-five years that I have sojourned in this strange land. One way or another, God will give you what you need, and will provide a place for you to live."

Following those words, Ishmael moves closer to his father and lays his head on his shoulder. His prickly beard and warm breath are comforting to him. Though the news has been disquieting, he rests assured in his father's love.

They stay, arms round each other for a while, each engrossed in their own thoughts. Then Abram speaks again. "As I mentioned before, as part of the covenant, God has set me a task. This is the main reason I called for you straightaway." Ishmael stretches his stiff limbs as he sits up. "Every man and boy must be circumcised. We will do this tomorrow, but I wanted you to hear it from me first, before all the servants know."

Ishmael frowns. He is disappointed. First his father tells him that he will not inherit the land. Now the camel jump competition will have to be canceled, too. It seems to him that God doesn't really care about him.

Abram notices the scour on his son's face and says, "Remember this, my son, through this circumcision we become part of the covenant."

When Ishmael hears this, he is visibly relieved. He is part of the covenant after all. He still doesn't understand all of it, but the anger he feels toward God has subsided a little. God has not completely rejected him.

In the meantime the savory aroma of roasting meat seeps into the tent. Ishmael smells it and his stomach growls in response. It is lunchtime.

One by one the men enter the tent of meeting. Abram reclines on a straw filled pillow at the far end, facing the entrance. Right next to him is Eliezer, his trusted right-hand man. Steaming teacups are placed on large copper trays in the center of the tent. Every man takes a cup and finds a place along the sides. The eldest and more esteemed men are seated nearest to Abram. As the men sip from the tiny cups, there is a buzz of excitement in the air. It is uncommon to be gathered in such a way on a normal workday. Under normal circumstances the men gather here on the seventh day, but that is still two days away. Something must have happened, but nobody knows what. No guests have arrived either. All they know, is that Abram called for Ishmael quite unexpectedly, and now they are very curious to see why the master has summoned them.

Abram addresses them and tells them about God's promises. While he is still speaking, most of the men allow their thoughts to wander. They have heard all this before; no longer are they fascinated. Some of them even begin to doze off. After a delicious lunch, followed by sweet tea, they are overcome with sleepiness. The hot, stifled air that penetrates the tent is not helping them. When Abram starts to speak about his meeting with God that very morning, all are suddenly wide awake. They sit up straight and try to absorb every word. God has spoken to Abram once again! None of them has ever met with any of their gods, but apparently their master has a special gift. And when his God speaks, it is time to pay attention. Abram has reminded them often enough, why it is that he is so wealthy, why his sheep or camels are rarely stolen, and why few of them get sick and die. The God that Abram serves must be a good God. The servants are glad to serve Abram.

"Each one of you has experienced the presence of God," Abram states, "God has entered into a covenant with me and all of you reap the blessings of this covenant." The men agree. "This morning God has set a task before me as part of the covenant." As Abram explains what this entails, the group collectively shudders. To cut off a part of that very sensitive part of the body must be very painful. Would they really have to go through with this to be part of the covenant God has made with Abram? The married servants worry about something entirely different. Would they still be able to have marital relations with their wives? No one has ever heard of circumcision. They have no idea how it will affect their manhood. Perhaps they won't be able to have children anymore.

Abram had struggled with some of those same questions. "I know that some of you are fearful. Don't worry. God has promised me a son. Even after circumcision I will still be virile, able to perform." The men roar with laughter. "What's learned in the cradle, lasts till the tomb!" one of the recently married servants shouts out.

Abram joins wholeheartedly in the mirth. Then he continues, "If this is the case for me, it will be the same for you." He sounds reasonable.

Some of the men are already convinced by Abram's words and they accept the task awaiting them. Others are fearful of the pain and are still worried about the risks. One of the servants, seated close to Eliezer, bends towards him and asks him quietly what will happen if they refuse to be circumcised. Eliezer doesn't know the answer to this question and turns to Abram. "What if you don't want to be circumcised? What then?"

As Abram surveys the circle of men, he knows that many of them are pondering the same question. This is a difficult moment. How can he convince his men that God wants to show them his great love, while all they can think about is the pain and fear? He thinks back to the events in the garden of Eden. Even though this gathering is an odd assortment of slaves, servants, and relatives from various areas, each one of them knows their ancestor was Adam. Some of them have come with Abram all the way from Ur, others from as far as Haran and Egypt, and still others are from right here, from Canaan.

"A few weeks ago, on the day of rest, I told you, how God created the first man. He placed him in a beautiful garden where everything was perfect. God gave him, Adam, the choice between life and death. We all know what choice he made. Today you too have a choice. Obey God and you will live. Disobey God and you will die; you will not be a part of this covenant. I will send that person away, as he can no longer be a part of this household."

Eliezer nods approvingly. He knows Abram better than anyone else in the room and he also knows that Abram doesn't say these things to be offensive or to hurt anybody. On the contrary, he wants the very best for each of these young men. The same is true for what he has just said.

After a few more questions, Abram gives orders for the tent of the night watchmen on the outskirts of the camp to be prepared. One question is on everyone's mind. Who will go under the knife first?

A little while later, one of the servants reports that everything has been prepared. Abram gets up and gestures to his son. Ishmael reaches for his father's outstretched hand and feels the sweat on it. Hand in hand they make their way to the tent. The moment is tense for all, even for his strong and wise father.

Before Ishmael realizes what is happening, it is done. His foreskin has been removed. If his father hadn't been such a quiet rock and if he didn't love him so much, Ishmael would probably have gone and hidden. But he wanted to be brave and he repressed his fears. Now that it is over with, he does feel some pain, but it is not as bad as he thought it would be. He marvels at the warm peace in his heart, a peace that is stronger than the physical pain. *I am part of the covenant too,* he senses deeply in his soul.

After all the men in the camp have been circumcised, Abram too takes his turn. Eliezer, his most trusted servant, must do the procedure. No one knows Abram as well as Eliezer and over the years they have been through a lot together. Eliezer would prefer for someone else to do this job, but he understands why Abram chose him. After it is done, he speaks emphatically, "Master A b r a h a m, may the Lord your God bless you and make you the father of many nations."

Abraham smiles. Eliezer had paid close attention to Abraham's explanation that afternoon. "May God bless you and keep you and your offspring, Eliezer," he answers.

While Abraham is resting in his tent to recover, he tries to digest everything that has occurred. As of now, he has a new name, given to him by God himself. That name will be a continuous testimony to God's covenant with him; a covenant by which God has promised to make him the father of many nations. He will even have a son by his own precious wife Sarai, to whom God has given the beautiful name Sarah. The covenant also means that God will bless Ishmael. Although Abraham is in quite a bit of pain, he rejoices. From a grateful heart, he whispers, "Lord, You are good."

4 Wise Lessons

"Ishmael, hurry up! Don't you see it is going to rain? I don't want everything to get soaked." The boy walks over to his mother's tent. Resistance is growing inside him. Ever since she has become pregnant, her attitude towards him has changed. Before that, she used to spoil him and he could do no wrong, but now…!

Why doesn't she call one of the menservants to do her bidding? Ishmael is irritated. He knows very well that it is not appropriate for a manservant to enter the women's quarters, especially when the women are not wearing their headscarves. It is one of his father's rules in the camp. He wants to prevent the young men who work for him from being tempted by the women's beauty. That is why his father upholds a high moral standard.

Although Ishmael respects his father for doing so, he is sure that his mother is taking advantage of the situation. Why does he have to do the work of a servant, with so many slaves around? Isn't he the master's only son? Soon he will be the camp's leader. Abraham has already started to teach him how to breed livestock, how to negotiate prices, how to maintain trade relationships within the different markets, and how to determine the right price of cattle. That kind of work is his future, not the menial chores of a slave. *She is just too lazy to put on her headscarf,* Ishmael concludes. As her son, he can see his mother with her hair uncovered, which is a privilege for family members only. For anyone outside of the family, they are only allowed to see the faces of the other women.

Besides, this is not the first time that Sarah has called him to do a chore for her. He has complained about it, too, and his father promised him to speak to Sarah about it, but nothing has changed so far. It is a shame that Sarah is pulling all the strings in the camp. His father competes effortlessly with the kings of the surrounding nations. They treat him as an equal; he is a strong and well-respected man in the entire community. Yet, when it comes to Sarah, he is weak. *When I am grown up, my wife will do as I say,* Ishmael resolves. *It is utter nonsense for my mother to order me around just because she is expecting a baby.*

As he nears the tent, Ishmael kicks a rock against a copper vessel on the side of the tent. Immediately Sarah shrieks, "For crying out loud, be careful! You are always destroying things."

"No need to exaggerate," Ishmael answers, irritated. "Nothing happened. Besides, that pot is already well and truly dented." *Ridiculous, the way she fusses over everything.* Fixing his dark eyes upon her, he tells her that she doesn't need to boss him around.

Sarah responds with a fierce look.

Ishmael notices her beautiful eyes with long lashes. Those eyes used to comfort him. They spoke of love and happiness. Now they only speak of rejection and condemnation. Trying to ignore the pain, Ishmael turns away. As the first raindrops start to fall, he unties the rolled-up goat hair canvas and lets it fall, enclosing the side of the tent. When he has finished, he waits in vain for a sign of appreciation from his mother for this humble slave deed, but there is only silence.

"Father, I can't take the way Mother treats me anymore," Ishmael says in a quivering voice. He knows his father esteems her highly and he is ever so worried about criticizing her openly. His father could easily become vexed with him. But today, it was the straw that broke the camel's back and he needs to get it off his chest. Night has fallen, and all the servants have gone to their tents. Ishmael is counting on his father's attention without any interruptions.

Abraham looks compassionately at his son. "What happened, my boy?"

Ishmael recounts the events of that afternoon. When he is done, his father asks him, "Is there anything else?" Ishmael relaxes considerably as he continues to relate more and more incidents of feeling rejected by Sarah. Occasionally, he looks up at his father. The only light comes from the flickering wood fire at the entrance of the tent, and Ishmael is not able to see his father's face very well. Is he laughing at him, or does it only seem like that?

"Son, that is a lot for you to deal with," Abraham responds and then he continues, "Do you understand why this is happening?"

"Because she hates me!" Ishmael bursts out. He hadn't meant to come across so strongly, but that's the way he feels.

Abraham puts his arm around his son, and pulls him towards himself. "Let me explain something to you about women," he begins. Then he tells him that women often feel unwell and a little depressed when they are expecting, causing them to be short-fused and irritable, though they don't mean to be. "It is important for us, as men, to be patient and tolerate their rude comments; especially when they are with child," he adds. "Your birth mother went through the same thing. She even ran away from home during her pregnancy."

Ishmael has never looked at it this way. He is glad to be able to speak openly with his father about these things.

"There is something else, my son," Abraham continues. "Your mother and I have weathered a great struggle in our life." Ishmael turns his head and looks at his father questioningly. "Do you remember the time that God spoke to me about the birth of Isaac?"

"Wasn't it at the same time He told you about the circumcision?"

"Indeed," his father confirms. "When you asked me if I was certain whether this was from God or not, I made it clear to you that I was convinced. But what I didn't tell you, is what your mother and I were dealing with at that time."

Abraham peers into his son's eyes to gage how much he should tell him about the pain he and Sarah had endured. Ishmael candidly looks at his father, expectancy seen in his brown eyes. He is an open-minded young man, and Abraham decides to teach him a new life lesson.

"As you know, there comes a time in the life of an animal that it is no longer able to have offspring. The same thing goes for humans."

"Do you mean that women who had children before, will at some point in their life no longer be able to bear children?"

"That's right, my boy," Abraham smiles. He enjoys seeing Ishmael's quick insight. "For your mother it was the case when she reached a certain age too. Since God did not bless her with children when she was young, we knew then that she would never have a child of her own. This has always been deeply hurtful for your mother. Every time she visited other women, they would look down on her. Sometimes the shame was unbearable for her. Men will never truly understand what infertility means for a woman. In a sense, it is a denial of their femininity. Your mother silently bore this rejection all these years ... without becoming bitter over it."

"But Father, can't a man be infertile too?" Ishmael asks. "When we tried to mate the ewes with the spotted nose ram nothing happened. But when we mated them with a different male the ewes did conceive. "

"They did indeed; you are a smart boy!" Abraham winks at his son approvingly.
Ishmael blushes a little, clearly enjoying the compliment. "That is the reason why we finally decided that I should take Hagar, your biological mother, as my wife. After all, God had promised me many descendants. You already know what happened next."

"Yes, I was born," Ishmael laughs.

"Exactly. To me that was enough confirmation that I was a healthy man, and that it was your mother who was infertile. This was hard for her to take on board. To add insult to injury, when Hagar started to show off about her pregnancy to her ... well, perhaps you can imagine how difficult this must have been for Mother."

Ishmael has never heard this side of the story. As he listens to Abraham speaking, he feels more compassion towards his mother, Sarah. At the same time, he still feels the pain over what happened today. "Since she is now expecting a baby herself, she really shouldn't be that sad and angry anymore."

"You are right, but do you at least understand that this pregnancy is quite the miracle for Mama and me?

Ishmael nods affirmatively.

"When the Lord first told me, I laughed. I could not believe it," Abraham continues. "Only when the Lord appeared to me a second time did I know for certain that your mother would conceive."

"When was that?" Ishmael inquires.

"Do you remember when the cities of Sodom and Gomorrah were destroyed a few months ago?"

As if he could ever forget that disaster! He had been deeply moved by the enormous clouds of smoke. He had urged his father to flee. Luckily, the fire had stopped raging just in time. It probably hadn't spread because of the arid landscape they lived in.

"The day before the great fire the Lord visited us," Abraham goes on. "He told us about the destruction of those cities."

Ishmael nods again. He remembers well those three peculiar men in shining white robes. He also remembers his father explaining that one of them had spoken as if he were God himself.

"The Lord told me other things as well; things you were too young to understand," Abraham continues. "He promised that Mama would bear a son. Even she heard him say this. At first, she laughed at him, just like I did the first time I heard. Just think about what I said before."

Ishmael tries to get his brain round all this new information. Imagine an old ewe that has never been successfully mated suddenly starts lambing. That has never happened.

Abraham continues his story. "Then the Lord said to me, 'Is anything too hard for the Lord?'[11] At first Mama still doubted, but after she saw the judgment on Sodom and Gomorrah, she became convinced too. We thanked God together for his promises and we committed ourselves to trust his word, and, as you know now, his promise has been fulfilled!"

"Father, as glad as I am to hear all of this, I still don't understand why Mama is so impatient with me. Shouldn't she be filled with joy instead?"

"Mother is definitely happy about her pregnancy, but she doesn't want to show that to you. Because you are not the son of the promise, she finds it difficult to be joyful around you. She just doesn't want to emphasize her happiness in your presence. Besides that, she is concerned about this pregnancy. What if she slips and falls and …?"

Abraham stops mid-sentence with emotion. Ishmael is sensitive to his father's struggle. He has many more questions he wants to ask, but he has learned to be patient. His father doesn't keep secrets from him and, when the time is right, he will tell him. While Ishmael waits for further conversation, his eyes rest on the old man who is staring into the smoldering fire in front of the tent. His lips move as if he is speaking with someone.

"God, your name be praised," Abraham's voice suddenly resonates.

Ishmael realizes whom his father is talking to.

Abraham looks at his son and says, "We must always continue to trust God, every single day of our lives. Hold on to that, my boy, and all will be well."

5 A Sad Feast

Fortunately, things are going well, Ishmael thinks. *Could it be because of what Father explained to me? Or did Mama change perhaps? Or is God helping us?* He doesn't quite know why, but these last few weeks the relationship between his mother and him has been more relaxed. But at this very moment he is not allowed to even see her. The women's quarters are buzzing with activity as the maidservants are running to and fro. "It is almost time for Isaac to be born," Hagar informs him.

Ishmael is lost in his own thoughts. He finds it strange that she calls this baby by his name. Why wouldn't she wait until she knows whether it will be a boy or a girl? Even if it is a boy, it is normal not to name him until the eighth day, when he is circumcised according to the new covenant. While listening carefully for the first sound of a crying baby announcing the birth, Ishmael continues his musings. What is God's plan for his little brother? And what does God want from him? Didn't he also receive his name directly from God? Ishmael can't fully comprehend, but he senses something special will happen in the future.

Suddenly he hears the wail of a new-born baby. His little brother! For a moment Ishmael wishes he were a girl so that he could go into the women's tent and see his brother, but he will have to be patient.

After what seems like an eternity, Hagar comes out of the tent. "Isaac is perfect and completely healthy!' she calls out happily.

Ishmael sighs with relief and exclaims the same thing he has often heard his father say, "God be praised!"

During the first few weeks after Isaac's birth everyone is happy and excited, but when the weeks turn into months the tension between Ishmael and his mother increases again. Ishmael is not allowed to hold or cuddle his little brother as much as he would like to. Sarah is worried that something will happen to Isaac, and as a result she tries to shield him as much as possible. Ishmael is annoyed by her over protectiveness and withdraws.

To Sarah, Ishmael seems careless, and this confirms her fears. She feels misunderstood over her concerns and this weighs upon her heavily. To protect herself, she becomes more and more detached from her older son. In turn, Ishmael becomes more and more frustrated as he feels her love for him diminish. He starts to avoid Sarah and is drawn more to Hagar, his birth mother.

On Isaac's first birthday, Ishmael is reminded of the years before God had spoken about Isaac. What a difference a few years can make. He was his mother's only son, and she had pampered him constantly. While his friends had to help at home with all sorts of chores, he had always been allowed to play and do as he pleased. He was never bored, for there was always something going on in the camp. The large flocks needed a lot of care, especially during lambing and shearing seasons. Father often received important guests as he had many friends, but he also welcomed travelers and strangers into his tents for a meal or for a rest. On market days Father used to allow him to go to town with some of the menservants. They would sell some of the animals and return with fresh vegetables and other necessities. Those had been the best days of his life. Ishmael would wake up at the crack of dawn, at the same time as the menservants. When the first sunbeams peeked into the valley they left the camp, riding on donkeys. The trip through the mountains was always exciting with surprises around almost every corner. Once they reached the town, the hustle and bustle of people offering their wares for sale provided an environment of endless excitement for a young boy. The traders spread out their goods on carpets and blankets under small pieces of tent cloth that provided shade. There were stalls with bowls, jugs, baskets, and other household items, as well as a varied assortment of farming tools. Fresh vegetables and sweet juicy fruits were available at other stalls. The sweet aroma of freshly cut wood permeated from the stalls of table and crate sellers and in another part of the market, the air was heavy with the scent of cinnamon, mint, and other spices.

Every time Ishmael went to the market with the men, he was allowed one purchase for himself. He couldn't get anything expensive or dangerous, of course; nonetheless, he had gathered quite a selection of goods with which he could play the game of bartering and selling just like the grown-ups did. Finally, at the marketplace he would hear all the latest news. Even though the servants had heard these stories as well, he was given permission to recount them to his father. After lunch he, Ishmael, was the one who was invited to sit with his father and relay all that he had experienced. He always felt very special as he told his father what he had learned and done.

No, Ishmael never had a reason to be bored. And even though he wasn't obliged to do any real work, he enjoyed watching the servants, and he often tried to copy them. Sometimes they would laugh at him as he chased runaway goats. Ishmael would then try to run his fastest. He was an excellent runner on the flat paths, but the rocky mountain slopes were a different story. One time he stumbled and hit his head roughly on a rock. Blood was everywhere. Sarah insisted on taking care of him herself. None of the slave girls could touch him, not even Hagar.

As Ishmael recalls the incident, an agonizing pain grips him. At that time, his mother had been willing to do anything for him, and Hagar was but standing on the sidelines. Now it seems the roles have reversed. His mother now keeps her distance and he feels safer with Hagar.

He remembers his father's guests, and their compliments, as they remarked to Abraham, "What a clever young man. Your son will be an excellent successor." That had made him happy, but now Ishmael is confused. On the one hand, he is the firstborn son who will take his father's place when he grows up. He has learned so much and his father has started to delegate small responsibilities to him. On the other hand, God has said that his half-brother Isaac will inherit the land where they currently live and that through him all people in the world will be blessed. Amazingly, Isaac has been born, so God must have a plan with his brother indeed.

Where does that leave him, Ishmael? What is God's plan for his life? What will happen to him now that Sarah's attitude towards him has changed again? When she was expecting Isaac, her relationship with Ishmael had already changed. After Isaac's birth, things had improved for a while, but now, she treats him with increased hostility. Pregnancy can no longer be blamed. Suddenly, a thought enters his mind like a dark cloud. *Instead of treating me like a son, she treats me like a slave! Instead of seeing me as her son, she sees me as her property!* Immediately, Ishmael is consumed with anger, and he tries to think of ways to retaliate.

Then another thought enters his mind. Is he imagining things? It is as if a soft, still voice speaks in his heart, "You will not be a slave, but a free man." Those words remind him of his mother's counsel. "You will be a wild donkey of a man," she had taught him. That was God's promise, given to him before his birth. Ishmael senses an incomprehensible peace in his heart and releases his anger.

As time goes on and the rhythm of rainy and dry seasons marks the passing of years, another milestone is reached for Abraham and his family. While the sun rays reach over the mountain tops, the camp slowly comes to life and people get ready for the special day.

"Good morning," Ishmael greets his father as he enters the men's quarters, "How are you?"

"To God be the glory, my son, I am well," Abraham responds with a smile on his face.

"You are looking tired this morning; did something happen last night?"

"No, all was calm and quiet."

"Yes, but you didn't sleep well, did you?"

Abraham appreciates Ishmael's perceptiveness. The boy senses immediately when something is wrong and Abraham recognizes himself in the boy. Thanks to his own discernment he has been able to solve many a conflict throughout his life.

"I did have a restless night," Abraham confides, "I was troubled by a disturbing dream."

"Are you worried about something, Father?" Ishmael questions him. "Isn't everything ready for the feast? Perhaps I can help you with some of the final details."

"I don't know, my son. These dreams seem to come when I am facing trouble. I sense a premonition from God, like a warning. But He hasn't given me any further insight. Come on, let us go and have breakfast."

Cheerfully, Ishmael accompanies his father as they walk towards the circle of men who are already squatting on the ground. They take their places among them, right in front of the steaming dishes of fried eggs and baskets with freshly baked flatbread.

That same afternoon it happens. The feast is a great success. Everyone is in high spirits when Abraham relates for the umpteenth time the story of the three visitors, and how one them had promised that Sarah would bear a child. Even though his friends have heard it multiple times, the story of the miraculously divine meeting remains fascinating to them. The promise made to Sarah continues to impress them tremendously. It was already miraculous that both Abraham and Sarah were still very healthy in their advanced age, but Sarah's pregnancy was unmistakably the result of Divine intervention by the God Abraham worships. Imagine, a ninety-year old woman giving birth. This was unheard of, but the living proof is in their midst.

Isaac sits quietly next to his mother in the women's tent, surrounded by chattering and giggling womenfolk. They have all come to celebrate with Sarah that her son has been weaned and enters a new phase in his life. Many babies don't survive the first three vulnerable years of their lives, but Isaac has remained healthy throughout his early childhood years. That's even more remarkable since his mother, though still looking attractive, is an extremely elderly woman.

Proudly, Sarah looks around the tent as she chronicles in detail the miracle of her pregnancy, after God had promised her a son. She then explains the things He has declared concerning Isaac's future. The women are a captivated audience, but Isaac is starting to get bored and runs off on his short, chubby legs towards the entrance of the tent. Several women kiss him on the forehead. He is such a delightful little boy! "This is my husband's heir; Isaac will inherit all my husband's possessions," Sarah divulges enthusiastically, "and all the people on earth will be blessed through him."

Coincidentally, at that very moment Ishmael passes by the women's tent. He has left the company of the men to relieve himself outside the camp. Just while he walks past, he picks up Sarah's last words. Ishmael feels as if he has been stabbed in the back. *What a terrible woman*, he thinks. He can't help but linger and listen to the rest of the conversation. "What about Ishmael? What will he inherit?" he overhears one of the women ask.

"Oh, well, he is the son of a slave girl. He should be grateful if he receives a present," Sarah answers.

With that, Sarah confirms what Ishmael has felt for a long time: she doesn't care for him anymore. At the same time, he notices Isaac bouncing out of the tent. *It is all because of him that I am now unhappy.* Jealousy takes hold of him. Then he hears the women bestowing all their affection and attention upon Isaac. In a fit of rage he kicks his little brother in the stomach. Isaac falls backwards, hits his head hard on the ground and begins to scream.

Later that evening, after nightfall and when everyone is ready to go to bed, Abraham and Sarah reminisce about the day's events. They rejoice about the attention they received from their friends. Abraham shares with Sarah the wonderful opportunity he had to tell them about God's greatness. "Some of our neighbors brought friends from another region. They had heard about us and couldn't believe it. For us to be so old, and yet to be given a child, a remarkably healthy baby, without defect or handicap. They had all wanted to hear how such a wonderful thing could have happened; for they knew this was impossible without the help of the gods. Then I told them about God, the Creator of heaven and earth."

Sarah smiles at her husband. How he loves God. Sometimes she wishes she had that same kind of love, that same kind of unshakeable trust. But the world is rough and one has to stand up for oneself, otherwise things can go badly wrong. That is her conviction. That is why she has this urgent need to tell her husband something.

Sarah waits patiently until Abraham has told her everything. When he has finished talking, he turns to her. "What is wrong? How come you are so quiet after having received such an amazing day from God's hand."

Sarah swallows. In her mind she's had this conversation with her husband many times. Yet she has a hard time broaching the subject. Overcome by her emotions, she blurts out, "Abraham, my love, there is something that has been bothering me for a long time."

"Just tell me; you know I love you."

Sarah bursts out crying. She is not that sad, she's more angry than anything, and she is well aware that her husband has a weakness for her tears.

Immediately Abraham pulls her tightly in his embrace.

"Ishmael hurt Isaac again," she continues, "and it keeps getting worse."

Abraham had heard about the incident and understands that the tension between his wife and Ishmael has increased greatly. His son has always treated him courteously and respectfully, but lately Ishmael's attitude towards Isaac has changed. Abraham can understand him. His son is a teenager and pushes the limits. Besides, he now frequently leaves the camp with some of the servants and sees how the families of the surrounding peoples treat their little children. Those kids endure much more than Isaac.

Sobbing, Sarah continues, "I don't want him to seriously injure Isaac. We have to protect the son God has given us!"

Abraham fully agrees, but he also doesn't think it is such a big deal. Ishmael will outgrow this phase soon enough. On the other hand, this is not the first incident, and things are getting worse.

Through her tears, Sarah peers at her husband. She knows he is deep in thought. "We can't take the risk," she persists. "That is why there is only one way out of this. Ishmael and Hagar have to leave." Well then, she said it. Sarah feels relieved. Finally she has mustered the courage to say what she has wanted to say for a long time. She looks at her husband intently. In the pale light of the oil lamp she notices the deep wrinkles on his forehead. As his eyes meet hers, they flicker dangerously. Sarah knows that whenever Abraham faces injustice he responds with indignation.

Abraham keeps himself under control, but his voice shakes when he responds with resolve. "That will never happen! Ishmael is my first-born son, and he was the first one to be circumcised." A bit calmer, he continues, "Make sure to treat him kindly. The boy needs your love."

Sarah attempts to defend herself, but realizes all too well that her husband is determined to keep Ishmael with him. Sometimes she can charm Abraham into doing what she wants him to do, but this time it doesn't work.

A little later, Abraham blows out the oil lamp and pulls the woolen blanket over himself.

Lying in the dark, Sarah quietly asks God to change her husband's mind. Soon after that she sinks into a deep sleep.

Abraham remains wide-awake next to her. Sarah's words have greatly disturbed him. He feels stuck between a rock and a hard place. He dearly loves his older son, but he also doesn't want his younger son to get hurt. What should he do? While stretched out on his bed mat, snug under the warm covers, he reflects on the previous night's dream. Again, he is beset by the same restlessness he felt when he woke up that morning. In his heart, he cries out, "God, please intervene! Help Sarah and Ishmael, so that we may all live together in peace."

6 *Living Water*

As the darkness of the night gives way to the early dawn, Abraham turns over under his blanket. He has hardly slept. God spoke to him in the middle of the night and his words keep milling through his head. "Do what Sarah has asked you to do" and "I shall make the son of your maidservant into a great nation."

Troubling thoughts run through his mind. How can God ask him to send his son away? How can He give him a son and then take him away? Why can't God just answer his prayer? Then everything would be fine. God is not being fair. Isn't it hard enough on Ishmael that Isaac is the son of the promise and not he? Now he must be sent away as well? That is a double rejection!

After hours of wrestling with his emotions, Abraham is still angry with God. He has tried to let go of Ishmael and leave him in God's hands, but in moments like these he just can't reconcile God's character with that of a loving Father. What devoted father would send his son away? God is the chief example of care. Often Abraham has watched how the donkeys show tender loving care for their foals. Even tiny birds feed their little ones with utmost care and protect them from all possible predators. The entire creation teaches how important and beautiful it is to care for one's children. In the same way, Abraham loves his son very much. He is proud of his clever and sensitive Ishmael. He tries to ignore the thought of sending him away. However, God's voice couldn't have been any clearer.

While Abraham is still struggling, he lifts his eyes and focuses on the tent cloth above him. Some of the knots in the fabric remind him of his circumcision. He had been lying on the floor then too and had concentrated on the texture of the tent cloth to distract himself from the pain. Abraham allows his thoughts to wander to that occasion. The circumcision had been a giant leap of faith. At that time no one knew what the consequences were going to be.

However, God has clearly blessed our obedience, Abraham realizes suddenly. He hadn't lost his manhood in any way and Sarah had conceived, just as God had promised. *If God took care of us then, He will take care of us now.* It is as if Abraham received an answer to his question with this thought. Deep inside he knows that God's way is the best way, and Abraham resolves to obey God, in spite of the harrowing pain. Instantly, he gets up from his bed and wakes Ishmael to let him know what God has said.

As the first sunbeams peek over the mountaintops and light up the valley below, the maidservant and her son leave the encampment. Hagar lets her tears flow freely. She is heart-broken. Her future is in shambles. *Once a slave, always a slave,* she thinks to herself. *God had promised all these wonderful things, but nothing came of it. Everything is hopeless. Abraham has not even given us a single thing. He is so immensely rich and yet he sent us off with only a water skin and a lump of bread. He could at least have given us a donkey to ride on, or some money to build a new life elsewhere. What a self-centered man! Claiming that God himself spoke to him! Well, if his God demands such things, I don't really care anymore.* She continues down the road in anger. Going where? It doesn't really matter anymore. Deep inside she wishes to die. What a miserable life! However, the footsteps behind her remind her of her son. He still needs her.

Hagar feels conflicted. Her mother's heart wants to give her son the best future, but her sense of justice tells her that he is the cause of her misery. If only he had behaved better, this all could have been prevented. They would have had a good life with Abraham. To be quite honest, she had not at all expected that her master would have resorted to this. Sending your own son away - what sort of father has ever done such a thing? "Abraham is nothing but a hypocrite!" Hagar exclaims to her son, "While he claims that he loves you and that it hurts him to send you away, he bans you from his presence at the same time. He doesn't practice what he preaches!"

Ishmael shares in the pain his mother experiences in her heart. His eyes burn in grief. He wants to be strong and not cry, and he tries hard to hold back his tears. *I should have never kicked Isaac. Then we wouldn't be in this situation now. How foolish of me not to exert more self-control. But Sarah was so mean-spirited. Anyone would have reacted the same way I did.* Only then do Hagar's words sink in. *His father a hypocrite? How does she come to that conclusion?* Ishmael doesn't really understand either why his father has sent him away, but he holds on to the positive image of his dad. "Mum, father truly loves me, I'm sure about that. He will regret what he has done and then he will send his servants after us to bring us back."

"Do you really think so? Of course not!" Hagar replies sharply. "As you know, I ran away when I was expecting you. When I returned, he told me that he had sent out men to search for me. Well, if that were really true, they would surely have found me." As Hagar speaks, she realizes that she is not entirely honest. For the first two days, she had purposely avoided the main road and had tramped across the mountain paths. The menservants had told her later how much time they had spent looking for her and she had been pleased to hear that.

While Hagar thinks about that, the meeting with that extraordinary man comes back to mind. At the well, God had given her such precious promises. Ishmael was supposed to become a great nation and a free man, enjoying his freedom just like the wild donkeys all around them. Ishmael's birth heralded blissful years during which Sarah finally treated her kindly. Even though she had remained a servant, her workload had been lightened and she was allowed to nurse Ishmael. She had been so thankful that God had spoken to her and really glad that she had obeyed his voice and returned to her mistress.

"Mama," Ishmael breaks the silence, "How is it possible that God first promised you that I will become a great nation and then to reject us? Did I lose that promise because of my jealousy of Isaac?"

"I don't know, Ishmael. It is a mystery to me as well. Can you believe what Abraham said to me this morning? According to him, last night God promised him again that He would make you into a great nation." Doubt resonates in her voice. She doesn't trust Abraham anymore. How could he just send them away like that? And since God commanded him to do so, she no longer trusts God either. She feels abandoned by both of them and decides that from now on she will take her destiny into her own hands. "Ishmael, forget about your father's God," she goes on. "It makes no sense to serve this God; He does as He wills. One day He loves you, the next day He rejects you."

Ishmael doesn't agree with his mother, but he wisely keeps his mouth shut. It would not do any good to contradict her just now.

Together they head south, every step taking them further away from all they have known and trusted. With the sun at its peak, Ishmael's stomach starts to rumble. At the top of a hill he notices a wild fig tree and he suggests, "Mama, I will pick us some fruit; it will be more nourishing than just bread."

"That's a good idea, my son; let me help you," she answers as she clambers up the steep incline behind him. The tree is heavy with rich red-purple figs. Birds have obviously already feasted on some of the fruits. Soon Hagar and her son enjoy the delicious bounty as well. Without giving it much thought, Ishmael continues to eat, and when all the ripe figs are gone, he picks the unripe ones. Hagar watches him, and warns, "Watch out, those white ones can make you sick."

"Oh, Mama, who knows when we shall find something else to eat? I am just so hungry."

Hagar knows this will easily turn into a senseless discussion and she lets him be. In the end, Ishmael has eaten so much that his stomach starts to hurt. This is a clear sign for him to stop.

After drinking some water and resting a bit, they continue down the road southwards. A few hours later, Ishmael's stomach hurts even more. All of a sudden, he feels the urge to relieve himself. Pulling up his long tunic he quickly squats behind a large rock. Then he carefully cleans himself with a small stone, but there is no relief. The cramps increase in severity and soon Ishmael has a serious case of diarrhea. He continues to walk with great difficulty. Meanwhile the sun has disappeared behind the mountains and it will soon be dark. Together they try to find shelter for the night.

Ishmael's throat is parched. He picks up the water skin and opens it. "Be careful not to drink much," says Hagar, "that is all we have. We don't know when we shall find another well."

"But Mama, I have to drink, otherwise I will get worse," Ishmael defends himself.

"What if we run out of water? Then I won't be able to go on, and then I won't be able to care for you either." Hagar responds worriedly.

"Don't worry. God will take care of us. He promised," Ishmael retorts confidently while taking a few swigs.

"How conceited you are; just like your father. You do just what you want to do and then say that God will take care of everything."

Ishmael is annoyed. Why is his mother always so negative? "You told me yourself that my name was to be Ishmael. It still means, 'God hears', whether you believe that or not."

Hagar had not thought about that for a while. "That's true," she reluctantly admits, but then adds, "Still, we have to do our utmost; otherwise God is not obliged to do anything for us. I even had to return to Sarah while she was still mistreating me."

Ishmael doesn't feel like contradicting his mother; he is too exhausted and too sick. A little while later, they both fall asleep under the stars.

The next morning Hagar and her son continue on their journey. Ishmael had not had a good night. The dysentery kept him up a lot of the time and the abdominal cramps continue to plague him. His skin feels hot with fever. He hobbles behind his mother as she searches for a well. There is not a drop of water left in the skin with which to alleviate his burning thirst. Finally, Ishmael can no longer put one foot in front of the other and he collapses.

Hagar looks back. "Ishmael, please, don't give up," she begs. Ishmael doesn't reply. He moans softly. Hagar is frightened. What can she do now? "Help! Help!" she cries. Her voice echoes a few times between the barren rocks and then fades away into a dead silence. No answer. After a while, Hagar gives up. It is useless to keep calling for help. They are all alone in the desert. Panic sets in. She has just enough strength to help Ishmael out of the sun. She bends down next to him, wraps his limp arm around her shoulders, and carefully drags him underneath a large bush where she lays him down in the shade.

Ishmael's whimpering becomes fainter. He seems to be saying something from time to time, but Hagar isn't sure. She thinks she can discern some words such as 'God', and 'father', and 'promised'. His face is so pale and he seems to be delirious.

Hagar fears the worst. Her eyes brim with tears as she realizes that her son is dying. She doesn't want to endure this trial up close. "Poor boy, why should your life end like this?" she whispers as she plants a farewell kiss on his forehead. Weeping she walks away and sits down at a little distance, waiting for the moaning to stop forever. *I should have stopped him from eating the unripe figs. No, it's Abraham's fault. He sent us away! But that was because of Sarah, that malicious woman! But no, it is really all God's fault. If only Isaac hadn't been born…*

Suddenly Hagar hears a voice. Someone is calling her name. The voice sounds familiar. Bewildered, Hagar looks around but sees no one. "What is troubling you?" the same voice resounds. The sound seems to come from above, but the desert is flat here. Only in the distance can one discern the outlines of the mountains through a haze of dust. Hagar lifts her gaze and notices a cloud straight above her. The cloud seems to be whiter and more radiant than any other cloud in the sky. *I have heard that voice before.* At once she remembers. It is the voice of the stranger at the well who told her she would bear a son. *But where is he now? Has he hidden himself behind the cloud?*

"Lord, there is no water and Ishmael is dying", she answers. "I am at the end of my rope. It is all over."

The voice Hagar heard so many years ago reverberates powerfully and convincingly from heaven. "Fear not for God has heard the voice of the boy where he is."[12]

Hagar is reminded of the beautiful meaning of Ishmael's name. It is true: God hears. Even when she couldn't understand Ishmael's soft moaning, God had heard him. The voice continues, "Up! Lift up the boy, and hold him fast with your hand, for I will make him into a great nation."[13] At those words, hope fills Hagar's heart. *God has not deserted me after all.* Almost immediately she is again gripped by fear and doubt. *What difference does it make now? Why give the boy false hope? There is no water anywhere around here and neither are there any rain clouds.* Her thoughts waver between hope and despair, between trust and distrust.

Hagar feels the weariness of her body and her parched mouth and cracked lips remind her of her own thirst. If they both die, their suffering will end. On the other hand, God has promised her a wonderful future, with the honor of becoming the mother of an entire people. Her soul struggles bitterly within her. In the end she decides to give God a chance. "I don't know how this will ever come true, but I want to trust you. I want to trust that you will keep your promises, even though it doesn't make sense to me," she prays silently.

Again she places her son's arm over her shoulder and carefully lifts him up. As she straightens up she notices a hole in the ground. *It looks like a well!* She lies Ishmael down on the ground and quickly runs towards it. When she peers down, she can hardly believe her eyes. It is indeed a spring with clear, fresh water. How could she not have seen it earlier? The well is not deep at all and she easily scoops up the water with her cupped hands. She quickly tries a few sips. Oh, how deliciously refreshing, not at all brackish or bitter. She can't recall a time when she has tasted sweeter water.

Within minutes Hagar has filled the water skin and she returns to Ishmael. As he tastes the refreshing liquid, he opens his eyes and smiles at his mother. It is as if he says, "You see, Mama, God really does hear and He keeps his promises."

7 Immanuel - God with them

Ishmael recovers remarkably quickly and the very next day he and Hagar continue on their journey. "Where are we going, Mama?" Ishmael wants to know.

Hagar is taken aback by the question. At first, she had been taken up with the thoughts of having been sent away from Abraham. After that terrible rejection, she never wanted to see him again; neither does she want to be reminded of him. That is why she wants to stay as far away from his shepherds as possible. She explains her plans to her young son.

When his mother finishes talking, Ishmael asks, "Would they really come all this way into the desert?"

"No, I don't think so; we don't need to go much further," she answers. *How wonderful that Ishmael is such a mature young man*, she thinks to herself. "What do you think we should do next?"

"Well, the water from this well is very sweet. If we can find food, we can stay here for a long time."

'That's true," Hagar agrees. "You know what, let's search the surroundings for fruit trees."

"Perhaps I can catch a hare, or a wild donkey," Ishmael adds.

Hagar bursts into laughter.

"What? Did I say something wrong?"

"Not at all, but when you mentioned the wild donkey, it made me think of what God said about you, my son."

Ishmael laughs too. After the encounter with God, who spoke to them from the air, they both feel more at ease. God has proven that He has not rejected them. He even answered Ishmael's simple prayer when he was delirious with fever. The knowledge that God sees and hears everything fills them with hope for the future.

One day, Ishmael rushes towards the tent. "Look at what I caught today, Mama!" he exclaims with excitement. Breathless he shows his mother the splendid catch.

"Great! That is amazing!" Hagar exclaims. "You are an excellent hunter!" Filled with pride, Ishmael basks in the approval of his mother. He is happy to see her respond so positively.

These past few months in the desert, they have had to work hard to carve out an existence from nothing. Fortunately, Ishmael had learned a lot from his father about the wildlife. Recognizing their tracks in the sand, he could easily see which animals had frequented the spot and in what direction he would be able to find them. From the dryness of the animal droppings, he could tell when the animals had been there and how far they would have gone. From the gnawed tree branches and shrubs, he could pick up whether they were adult animals or young.

After a while, he had finally gathered enough animal skins for his mother to make a tent. This was a welcome shelter from the scorching day-time sun as well as a protection from the cold desert nights. Together they had made all sorts of wooden utensils and the area around the well was beginning to look like a little encampment. Additionally, Ishmael had made bows and arrows. When he thinks back to the first set he ever made, he laughs. Compared to the bow and arrow he has now, that first one was child's play. And the difference in results is obvious. For the first time in his life he shot a gazelle. Because they are so skittish, you must shoot them from a great distance, and because they are such fast runners, they are gone before you know it. *But today my arrow was faster*, Ishmael muses with a smile on his face. With his mother's help, he constructs a tripod from long slender branches. To hang the lifeless animal from its hind legs. A little while later, the meat is roasting on a stick above the fire. As Hagar turns the spit, she remarks, "You know, it is really amazing how you have learned to hunt so rapidly. I have seen many boys grow up, in Egypt as well as in Canaan, but I never saw anyone learn to hunt as fast as you have."

"Well, I do think my catch was pretty significant today. But isn't it normal to improve over time?"

"That's true, but as fast as you have learned ..." Hagar doesn't finish her sentence because she thinks of God's promise to her. Ishmael will become a great nation. "I think God must be helping you," she concludes.

"That's quite possible. I regularly ask him to help me," Ishmael responds shyly.

"Well, my boy, He does. May his name be praised!"

Months turn into years. Hagar and Ishmael have moved to another region. One year there had hardly been any rainfall. The trees had stopped bearing fruit and the animals had moved away. In order to find enough food to survive they had decided to go to another area and have ended up in the wilderness of Paran on the east side of the Red Sea.

Ishmael is now a grown man and his mother thinks it is about time for him to get married.

"Well, Mama, I don't want a wife from the tribes where we live; they don't care either about God or his commandments. I want to stay faithful to God."

"I understand, my boy, but where are we going to find you a bride? Your father's relatives live too far away. It is impossible for us to go there. Besides, I doubt that any of your father's brothers would give you a daughter as a bride after your father sent you away."

"I would also be happy with a girl born in my father's household. She would know what it means to worship the God of heaven and earth and she would encourage me to stay faithful to him even through the difficult times."

"I understand that that's important to you, but then you would be marrying a slave-girl and that would mean you voluntarily tie yourself to the world of slaves. I am just so glad that you've got a different future ahead of you now." As Hagar speaks these words, she suddenly realizes something that has been in her thoughts before, but only now does reality set in. She exclaims, "Ishmael, you are truly free, and so am I! When Abraham sent us away, he set us free. This is amazing! Never before have I understood it in this way!" Hagar's face radiates.

"God be praised. It really wasn't such a bad thing then that he sent us away without any gift", Ishmael adds enthusiastically, "He could have sold you instead, but he didn't do that." When Ishmael utters these words, a lump rises in his throat, and he has to swallow a few times. He has always believed that his father was a good man, even though his mother had been right about the fact that he had not asked them to return to him. It was as if he had completely forgotten about them, but the words he had spoken at their farewell had been sincere. "I love you, my son, and will always love you. Remember that," he had said.

Ishmael treasures those words in his heart like a promise, and whenever he experiences rejection, he recalls them. In the meantime, the painful memories from the past no longer haunt him. When he was dying, it was God himself who rescued him and this has left a deep impression on him. Afterwards many other wondrous things had occurred, and as a result Ishmael feels safe and at peace.

"… in Egypt. What do you think about that?" Ishmael is brought back from his thoughts. "I'm sorry, what did you just say? I was thinking of something else."

Hagar repeats her idea. "I still have relatives who could help me. Surely, I would be able to find you a proper wife in Egypt. What do you think?"

Ishmael finds it a difficult subject to talk about. "Aren't all your relatives slaves as well? What good would that be to me?" he asks his mother.

Hagar eyes him mournfully. She would love for him to have a sweet and pretty wife, and she herself is not getting any younger. One day, she will no longer be able to cook, clean, and do all the other chores around the camp on her own. "I have an idea!" she exclaims suddenly. "You have already amassed quite a collection of skins. If you sell them, you will have enough money for a dowry for the daughter of a slave owner."

Ishmael's eyes light up. He hadn't thought of that before. Besides, an Egyptian woman would fit well. His mother had been born and raised in Egypt and he is half Egyptian, after all. Excitedly they plan for Hagar to travel to her homeland. Ishmael stays behind to take care of their chickens and two goats.

After a few months, Hagar returns with a sweet girl. With her strong build she is well suited for the Bedouin way of life. After the wedding ceremony, Ishmael thanks his mother for finding him a bride. He is surprised at how quickly his wife adapts to life in the desert. His mother clearly picked the right woman for him.

Hagar hides her son's words in her heart and for the first time in many years she feels completely at peace. Life in the desert is not easy, and she must work very hard. Yet, they experience a measure of prosperity. "Ishmael," she whispers as she looks deep and long into his eyes, "I believe God's bless ing to Abraham is upon us."

"Of course, Mama," comes the confident response, "don't you remember what Father asked God when He promised him another son?"

Hagar makes a clicking sound in the back of her throat, indicating she doesn't know what he means and gives him a puzzled look.

"God told Father, 'Behold, I have blessed him.'[14] So my entire life, ever since I was born, I have been blessed by God," Ishmael explains. He has hardly finished speaking, before something else occurs to him. "No doubt this is why I didn't die, when you thought I would, when I was so sick." Suddenly, it dawns on him that all these years in the desert God has protected him too. Since then he hadn't been really ill, nor had he been attacked by a lion, while others had been mauled or even killed by predators. Several situations throughout his life come to mind in which he now clearly sees God's hand of protection. Tears well up in his eyes. "God is with us, Mama. He loves us." He tries hard to hold back the tears, but Hagar sees them and she cries too. She still has a lot of unanswered questions, but she also must admit that God is truly with them.

Whenever Ishmael goes to the market to trade goods for grain and other necessities, he meets traveling merchants. Sometimes they have news about his father.

This is how he found out that his father had moved to the same area where he and Hagar had first lived. That's where his father had quarreled with Abimelech, King of the Philistines. Ishmael was very surprised when he heard about it. He couldn't remember any time that his father had been at odds with anyone. He had always been such a humble and generous person. Once, there had been much tension between the shepherds of Father's flocks and those of his older nephew, Lot. His father had been remarkably generous. As Lot's uncle, Abraham had every right to choose first, but he had left the decision to his nephew, who had proceeded to take the better piece of land for himself. If only Ishmael had been in charge, then surely things would have ended differently. Fortunately, it seems that his father was able to resolve the conflict with the Philistine king wisely as well. By giving Abimelech a sizable gift, he had gained favor with him, and they had made a treaty. Ishmael thinks his father has been rather generous by giving him seven valuable lambs, in addition to all the sheep, goats, and cows. *I, his firstborn son, did not receive anything, while he just spoiled that foreign king.* Ishmael realizes that his father is a foreigner, living in the land of the Philistines by the grace of their king. Still, at times like this he feels the wound of rejection raw in his heart. He then quickly reasons that at least his mother is no longer a slave, but a free woman.

Sometime later, Ishmael picks up a very strange story. Rumor has it that his father had wanted to kill Isaac. "He did it in obedience to God," it was said. Ishmael doesn't understand it at all. It seems that God had later stopped his father from doing it and that's a good thing, too, since Ishmael secretly hopes to meet his half-brother one day. He then decides that when Isaac's parents have passed away, he will visit him and ask him what exactly happened.

Nine months after the wedding there is cause for celebration. Ishmael's wife delivers a beautiful strong baby and it's even a boy!

Ishmael understands that this too is a blessing from God. He thinks back to the conversations he used to have with his father in front of the tent after sunset. It had been repeated often. "You will father twelve princes, my son, this is what God has promised me. The Lord will bless you richly. Be assured that He loves you." Ishmael knows these words by heart and now experiences the fulfillment of them. His first prince has been born.

When Ishmael thinks about a name, his mother suggests, "Why not Terah, after your grandfather?'

"That is a beautiful name, Mama, but I would rather honor God and thank him for his blessings."

"Then why don't you call him Noah. It means 'rest', and God has now given you rest."

"That's a great name as well, but I also want to express something of the promise given to me by God. Something that points to the numerous descendants he spoke about."

Ishmael looks at his mother and notices she is in deep thought. Then she shakes her head. She can't think of any name that adequately reflects that thought.

"I know!" Ishmael suddenly exclaims. "I will call him Nebaioth; 'fruitfulness' articulates exactly what I want to say." Ishmael first looks at his mother and then at his wife.

All the time she has been quietly listening to their conversation. She understands that the bond between mother and son is stronger than between a wife and her husband.

Both nod approvingly. Hagar thinks quietly to herself, *Sarah can't do any better than this, with her only son. She may laugh because she received a child at an advanced age, but the promise of the twelve tribes is for Ishmael. Nebaioth is proof that Ishmael is the fertile one.*

When the new-born baby is eight days old, Ishmael does what he has seen his father do to the sons of the servants in his household. With a razor-sharp stone he carefully cuts away Nebaioth's foreskin. He wants his children to remain part of God's covenant with his father. This will always remind them that their Creator will continue to be with them as He has been with him.

8 Reconciliation between Patriarchs

Dust clouds rising in the distance announce a visitor. A man riding a camel approaches the camp. His clothes as well as the way he rides the animal, betray that he is from a different tribe. As he peers at this stranger, Ishmael tries to guess where he might be from but he just can't place him. Somewhat hesitatingly, the man follows the path to the watering hole in front of the encampment. Even before he reaches the well, Ishmael sends his youngest son to welcome him. Enthusiastically, Kedemah runs barefoot towards the visitor. After greeting him, he runs back to his father just as fast and calls out, panting, "Daddy, I can't understand him."

"Ok my son, let me go and see what he wants." Ishmael gets up and goes out of the tent. Meanwhile, the man has dismounted and is now watering his camel. As Ishmael approaches him, he is startled. The man looks so familiar. He looks like Eliezer! What a surprise! But what does he want? An old wound opens as pains of his father's rejection resurface. The scene springs back into his mind. After saying farewell, his father had immediately turned around and walked away. Ishmael's last memory of him was his back and the long white strands of hair fluttering in the wind. He hadn't waved or walked along for a short distance, as he always did with visitors. No, Abraham hadn't shown any respect during their parting. Eliezer had waved goodbye and called after him, "Go in peace!" Not his father. No, he had completely dismissed and rejected him. Ishmael feels a lump in his throat, but he controls himself. He doesn't want to show his emotions; it would be a sign of weakness. After all, he is a strong desert dweller now and has a large household for himself. With his twelve sons, not to mention all the sheep, donkeys, and camels, he has become a respectable man.

As the guest approaches him, Ishmael is sure. This is indeed Eliezer! The callous on his forehead gives away his frequent bowing and touching the ground with his face. He has learned this from Abraham, who often humbles himself in front of his Creator and kneels to the ground to worship him.

Eliezer greets him and says, "Peace be with you."

"Peace be with you, too. Welcome to my humble home," Ishmael replies, while shaking his hand. He pretends not to recognize Eliezer.

Eliezer hesitates for a moment but then he says, "I bring you greetings from my master, Abraham."

At the sound of his father's name, Ishmael blinks a few times to hide the pain. Should he pretend to be someone else or should he confirm to Eliezer that he is in fact, Ishmael? Eliezer's wrinkled face looks so kind and friendly. Ishmael remembers how he used to play tricks on him. Eliezer had put up with a lot when he was a young boy. Sometimes his father's head servant had even been the target of his mischief, but Eliezer had never really got angry with him. He truly was a kind man. The realization that he can't really blame Eliezer for anything breaks the ice between them. He puts his left hand on Eliezer's shoulder and kisses him on both cheeks.

The old man's eyes fill with tears as he draws Ishmael into a tight embrace. After Eliezer has dried his eyes with his dusty headscarf, he turns to the boy next to Ishmael and shakes his hand as well.

"This is my youngest son, Kedemah," Ishmael explains.

Eliezer looks at him wonderingly and asks, "How many sons do you have?"

"God has blessed me with twelve sons."

"Praise be to God, to him be all honor!" Eliezer proclaims. "He is faithful to those who serve him. Do you remember what God promised your father?"

Ishmael remembers that very well and confirms that God indeed has been true to his promises. As the conversation proceeds, Ishmael begins to relax and enjoy the visit of his old friend.

In the evening, after sunset, when the stars adorn the heavens, Eliezer knows the moment has come to reveal the purpose of his visit. He reclines by the campfire with Ishmael, his sons, and his mother, Hagar. Because Eliezer speaks in a different dialect, Ishmael occasionally explains to his sons what he is saying. They have already learned from their grandmother that their guest is originally from far away Damascus and that he has worked many years for their grandfather. They can't get enough of the fascinating stories about their ancestors. Their father hardly ever talks about his past. He has taught them about the God their grandfather worships but rarely about their grandfather himself.

Eliezer tells the family about Sarah's death and about the land Abraham purchased from the Hittites. In detail, he relays how God led him to the right wife for Isaac.

Ishmael nods. He understands God's hand in these events. Then there is a silence.

Eliezer looks Ishmael in the eyes and silently asks God for wisdom. Then he says, "Your father misses you."

Ishmael's heart skips a beat. He can barely contain himself.

Eliezer notices the tension in his face. "He sent me to you to tell you that," he continues.

Ishmael can't believe it. *My father rejected me so long ago. And now all of a sudden he misses me? Must be because Sarah has passed away. Now he is sad and needs me to comfort him. Well, that's never going to happen. He should have come to me himself.* Ishmael glances at his mother and the hardened look in her eyes confirms his own feelings. "That's too bad for him," Ishmael replies. His words sound cold compared to Eliezer's gentle voice.

He was prepared for this answer and continues, "Your father is sorry for the hurt he gave you." Then he turns to Hagar and says, "He also apologizes to you for the way he treated you both."

"Well, if he is that sorry, why didn't he come himself?" Ishmael retorts sharply. "When we said 'goodbye' he didn't even wave at me. He treats all his guests with the utmost respect but he chased us away like a pack of wild dogs."

Eliezer remains calm. "I know how you feel, Ishmael," he says. "You feel forsaken and rejected by your father. To be sent away like that must have been extremely painful. I was surprised myself at the time, but the fact that he didn't wave at you had nothing to do with you but rather it was the heart-wrenching pain he felt at having to bid you farewell. Don't you remember how he personally, placed the water jug on your mother's shoulder, instead of getting one of the servants to do it? In doing so he was paying you respect. I am sure your father wanted the best for you. He often prayed for you and I could see how much he missed you."

"Well, he could have sent us word before this. We are only a four-day journey away from him!" Ishmael lashes out.

"Ishmael, your father did not act on his own volition. He sought to do the will of the Creator. I can't fully understand it but I can see that God guides him. Do you know that, before you were born, I was going to inherit everything from your father?

Ishmael looks at him puzzled. He doesn't quite understand. "So, he rejected you too?"

"No," Eliezer replies, "I have not been rejected. At first, I thought I might have been but later I realized God has a plan that I can't fathom." Eliezer notices that Ishmael begins to relax and he continues, "Even Isaac felt rejected at times. At one point your father was going to sacrifice him. Your father was fully convinced that God was asking him to do this."

"Yes, I heard about that," Ishmael replies with a look of disdain. "Such a bizarre story. I could hardly believe it. So it really happened?"

"Yes, but your father sincerely believed that God would raise Isaac from the dead." Before he continues, Eliezer allows some time for his words to sink in. Then he says, "Now he hopes to see you again, too."

"What does Isaac think about nearly being slaughtered?" Ishmael asks, carefully avoiding a direct answer to Eliezer's invitation.

"Isaac has matured and his trust in your father has grown. Even his faith in God has deepened through that experience. I am starting to see similar faith in him as your father," Eliezer explains. "As a matter of fact, not only your father, but also Isaac would like to meet you. You are his only brother and, except for the stories he has heard about you, he has no memories of you."

Those words touch Ishmael deeply: his own brother wants to see him. "It is late now and time to go rest," he decides. "I will let you know in the morning if I will go with you to meet Abraham."

That night Ishmael dreams peacefully. It is the gentle push that helps him make his decision.

Meanwhile, Abraham eagerly awaits Eliezer's return. Every afternoon he reclines under the large tamarisk tree that he planted on the edge of the camp. From there he gazes across the sloping landscape with his experienced eye. Now that Sarah is gone, he feels free to meet his firstborn son again. When he had discussed the idea with Isaac, he had agreed enthusiastically. That meant that there was no longer any reason not to invite Ishmael.

Finally Abraham sees his servant appear in the distance. Eliezer is still far off but Abraham recognizes him from the way he rides his camel. His heart starts to beat faster. Eliezer is not alone! Immediately Abraham gets up and as fast as his old legs can carry him, he rushes towards the approaching party. When Ishmael sees the old man running at them, tears well up in his eyes.

Nebaioth, who is riding next to him, is embarrassed. His father had always impressed upon him and his brothers never to cry in public, as that is a sign of weakness. He is very proud of his father who has built a life for himself and his family out of nothing. How can he then care so much about this elderly man who abandoned him when he was still a boy?

But Ishmael's heart has melted and he skillfully makes his camel kneel down quickly. Father and son embrace each other straightaway and both weep. After wiping away his tears, Abraham greets the young man next to Ishmael. "Nebaioth, this is your grandfather, Abraham," Ishmael explains needlessly.

Nebaioth politely shakes his grandfather's hand, but that is not good enough for Abraham. The old man pulls his grandson into his arms and hugs him tightly. On the one hand Nebaioth is upset about the past, but on the other hand he experiences a warmth and peace from his grandfather such as he has never felt before. Together they walk to the camp and sit down in the shade of the large tamarisk tree.

As the daylight slowly retracts from the valley and the grounds and tents are enveloped in the fast-growing shadows, Isaac returns home. The large circle of children near the tree reveals that his father must have interesting visitors. *Ah, maybe Eliezer is back,* is the first thought that comes to mind. He quickens his pace and tries to distinguish who all the different people are.

One of the children looks towards him and then calls out something which he can't understand. Immediately a stranger gets up from the circle of men and comes towards him.

Strange, he looks just like my father. At first Isaac is surprised but then he realizes who this is. This is his brother, his only brother! He sees the tears in his brother's eyes and feels a great sense of relief. "Ishmael, welcome! A thousand times welcome!" he calls out while affectionately kissing him on both cheeks. He greets Nebaioth with the same enthusiasm, but Ishmael's son still acts slightly reserved with these new people, although inside he feels strangely relaxed. He is glad to get to know his grandfather and uncle. He has never met a relative from either his father or mother's side before. He remembers how he used to feel a little envious of his peers who received attention from their grandfathers.

That day marks a new beginning in the relationship between the relatives. Unfortunately, all too soon Ishmael must return to his family and livestock. At their parting, he promises his father and brother that he will visit them again. "You must bring your entire family next time," Isaac states emphatically.

"I'm afraid that won't be possible, as my sons are responsible for the livestock; it is work that I can't leave to my servants," Ishmael indicates. "When danger comes, the workers tend to think of themselves first and they easily forget about the sheep and goats."

Isaac hadn't thought of that. Then he realizes how difficult it must have been before for his own father, before he had sons to whom he could entrust such responsibilities.

On the way back Nebaioth has many questions for his father. He wants to know what exactly happened between his grandfather and grandmother. Ishmael explains in detail the reasons why Abraham had sent him away.

"Father, I just don't understand. It seems to me that Grandfather is a very kind man, and yet he was so cruel to you and Grandmother Hagar."

"I don't understand either, Nebaioth, but I do know it has a lot to do with God the Creator. Grandfather was being obedient to him."

"Well, I don't really want anything to do with a God who demands such cruelty from his people."

"Nebaioth, I understand how you feel. Sometimes I find it difficult to accept as well. In the meantime, I have experienced enough with God to see that He is with me and that He loves me."

"Really, like what?" Nebaioth asks coldly. He is clearly struggling with the rejection, which has had an effect on him in that he missed out on being a grandson. He didn't have a grandfather to tell him stories about times long ago. No one to go to when you can't talk to your parents, no one to listen to your own adventures.

Patiently, Ishmael answers his son's question. "When the water ran out, I really thought I was going to die. I had a high fever and was unable to walk because I had become so weak. Only by leaning on Grandmother Hagar's slender body was I able to stumble along for a while. Wherever we looked, there was no water to be found anywhere. Grandmother finally laid me down in the shade of some bushes and moved away from me so that I wouldn't see her tears as she wept. At that very moment, I thought about the meaning of my name."

"God hears," Nebaioth interrupts slightly annoyed. "You told me that many times."

"Indeed, my son," Ishmael continues. "Then I called upon God with all my strength, 'If you are truly alive, save us!' Suddenly a voice rang out from heaven. I couldn't see anyone but Grandmother recognized the voice. It was the stranger whom she had met years before. I am sure it was God's voice for He hears and He speaks. Even Grandfather heard him speak many times."

As Nebaioth listens to his father's story, something transpires in his heart. The pain and anger give way to different feelings, something new. He senses the same sincerity in his father's words as his Grandfather's. By the time Ishmael has finished the story, Nebaioth has learned an important lesson. God's ways are unfathomable but He gives us enough evidence of his love and blessings for us to be able to trust in him. The Lord is good and loves those He created.

9 A Puzzle Solved

"Mibsam, Kedar, and Adbeel, you will come with me," says Ishmael. The men are happy that it is finally their turn to go. Ever since Nebaioth returned from the visit to his grandfather, they have been looking forward to meeting him as well. Meanwhile, almost a year has passed, a year of waiting, until their father deemed the time to be right. Occasionally they would ask him about it, but they knew that, if they would pester him too much, it would have the opposite effect. Finally, it seems their patience is rewarded. The other brothers in the tent are somewhat jealous.

"When can I go?" Kedemah asks. He is the youngest and not the least bit shy about asking his father for a favor.

"One day it will be your turn," his father replies.

"But you said that Grandfather is one hundred and forty-five years old!" Kedemah protests, "we have never even heard about anyone living that long. Surely, he will die soon."

"Ha-ha, don't worry about that," Ishmael laughs. "Do you know how long your great-grandfather Terah lived?" Kedemah doesn't know. Ishmael looks around the circle to see if any of the others know. He winks at Nebaioth, who has personally heard the answer from his grandfather's mouth.

Speaking slowly and emphatically, Nebaioth responds, "Grandfather's father lived two hundred and five years."

Kedemah looks perplexed. "How is it possible for someone to live that long?" he wants to know. "Grandfather's wife, Sarah, died a long time ago and even she was very old."

"It has to do with Creator," Nebaioth explains, and then he proceeds to tell them all the things he learned about God from his grandfather.

Listening to the conversation that follows between the brothers, Ishmael realizes how much Nebaioth has benefited from seeing his grandfather. He should really give each one of his sons that same opportunity. On the other hand, he must be practical and think about the livestock that needs to be cared for in his absence.

"Alright, if Nebaioth is ready to look after the camp with the help of your six younger brothers, I can allow Mishma and Dumah to come with us as well."

Nebaioth heartily grants his brothers this trip and nods his head in approval. A few days later, a caravan of camels and their riders are on their way to Beersheba.

After a three-day journey, Ishmael sees the old familiar tamarisk tree in the distance. Fortunately the tents are still there, which means that his father hasn't moved yet. As he comes nearer, he sees his father seated under the large tree. It's easy to recognize him by his long, white hair, and it doesn't take long before Abraham spots him, too. Quickly he rises to his feet and greets his beloved son. "It is such an honor to see you again, Ishmael," he says joyfully.

"It is I who am honored by meeting you again, Father," Ishmael responds. Then he introduces the sons who are with him to their grandfather. Filled with pride, Abraham greets each one and gives them a warm embrace. A little while later they all sit down in a circle under the tree. Scattered around are some square rocks. Abraham has ordered two of his servants to bring the guests goat hair blankets, one each. They drape one part over the rock and spread the rest out on the ground. This way they turn the rock into a pillow, creating a comfortable spot for every guest. Now the men can relax from their arduous journey on the camel backs. When the tea is being served, Ishmael hears a baby cry. He turns his head in the direction of the sound and notices it coming from Abraham and Isaac's tents. "Father, blessed are you, now that Isaac has become a father as well." For a moment Abram looks at him in puzzlement, but then he understands what Ishmael said. "Indeed, I am blessed, my son, but not in the way you think. The baby you hear is my son." Then it is Ishmael's turn to be surprised. His sons have their ears wide open. *What is Grandfather saying? Has he had another child? That's impossible! He's far too old for that!*

Grandfather gets up, walks towards the tent and returns with a beautiful baby boy in his arms. "I remarried and this is Zimran; he is only six weeks old."

This is not at all what Ishmael had expected, but he does think it is quite amusing that his father is still so vigorous. Then his thoughts go back to the conversation they had at home. "Boys, now you can see with your own eyes: Grandfather is a strong man and still has many years ahead of him."

Abraham smiles. "To be honest, I was a little surprised myself at being a father again but God has kept me in good health and I am really enjoying it." The men in the circle chuckle. They secretly hope that they will grow old in the same way, enjoying intimacy with their wives for a long time to come.

"What about Isaac?" Ishmael asks, "How is he?"

"Not so good," Abraham responds. He has been married for many years now, but for some reason God still hasn't blessed him with a son."

Ishmael notices the hesitation in his father's voice. He realizes the struggle Abraham faces. The son he sent away has been richly blessed with twelve sons, while the miracle son remains childless. "Father, I will pray for him, I promise."

"Thank you, my son. I really appreciate that," Abraham replies. "I believe with my whole heart that God will honor his promises through Isaac; I just don't understand why it has to take so long."

The five young men, Kedar, Adbeel, Mibsam, Mishma, and Dumah, listen breathlessly to the conversation between their father and grandfather. Grandfather's steadfast faith in the Creator deeply moves them.

"One day," Grandfather continues, "God will fulfill his promise to Isaac and bless him with many sons, just like He has done for you."

Ishmael agrees. He decides to let Isaac know that he will pray for him.

During breakfast the next morning the plans for the day are discussed. "Father, this afternoon I would like to show Ishmael around a bit," Isaac offers.

Abraham senses that his two sons need to spend some time together. "Absolutely, that's fine. Actually, while you guys do that, I will entertain Kedar and his brothers with some of my stories," Abraham suggests. With a twinkle in his eye he looks at both of his sons and continues, "Stories that you have heard many times before. "

Frankly, Ishmael never tires of his father's stories, but he also wants to spend time alone with his brother. He happily agrees with his father's suggestion. As for his sons, they can hardly wait to hear more from their grandfather.

After lunch and a short nap, Ishmael and Isaac go to the hills. They have been looking forward to time alone as brothers. Since there is no real privacy in and around the campsite, it is better to go for a walk if you want to speak confidentially. The only people outside the camp are the shepherds, but they mostly keep to themselves. When the two brothers are well out of range of the camp, Ishmael carefully broaches the sensitive subject. "I am sorry, Isaac, that you are not yet a father."

"God is good," Isaac replies.

Ishmael picks up the coldness in his voice and probes a little further, "How are you coping with that?"

Isaac senses his brother's concern and begins to be more open with him. "It is not easy, Ishmael, especially after all the miracles my father experienced and after all God's promises. The people around us have expectations of us. At first they were impressed with our God, but now they regularly mock him. Father says that he is used to their taunts and that I shouldn't let it affect me, but actually, whenever a visitor jokes about it, or when I hear the people in the market speak about our God with disdain, it hurts." Isaac controls himself, but Ishmael feels his brother's pain.

"Sometimes, I can't understand God either," he admits. When Father sent my mother and me away, I was furious with him. I never wanted to see him again and wished he were dead. Then, as I lay dying in the desert, I called on the Lord and He saved me."

Isaac eyes his brother curiously and wants to know, "How did you deal with your feelings of rejection?"

"To be honest, I continued to hold a grudge against Father until Eliezer came to see me last year. He told me about his own feelings of rejection, but he also shared with me how he had come to have peace about it."

"Yes, I know, Eliezer told me," Isaac remembers. "He trusts God, just like our father."

"That's exactly what happened to me," Ishmael adds. "My life hasn't been all that easy, and I have experienced my share of painful moments. At the same time I have been able to see God's hand in so much of it." Seeing that Isaac is eager to learn how, Ishmael continues, "After God saved me from death in the desert, He helped me build a life for myself and my family in a relatively short time. It wasn't until later, however, that I saw God's blessing upon my life. Never again did I fall seriously ill and God has given me twelve healthy sons. I became an accomplished hunter, and by selling hides I have managed to build up quite a flock. So far, I have not been robbed by any of the other desert dwellers, and I've never been attacked by a lion. Well, the area where I live is probably too dry and desolate for lions anyway," he jokes.

"You are truly a man of the wilderness," Isaac laughs as he gives his brother a friendly jab in the ribs.

"By the way, what exactly happened when you were to be slaughtered?" Ishmael wants to know. "I heard this bizarre story. Did Father really try to sacrifice you on an altar?"

"Actually, Ishmael, it was the most amazing miracle I have ever seen."

"So, it really happened?!" Ishmael exclaims in surprise. He looks at his brother in disbelief.

"I know it is a strange story, but God had indeed given the order to Father to do it."

"What about you? Were you not frightened when Father tied you up?"

"Of course, I was. I was scared to death!" Isaac confirms, "but he kept reassuring me, reminding me that nothing is impossible for God. That day I experienced how true that is."

"You are indeed alive and well, and sitting right here next to me," Ishmael laughs happily. "But tell me, how did it come about?"

"The moment Father got hold of the knife, a voice came from heaven, saying, 'Abraham, do not lay your hand on the boy'[15]."

"Unbelievable! You heard the voice from heaven, too?" Ishmael is overcome with emotion and seems nailed to the ground. "I had the same experience, brother."

"You're not kidding!" Isaac cries.

"Really. After my mother had said her farewells to me, while I lay dying, she heard the voice of a man. There was no one there, only a white cloud above us."

"That's incredible!" Isaac cries out amazed. "When I was tied up on the altar, it seemed to me that this heavenly voice came from a cloud as well." Both brothers sense an intimate kind of bond as they enthusiastically fill each other in on the details of their individual experiences.

"Listen, Isaac, I believe that God will bless you with a family of your own,' Ishmael says. "I don't always understand his ways, but I will continue to pray until God's promise to you is fulfilled as well."

Isaac looks his older brother in the eye and feels proud of him. "Thank you, I really appreciate that. I will also continue to pray with great expectation. Surely, God has a plan for both of our lives."

Ishmael nods in agreement, and with a strange certitude in his voice he says, "God is pleased when we trust him, even if we don't understand his ways."

These are the last words on the subject. Isaac peers at the setting sun and realizes it will soon be dark. "Let's go and see how your sons are faring," he suggests. "Perhaps Father has fallen asleep and now they are bored."

Ishmael bursts out laughing and grabs his brother's hand. "You know very well that Father will only stop talking when he breathes his last!" he exclaims.

Laughing together, the brothers walk back to the camp and there they find Ishmael's sons engrossed in the stories their grandfather is telling them.

Following this visit, the whole family enjoys several happy years. At least once a year Ishmael goes to visit his father and his brothers. The family continues to grow and Abraham has five more sons with his wife Keturah. Then, after a long wait of twenty years, Isaac finally becomes a father as well. God has given him a double blessing in the form of twins. When the two boys grow up, Ishmael is amazed at the difference in their characters. While Esau's temperament reflects the adventurous side of Abraham, Jacob seems to have inherited his grandfather's sensitivity. Strangely, Isaac has no more children after the twin boys. To Ishmael that shows even more how much he has been blessed by God, having received twelve sons. One day he mentions this to his father. Abraham wisely replies, "God always fulfills his promises; it is up to him to decide how and when."

One day, one of Abraham's servants shows up unexpectedly at Ishmael's camp. Ishmael recognizes him as one of Eliezer's sons and knows that he is a trustworthy messenger. "Your father wants to see you urgently" the man says.

Ishmael immediately makes the necessary arrangements and that very day he accompanies the servant to see Abraham together with his first-born son Nebaioth.

As soon as they arrive, Ishmael hurries to the tent where his father is resting. Abraham struggles to sit up to greet his son. "I am glad you have come quickly," he begins weakly. "There is something important I need to tell you."

Ishmael realizes that his father's health has declined to the point of death. He is surprised that there is still something that has to be discussed between them. "What is it Father? Did we not resolve everything between us a long time ago?

"This is true, my son. And yet, there is something I need to make amends for." Abraham notices the confusion in Ishmael's eyes. "A long time ago, I sent you away empty-handed, but today I want to fill your hands," Abraham continues.

"You don't have to do this, Father. I have all that I need," Ishmael responds.

"It is what I desire and thus it will happen," Abraham persists. "I have given all of Keturah's sons a share of my possessions, and you will receive your share as well." With great difficulty and using all of his strength, Abraham speaks the words. This message is important to him.

Ishmael, meanwhile, is deeply concerned about his father. Though he knows that the day is approaching when he will have to say farewell, he truly wishes for his father to live longer.

"Ishmael, my son, be blessed and be a blessing," his father continues. "God has a special plan for your life. He will surely use you and your offspring to bring glory to his name."

"Yes, Father, I believe so too."

"Do you remember how you prayed for Isaac?" Abraham says. "God has answered your prayers and blessed Isaac with two precious sons. He will surely make Isaac's offspring into a great people, just like He is doing for you. Continue to bless your brother, and you will be blessed as well."

"I will certainly do so, Father," Ishmael promises.

Abraham concludes, "Never forget that it was God himself who has given you your beautiful name. He hears you."

"I know, Father, I have experienced this firsthand," Ishmael affirms.

Abraham is visibly satisfied with his answer and he slowly leans back on to the soft pillows. Then Ishmael kisses his father on the forehead and leaves him to rest. That same night Abraham falls asleep peacefully, never to wake again.

Isaac and Ishmael now make some decisions together, but first they take time to properly mourn their father's death. They reminisce about the miracles Abraham experienced throughout his lifetime, some of which they themselves have witnessed. This helps them process the loss. Their father truly was a man of God and a powerful example of a life, lived by faith.

As soon as the sun starts to warm the earth, Ishmael and Isaac arrange for the body to be preserved and prepared for burial according to the latest knowledge from Egypt. The next day, both brothers prepare for a long journey. Isaac has promised to bury his father in the same grave as their mother on their own plot of land in the mountains of Mamre. Because the road is too difficult for carts, several servants carry the body on a litter. The fifteen-year-old twins, Esau and Jacob, would love to join the funeral procession but Isaac does not allow them to. They need to stay behind to take care of their mother.

As the funeral procession leaves, the two sons walk in front, immediately followed by the pallbearers. At the rear of the procession are those carrying supplies for the journey.

As they walk, Ishmael muses about the things God told him regarding his future. He will be wild donkey, a free man. In a sense, the death of his father has opened a new kind of freedom for him. As the first-born son, he is now the elder in the family. That would normally make him responsible for all his younger brothers and their families, as well as for the older widows. Now Isaac carries that responsibility, while he himself is free to determine his own future. Ishmael hopes that, when life is back to normal, Isaac will not reject him. Time will tell.

10 Wise Counsel

After the funeral, the brothers ride their donkeys leisurely back home. Ishmael accompanies Isaac to his encampment in Beersheba. From there he will continue to the desert of Paran, where his own family is awaiting him anxiously.

"I will miss you, Ishmael."

"I will miss you even more," Ishmael replies. Silence envelopes the two brothers as they reflect on the future.

"I wish we could live together," Ishmael breaks the silence.

"I do as well," Isaac reacts, "but I'm afraid that there won't be enough food to feed both of our flocks. I don't see a solution for that, but perhaps we can move closer together."

"Yes, I don't see why not. I have thought about it many times, and I think it would be good to move elsewhere, but we will have to be careful not to be in each other's way, otherwise history will repeat itself," Isaac chuckles.

"What do you mean?" Ishmael acts surprised. Then he remembers the incident with cousin Lot, and after all, forewarned is fore armed.

Isaac looks at his brother; he is proud of him. Because Keturah's sons are a lot younger, he doesn't have much in common with them. Ishmael, on the other hand, is his big, strong older brother. He has proven himself by surviving in the harsh desert. In fact, he didn't just survive; he became very fruitful. Suddenly Isaac has an idea. "Ishmael, isn't there a sweet water well, not too far away from where you live?

"I don't think you'll find a well similar to Beersheba," Ishmael responds.

"I was thinking of the well Lachai-Roi, where your mother met with the Lord. Not too long ago I went there with some of my flocks."

"That's odd, I didn't even think about that," Ishmael reacts enthusiastically. "I am pretty sure that one has sweet water all year around."

"I wouldn't expect differently," laughs Isaac, "God himself used that well to save you. That place is blessed. How far is that away from you?"

"Well, on a fast camel you can easily make it in one day." Ishmael replies cheerfully. The thought alone that his brother might move closer to him fills him with joy.

"That would be great!" Isaac exclaims. "We could see each other every new moon. I really enjoy seeing your children and I would also like to get to know your grandchildren better."

"Then perhaps I can be useful to Esau and Jacob as well, in case they need advice from their uncle." Winking, Ishmael adds, "and keep an eye on them at the same time."

"You're quite a character!" Isaac blurts out laughingly. "Spoken just like a first-born son!"

"I believe you are right, Isaac, but I don't want to meddle in your affairs," Ishmael reassures him. Happy about their new plans the brothers continue on their way.

Suddenly Isaac becomes quiet. He is overwhelmed by fear. What if Ishmael wants to get rid of him, to obtain Father's inheritance? Jacob and Esau would not be strong enough to stand up against their uncle. "How do you feel about the situation now?" Isaac asks his older brother.

"What situation are you talking about?"

"Well, the time when father sent you and your mother away to please my mother." Isaac purposely leaves out God's part in that event. He wants to know how Ishmael feels about it from a human viewpoint.

"I thought your mother was a terrible person, and in the end I even hated her. She continually criticized my mother and me and at the same time always thought quite highly of herself, typically a beautiful, but spoiled and pampered woman."

Isaac is taken aback by his brother's words. As Ishmael expresses his remaining feelings of bitterness, Isaac realizes that he has correctly assumed his brother is still troubled by the past. Carefully he probes a little deeper, "But wasn't it Father who sent you away in the end?"

"For a long time I was angry with him as well," Ishmael explains. "Even when many years later Eliezer came to ask me to visit him, I didn't want to go at first.

"Why then did you do it after all?"

"Eliezer was very soft spoken, and he reminded me of Father. His gentleness and patience in dealing with problems made me love him even more. So on the one hand I was furious, but on the other, something inside me longed to see him. When Eliezer said that you missed me, too, and wanted to see me, it touched me deeply."

On hearing these words from his half-brother's mouth, Isaac feels a lump in his throat. Ishmael really loves him. How comforting it is to know that.

"You were my only brother and I still feel the same way about you," Ishmael continues. "I was confronted with a great dilemma, but that night I had a dream which instilled peace in me, so the next morning I decided to go with Eliezer."

Isaac sighs with relief. Clearly, Ishmael has chosen to accept Father, as well as everything that has happened in the past. No one had talked him in to it. Isaac steers his donkey next to his brother's and grabs his hand. "I am so glad you did that," he says, and then he adds, "You are very much like Father."

Ishmael feels a little embarrassed, but happy as well. "Thank you," he whispers.

Two months later, Ishmael travels with several of his sons to the well of Lachai-Roi, and a warm reunion between brothers and cousins takes place. That night, Isaac and Ishmael exchange the latest news.

Nearby, their sons are enjoying each other's company, though only Esau is actually having fun with his cousins. His brother, Jacob, quietly watches from a distance, feeling jealous. Esau is well-built, strong and is often the center of attention with his wild tales about hunting adventures, while he, the quiet Jacob, knows more about cooking than anything else. His father is a little ashamed of him. Not that he has ever said so in so many words, but Jacob senses it. His father always tells others in detail about Esau's exploits but he hardly ever mentions Jacob. The only one who really cares about him is his mother; at least, that's how Jacob feels about it.

His mother often compliments him. She is also the one who continually reminds him that God has a special plan for his life. Her words often comfort him. "One day Esau will serve you, even though he is the oldest. You will be a great nation." That's what God had told his mother when they were born. How this will ever take place is a complete mystery to Jacob, however. Esau has great leadership qualities and doesn't flinch at anything. In contrast, he is shy and prefers to stay within the safety of the camp. These are Jacob's daydreams about his life. *I wish that one day I could get my own back on Esau.* In his mind, he contrives all sorts of scenarios to trick his brother. He then notices his father and Uncle Ishmael get up from the thick animal hides where they had been sitting. It is time to go to sleep.

Not long after that, Jacob sees the opportunity of a lifetime. Esau has just returned from hunting and is worn out. He has carried a massive dead ibex on his shoulders. It was a superb but heavy catch. He would much rather have left the animal behind to bring home on a donkey, but he didn't want to take the risk of a lion or some other predator making off with it. After stringing the dead animal up in a safe place, Esau drags himself round to the kitchen tent. "Hey Mom, any food ready for a hungry bear?" he calls out. There is no answer. Esau hears the crackling of a fire and trudges around the tent to the front entrance, where he notices Jacob busy stirring in a big pot of soup. The savory aroma wafts gently from the cooking pot making his mouth water and his tummy rumble. "Quick! Give me some of that red stew you are making," he orders his brother.

Jacob looks up from the cooking pot and scrutinizes his sweaty and exhausted brother. *He may be the master of the outdoors, I can't change that; but this is my domain.* "We will eat shortly. You can wait," he replies curtly.

"I'm so hungry, I'm practically fainting. Come on, now, don't be so childish," Esau reacts impatiently.

When Jacob hears the word 'fainting', he gets an idea. With a scorning voice he says, "Okay then, I'll give you some of the stew… if you sell me your birthright."

Without giving it a second thought, Esau replies, "I am about to die; of what use is a birthright to me?[16] Be my guest. Now give me the stew."

Aha! I've got him now, Jacob thinks, as he feels the power over his brother growing. Even though Esau is much stronger physically, Jacob has now skillfully succeeded in making his brother do what he wants. *But what if Esau later denies that he sold him his birthright? There is no one here to witness it.* Then Jacob has an idea. With his heart pounding in his throat, he says, "Swear to me by the name of the living God that you are selling me your birthright." Never before had Jacob felt so full of courage.

"I swear," Esau answers right away.

Jacob can't believe his ears, but he is not quite satisfied yet. "Swear by the name of the living God," he insists.

Then it is as if Esau hears a still small voice deep inside, '*don't do it; this is not right.*' At the same time, the hunger pangs are stronger than ever, and he says, "Oh well, what use is my birthright, if I am about to die?" Again, the voice inside tries to stop him, but he ignores it. "I swear by the name of the God of heaven and earth. Now, give me the stew!"

Without a moment to lose, Jacob fills a bowl with the steaming red lentil stew and hands it to his brother. *But what if Esau changes his mind?* So, quickly he hands him a freshly baked flatbread as well.

Esau devours the meal. He dips the bread in the soup and gobbles it up, almost burning his tongue. When the contents of the dish have cooled off a bit, he quickly slurps the rest and then disappears again.

Jacob stands, shaking by the cooking pot. He can hardly believe what just happened. For once, he, the weak, has overcome his strong twin brother.

One day, while Isaac is enjoying the coolness of the evening outside his tent, Esau joins him. "Father, I would like to get married," he says.

"That's great, my son," answers Isaac. "I believe you are ready."

"That's just what I was thinking. Weren't you forty years old yourself when you married Mother?"

"That's right," Isaac confirms, "and who would you like to marry?"

"I know a beautiful girl who would suit me well, Father. She is the sister of my friend, Zohar, from Mamre."

"And where is she from, my son?"

"She is the daughter of Anah, the Hittite."

When Isaac hears that she is a Hittite, he frowns. His own father had emphatically warned him not to marry the people of the land. "My son, this is not a good idea. Have you forgotten why Grandfather brought your mother to me all the way from Paddan-Aram?"

"But Father, her family is very influential. This is a great opportunity for us to strengthen our position in the land," Esau objects. He has carefully thought about how he would word his request beforehand, and now he is ready to argue his case with his father. "Look at all the problems we have faced with the Philistines, Father. When we lived in Gerar, they would fill our wells with sand. If we make an alliance with the Hittites, the Philistines will no longer be in a position to harm us." Esau goes on and on, pursuing his case. He senses his father's reluctance and realizes he needs to do all he can to try to convince his father that Adah_is the best choice. "You also made an agreement with the Philistines, which resulted in peace. What if the Hittites decide they want to take the land that Grandfather bought a long time ago?"

Isaac never really thought about that. But even though the people of Canaan might deceive him, for they do not fear God, he has been through enough to know that God himself will look after him.

"Esau, your arguments sound very convincing. Yet, I still don't believe this would be a wise move," Isaac decides, "but I will give it some thought."

Later that evening Isaac tells Rebecca about Esau's plans. Rebecca is appalled. "A Hittite woman in our family? Over my dead body! I have seen how filthy they are. Can you imagine her cooking us a meal? We would all get sick!"

"It wouldn't be hard to re-educate her. Personally, I am more worried about their immoral ways of living. They don't even trust each other; how are we to trust them?

"I have an idea," Rebecca says, "Why don't you get Ishmael speak to him about it? I know Esau respects his uncle."

Isaac thinks that's a great idea and decides to discuss the matter with Ishmael the next time they meet.

When Ishmael visits them again, Isaac takes him aside and explains the delicate situation to him. "No problem," his brother answers reassuringly, "leave him to me."

That afternoon Ishmael suggests to Esau that they go hunting the next day. Esau is thrilled; his uncle is an experienced hunter. When he tells his father about the plan for the following day, Isaac sighs with relief. *Everything is going to be all right.*

The next day, while they are out in the fields, Esau excitedly brings up the subject of his forthcoming marriage. "Uncle Ishmael, I have found a beautiful bride," he blurts out, and with passion tells him the reasons why.

"What does your father think about it?" Ishmael wants to know.

Esau's excitement turns to frustration. "He isn't happy about it. Perhaps he is too old to understand. Please, could you talk to him? You understand about life in the desert better than he does."

Ishmael affirms that he has indeed learned to survive in the desert as a lone wanderer. "But above all, it is God who gives success."

"But Uncle Ishmael, God didn't give us common sense for nothing; we need to use our brains."

"True, but why would you think the Hittites would want to make an alliance with you?" he asks Esau.

"Well, I think they feel inferior because of our wealth and influence. An alliance with us would reassure them that we wish them no harm."

"That's a clever thought, Esau, but these people do not care about God or about his commandments. Don't you realize that when you marry Adah, she can also claim part of your inheritance?"

Esau admits he hasn't thought about that. "But didn't the Philistines respect the agreement Grandfather made with them? As far as I know, they never took any land away from him. The people here in Canaan aren't that bad!"

"Esau, I urgently advise you not to go through with this marriage. Nothing but problems will come from it."

At those words, Esau looks down in disappointment. He had been so hopeful that his uncle would help him. Now it turns out to be the opposite. Even this man, who has learned to survive in the wilderness, disagrees with his plans. *They just don't understand what a smart move it would be to make an alliance with the Hittites through marriage,* Esau thinks. What motivates him even more is Adah's beauty. There are not many women like her, so he cannot let this chance pass by. Also, he would gain respect in the community because of her. He has often heard the stories about the privileges his grandfather received because his grandmother was so stunningly beautiful. Besides, isn't it every man's desire to marry a gorgeous woman?

Thinking about why he wants to marry Adah, Esau becomes more and more convinced within himself that this is the right thing to do. Perhaps his father and his uncle don't think it's a wise decision, but what do they know? Times have changed. Things are no longer the way they were forty years ago. One has to adapt to the time one lives in and because his father is wealthier than his grandfather ever was, an alliance is sensible.

On the other hand, Esau can't help but respect his uncle's views. He has seen many times that what Ishmael said, has turned out to be true. Indeed, it is impossible to foresee all the consequences of this marriage. Suddenly, a new thought comes to mind. *King Abimelech expelled Father because we own so many animals. Perhaps other kings in the land will do the same, and we will end up living in the desert again. That would be unacceptable. After all, God has promised us this land.* That's the decisive argument. Now it is completely clear that Adah is the right woman for him. As soon as the opportunity presents itself, he visits Zohar's father. They agree on the dowry and only one week later, Esau marries Adah … without the consent or blessing of his own father.

Once Adah has moved into his tent, Esau discovers and fully enjoys the pleasures of married life. But during the few days each month his wife is unclean, Esau is not able to touch her and must control himself. That doesn't suit him at all and he thinks about solutions to his problem. Of course, he could follow the ways of the men in Canaan and sleep with other women, but that doesn't feel right. He knows very well that that's against God's will. Suddenly, he has a brilliant idea. *What if I take a second wife? That way one of the two should always be available to me; it would be easier to avoid committing adultery.* Esau doesn't need to think about it for very long. The next day he consults with his friend Zohar, who instantly recommends a suitable second bride for him.

One month later, Esau marries Oholibama, the daughter of the Hittite, Elon. The dowry had been enormous, but what does that matter? His father has plenty of camels and sheep, and doesn't a large part of the flock belong to him anyway? He only must share his father's inheritance with Jacob. In contrast, Uncle Ishmael's sons will have to divide their father's possessions between twelve.

As is the custom, after the marriage Esau continues to live with his parents. Both Adah and Oholibama have been raised with worshipping idols and their families have given them beautiful new statues of their gods as wedding gifts. Their mothers have taught them the importance of passing on the traditions of their religion to the next generation. They meticulously follow all the rules as they faithfully worship the carved images of their gods.

Soon tensions between the two women and their mother-in-law escalate, as the women share all the household chores. Rebecca is greatly upset when she sees them offering the best food to their little stone gods. Only God the Creator is worthy of the best they have to offer. Besides, the young women do not even respect the God of Esau's grandfather Abraham. Even Isaac becomes irritated with their behavior. Esau may be his favorite son, but he is sick and tired of all the quarrelling. How he longs for the peaceful days before Esau's marriages.

11 Family Problems

Two elderly men are sitting on a mountain edge, enjoying the view across the desert plains. In the valley below lies the encampment of the younger of the two. The tents and the cultivated fields resemble a piece of mosaic art. Squares of black goat hair alternating with patches of bright green are surrounded by an undulating carpet of sand and stones that reaches far into the distance. The laughter of playing children, blended with the voices of chattering women, rises from the valley. A lazy sun creeps along the blue skies towards the horizon, dousing the landscape in a balmy glow. The afternoon is ending and the radiant orb has already lost most of its intense heat. The light breeze makes the little plateau a good place for the men to relax. From a small bowl they pick sunflower seeds, which they skillfully crack open between their teeth. Occasionally one of them spits out some of the shells, which now litter the ground around their feet.

"What do you think about all of this?" Isaac asks his beloved half-brother.

Ishmael stares straight ahead. He has just learned about Isaac's family problems. Esau's wives are extremely stubborn. Added to that, instead of honoring and respecting his parents, Esau often takes their side. His attitude is diametrically opposed to Isaac and Rebecca's customs and values. He appears to be under a type of spiritual influence, which has blinded him to their ways of thinking. Isaac is tremendously bothered by the problems. It has taken much effort to teach the two young women respect for people and animals, but they refuse to honor their Creator. Instead, they stubbornly continue to worship their own carved idols. Ishmael is grieved that Esau has disregarded his advice. How is he to help Isaac now? While he is still mulling over the things he has just learned, Isaac continues, "I have thought of sending him and his wives away..."

"What? You can't be serious?" Ishmael interrupts. Immediately he sits up straight. "May God forgive you for harboring such thoughts!"

"...but because I have seen your pain and our father's, I couldn't go through with it," Isaac continues.

"Oh, thank goodness." Ishmael lets out a sigh of relief and leans back against the rocky outcrop. He doesn't want his nephew to experience the same pain he went through. "We can be thankful that the Hittites haven't caused any problems yet," Ishmael points out. "When Esau came to me for advice, I warned him that they have their own reasons to marry their daughters to him."

"Thankfully, God protects us," Isaac shares. "They hardly ever harass us. The animals are doing well and we are seldom robbed."

"Yes, indeed, God is with you and blesses you immensely," Ishmael agrees.

"Yet the dowries for Ishmael's brides were exorbitant. They cost me an arm and a leg. I can only hope Jacob doesn't have similar plans."

"Speaking of Jacob; isn't it about time for him to get married too? He must be over fifty now?"

"That's true, but I definitely don't want him to marry a Canaanite woman," Isaac adds emphatically.

"What about my daughter Mahalath? I wouldn't mind him marrying her," Ishmael offers spontaneously.

Isaac laughs heartily. "That's not a bad idea, really, but because God has specifically declared that He desires to bless the world through my off-spring, I don't want to create confusion. What if it caused a quarrel between our children and grandchildren?"

Ishmael doesn't want that to happen either and he quickly abandons the idea.

"I would love Esau to be more devoted to our God and Creator. It seems that faith is of little importance to him," Isaac continues. "He talks a good talk, but in the meantime, he allows his wives to do whatever they please."

"Continue to pray for them, Isaac. And even when you doubt whether God hears you, remember my name and the well that's here beneath us. God sees and hears the cry of your heart." This is the best advice Ishmael can think to give his brother at this difficult time.

The memory of God's faithfulness in humanly impossible situations encourages Isaac. Wasn't that the reason he went to live close by the well after his father's death and hasn't God blessed him abundantly throughout his life?

"Recently something fascinating happened to me," Ishmael continues. Enough has been said about the problems regarding Esau; now he wants to lighten his brother's mood. Captivated by Ishmael's anecdotes, Isaac relax-es. At the hilarious culmination of the tales, he bursts into laughter. If the camp had been entirely silent, one could have heard the sound of the two men reverberate throughout the valley. The brothers are glad for this and every other opportunity they get to spend together.

"Uncle Isaac, please, come quickly," a man gasps as he rushes into the tent, interrupting Esau's conversation with Isaac. Although his eyesight is gone, Isaac immediately recognizes his nephew's voice. "What's the matter, Kedar? Why are you in such a hurry?"

"Father has weakened a lot over the past few days, and he feels the end is near. He wants to say his last goodbye to you." Isaac understands the gravity of the situation, and he immediately orders his servants to prepare the camels for Esau and himself. Esau was busy bragging about his latest hunting exploits, but as soon as he hears the news, he jumps up and helps his father to his feet. Walking out together, Isaac instructs his older son, "Esau, you are coming with me. Tell your mother, I will be gone for a week. Also, tell Jacob he will be responsible for the camp and the animals." Esau immediately does as he is told and then helps his aging father onto his camel.

A little while later, Kedar and his uncle and cousin head towards Paran where Ishmael lives. With every step, the camels toss up fine desert sand and soon the travel party disappears behind a cloud of dust.

"They're here," Nebaioth whispers. Ishmael's weary eyes light up when he hears that his brother has arrived, and with great effort he tries to pull himself up on the bed.

"Father, lie back down. You are too weak," Mibsam admonishes him.

Ishmael disregards his son's words, and uses the last bit of strength left in him to push himself into an upright position. Quickly, Mibsam supports his back with a comfortable straw-filled cushion. Now Ishmael can see the entrance to his tent perfectly.

A moment later, Nebaioth leads the visitors into his father's tent while holding his uncle's hand.

"Peace be with you," Isaac says as he shakes hands with his brother and kisses him.

"Peace be with you, too, my brother,' Ishmael replies. "Thanks be to God for your safe travels."

Mibsam, who is seated close to his father, swiftly gets up to make a place for his uncle. Leaning heavily on Esau, Isaac carefully bends his stiff knees to recline on the pillow provided by Mibsam. It takes a while for him to get comfortably seated next to his beloved brother.

One of Nebaioth's sons carries in a wooden tray with four cups of steaming hot tea. He puts the tray in front of Isaac and politely offers him a cup. Isaac is glad for the hot drink and as he sips loudly, he turns towards Ishmael. After the usual exchange of pleasantries, the conversation changes to deeper issues. "Do you remember how I used to think you look like father?" Isaac asks.

"Yes, I do. Why?"

"Now that you are older, even your voice sounds like his."

"Well, I can say the same about you," Ishmael answers. A cautious smile appears on his deeply lined face. Immediately the pain in his worn-out body flares up again, reminding him that the end is approaching. He winces and after it passes he continues weakly, "I am glad you have come, Isaac. I will miss you."

Isaac inclines his ear to Ishmael's face so that he can hear him and answers, "I will miss you, too, brother. But one day soon, we shall see each other again. This is my certain hope."

"That hope is mine, too, just like Father taught us." Although Ishmael's voice is barely audible, the conviction of his heart rings out. "Do you remember how he often used to tell us that true life is not here on earth but in the hereafter?"

"Definitely," Isaac confirms, "that's why I still live in a tent, as then I'm always reminded that life on earth is temporary."

"Isaac, you are an amazing example to all of us. I hope that our families will always keep this close connection."

"As surely as God the Creator lives, I will commit myself to that, my brother," Isaac promises.

Esau and the others present are witnesses to Isaac's promise to Ishmael.

After a while Isaac notices his brother drifting off to sleep. He takes his weathered hand into his own hands and remains quietly seated next to him.

Two days later, Ishmael breathes his last. All the neighboring nomadic tribes and their chieftains attend the funeral. Ishmael has become known as a powerful man and because his twelve sons have their own large families, the clan has become a force to be reckoned with in the surrounding areas.

For seven days Isaac, Esau, and the rest of the family continue mourning. Finally, it is time to return home. When they say goodbye to each other, Isaac reassures all his nephews that they are always welcome in his camp. Esau confirms his father's words, "Yes, please come anytime. We will be honored by your visit."

"You are also most welcome here, Uncle," Nebaioth, the new clan leader, answers. "And whenever there is a need, do not shy away from asking us for help. We will always be there for you."

When Isaac arrives home, he mourns the loss of his brother for many more weeks. He feels very lonely. His parents died many years ago and he has little in common with his younger brothers. It's not to say that Zimran and the others are not kind; they are just so much younger than he is. They were born after he got married and are from a different generation. There is no one left now who went through the same ups and downs of life that shaped him into the man he is.

"Ishmael often understood me without me having to say anything," Isaac shares with his sons. "We have gone through so much together."

Puzzled, Jacob asks his aged father, "Didn't Grandfather send him away when you were only three years old?"

"That's true," Isaac sighs, "yet we have so much in common."

"You told me once that you both met with God."

"Indeed," Isaac confirms, "Those were powerful experiences. It happened to both of us when we were near to death. Nobody ever faced a crisis like ours."

"But I thought that Grandfather knew for sure that, after the sacrifice, you would be coming down the mountain with him?" Esau says. "So you were not really about to die, were you?"

Isaac looks at his son. The deep lines in his forehead testify to a troubled life. "I can assure you that I really felt like I was going to die then. After my father had tied my hands and feet with rope, I was terrified. Then he held the knife..." Isaac chokes back a tear when he thinks about that time. How rejected he had felt. He instantly remembers that Ishmael experienced a similar fear when he lay dying in the desert.

"Your uncle really was an amazing man," he continues. We both experienced what it is like for a man to be sentenced to death by his father. My fear only lasted a moment, but for Uncle Ishmael life in the desert was a daily battle against death. Grandfather cut me loose as soon as God provided a way out, then we were able to sacrifice the ram that took my place."

For a moment the two young men are silent; their father's words have made a deep impression on them. Then Isaac continues, "Thankfully, God blessed him by giving him many heirs, just like He promised Grandfather He would do."

"Didn't God promise us the same thing?" Jacob asks. "Grandfather often told me about that when he was still alive."

"Yes, he did," Isaac confirms, "that too is something Ishmael and I have in common."

Esau prefers not to talk about that. He knows that Jacob is the son of the covenant, not himself. Then he asks, "Is there anything else you had in common with Uncle Ishmael?"

"Even before we were born, God gave us our names," Isaac shares. "In the entire history of mankind that has never happened before."

"Is that so? Didn't God also give Grandfather and Grandmother their names?" Esau reacts in a matter-of-fact way.

"The difference is that they were elderly when God gave them a new name. God gave us our names before we were born," Isaac explains. "Besides, in both cases God sent a unique messenger to announce our names to our mothers."

"In fact, who was that?" Jacob inquires.

"It's hard to describe him," Isaac replies. "Sometimes He appeared to me in human form, while at other times He was invisible. He would always say, 'This is my will' or 'I shall do this', just as if He were God himself. And yet, no one has ever seen God, except Adam and Eve when they were still living in the garden of Eden."

Jacob is fascinated and deep in his heart he would like to meet that man. At that moment he has no idea that many years later his wish will be granted. One day he will even wrestle with him.

"Yes, your uncle was an amazing man," Isaac concludes. As he utters this, another thought about Ishmael's uniqueness comes to mind. "Don't forget that he was the first one to be circumcised. He was before me, and not only myself, but you too," Isaac adds with a chuckle.

A question occurs to Jacob. "By the way, how do you see this, Father? Does that mean that Uncle Ishmael is part of the covenant God made with you and Grandfather?

Esau pricks up his ears. He wants to hear about this. He has been circumcised, too, and he would really like to understand what this means with regards to his relationship with Jacob.

Isaac stares straight ahead, searching for the right words. Finally, he breaks the silence." That's a good question but difficult to answer, my son. I don't quite understand it myself, but I can clearly see God was with Ishmael and He is blessing his children and grandchildren." Then Isaac turns to Jacob, "God has a unique plan for you and for your offspring, but everyone who is circumcised can expect God's presence and protection." As he says this, Isaac worries about the adverse influence of Esau's wives upon his eldest son. He realizes that Esau tends to think that circumcision itself has made him right with God. Even though circumcision is important, as an act of obedience to God, there is more to it than that. He adds, "Above all, God asks that we walk with him. Whoever loves God Almighty with all his heart belongs to him. God will bless him with long life, just like he did for your grandfather and your Uncle Ishmael. "

"So what about circumcision then? Why is it so important?" Jacob asks his father with curiosity.

"God desires a personal relationship with every person on earth. He told Grandfather that it is his plan to bless all people on earth through him," Isaac explains. "Circumcision is only the outward sign of inner devotion to him."

Jacob nods; he understands.

Esau sighs deeply and says, "It's not easy to please God." To him, serving God feels more like a duty than a joy. There are so many things God doesn't want you to do; life is so much easier if you don't have to reckon with him so much.

Isaac knowns how his son struggles and it makes him sad. *"Lord, help me to put Esau back on the right track,"* he prays softly. Then he answers his son, speaking emphatically. "Forgiveness, Esau, forgiveness is the road to a clean heart. Forgive those who have treated you wrong and receive God's forgiveness for your own wrongdoings; only then will you find joy in serving God. Your Uncle Ishmael forgave Grandfather for rejecting him and after that found joy in the restored relationship. God also rewarded him with the friendship and intimate brotherly love he and I were able to share for a long time. Follow your uncle's example and everything will turn out well."

Have you been touched by Ishmael's life? Are you surprised that God blessed him the way He did?

The Lord's hand on Ishmael's life is evident from the moment his mother ran away from her mistress, Sarah, and met a stranger near a well in the desert. That meeting touched Hagar so deeply that she obediently returned to the one who had been mistreating her. She believed his promises. Let's take one more look at this meeting as described in Genesis 16:7-12. It is here that we encounter the following unique events:

1. For the first time in the history of mankind the Angel of the Lord appeared. Hagar was privileged to be first human being ever to meet God's heavenly messenger.[17] This had not occurred during the preceding 2000 years of the existence of mankind. Throughout the ages the church fathers have understood the Angel of the Lord as an appearance of the Lord Jesus Christ, the Word of God, in human form. For more information, please go to www.godlovesishmael.com/angel.

2. Apart from Eve, who had been with God in the garden of Eden, Hagar was the first woman to address God directly.

3. Hagar was the first woman on earth to receive a promise from God. God had made Eve a promise as well, but that happened while she was still in paradise.

4. God promised Hagar that her son would become a great nation. No other woman received a promise of such extraordinary blessing directly from God. Only Abraham, Isaac, and Jacob received the same promise directly from God.

5. Ishmael became the first person who received his name from God before he was born. Only three other people in the history of mankind received their names from God before birth: Ishmael's half-brother, Isaac, John the Baptist, and his cousin, Jesus.
See www.godlovesishmael.com/4named.

6. God gave Hagar's son a special name. The name Ishmael means "God hears" and contains a wonderful promise in the context of prayer. God made himself known as the God who would hear both Hagar and Ishmael's prayers.

7. Ishmael would become a "wild donkey of a man." In Scripture the wild donkey is an image of freedom and independence, contrary to the domesticated donkey that has to mind its master. So, while the

Angel called Hagar "servant of Sarah," He promised her that Ishmael would not be a servant but a free man.

8. Hagar was the first person to give a name to God. She named him "the God who sees," pointing to his attribute of seeing, in addition to the attribute of hearing, by which He had made himself known to her. The fact that the name Hagar gave was recorded in Scripture, shows the pleasure God took in this interaction with her.

The seventh point needs additional explanation. Throughout the ages, most Bible scholars have interpreted the phrase, "wild donkey of a man", with a negative connotation, referencing to the "wild Arabs". This view has even impacted some Bible translations, in which Ishmael and his offspring are depicted negatively.[18]

The original text in the Hebrew Torah, however, is neutral. Furthermore, the expression 'hand upon' indicates who is the most powerful. According to the text, Ishmael will not be ruled over by any other people, nor will he rule over others. How true this has been of the Bedouin people on the outskirts of the Arabian deserts. It seems that the advent of Islam and tales of barbaric Arabic Bedouins have negatively influenced the interpretation of the original text.

In his book, *Arabs in the Shadow of Israel*, the Lebanese scholar Tony Maalouf maintains that every single part of the prophecy spoken by the Angel of the Lord, was meant to comfort Hagar.[19] The command to return to Sarah was an extremely difficult one to obey. No counselor would ever advise his mistreated client, "Submit yourself to your abuser." Would God, after the previously mentioned blessings, conclude his message to Hagar with a curse over the delicate life in her womb? Would He not rather encourage her with a promise of further blessing?

The gravity of Sarah's mistreatment is made clear by what the Angel of the Lord says about it. He speaks of oppression (Genesis 16:11). The Hebrew text uses the exact same word to describe the immense oppression of the Israelites at the hand of the Egyptian Pharaoh (Exodus 3:7,17), as well as the grievous suffering of Job under Satan (Job 10:15, 30:16, 27).

A detailed study on Genesis 16:12 can be found at
www.godlovesishmael.com/genesis16

It should also be noted that for a period of over thirteen years Abraham and Sarah lived with the expectation that Ishmael was the son of the promise. Why did God wait all this time to reveal to them that he wasn't? Could it be that he wanted Ishmael and his descendants to realize that they are indeed deeply loved?

When God announced to Abraham that Sarah would conceive a son, Ishmael was thirteen years old. His childhood behind him, he was now a young man. He spent the most vulnerable years of his life being loved by his earthly father. Even when it became known that he was not the son of the promise, he was still loved. The following unique events and blessings can be seen in the life of Ishmael.

1. The first intercessory prayer recorded in Scripture is Abraham's prayer for Ishmael, and God heard his prayer too!

2. God promised Abraham that Ishmael would become the father of twelve sons. This is equal to the number of sons that God blessed Isaac's son Jacob with.

3. God heard the voice of the young Ishmael when he lay dying. In doing so, He showed himself as the God who indeed hears.

4. The phrase, "God was with…" is used for the first time in Genesis 21:20. Centuries later, the prophet Isaiah, spoke about Immanuel – God with us (Isaiah 7:14). Those were comforting words for the descendants of Isaac and Jacob: the Israelites. The New Testament shows us the fulfillment of Isaiah's prophecy in the person of Jesus Christ. When Jesus said farewell to his followers, He comforted them with the words, "Behold, I am with you always, to the end of the age."[20] Ishmael experienced his presence ages before that in a very real and personal way.

5. According to Genesis 25:6, Abraham gave gifts to the sons of his concubines. Two of them are named in Scripture: Hagar and Keturah. Thus, we know that Abraham did not reject his first-born son forever. He met with Ishmael before his death, in accordance with his love for him (Genesis 21:11).

6. After the death of their father, Isaac confirmed his love for Ishmael by living in Lachai-Roi (Genesis 25:11), the same place where the Angel of the Lord had spoken to Hagar. Rather than staying in Mamre of Beersheba, he moved closer to Ishmael.

7. The Bible doesn't necessarily mention the age at which important characters died. For example, it is not known at what age Lot, Esau, or eleven of Jacob's sons died. On the other hand, the Bible does mention that Ishmael reached the age of one hundred thirty-seven years. The record of the length of his life indicates that Ishmael was important to God. Because we know that he had a long life, we can conclude that God's blessed and loved him.

All these unique events and blessings express God's love for him. Beside this, many similarities between the life of Ishmael and his younger half-brother can be noted.

	Event	Ishmael	Isaac
1	Supernatural birth announcement to the mother (by the Angel of God)	Genesis 16:11	Genesis 18:10-15
2	Received name from God before birth	Genesis 16:11	Genesis 17:19
3	Circumcised	Genesis 17:23	Genesis 21:4
4	Rejected by their earthly father at God's command	Genesis 18:14 Sent into the desert	Genesis 22:9-10 Threatened with a knife
5	Near death experience	Genesis 21:16 Under a bush	Genesis 22:10 On an altar
6	Personal encounter with the Angel of God	Genesis 21:17	Genesis 22:11
7	God intervenes and provides	(living) water	(living) sacrifice
8	Buried their father together, without Keturah's sons	Genesis 25:9	Genesis 25:9
9	Received the promise of becoming a great nation	Genesis 16:10, 17:20	Genesis 17:16, 26:24
10	Blessed by God	Genesis 16:11, 17:20	Genesis 25:11, 26:24
11	Father of twelve tribes	Genesis 17:20, 25:16 12 sons	Genesis 35:22b-26 12 sons (through Jacob)

All these parallels point to the fact that the forefather of the Ishmaelites has a very special place, not only in biblical history, but even more so in the heart of God.

We can safely conclude that the life of Ishmael was no accident. God allowed Abraham and Hagar to have a son. When Hagar fled, He did not let her go, but instead he purposefully intervened. This reveals that God had a plan with this yet unborn child. Also, even though at the age of thirteen Ishmael learned that he was rejected as the son of the promise, he was deeply loved, especially by God, but also by Abraham and Isaac.

How did the relationship between the offspring of these two patriarchs develop? Did the Ishmaelites live like savages? Did they quarrel with the Israelites? Or did they live together in peace and harmony? These questions are tackled in the next part of the book.

Part 2

Joys and Sorrows Between the Descendants of Two Half-Brothers

A journey with the descendants
of Ishmael and Isaac
until King Jehoshaphat of Judah.

"He shall be a wild donkey of a man, his hand against everyone, and everyone's hand against him, and he shall dwell over against all his kinsmen."
Genesis 16:12

Peoples from Abraham

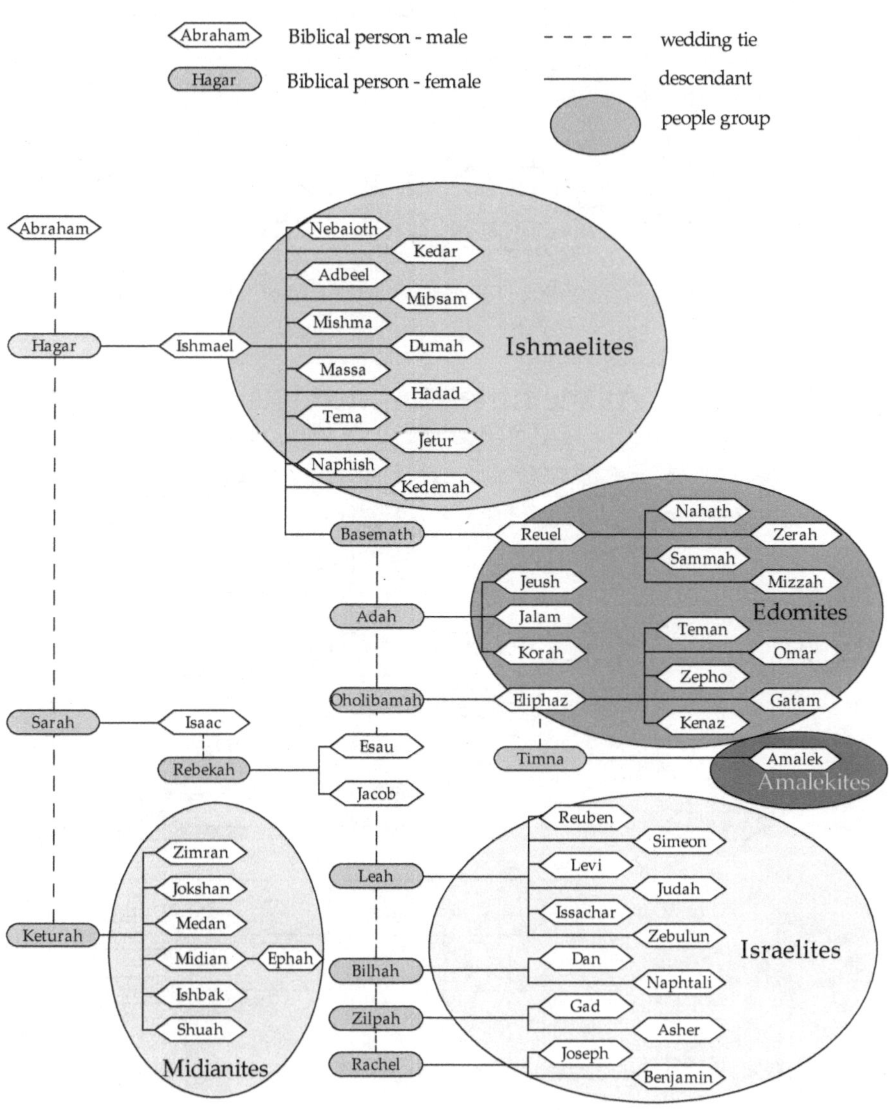

At the time of Joseph

Abraham
Ishmael
Isaac
Nebaioth
Kedar
Esau
Jacob
Ishmael
Sammah
...
Eliphaz
Joseph
Massa
Baraka
Naim
Job
Teman
Eliphaz

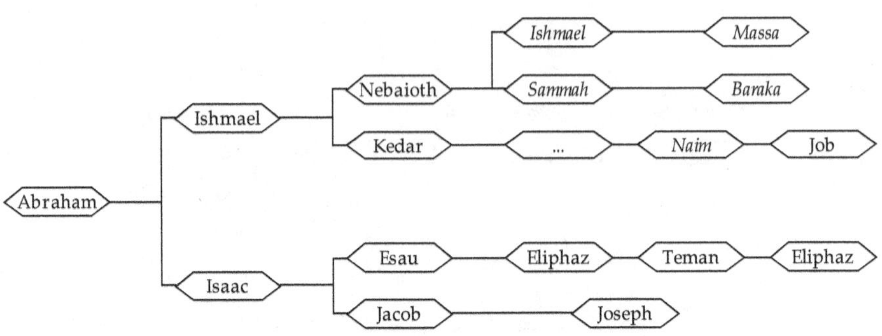

Note: the relationship between Job and his ancestors is based on interpretation

At the time of Gideon

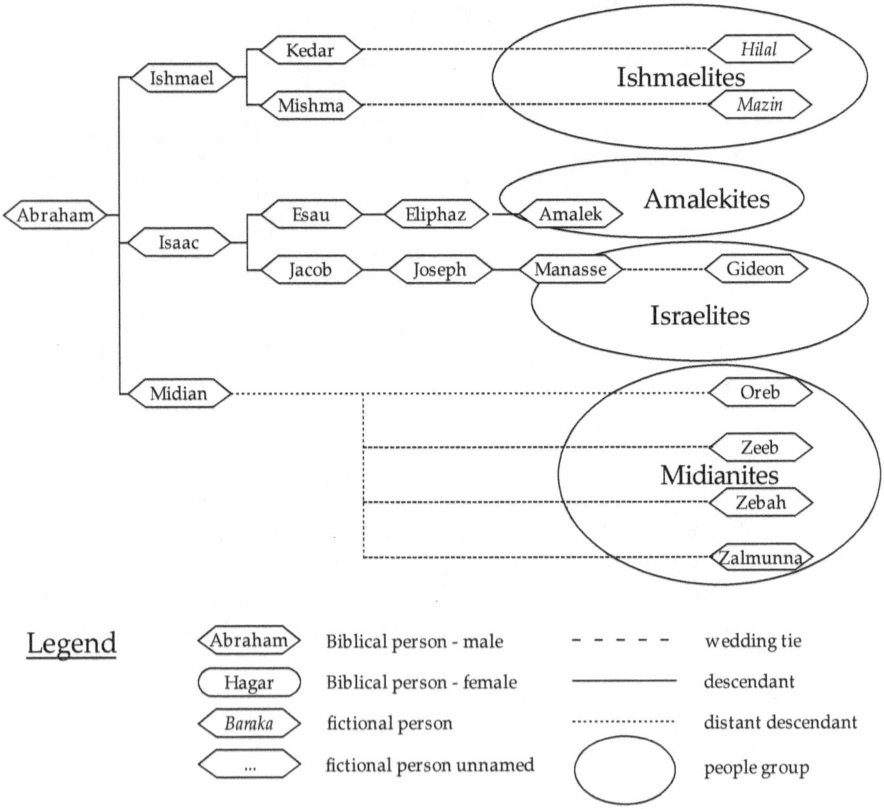

Abraham
Ishmael
Isaac
Midian
Kedar
Mishma
Esau
Eliphaz
Amalek
Jacob
Joseph
Manasse
Gideon
Hilal
Mazin
Ishmaelites
Amalekites
Israelites
Oreb
Zeeb
Zebah
Zalmunna
Midianites
Legend
Abraham
Biblical person - male
Hagar
Biblical person - female
Baraka
fictional person
...
fictional person unnamed
wedding tie
descendant
distant descendant
people group

At the time of king David

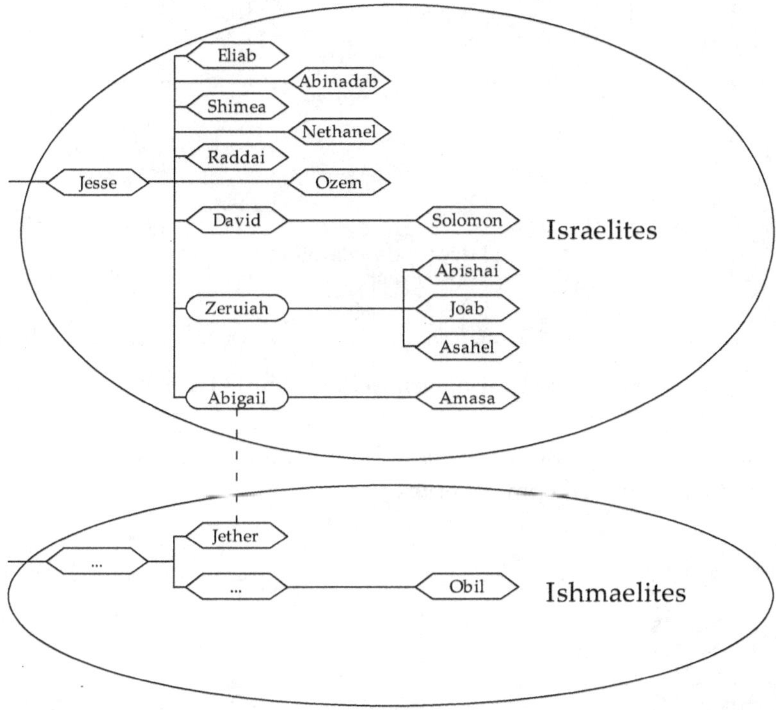

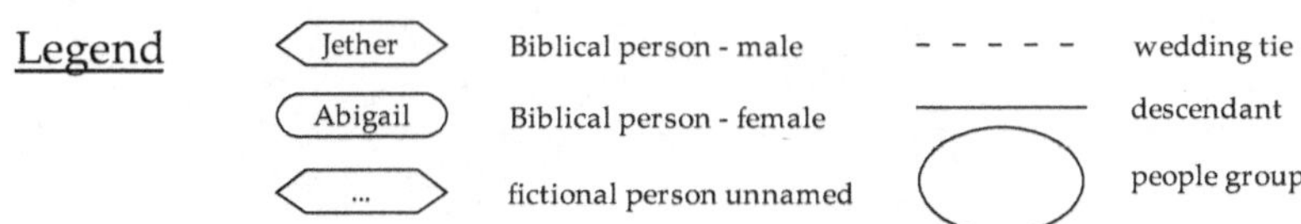

Note: the relationship between Jether and Obil is fictional

Legend

Jether	Biblical person - male	- - - - - - wedding tie
Abigail	Biblical person - female	descendant
...	fictional person unnamed	people group

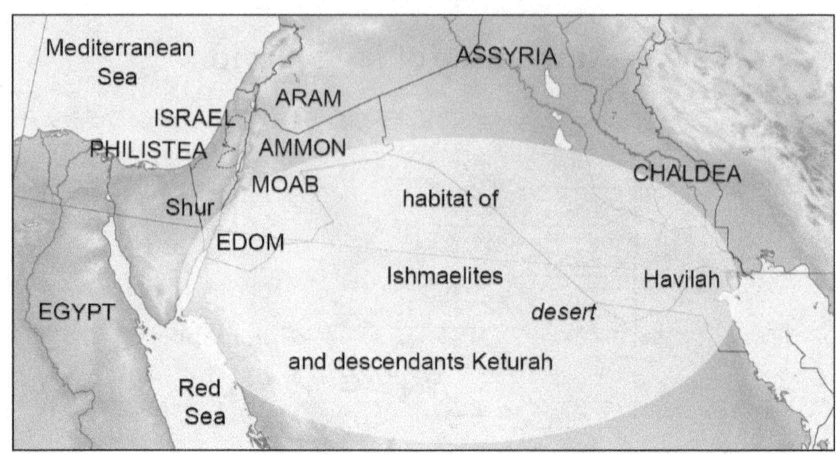

Habitat of the Ishmaelites from Shur to Havilah

For an animation clip about the spread of the Ishmaelites, go to www.godlovesishmael.com/peoples

Several years after the death of Ishmael

12 Migrations

At the rock with the oval aperture take the path on the left and continue until you reach the wadi. Then turn left and follow the riverbed past the sixth bend. Immediately after, leave the main wadi and take the arm that curves to the right. Stay on this path until the second well, which is a good place to rest, as you will find water there throughout most of the year. Next take the path on the right, at three stones' throw distance from the well.

Esau has made the journey many times and knows the trail like the back of his hand. *After the cloven tamarisk tree follow the trail in the direction of the 'camel mountain' and then…*

When Esau sees the mountain in front of him, a smile appears on his face. *Such a fitting name; approaching the mountain from this area, it looks just like a resting camel.* Esau veers left around the mountain and then the familiar ridge comes into sight on the horizon. At last he spots his destination; nestled in the foothills of the mountain range lies the encampment. Immediately, he notices it is quite a bit smaller than it used to be. *Strange! Could this be a different tribe of nomads? Is it possible that my nephews have moved and pitched their tents elsewhere?*

A few of the young men are sharpening their arrows outside on the ground. Esau approaches the youths, but he doesn't recognize any of them. After exchanging greetings, he asks, "Whose camp is this?"

The eldest replies politely, "This is the camp of Nebaioth, son of Ishmael, son of Abraham."

"And you are?"

"I am Massa Bin* Ishmael Nebaioth."

"Great, call your grandfather and tell him that his nephew is here."

"Are you Uncle Esau?" the youngster asks him eagerly.

Esau nods while he makes his camel kneel down, then adds with a laugh, "Quickly now, fetch your grandfather."

Soon, both relatives warmly embrace one another. After exchanging the latest news, Nebaioth explains why the camp has shrunk. "God blessed us all with rather large families, so we've had to spread out."

Esau nods. "I didn't even recognize the children when I first arrived. Massa has grown so tall, and you have so many grandchildren. "Pretty soon you people will take over the whole world!" he adds jokingly.

---

* Bin is Arabic for "son" or "son of".

"Have no fear," Nebaioth smiles. "We will never bother you and your brother. Nearly all of my brothers have moved eastwards, where there is plenty of room for them and their flocks."

Esau is surprised. "What a coincidence! Jacob also seems to have settled in the East."

"Oh really?" exclaims Nebaioth. "What a shame! How could he just have left your father?" While he is still speaking he recalls the things Esau told him last time about Jacob. He had pretended to be his brother and, in this way, stolen the blessing of the firstborn son from Esau. The mere thought makes Nebaioth angry. He adds, "Jacob is a dirty trickster."

Esau is glad to have his nephew's support. He would rather see Jacob dead than alive and for a while he even contemplated ways of getting rid of him. Then he would still inherit everything from his father for Jacob didn't have children or even a wife yet. Anyway, with his brother gone now, it doesn't really matter anymore. When father dies, Jacob's stolen blessing will be his after all.

In the afternoon a lavish meal is served, specially prepared to honor the visiting relative. After all have eaten their fill, they recline against the pillows and are served freshly brewed tea. As each is sipping his beverage, Esau explains the reason for his visit. "Father has instructed Jacob to choose a wife from among our relatives in Haran. I, too, would like to honor my father and marry a girl from our extended family. That is why I would like to suggest an alliance between us through marriage."

Nebaioth immediately welcomes this idea. "Of course! It would be an honor to be allied with your family. What about your father, what does he say?"

"He is old and blind. I am responsible for all the affairs of the camp now. He doesn't really deal with anything anymore and pretty much lets me do whatever I think is right. So, don't worry about him." Esau replies.

"I would still like to have his consent. He is your father after all, and as long as his mind is still sound, we must respect his leadership," Nebaioth points out. "I would really prefer to have his blessing on this agreement."

Esau is a bit taken aback by his nephew's reaction. *What if Father rejects this idea?* At the same time, he realizes full well that Nebaioth is right.

When Esau gets home, he waits for the opportune moment to inform his father about his plans. When the time comes, he emphasizes in detail how delighted Nebaioth is by the idea. Fortunately, Isaac agrees and shortly after, Esau makes the long trek back to the camp of his relatives one more time, taking a generous dowry with him. He has noticed that Nebaioth has a beautiful and sweet granddaughter named Noura and is dreaming about getting married to her.

After Nebaioth has discussed the matter with his son, he lets Esau know that they have no objections. Esau breathes a sigh of relief and fantasizes about the upcoming wedding night, but Nebaioth hasn't finished speaking yet. He continues, "We shall also ask the girl if she agrees."

Esau now must exercise patience. First of all, the father will speak with the girl, then her mother. After that, she will have some time to think about it before giving her final answer.

Three days later, Nebaioth takes his nephew aside and says, "We asked Noura and her mother."

Bursting with curiosity, Esau tries to read Nebaioth's facial expression. His nephew speaks with a warm smile, but hides his true emotions. *What will the answer be?*

"We are very excited with such an alliance between our families through marriage," Nebaioth adds.

Esau is used to lengthy dialogs and indirect speaking but this time he wishes his nephew would be more straightforward.

"But Noura is too young to be married."

Too young? Esau is outraged. *This is ridiculous. She is at least seventeen years old and surely a mature young woman.* He wants to discuss the matter further but before he can open his mouth, Nebaioth continues, "I know that you are a strong and healthy man, and that is why I have another proposal." He pauses so that the words sink in.

Esau's curiosity is aroused, and he listens intently. He allows his thoughts to wander a little, as he recalls all the other lovely nieces and second nieces. Some of them would be agreeable to him as bride as well.

"You may marry my sister, Basemath," Nebaioth offers. "She is your age and has been a widow for a few years. I have already spoken to her and she is ready to join your family."

Visibly disappointed, Esau stiffly thanks his nephew for the offer. He tries to change Nebaioth's mind and attempts to negotiate for one of the virgins, but his words fall on deaf ears. Nebaioth remains unmoved. In the end, Esau makes the best of a bad bargain. After all, this alliance between the two families may prove to be beneficial to him in some way or other in the future.

Several days later, Esau leaves the camp with his new bride, hoping she will bring him prosperity.

Regrettably, Esau's third marriage does not improve the situation at home. Although Basemath adapts well to her new family, problems steadily increase with his other wives, Ada and Oholibama. Both argue continually with their mother-in-law, and especially during meal times the tension is often palpable. Every time he returns from the hunt, Esau must mediate the conflicts that have arisen in his absence.

After intense deliberation, Esau decides it is time to move away. The warm relationship he used to enjoy with his father has cooled off significantly and he is sick and tired of the bickering between his Hittite wives and his mother. Since he has never been very close to his mother anyway, he won't really miss her.

Not long after he has made his decision, a long procession of people and animals leaves Mamre going south. Esau had explored the mountains of Seir earlier and he likes the look of that area. There's plenty of room for his cattle to graze and the inhabitants are friendly, making it an inviting place to live.

Isaac is saddened by his son's departure for now there is no one left. His other son, Jacob, never returned home. Perhaps a wild animal killed him, or maybe robbers attacked him and sold him as a slave. Every day anew, Isaac must consciously decide to trust God to take care of his son. Now his remaining son has left him as well. He especially misses his grandchildren; they would often come and spend some time with him. Isaac is lonely and with little hope of hearing news of his youngest son. Will he ever embrace and kiss Jacob again? Will his family situation ever take a turn for the better?

Unbeknown to Isaac, something beautiful will happen a number of years in the future.

"What are you saying? My brother Jacob is coming?" exclaims Esau.

"Yes, indeed," the strangers answer. "Your servant Jacob has sent us to you to tell you of his arrival and he beseeches you to receive him mercifully."

"This is good news," responds Esau, "I will greet him appropriately." Immediately he instructs his servants to arrange a welcoming party and he sends Jacob's messengers ahead. Esau hasn't seen his brother for more than twenty years. The pain from Jacob's deceit is now a distant memory and the anger is gone. It no longer bothers him that he won't be the recipient of the lion's share of their father's inheritance. He is a rich prince in his own right with a private army of four hundred faithful men to fight for him, more than even his grandfather Abraham could boast of.

As soon as Esau can see his twin brother limping forward, he runs to greet him. He warmly embraces Jacob and kisses him several times on both cheeks. Both brothers allow their tears to run freely.

Jacob feels the tension drain from his body. All along he has been scared that his brother might want to kill him, but now Esau accepts him. In fact, he senses Esau's love for him in his heart.

Indeed, Esau is overjoyed to have his only brother back. Looking at Jacob's retinue, he asks, "Brother, what is all this?"

Beaming, Jacob answers, "God has blessed me." Proudly, he introduces his eleven sons to his brother.

"Well, Jacob, only one more, and you will have as many princes as your uncle Ishmael," Esau says jokingly. "Then your family will be complete."

Esau doesn't realize the depth of what he has just said, but his words leave an impression on Jacob. He has a feeling that God will indeed bless him with a twelfth son. God has a plan for his offspring as well as with the children of his uncle Ishmael. Only time will tell what that plan is.

13 Unexpected Salvation

A long caravan passes through the valley. At the head of the long undulating line walks a man leading a camel by the hand. Another camel follows its trail. It has no other choice, for its head is tied with a rope to the tail of the animal in front of him. In the same way a third camel follows… and a fourth one… and a dozen or so more. Joined together head-to-tail, they form a long chain of gently swinging desert ships moving steadily through the arid landscape. Once in a while, one of the animals snorts in mild protest. A fine dust is blown upwards from time to time by the east wind through the valley. The men cover their faces with their headscarves to keep the powdery sand out of their eyes, nose, and mouth. Meanwhile they constantly peer into the distance and listen carefully for any unusual sounds. Their cargo is costly and must be well protected. They need to keep out a watchful eye, because caravans such as theirs are an easy target for robbers.

Thankfully, the most perilous part of the road lies behind them. They are especially vulnerable in the eastern parts of the desert, where help is hard to find if one is attacked. But here in the valley, scattered Bedouins have made their home and shepherds are constantly about. And yet, one can never be too careful, the seasoned caravan drivers know. They are all familiar with this particular trade route and prefer to travel in large groups, as there is safety in numbers.

"Attention, men," the front man suddenly warns. "Someone is running toward us; he seems unarmed, though."

The men directly behind him pass on the message and in no time at all the entire procession has been informed about the approaching stranger. When the man gets near the caravan, he calls out loudly, "Peace be with you all!"

"Peace be with you too," comes back the response.

As soon as he reaches the front group, the stranger seeks out their leader.

"What do you want?" the leader answers gruffly. He doesn't want to stop, for the camels are tired and once they lay down, it will be hard to get them moving again.

"Where are you traveling to?"

"We are on our way to Egypt. Why?

"Excellent," the man answers. "I have a strong, young slave for sale. He will bring good money on the Egyptian slave market."

This sounds like something they might be interested in and quickly the caravan leader discusses the proposition with the other merchants in the caravan. Most of them continue to trudge on sullenly to their next resting place, but one merchant brings his animals to a stop and instructs one of his servants to make sure that none of them lay down. Within minutes he finds himself surrounded by curious onlookers. A couple of the stranger's brothers have joined the group as well.

"So, you have a slave for sale? Where is he?" demands the trader.

"Simeon and Levi, quickly, bring him," the stranger orders his brothers. In the meantime, he extols the virtues of the slave to this potential buyer.

When he sees the boy, the trader is intrigued. He is indeed as his owner described, a strong and healthy young man, with a muscular body and fine facial features. "How much do you want for him?"

The man looks at his brothers and one of them says, "Judah, he is at least worth thirty." The others nod in agreement, and Judah replies, "I will sell him to you for 30 pieces of silver."

Meanwhile the boy calls out, "Let me go, I have done nothing wrong." His eyes plead with his captors, but Judah ignores him and focuses on his negotiations with the merchant. That requires much effort and the trader realizes he could take advantage of the situation to strike a good bargain. With a loud voice, he rudely says, "Look at his smooth hands; surely this boy has never worked in his life. He is not even worth ten."

Ten pieces of silver is the price for an old female slave and far too low. But the brothers are uncomfortable, and they want to conclude the deal as quickly as possible. Judah tries hard to negotiate further and finally they settle on twenty pieces of silver. They count the money and turn over the boy to the buyer. He continues to cry for mercy from his captors, but they only laugh at him. When the caravan starts up again, one of them calls after him sarcastically, "Hey dreamer, good luck in your new position!"

Just before sunset, the caravan arrives at a suitable place to spend the night. The camels are untied and given food to eat and water to drink. The servants cook food above wood fires, first for their masters and then for themselves. During the meal, they leave the hands of the slave untied. With a rope around his waist tied firmly to a tree, he is unable to escape. A nearby servant keeps watch over him.

When the men have eaten, they stretch out their tired limbs and recline against the camel packs. As they sip steaming hot tea, the main camel puller pipes up, "Hey Massa, what is it that you have bought?"

"This was a really good deal; a well-built and clever boy, and I got him for next to nothing."

"What people and what tribe does he belong to?"

"The men who sold him wouldn't say; but look at him, who cares where he is from? I know he will bring a fine price."

After the meal, Massa walks over to check up on his new acquisition. "My boy, what is your name? "Joseph bin Jacob bin Isaac, Sir.

Massa blinks momentarily. "Who is the father of your grandfather?"

"Abraham, the Hebrew, Master," the boy answers politely.

"What? Impossible!" Massa exclaims greatly surprised. "Do you truly descend from Abraham?"

"Yes, Sir, I do."

Massa can't believe what he is hearing and calls out to his friends, "Listen to this! You won't believe whose tribe the boy is from!" The others interrupt their conversations and look up towards him.

"This is a great-grandchild of our forefather Abraham!"

"That makes him a relative of ours," one of the others concludes.

"The way those men spoke," a third one calls out. "It sounded so familiar; very different from the languages of any of the Canaanites that inhabit that land."

Joseph is taken aback as well. "May I ask you something, Sir?" he says with a timid voice, as he turns to Massa.

"Certainly, my boy."

"Who are your forefathers?"

"I am a grandson of Nebaioth, the grandson of Abraham."

"Are you an Ishmaelite then?" Joseph asks carefully.

"All the way, boy, from head to toe," Massa smiles.

Then everybody laughs and for the first time Joseph relaxes a little. He even dares to ask another question, "Are all of you Ishmaelites?"

"No," replies Massa, "some of us are from the tribe of Midian."

"But you are all somehow related, right? Wasn't Midian also a son of Abraham?"

"That's right," Massa confirms. "You are a clever boy."

A short while later, as the men settle down to sleep, Joseph lies on his back watching the stars. He tries to figure out what exactly has happened to him. It had been a momentous day; he had finally found his brothers, but then they had suddenly grabbed him, ripped his coat off of him and thrown him into a deep pit. Fortunately, the well had been dry; otherwise he might have drowned, too. After some time, they had pulled him out of the pit and tied him up, only to be dragged before these merchants and sold to them, as a slave. Here he is, far away from his father's home and on his way to Egypt.

"Oh God, where are you?" Joseph prays silently. "Why have you forsaken me?"

Overcome by grief he begins to cry softly. He would like to cry out in despair but controls himself, for he doesn't want to show weakness to the others. Tears roll down his temple and land in his dusty curly hair. *What have I done wrong for God to forsake me in this way?* In the midst of the pain of rejection and fear for the unknown dark future, another thought comes to mind. *It cannot be a coincidence that these men are my relatives and not complete strangers.* This knowledge encourages him, and he thanks God for the little spark of hope in his heart.

A short distance away, Massa is tossing and turning in his sleep. He dreams that robbers are raiding him. A group of marauders, armed to the teeth with swords and clubs, come straight at him. Their hawk-nosed faces are hidden behind headscarves, only their dark-brown eyes and bushy eyebrows are visible. They grab him roughly by the arms and tie him up. "Have mercy!" he cries, but they don't care. He can hear them snicker; pleased with their booty. Someone pushes him hard down to the ground. He barely avoids hitting his head on the edge of a sharp stone. While lying on the ground, he can feel the wind in his hair.

Slowly Massa emerges from the dream. He opens his eyes and tries to get his bearings. Everything around him is peaceful. There is a guard by the smoldering campfire. The camels are snoozing on their bent knees. *Whew! It was only a dream!* Massa turns around to get comfortable and soon dozes off again.

Early the next morning the merchants break up camp and before the sun is fully risen they make their way to Egypt. The mountains are behind them and rolling hills stretch out before them. The wide riverbed offers a smooth and easily passable road for the travelers and their heavily laden beasts. The tiny brook in the center meanders peacefully to the lower parts of the glen. Both sides of the stream are covered with lush grass. The men, who are so used to the desolate regions of the East, find respite here. Even the camels find fresh energy as they feast on the abundance of fresh green leaves and copious amounts of water.

Massa enjoys this part of the journey the most. There is no worry here of bandit raids. The Philistines inhabit these low-lying plains of Canaan, and thanks to his ancestors they are on friendly terms with them. The king in Gerar has even sworn to severely punish anyone who harms the descendants of Abraham.

Massa muses about the arrival in Egypt and all the friends he will meet again. As he turns his head around to assess the situation behind him, his eyes fall on Joseph, the slave, who is peacefully walking along in the procession of man and animal. Suddenly he remembers his dream. He had cried out, "Have mercy!" but the robbers had known no mercy. This young man had also asked for mercy, Massa suddenly realizes. During the negotiations with Judah and his brothers, he thought that Joseph was like any other slave. Only later that night, it had become clear that Joseph was related to them. But business is business and this was the opportunity of a lifetime to make a lot of money.

Ever since his dream, Massa has felt restless. His anxiety increases as he observes Joseph's attitude. He is such a gentle character. Despite the rough treatment he underwent at the hands of his captors, not even once has he grumbled. On the contrary, whenever Massa tells him to water the camels, he does as he's asked without complaint. Afterwards, he even asks politely, "Is there anything else I can do for you?"

As Massa's anxious thoughts grow, his conscience begins to bother him. *I should return him to his father's house.* But he immediately wonders about the wisdom of that idea. *What would the others think of me if I did that? Surely, they would mock me. It would be shameful to display such weakness. Besides, I probably wouldn't even be able to ever find his family anyway. Judging from their dialect, his vendors were clearly from an unfamiliar region.*

That same night, while the men set up the camp, Massa invites his cousin and good friend Baraka to help him find dry twigs for the fire. As soon as they're out of earshot of the others, he asks him, "What do you think of Joseph?"

"You made an excellent bargain. He is strong, healthy, and intelligent. But you already know that." Baraka responds.

"True, but what bothers me is that he is our relative and moreover, he didn't really deserve to be sold as a slave."

"What do you want to do? Let him go? Perhaps you can sell him back to his father," Baraka jokes. "You realize that would make you a laughing stock?" Reassuringly he adds, "Don't worry so much about it."

"No, I don't really want to send him back, but I can't sell him for profit with a clear conscience."

Baraka's eyes light up. "I've got an idea. Let me buy him from you for 20 pieces of silver. That way you won't make a profit, and your conscience will be clear."

"No, Baraka, you shouldn't profit from this either, after all you're an Ishmaelite too," Massa replies confidently.

Baraka nods in agreement with his friend.

Their arms filled with twigs, they return to the others. As Baraka observes them going about, he suddenly gets an inspiration. "Massa, listen. It just occurred to me that Imad and Waqqas are Midianites.* They are not

---

* For the relationship between the Ishmaelites and Midianites, see
   www.godlovesishmael.com/midianites.

as closely related to Isaac's tribe as we are. Sell Joseph to them for the same price. You will not make a profit and neither will you bring shame on our family."

Massa looks up surprised. This seems like a welcome compromise. "Baraka*, once again you bring honor to your name," he says. "Why didn't I think about that?" The men exchange looks of mutual admiration. Massa is thankful for his friend. Baraka is often a blessing to him.

Imad has no objection whatsoever to purchasing the young man, so Joseph ends up in the hands of the Midianite, whom he serves during the remainder of the journey. Upon their arrival in Egypt, Imad promptly sells him to a slave trader for a good sum of money. When the group of merchants returns home, he is very pleased about the large profit made on Joseph.

Massa can't forget the matter. Joseph was such a kind fellow; he didn't deserve to be sold as a slave. He prays regularly, "God, please, bless Joseph in Egypt. May his master be kind to him." After a while, he feels hopeful. Perhaps Joseph will be all right after all. God will take care of him, just as He cared for Abraham, Ishmael, and Isaac in the past.

And Joseph? He is thankful that God has preserved his life. Confronted with his brothers' hatred, he realizes that things could have ended up much worse. For now, he is alive and well, thanks to the distant relatives who happened to be passing by.

---

* Baraka means 'blessing'.

14 A Familiar King

"Massa, listen to this. A slave has become a king," a man calls out as he approaches the tent.

The front of it, as well as part of the back wall, has been rolled up, so that the wind has free reign. The light breeze doesn't really bring much refreshment in the heat of the day, but still every little bit helps. Fortunately the thick goat hair cover, on top, keeps out the powerful rays and provides some shade from the scorching sun. The tent is the best place to be, for even the acacia trees with their tiny leaves offer little protection in the sweltering heat. Massa is slightly bent over as he works on his dagger. He is sharpening the knife blade by rapidly moving a hard stone over it. He had already noticed the man in the distance and immediately recognized him as his good friend, Baraka. They had already spoken with each other earlier that morning.

Without looking up from his work, he shouts back, "A slave turned king? Impossible!" *Baraka so easily believes the local gossip*, Massa thinks to himself.

"Really, it's true. It happened in Egypt," says Baraka as he arrives at the tent. "Unbelievable, isn't it?"

"You are taking the words out of my mouth, Baraka."

"It's the truth, though. Do you want to know his name?"

Massa is not really interested and shrugs his shoulders.

"Joseph! His name is Joseph!" exclaims Baraka.

"That's impossible. Joseph is not an Egyptian name."

"Well, his Egyptian name is Zafnath Paaneah, but I heard that he has a Hebrew name as well. Do you remember the young slave you once bought and then regretted it afterwards? His name was Joseph too."

"What are you saying?" Massa cries. Suddenly he is full of attention and carefully studies his friend's face. "Do you mean the Hebrew boy that I later sold to Imad?"

"Yes, that's right, that's the boy I am talking about. It has to be him!" Baraka responds excitedly. He then recounts the entire story as he heard it from an acquaintance during the midday meal.

Massa stares at his friend. *An imprisoned slave who interpreted Pharaoh's dream. A curious incident indeed.* "I can just about imagine that a slave would interpret Pharaoh's dream, but I cannot imagine that the same Joseph who I bought would have been put in prison. That boy was so gentle; he wouldn't hurt a fly."

"Well, I am convinced it is him. Even then he spoke about God and how He cares for us. Remember the dreams he told us about?"

Massa digs deep in his memory. "Do you mean the one in which the stars and the moon would bow down before him?"

"Exactly," answers Baraka. "Then he said that his brothers would bow down to him. According to him that was the interpretation of the dream. That's what had made his brothers so angry with him, even to the point of selling him as a slave."

"What you are saying sounds intriguing, but I haven't seen his brothers bow down to him at all. In fact, he bowed down to them when he begged them for mercy. So, his dream didn't really come true. And now that he's a slave in Egypt, there is no chance at all for it ever coming true."

"Well, I don't understand that dream either, but I am sure that this is the same Joseph. Don't forget that he is a son of Jacob and a grandson of Isaac. Those were men who knew God well and had personal encounters with him."

Massa can't deny all of that. "Well, if it's the same Joseph, then God at least did hear my prayers for him," he concludes in a matter of fact manner; then he bends over to continue sharpening his dagger.

During his next trade expedition, Massa decides to investigate. On arrival in Egypt, he curiously inquires after the new viceroy. To his great surprise, all Baraka's stories are confirmed to be true. The second most powerful man in the country was at first an imprisoned Hebrew slave. *But how strange for a slave to be put in the prison of the king's court. Such prisons are usually reserved for high-ranking officials. Slaves are thrown into the deepest and darkest dungeons, or else they are simply executed.*

Massa tries to find out why this slave had been convicted, but it remains unclear. Some say that he had tried to rape his master's wife. That, however, is very unlikely the reason for putting him in jail. His master would have killed him on the spot.

"Make way, make way for the king!" the officials on horseback call out. The main thoroughfare of Avaris is buzzing with activity. Following the other bystanders, Massa swiftly moves over the cobblestones to the side of the street. Shortly after, a long procession of chariots passes by. The first ones carry dignitaries, but then one appears that is completely covered with gold leaf. Seeing all that pomp and circumstance pass by, a shiver runs up Massa's spine. He realizes that is the carriage of the king of Egypt. Next to the king, on his left-hand side, there is a young man, a little taller than the king. As the chariot approaches, the young man turns his head and looks in his direction. Massa is startled. It feels as if the man is looking directly at him and recognizes him.

Bah, nonsense, there are hundreds of people standing along the road; he only casually looked in my direction. But those eyes… and that face… They are burned into his memory. Once the procession has gone by, he asks one of the bystanders, "Who was that man next to the king?"

"That is the ruler, Zafnath Paaneah."

"Do you mean the viceroy of Pharaoh?"

"Of course, who else would be standing next to his majesty in his chariot?"

Massa feels conflicted. Could that be Joseph, the youth of so long ago? The look in those eyes… was that why Zafnath's glance toward him had affected him so much? *No, it was just coincidence. I really shouldn't be so gullible,* Massa decides and he continues on his way to buy the last of the supplies for the long journey home.

A few years later, the East is hit by a famine. Because of the lack of rain, the seedlings have not matured properly, and the harvests have been too meager to live on. The leaves on the trees are unusually small and it is difficult to find enough feed for the herds of camels. Massa and Baraka consult with their relatives as to what is to be done. Trade with Egypt has diminished, because the people there suffer the same problem. They haven't been there for a long time.

"I think we should be able to make some money with the spices," says one of the men in the circle. "The market isn't what it used to be, but the Egyptians love to burn incense in their temples. Perhaps that is what we should focus on, and then…" A lively discussion follows with much shouting and many hand gestures. Finally, the decision is made and the men immediately start to make preparations for a new trip.

"You are Ishmaelites and not citizens of Egypt, therefore I can't help you," the official firmly states.

"But we have been trading with your people for years; we are friends," Massa argues. "You must help us."

"I am sorry, but there is nothing I can do for you."

"Bring me to your overseer; I want to talk to him."

The official reluctantly explains where they can find him but unfortunately, he can't help them either.

Finally, Massa learns that all decisions with regards to foreigners are taken by the viceroy himself. "Well, let's go and see him," he says resolutely to the men in his traveling party. He is in fact looking forward to meeting Pharaoh's second in command. Perhaps then he can prove to Baraka once and for all that this man is not the same Joseph, who he bought as a slave long ago. At the same time, he has more or less given up hope to securing any amount of grain. *Why would the viceroy help us?* he thinks despairingly.

Once outside, Massa vents his frustration to his companions. "This is ridiculous. The Egyptians are worried that they won't have enough for themselves but look at all the immense storehouses! They are filled to the rafters. When there is a good harvest again next year, they will be stuck with an enormous surplus and the bulk of the grain will go to waste."

Baraka doesn't agree with his friend and says, "I can understand why. Do you remember Pharaoh's dream? That one really came true."

"That's pure coincidence, Baraka! It's true that we have seen seven years of great prosperity, just like in the dream, but that doesn't necessarily mean that we are now facing seven years of drought. God won't do that! He blesses those who keep his laws!"

"I used to think that too, Massa, until I heard the story about the man from Uz."

"You mean, Job bin Na'im? That is certainly a curious case. I understood that he was the richest man in that country."

"He was indeed, and he was known to everyone as the most God-fearing man around. He faithfully walked in the footsteps of our forefather Abraham and yet, everything was taken away from him." Baraka sighs deeply. He hopes something like that will never happen to him: losing all your livestock in a single day and, added to that, all of your children.

"Well, I'm pretty sure that he cursed God at some point. The Almighty would never allow something like that to happen to a righteous man," Massa says flatly.

"You would think so, but why would Job curse the God who had blessed him so tremendously? There is no just reason. I don't understand it either, but I just cannot imagine Job would have committed any punishable sin."

Still engaged in their conversation, they arrive at the viceroy's conference room. After explaining to the guards the reasons for their visit, they are ushered inside where they queue up with dozens of other people who are idly waiting for their turn.

"So according to you this is Joseph, the slave?" whispers Massa, as he peers over the mass of heads to catch a glimpse of the person seated behind the enormous stone table.

"You still don't believe me, do you?" Baraka whispers back. "In a moment you will see for yourself," he adds with a smile and a wink.

Finally their turn comes. Sitting at the table is a scribe who documents all decisions made. Behind him is the viceroy, seated on his throne. On each side, servants with enormous fans keep their master cool.

Just like the others before them, Baraka and Massa respectfully prostrate themselves before the king. While their heads touch the ground, the ruler takes a sip from his bronze goblet. After they straighten up, he asks them, "Who are you and where do you come from?"

"We are Ishmaelites from the East, Your Highness," comes the answer. "I am Baraka bin Samma bin Nebaioth."

"And I am Massa bin Ishmael bin Nebaioth."

Upon hearing those names, the viceroy squints and looks them both in the eyes. "What is your occupation?"

"We are merchants, Your Highness. We have come to trade spices and incense in Egypt," replies Baraka, the eldest of the two friends.

Massa feels uncomfortable. Little beads of perspiration appear on his forehead and cold sweat runs down his back as the viceroy asks these direct questions. In the meantime, he is very anxious to find out for sure whether this man is Joseph or not, but doesn't dare ask him, at least not in this official setting. If this is not Joseph after all, then Massa would look rather stupid and they might lose their last chance of obtaining some grain.

Suddenly, the ruler begins to laugh. He barks an order to his servants, and then tells the two friends, "Follow my servant." Massa is petrified. *What have I done? Why doesn't the king just give us what we have asked for?*

As they follow the servant to another hall, Massa has a lump in his throat. "Wait here until lunchtime. I will come back for you," the man says.

Baraka enjoys looking at the Egyptian artifacts that are tastefully displayed in the room, but Massa can't relax. After waiting for what feels like an eternity, he and his cousin are led to the dining room. They are given seats near the head of the table. They are well aware that they are being honored and Massa's nervousness gives way to curiosity and excitement. Here they are, not only meeting the viceroy of Egypt for the first time, but even sharing a meal with him. This is a sign of friendship and trust.

As usual, during the meal no one really talks. Only later, after everyone has eaten their fill and hot tea and fresh fruit have been served, does the conversation start to flow. It is during this lively exchange that the viceroy makes himself known to Massa and Baraka. Massa almost keels over in astonishment. It is true after all!

The ruler reminisces with them about their journey from Dothan to Avaris. Contrary to what Massa had expected, Joseph doesn't show any anger over the things that happened to him.

"Why did you end up in prison?" Baraka ventures.

Joseph then explains in detail what happened shortly after Imad had sold him to the Egyptian slave trader.

When he tells them about Potiphar's wife, Baraka becomes furious. *How dared that woman deceive him so?* "I have always maintained that you were innocent," he says passionately. Hoping that Massa will confirm his words, he turns towards him, only to see him looking downcast.

Massa feels downcast. He is responsible for the pain in Joseph's life. He should have taken him back to his father after all; or at least, he should have set him free.

Joseph senses what he is thinking and feeling and reassures him. "Massa, my friend, I am not blaming you. What you did was part of God's plan."

When Massa hears Joseph say his name, he looks up, straight into the eyes of the viceroy. "But I have caused you so much suffering and you were innocent!" he stammers. He is deeply ashamed of his actions and continues, "I am so sorry, Your Highness, please forgive me."

"I am not angry with you, Massa. Everything is all right," Joseph replies tenderly. The warm look in his eyes and the smile on his face attest to his words. As Joseph continues to unfold the events of the past years, it becomes obvious to the cousins that God has worked out everything for good, not only in Joseph's life, but also in the lives of others. "God sent me here to save us all from this famine," Joseph summarizes.

"Even foreigners?" Baraka carefully inquires.

"Even the foreigner," Joseph answers emphatically.

Massa is overwhelmed. He understands why Baraka asked the question. They still need to secure grain for their hungry people. What the vice regent has said means that he is giving them his word that he will sell them some of the stocks from the Egyptian storehouses. *Would he really be so kind to me even though I caused him so much pain? Is it possible for God to love me so?* Then he thinks back to the conversation that morning about the question whether good people may be punished by God "Majesty, do you know the story of Job bin Na'im?" he asks.

Joseph nods and shares what he has heard about this man who once was so extremely wealthy. Then he asks, "Is he well again?"

"The latest we have heard is that he is deadly ill," Baraka replies.

"May God bless him with patience to endure his suffering," Joseph sympathizes.

Massa and Baraka look at each other and both realize they want to ask the same question. Baraka is the one brave enough to ask Joseph directly, "Why does God punish him so severely?"

For a moment Joseph is silent. He tries to find the right words to express what he is thinking.

Massa feels a bit nervous. Perhaps this question will open deep wounds for Joseph.

Then Joseph responds calmly, "Sometimes God allows bad things to happen in our lives, for us to bless others. God uses everything for good for those who love him. These things test our trust in him."

On hearing this Baraka's eyes light up. Wonderfully, this man is saying exactly what he himself has felt in his heart. Now he knows for sure that Job didn't sin at all, despite all his harrowing afflictions.

Massa struggles to grasp it. "I can clearly see how God used everything that happened in your life for good, but, for Heaven's sake, what good can come out of losing all of your possessions and eventually even your life?"

"Massa, haven't you heard the stories of our ancestors, Adam and Eve?"

No one utters a sound. As Massa contemplates Joseph's question, he tries to understand what he means. What do Adam and Eve have to do with Job's trials?

Joseph explains, "In the Garden of Eden, there was no suffering and no death. After Adam and Eve had disobeyed God, however, they became ashamed and fearful. Then God took an unblemished animal out of his precious creation and killed it to provide clothing for them. God allowed the suffering and death of a perfect animal to cover their shame. The animal hadn't done anything wrong and didn't deserve to die. God used the life of an innocent beast to bless Adam and Eve."

"Hmmm, I have never looked at it like that before," Massa exclaims thoughtfully. "But I still can't see what the suffering of an animal has to do with the suffering of a human being. We often slaughter animals, in fact we usually slaughter one or more lambs for every feast."

"It is exactly through this sacrifice that we can understand the character of God," explains Joseph. "He allows that which is innocent to take the place of the guilty, to bless him. I was not at fault either and yet God has used my suffering to bless the Egyptians, even though they don't believe in him and still worship their idols."

While listening to Joseph, Massa watches him attentively. The ruler's face radiates peace and you can tell that he means what he says.

"God blessed me as well," Joseph adds, his eyes sparkling. "If you would have told me when I was seventeen that one day I would be the viceroy of Egypt, I would not have believed you." Taking another sip of tea, he gestures to one of his servants to refill the guests' cups.

When their meeting comes to an end, Joseph impresses on both men that they are always welcome at his palace. Whenever they are in Egypt, they must come and visit him. Massa and Baraka feel honored and promise him that they will certainly return.

When the cousins set out on their journey home, their packs are laden with so much grain that the camels almost give way under the weight. On the way, Massa thanks God for a successful trip. "God, you are good," he prays silently. "Thank you for using the suffering of Joseph to save us and many others from starvation. Thank you for the new insight into the lives of Adam and Eve and how you blessed them through the suffering of an innocent animal."

As he pours out his heart to God, his thoughts go out to Job bin Na'im. *Perhaps Baraka is right after all and Job hasn't sinned.* Massa feels compelled to pray for him on the basis of what he has understood so recently. Choosing his words carefully, he prays, "O God, bless Job and use his sufferings for good and for your glory."

Suddenly a deep sense of peace and calm fills his heart. He still has no explanation for unjust suffering but is convinced that God will hear his prayers.

15 A Speaking Thunderstorm

"Are you really serious?" Massa exclaims surprised.

"I am. I already told you years ago," Baraka says, with a grin on his face.

Filled with amazement, Massa looks at his cousin. He knows him well enough to understand that he is not joking, and yet, this news catches him off guard. "Is he really completely recovered; are you saying that he regained all of his former wealth?"

"Yes, God's blessing is on him again."

"Surely, he must have confessed his sins and turned back to God," Massa insists.

"Not at all, God actually came to him and spoke with him."

"Of course, God, in his great mercy, told him what he did wrong."

"On the contrary, Massa. God commended him for having spoken favorably of him.

"I can hardly take it in! It makes my head spin!"

"Come on, Massa, you're a sensible man, which I truly appreciate about you, but there are things you must accept by faith. Don't you remember Joseph?"

There's a lot more Baraka would like to say, but he sees that his friend is struggling to take it all in. What can he do to help Massa to believe, too? Then an idea pops into his mind. "If you really want to be sure, why don't you go and find out the truth for yourself?"

Massa's eyes light up. *Not a bad idea, except that it's a long and costly journey.*

Baraka notices the hesitation and he nudges a little further, "Aren't the things of God more important than anything? When you focus on them, everything else falls into place."

Recognizing his friend is right, Massa gives in. "All right. I'll go, but only if you come with me."

"It will be an honor to accompany you, dear cousin," Baraka responds. Immediately the two deeply engage in making plans to visit Job.

"Where is the house of *Sayyed** Job Bin Na'im?" Massa asks a lone shepherd boy.

---

* The Arabic *Sayyed* means Mister in English.

"He lives by the oasis of Hadad. Follow the wadi until the black rock and there take the trail that veers slightly to the left. At the very end of the mountain range, you will see the oasis."

"How far is it from here?"

"You will get there before midday," the boy replies politely.

Carefully following the directions of the young shepherd, Massa and Baraka continue, until a large grove of tall palm trees appears in front of them. The treetops are heavy with enormous clusters of dates. Very soon they will be ready to be harvested. Between the trees are several Bedouin tents. The friends also notice a tall mud house, with its window frames and roof top lined with white gypsum powder. The dwelling looks well maintained and clearly belongs to a wealthy man.

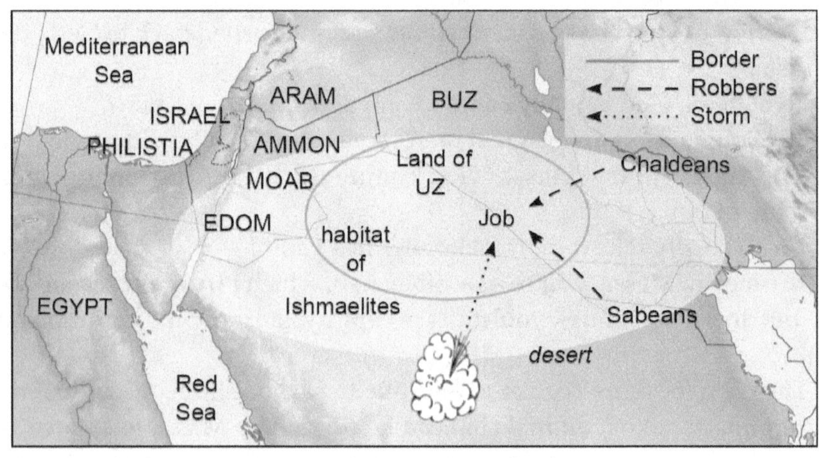

Probable habitat of Job

As soon as the two men arrive at the house, a servant welcomes them warmly. "Please, leave your camels with me. I will give them water, and care for them." Although they are complete strangers, the weary travelers immediately feel at home.

"This is our kind of hospitality," Baraka comments laughingly. Massa nods, while following another servant towards the house. Inside, the coolness is a welcome relief for them after the stifling heat of the burning midday sun. The man allows some time for their eyes to adjust to the dimness, before taking them up the stairs. They climb to the top floor where the servant offers them a seat in the lavish guest room. Shortly after they have sat down on the comfortable floor cushions, a grey-haired man with dark piercing eyes enters the room. *So, this is the man we've heard so much about,* thinks Massa.

Job greets each of them by kissing them on both cheeks. Immediately after exchanging the customary pleasantries, a servant comes in and lays out refreshing drinks and an array of fresh fruits. Their host leaves them again to attend to unfinished business but returns at lunchtime.

After a wonderful meal with plenty of meat, the men lay back and take time to get to know each other. Job gets interrupted regularly by servants needing instructions, all the while managing to give his guests his full attention. Despite his age, his mind is sharp.

After a while, Massa feels the time is right for him to question him. Not wanting to be too direct, he asks Job first of all how he came to know God.

"When I was young, my father used to tell us the stories about our forefathers," Job begins, and then names Adam, Enoch, Noah, and several others. When he tells them about how God called Abraham out of Ur of the Chaldeans and brought him into the land of Canaan, his eyes light up. Job is visibly proud and grateful for the heritage that his ancestors have left him.*

"Abraham is my example regarding offering sacrifices to our God," Job explains. "Isaac and Jacob followed their father's example and built altars to our God as well. During those times God would often speak with them."

Baraka and Massa are captivated by the stories of their distant relative. What he says reveals that he has a deep knowledge of God and of his dealings with mankind. But there is something unusual about him. On the one hand, Job displays much respect and reverence for God, on the other hand it sounds as if He is his most trusted and close Friend.

"You know," continues Job, "the most beautiful sacrifice is the one God himself made on our behalf."

Massa looks at him not understanding and asks, "What do you mean?"

Job explains, "After Adam and Eve sinned in the Garden of Eden, God sacrificed some of the precious animals He had created to make them skins to cover up their shame."

Baraka looks at his friend and winks. Then Massa remembers Joseph's words. He had said exactly the same thing.

"The sacrifice of an innocent animal reconciles man with God. Therefore, I make such a sacrifice regularly," Job continues.

Massa is deeply moved by the faith of this man. He can no longer contain his curiosity and musters up the courage to ask his burning question. "Why did God punish you so severely? How could God do such a thing, when you were endeavoring to be reconciled to him?"

The silence that follows seems to last for an eternity. Massa starts to feel uncomfortable. *Perhaps I was a little too forward. Have I dishonored my host in asking this?* He begins to regret his words, but before he can apologize for his presumptuousness, Job breaks the silence.

---

* For Job as a descendant of Ishmael, see www.godlovesishmael.com/prophet-job.

"When God took everything away from me, everyone, including my best friends, was convinced that I had committed a grave sin. They didn't hesitate to tell me so. How I suffered then." As Job speaks, his eyes brim with tears.

Massa notices and tries to comfort him. "Thankfully, all that has passed; you seem to be doing so well now."

Job looks at him for a moment before he responds with words that come from the depth of his heart, words that Massa will never forget. "God gives and He takes. God takes and He gives again. The name of God be praised into eternity."[21] With this powerful statement, Job shows that he sees no room for coincidences or mere fate in life. The immense losses and the countless blessings in his life are all in God's hand.

Job's words make a profound impression on Massa. His respect for the white robed man sitting across from him has greatly increased in the last few hours. Job is a man of flesh and blood, just like he is, but with an unshakable faith in the goodness of God. Massa realizes that he still has a lot to learn.

"Come," says Job, "let's go outside. I will show you the fields."

Once outside, the men blink a few times. Although the sun's strength is waning in the late afternoon, the contrast between the dark room and the bright daylight is still strong. As they stroll around the back of the house, Massa hears the bleating of sheep. A perceptive host, Job continually watches his guests to make sure they are comfortable and he immediately notices the curiosity on Massa's face. "Come and see the newborn lambs," he invites as he walks over to a clay fence. Inside the pen are a few ewes that have recently lambed. Instinctively, Massa counts their offspring. It has been quite a few years since he has dealt in livestock; nevertheless, he remains a Bedouin at heart with a lot of knowledge and experience. He notices there are too many lambs for the number of ewes present. Surprised he asks, "Where are the other ewes?"

Job understands his question and chuckles, "What you see here is nothing less than God's hand upon my life." Before Massa can respond, he continues, "Every single ewe has given birth to three or four lambs instead of one or two."

"Praise be to God!" exclaims Baraka.

Massa adds reverently, "Thanks be to God!"

A little while later the three men enter Job's vineyard. Suspended beneath the thick canopy of dark green leaves they see deep blue clusters of grapes. Job picks off a bunch and divides the fruit between the three of them. Enjoying the lush green around them, they find a place to sit in the cool shade of the vines.

Meanwhile, it is clear to Massa that Job is a righteous man who has not been punished by God for his sins, but that still leaves the question of Job's suffering. "Uncle Job, you are convinced that God allowed you to suffer, even though you didn't deserve it. Did you never doubt God's goodness?"

Job senses his guest's sincerity. For a moment he looks Massa in the eyes, but then he stares off into the distance again. "In the midst of my circumstances at the time, I did doubt. Sometimes, I almost cursed God but I'm glad I never did. When I was at my worst, I did curse the day of my birth.

Listening to Job tell his story, Massa can't help but sympathize with him. He realizes that, if he had been in that situation, he would have most likely cursed God.

"Whenever I focused on God and poured my heart out before him, I found some peace of mind. He did not answer me, but I felt relief in crying out to him."

"I feel the same sometimes," affirms Baraka.

"I often thought back to Noah Bin Lamech," Job goes on. "He was a righteous man and yet he had to work harder than anyone else. When his neighbors had finished their work on the land, they were able to sit back and rest, but God had given Noah orders to build an enormous boat. Think about that, while his friends were enjoying themselves, eating and drinking with their families, Noah was busy building his ark. On top of that, while he worked day in and day out, the people around him ridiculed him. Finally, after the rains came, Noah was marooned on that boat for months and months. Yet, the ark became his salvation. God rewarded Noah for his obedience and blessed him with a beautiful new earth, just for him and his family. God then made a covenant with Noah and sealed it by giving him a new sign in the heavens.

"Ah, yes, the rainbow!" Massa exclaims.

"Exactly! This encouraged me to trust in God. Noah didn't give up and was eventually blessed. Knowing this helped me to persevere, even to death if that came. I was sure that one day God would reward me, if not on earth then surely in heaven."

Baraka and Massa listen attentively to Job's story. While they are amazed by his insightfulness and wisdom, it is the child-like simplicity and humility of Job's faith that really grips their hearts.

Suddenly Massa thinks back to his visit with the viceroy in Egypt. "Your story is so similar to that of Joseph's," he asserts. "He also suffered a lot, even though he didn't do anything wrong, but later God blessed him abundantly."

Now it is Job's turn to listen, and while Massa outlines the story of Joseph, Baraka fills in the details.

When they have finished, Job exclaims, "Praise be to God." He has enjoyed hearing it and is thankful that God has used Joseph to save the lineage of Isaac. "That's a beautiful example of how God uses the suffering of the righteous for good, Massa," he concludes.

"But what finally happened to you? How did you get back to being well again?" asks Baraka.

"Well, let me finish my story," Job replies. "I was close to dying, when a violent storm arose. Within moments the entire sky was full of gray dust clouds, completely blocking out all sunlight. We heard loud thunderclaps, but there was no lightning. Suddenly, I distinguished words in the rolling thunder and I realized that the loud noise was a voice speaking from heaven. I was frightened and shook with fear. When I listened carefully to the words, I realized that they were directed at me. God the Creator was speaking to me. Praise his name!" As Job relates the events of that day, he is visibly moved by the memory of that dramatic moment that changed his life forever.

Massa appreciates the profoundness of the experience and shivers.

Baraka, who is soaking up every word, inquisitively asks, "What did God Almighty say to you?"

"He challenged me, questioning me about creation, for example the foundation of the earth; the storerooms filled with snow; who placed the stars in the sky and who sustains them. He wanted me to tell him who restrains the wild animals. As you can understand, I didn't even dare open my mouth."

Baraka and Massa nod.

"I became intensely aware of my own insignificance; that I am but a speck of dust to God the Creator within the vast universe. I admitted that I am nothing before him." While Job is speaking, a tear rolls down his face. "I confessed that I had spoken about things too wonderful for me to comprehend and that I was sorry for what I had said."

A reverent silence follows. The two friends feel in awe of God's greatness. Massa feels small and ashamed in the presence of this godly man but strangely, he doesn't feel condemned. Rather, he senses an invitation in his heart to fully commit himself to God.

Meanwhile the afternoon slips into evening. Groups of shepherds are returning from the fields with their flocks of sheep and camels. Job reiterates the invitation he gave his guests at lunch time. "Tonight you are staying here. My house is your house."*

The men gratefully accept the invitation. They had already assumed that Job would adhere to the unwritten laws of Bedouin hospitality.

After having enjoyed Job's company and generosity for three days, it is time for the men to return home. While servants prepare their camels, Massa and Baraka say their farewells to their distant relative.

"There is something I would like to give you," says Job.

---

* Arabic expression, meaning "consider this your home."

The men look at each other; they have already been blessed beyond their wildest dreams. "A thousand times thank you, Uncle Job. You have been generous towards us and given us plenty of food and drink for our journey. Our camels are weighed down with gifts," replies Massa, underlining his words with overt hand gestures.

Job acts as if he hasn't heard Massa and says, "My friends, what did God promise our forefather, Ishmael?"

"Well, God promised him that he would become the father of twelve tribes," Baraka volunteers.

"This is true indeed. However, I am thinking about something else God promised."

Neither has an answer.

"He would be a wild donkey of a man," Job continues. "Now God spoke about that to me as well."

"Really? What did He say?" both friends ask in unison as they look expectantly at him.

Job continues solemnly, "God said, 'Who has let the wild donkey go free? Who has loosed the bonds of the swift donkey, to whom have I given the arid plain for his home and the salt land for his dwelling place? He scorns the tumult of the city; he hears not the shouts of the driver. He ranges the mountains as his pasture, and he searches after every green thing.'"[22] With a big smile on his face, he adds, "I leave it up to you to work out what this means for us Ishmaelites."

After the men have mounted their camels, Job blesses them with these final words, "Go in peace under the protection of the Almighty."

"May the peace of God be with you also," Massa and Baraka respond. Then they indicate their camels to go.

When the oasis behind them is nothing more than a green dot in the distance, Massa looks over his shoulder and gives glory to Whom all glory is due, "Almighty God of Abraham, Ishmael and Isaac, You are good."

16 The Consequences of Jealousy

"Oreb, your sheep are looking healthy and well fed. I wasn't aware that you had had so much rain this year!"

"We didn't, Zalmunna. These sheep are from the other side of the Jordan."

"Well, well, you have started up a new trade then?" Zalmunna laughs.

"You could say that, but not in the way you think."

"Come on, tell me your secret."

"We trade with the Edomites, but the Israelites… well, their sheep are for free," Oreb replies, grinning from ear to ear.

"Free… from the Israelites? Impossible, they are born merchants."

"You are absolutely right. That is why we don't deal with them at all. We just take what we want, without asking their permission, haha."

"I'm supposed to believe that? You can just go and take away their sheep without any repercussions? The Israelites are really powerful!"

"Oh Zalmunna, I know the stories, but they can't harm us!"

"Why not? Their God always protects them. Don't you remember how they defeated the mighty Egyptians? Later, they slaughtered all the Amorite kings. And don't forget, they even killed some of our kings as well."

"I know, but those things happened more than two centuries ago, Zalmunna! You are aware, of course that they don't have a king; these days they don't even have a strong leader. I'll tell you what, come with me around harvest time. There will be more than enough for both of us."

And so, it happens that Zalmunna, the Midianite prince, gathers a large group of clan members to go and raid Israel. They circle the area where the Israelite tribe of Manasseh is before following the Yarmuk River valley in a westerly direction. As soon as the Jordan River comes into sight, Zalmunna notices a large encampment in the valley. Immediately he orders his men to stop. Although this is the place where he has agreed to meet his friend, Zalmunna is alert. As a Bedouin he has learned to never trust anyone's word. If you want to survive in the desert, you must be very sure about everything you do. Zalmunna peers into the distance and carefully studies the men and their camels. "They are the Midianites from the tribe of Oreb," he finally calls out and beckons to follow him.

Upon arrival, the friends exchange the customary greetings by kissing one another enthusiastically on their bearded cheeks. First the left side, then the right side, then left again and a few more times on the right. Afterwards, Oreb instructs his men with a loud voice to help Zalmunna's tribesmen pitch their tents. Then he takes the prince into his own tent where they exchange the latest news with each other. The camels, meanwhile, enjoy a little respite in the lush green valley.

Two days later, the entire company of men crosses the Jordan River. They must take extreme care, since the water level is still high this time of year. Due to the melting snow in the mountains and the spring rains from the north the banks are flooded, but Oreb knows all the passable areas like the back of his hand and, perched high atop their camels, all safely reach the other side.

When Zalmunna sees the Valley of Jezreel, he is astonished. As far as the eye can see, there are auburn fields of barley, ready for harvest, interspersed with fields of golden wheat. "This place looks like paradise," he says to his friend who is riding next to him. "Such riches!"

"Yes, isn't it great! And it's all here for the taking. Not one Israelite in sight."

"Where are they all? They must be lying in wait to ambush us," Zalmunna responds suspiciously.

As they approach a village he watches the walled houses like a hawk. Donkeys are tied to trees and walls and sheep lazily crisscross the rocky paths through the village. There is no other movement.

Oreb looks at Zalmunna. "The village has been deserted. Believe me, there is no need to be afraid," he asserts confidently.

"I'd rather be safe than sorry," Zalmunna responds.

Oreb, ignoring his friend's remarks, instructs his men to round up all the healthy animals. Visibly pleased with himself, he turns to his friend and superfluously adds, "See how easy that was?"

To Zalmunna's great surprise, they indeed don't encounter any resistance from the Israelites. Emboldened by Oreb's action, he orders his men to remove all the sheaves of barley that have already been harvested.

As dusk falls, small fires are lit everywhere in the surrounding mountains. "Look," says Oreb, "the Israelites are crawling out of their caves to prepare food."

"So that's where they were hiding. Unbelievable, they are too scared to even defend themselves."

A few days later, their camels laden with plunder and driving large flocks of livestock ahead of them, the Midianite tribes return to their homeland.

Upon arrival, Zalmunna relates in detail to the other Midianite tribes what he has done. Traders from the surrounding tribes also hear about the profitable raids into Canaan, and the news spreads as far as the neighbors in the east. When the Ishmaelite tribal leaders meet one another, the raids are all they talk about.

"I am seriously considering joining them next year," says Mazin, sheikh of Mishma. "Will you join us?"

Hilal, the leader of the Kedarites, the largest Ishmaelite tribe, is puzzled. "How can you justify such actions before God?"

Mazin is taken aback by his reaction, "What do you mean, my brother? The Israelites are so affluent., they can easily share some of their wealth with us. We live in the desert and have to labor every day just to survive."

"So, are you lacking anything?" asks Hilal.

"It's not that we lack anything, but a bit more prosperity wouldn't hurt. I think we deserve it. Moreover, the land used to belong to our forefather Ishmael. He was Abraham's firstborn son."

Hilal shakes his head in disgust and in disbelief. "You are still angry about that then? I think those Midianites have a bad influence on you."

"How can you say that?" Mazin is irritated and speaks loudly, more than he intended. "I was talking about our side of the family, not theirs." In his heart he knows Hilal is right but he would rather swallow his tongue than admit he is wrong.

"We should be content with what we have and accept God's allotment to us," Hilal states. "Our forefather Abraham set us this example, which we should follow."

Mazin has nothing else to say, but he doesn't want to be disgraced, so he cleverly changes the subject. A little while later, he has captured the attention of all those present with a tale about one of his adventures and everyone laughs.

Several years later, an enormous army marches towards Israel. All the Midianite kings have gathered together. The Amalekites, who still have an account to settle with the Israelites, have joined them. Defeated by Joshua years earlier, they now want revenge.

Mazin and a few men from his Ishmaelite tribe have come as well. After years of indecision, the temptation of rich plunder proved to be too strong. He reasoned that they wouldn't kill anyone and that it couldn't even be considered stealing. Hadn't Zalmunna told him that the Israelites had abandoned their villages? Also, his tribe has become closely related to Zalmunna's through intermarriage and they have become like brothers. The difference between Midianite and Ishmaelite is not so obvious anymore. Mazin is responsible for those who live to the east and belong to the tribe of

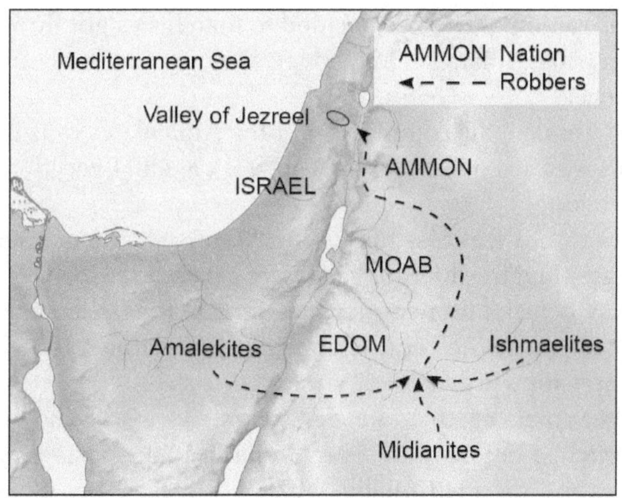

Possible route of the allied warrior tribes

For an animation clip, go to
www.godlovesishmael.com/gideon-battle

Mishma. The family name is the only remaining indication of their original roots.

The Midianite tribal leaders have decided to go out to battle regally. Their camels are adorned with gold trinkets around their necks, while they themselves are wearing purple robes and heavy gold rings and chains. Usually, these ornaments are worn during official royal visits. When confronting enemies, the treasures are left at home, but in this case the situation is different. The Israelites are afraid and hiding in caves, so they can hardly be considered an enemy. The various tribes are a spectacular sight, as they advance through the desert decked out in their finery.

Everyone is in high spirits. After having suffered humiliating defeats in the past, the time has come to restore their honor. Excitement is high as they expect to be victorious, which softens the pain over Isaac being the chosen son of the promise. They, the other descendants of Abraham, had been sent eastwards. Bitterness has become deeply rooted in their hearts. Isaac's descendants through Jacob have inherited the best land in the whole region, while they have had to survive in the arid desert for centuries.

This time the raiding party has decided to march straight through the three most eastern tribes of Israel. On the way, they plunder without meeting the least resistance.

"This is unreal!" the commander of the Amalekites calls out. "If things continue this way, we will never have to work again! Everything we want is here for the taking!"

"Just wait until we cross the Jordan," Oreb tells them. "There you will find the biggest and most fertile valleys you have ever seen."

Indeed, when the immense armies invade the Valley of Jezreel a few days later, the Amalekites and Ishmaelites are stunned by what they see. "Let's stay here for a little while," suggests Oreb.

The other chiefs agree and everyone gets to work. They want to have their tents pitched before dark. The Midianites take possession of the best spots. Mazin and his men finally settle in a reasonably pleasant area on the eastern side. Even though Mazin laughs and jokes with the other men, something has got to him. The thought of oppressing the Israelites bothers him. The way they have hidden themselves tells him that they must be terrified. Then he remembers Hilal's words. "We must be content and follow the example of our forefather, Abraham."

A few days later, rumors spread in the invading camps that the Israelites are rallying troops. The tribal chiefs get together to discuss their strategy. The atmosphere is relaxed, and the meeting seems but a formality. "How many are there?" Zalmunna wants to know. "I heard thirty thousand, give or take a couple of thousand," someone replies.

"There are over one hundred thirty thousand of us, which means we outnumber them four to one," Oreb calculates confidently.

"Plus the fact that we have the advantage of sitting high on our camels," someone else adds.

"All right then, just in case the Israelites are foolish enough to attack us, we will be ready to destroy them quickly," Zalmunna concludes dryly. Everyone bursts out laughing.

"They will flee before us, like dogs with their tails between their legs," jokes the leader of the Amalekites. One after the other starts to brag about the coming victory, until the men are roaring with laughter.

When they finally calm down, Zalmunna admonishes them, "Just to be on the safe side, let's station a few night watches." Not everyone thinks that that's necessary, but since they are doing this together, they all need to share the responsibility and so each of the encampments choose a few men to stand guard.

Something startles Mazin and he is wide-awake. *What is that? It sounds like pottery being smashed.* When he opens his eyes, he notices a weak flickering light through the cracks in the tent cloth. *Something is definitely wrong!* In a flash he reaches for his sword and jumps into action. Suddenly, powerful trumpet blasts resound throughout the valley, followed by loud shouting. Mazin attempts to make out the words, but the dialect is foreign to him. *Could they be Israelites? Impossible! They must have hired armies from other nations! With so many trumpets, they must have got a gigantic army together!* When Mazin leaves his tent, he sees burning torches everywhere he looks. They are surrounded!

He needs to decide quickly what to do. As their leader, he is responsible for the Ishmaelites that are with him. Everyone is awake now and the camp is in utter chaos. Swiftly, Mazin jumps onto his camel and tells it to get up. It's a good thing that these animals only need a few hours of sleep. While the camel rises to its feet, Mazin looks around to survey the scene. Enemy armies are positioned on the hills but the eastern side of the valley is shrouded in darkness. "Come. This way!" he shouts.

Several of the men hesitate. "What do we do about the sheep?" one calls out.

"Leave them and come quickly," Mazin commands. He knows in his heart they weren't theirs to begin with and now they must run for their lives.

Some of his people heed his warnings, but others can't bear the thought of leaving their rich spoils behind and begin to drive the sheep ahead.

In the dim light of the new moon, Mazin has great difficulty making out the narrow path. Fortunately, he is an experienced rider and he skillfully guides his camel. Behind him he hears the clattering of swords. Shrieks of panicked fighters pierce the darkness. Relieved not to be stuck in the middle of the camp, Mazin moves further and further away from the enemy. A short while later, a soft glow in the eastern sky announces the dawn of a new day. Mazin slows down and looks over his shoulder. Several members of his clan are behind him. He waits until the last person has caught up with him and asks, "Where are the others?"

"I don't know. They were busy rescuing their spoils when you gave us the order to leave," the man responds.

Mazin is upset that they haven't all obeyed him. What should he do now? As leader of the tribe he should defend his people, but it would be suicidal to return to the battlefield and face that massive army.

Now he is inwardly torn. On one hand, his honor as tribal leader is at stake, on the other hand, it was the stragglers own decision to disobey him. "Who of you will join me to go back and help them?" he asks. The men are too afraid. No one responds.

Well then, at least no one will be able to say I didn't try, Mazin thinks to himself. He turns his camel around and yells, "Come, we are going home!"

A few weeks later Mazin meets a local merchant who has just returned from Judah. The man is full of stories about the battle in the valley of Jezreel. "The Israelites only had 300 men and yet they were able to chase away an entire army. What a blow!"

Embarrassed, Mazin wants to defend himself and an angry retort is at the tip of his tongue, but he controls himself and continues to listen.

"All the Midianite leaders have been killed. They got hold of King Oreb and Zeeb even before they were able to cross the Jordan. Only Zebah and Zalmunna escaped, together with some of the members of our own tribe, but while recovering from the flight in Gilead, they were suddenly attacked. All of them were killed by the sword."

"How many casualties were there?" asks Mazin.

"The Israelites claim that they killed more than 200,000 men," answers the merchant confidently. Knowing he is exaggerating, he gestures wildly with his hands to make his words more convincing.

Mazin quickly does the math. *That is impossible; at the most there were 145,000. I escaped with about one hundred, and surely there must have been others who got away.* For a minute or so, he considers correcting the trader and putting him in his place, but then he changes his mind. He really doesn't want to dwell any longer on this incredible defeat.

Suddenly Mazin realizes how lucky he is. *I am the only prince who survived this unfortunate adventure. It's all because I was on the east side of the valley: which at first looked like the least desirable place to erect a camp. A good thing too that I didn't wait for the other men; I probably would have been killed as well.*

Not long after that, Mazin receives a visit from his closest ally. Having heard the stories about the battle, Hilal wants to talk to Mazin personally.

Abashed, the sheikh of Mishma relates the course of his little venture. "Luckily I set up camp in the eastern valley. That's the only reason I survived," he concludes.

"Luckily?" exclaims Hilal aghast. "It has nothing to do with luck, my brother. That was purely God's grace. He has protected you, despite your foolishness."

Mazin casts down his eyes in shame as he recognizes Hilal's wisdom.

"I hope you have learned your lesson," the sheikh of Kedar says in a gentle voice.

Indeed, Mazin does not need a reminder. Once and for all he has learned that one does not touch God's chosen people without repercussions. Things will eventually end badly for those who ignore this. Mazin knows this from experience.

17 Conversion

After the defeat at the hands of the Israelites and their God, Yahweh, Mazin decides he will never again fight with them. He joins the other peace seeking Ishmaelite tribes, with Hilal as their commander.

Mazin and his children focus on trading with neighboring tribes, near and far. Whenever they are in Israel, they glean the latest news. Over the years, the Israelites regularly clash with their neighbors. When they are not battling the Philistines, they fight the Ammonites or the Moabites. Often, these peoples are more powerful in the beginning, but in the end, the Israelites are victorious; every single time! God's blessing clearly rests upon them.

One day there is exciting news: Israel has a king! The Ishmaelites follow the developments with great interest and are curious to see how their half-brother's descendants are faring. There are continually success stories that they hear about; the Ammonites, the Moabites, the Philistines. Every single nation that takes up arms against Israel, is defeated at the hands of King Saul.

The most shocking news, however, is the Israelites' attack on the Amalekites, who have been close allies of the Ishmaelites. The King of Israel has nearly annihilated the Amalekite tribe, killing not only the men, but also the women. He hasn't even spared the children or the livestock. At first the Ishmaelites can't believe their ears, but when more and more fugitives from Amalek come to seek refuge with them, they realize the stories must be true.

Tension rises in the community. The big question on everyone's mind is whether Saul is planning to attack them as well. Will he come after the Amalekites who have taken refuge there or will he even obliterate them all?

Fortunately, it appears that King Saul's power is declining. More and more, he is forced to focus on the attacks launched by the Philistines from the West. After the major conflicts between Saul and his eastern neighbors have stopped, the Ishmaelites feel safe and resume trade with Israel.

One of the descendants of Ishmael is genuinely impressed with the Israelites' way of worshipping God. He regularly travels with his father to Judah to sell incense and other merchandise and each time he notices that the Israelites don't work on the last day of the week. At first those Sabbaths seemed an utter waste of time to Jether, but over time he has come to appreciate the weekly day of rest.

One day he witnesses an accident. At the edge of the marketplace, Jether sees a man preparing bundles of firewood for sale. The man chops up long branches to make them fit the clay ovens people use. Suddenly, his axe breaks and the blade hurls into the air. The woodcutter shouts out a warning but the man standing in front of him doesn't react fast enough. The sharp edge of the axe blade lands on his head and, bleeding heavily, he falls to the ground. Immediately, the lumberjack runs away. In the meantime, men come rushing from all directions to see what has happened. Jether watches everything in amazement. *How odd, no one stops the lumberjack from running away. Why do they allow him to escape?* He decides to ask one of the bystanders.

"Chances are, the wounded man will die. Killing someone by accident, you have the right to flee to one of the appointed cities of refuge," the Israelite explains.

Jether is surprised. He has never heard anything like that before. "What happens next?" he asks.

"The city of refuge is a safe haven for the accused, until the victim's family takes him to court. If the culprit is found guilty, he is given up to the victim's family, who will then be able to take blood vengeance. But if the judge decides it was an accident and the perpetrator is found not guilty, he is not killed. Instead, he may live his life in the city under the protection of the elders."

All that makes a lot of sense to Jether. He thinks of his own people. If they were to apply a similar practice, instead of just blindly following the 'eye for an eye and tooth for a tooth' principle, there would be a lot less family feuds.

The more Jether learns about the laws of God, the stronger his desire to belong to his people becomes. One day he blurts out to Ozem, his Israelite friend, "If only I were a descendant of Isaac!"

"What's stopping you from joining us," Ozem says warmly. "I heard about a Moabitess who did the same thing. From the day she came to live here in Bethlehem, God blessed her, and if God accepts a Moabite, He will certainly accept you."

"Why is that?" asks Jether.

"Well, it's simple. You Ishmaelites are Abraham's direct descendants, just as we are. Therefore, you are closer to us and to Yahweh than the Moabites, who are the descendants of Lot, Abraham's nephew.

Jether can feel his heart pounding. *Wouldn't it be wonderful to know God personally, just like the Israelites know him? They always speak about Yahweh as their God, who dwells in their midst in a special holy tabernacle. This is the God who made himself known to their prophet, Moses.* Jether only knows God as the Almighty Creator, whom he respects and serves. *Would God really want to be my personal Yahweh? Would He speak to me through his prophets too?* Jether is reminded of stories about the prophet Samuel, who heard God's voice, while serving him in the tabernacle as a young boy. *Imagine, experiencing God's presence like that! That would be marvelous!* Suddenly, something clicks in Jether's mind. *God is like a Bedouin amongst Bedouins. He lives in a tent, just like my people and me. Does God really want to be that close to his people?*

"What's stopping you, Jether?"

On hearing his name, Jether looks up. "What do you mean?" he asks his friend.

"Well, what's keeping you from becoming an Israelite?" Ozem repeats his question.

Jether feels vulnerable. He doesn't want anyone to know what he is contemplating so he shakes his head. "No, I can't; it would mean betraying my people and my family," he explains and then quickly changes the subject.

However, before going home, Jether decides to pay a visit to an Israelite priest. He is still very curious to learn what one needs to do to become an Israelite. On arriving at the priest's house, he asks some children playing outside to call the servant of God for him. He politely waits by the gate of the walled courtyard for the priest to come out to him.

When the priest sees the Ishmaelite, he acts distant toward him.

Jether immediately feels unwelcome but he needs answers and decides to ask his questions anyway.

"The most important requirement for an alien to be accepted into the people of God is circumcision," the priest explains.

Jether can't believe his ears. *I am already circumcised.*

"Also, one must follow the law of Yahweh; the same law He gave our prophet Moses," the priest continues. "The most important commandment is this, 'Hear, O Israel: The LORD[23], our God, the LORD is One! You shall love the Lord your God with all your heart and with all your soul and with all your might.'[24] God has given us ten specific commandments to help us in our daily life. He himself wrote them on two stone tablets and gave them to the prophet Moses. In short, loving Yahweh means that we consider him more important than anyone else. We don't make ourselves idols to worship; we don't even make images of God or bow down to them. It also means that we rest from all of our labors one day a week."

"The Sabbath," Jether says enthusiastically.

"Indeed," confirms the priest. "Furthermore, God wants us to treat our fellowmen with kindness. He commands us to honor our parents and never to hurt anyone. That means we are not to lie, steal, kill, or commit adultery."

Jether has never heard these things so clearly explained. He is so impressed by the faith of the Israelites and yearns for the same kind of faith. *If only everyone would obey these commandments, there would be no more quarrels between families, no more wars between nations. Instead, there would be peace.* He thanks the priest for his time and returns home full of joy.

When Jether tells his father what he has learned, the old man is not pleased at all. He voices his concern and says, "Surely, you don't want to become one of them, my son? It would be considered a betrayal and you would bring great shame on our family."

Jether's joy is quickly quenched by what his father has said but he doesn't want to give up yet.

"But father, those commandments are good for everyone, they are good for the whole world. If our tribes were to keep them, we wouldn't have to worry so much about being robbed. And you wouldn't have to worry about your daughters being taken advantage of while they are pasturing the sheep."

Jether's father looks dismayed. He knows his son is right. He likes to trade with the Israelites. They are more trustworthy than any of the other tribes. *But they are still Israelites and I am still an Ishmaelite. God has ordained it this way and no man can change that. What would the religious leaders say if they heard …?*

The longer the conversation between father and son drags on, the deeper emotions run. Finally, Jether's father declares in a shaky voice, "If you decide to become an Israelite, you are no longer welcome in my house." Jether hangs his head. *So, this is the price I must pay to follow Yahweh.*

That evening Jether can't sleep. A deep inner struggle causes him to consider his options. On the one hand he longs to know God personally, but on the other hand he wants to stay close to his family. He can't bring himself to decide because he wants both, but now his father is forcing him to make a choice. Jether is confused. *Yahweh wants me to love him above all; at the same time, He commands me to honor my parents. But if I obey my father, I will have to disobey God in other things. Then again, I am already circumcised; doesn't that, in itself, make me an Israelite? Didn't Ozem say that I am much closer to Yahweh than the other peoples?* Jether just can't work it out. In desperation he calls out, "God, please make yourself known to me, so that I may know what to do!" Finally, he drifts off to sleep.

"I am the God of Abraham, Isaac and Ishmael!"

Jether wakes up startled. *Was that a voice I heard, or was I dreaming?* Immediately he is reminded of Ozem's story about the prophet Samuel, who also heard God's voice in the middle of the night. *No, it must be my imagination. I am but a simple merchant; not a prophet.*

Jether rolls over and tries to go back to sleep. As he dozes off, he suddenly sees a bright light. Again there is a voice. "I am the God of Abraham, Isaac and Ishmael. Follow Me." Jether is startled again. As he tries to digest the implications of what he just heard, he remembers his prayer earlier on. *Could this be God answering me?* "Lord, Yahweh, if this is You, please let me know for certain. Then I will follow You," he prays silently. Shortly afterwards, Jether falls asleep again.

"Jether, I am Yahweh, I am the God of Abraham, Isaac, and Jacob."

Now he hears God's voice very clearly. Spontaneously and from the depth of his heart, Jether answers the call, "I love You, Yahweh." Immediately an inexplicable peace fills his heart.

A little while later, chirping birds slowly arouse Jether from his deep sleep. Straightaway, he remembers his dream. Could it have been real? Did God really speak to him? As he thinks about it, he again experiences that deep sense of inner peace from the previous night and stops wondering about it. Instead, he prays, "Thank you, God, for answering my prayer."

Jether's new life then begins. When he returns to Israel, he can hardly wait to tell his friend about what has happened. Ozem is astonished by the news. He is even jealous of his friend for having had such a personal experience of God. He would like to have the same thing happen to him, but joy outweighs his jealousy. Together they visit the priest in Bethlehem to inform him of this good news and to fulfill the official requirements to become an Israelite.

"So, you have been circumcised?" the priest asks emphatically. "I will have to see proof of that." The priest is surprised when he sees that the man has spoken the truth. He has always been under the impression that circumcision was solely meant for the Israelites, God's chosen people, but Jether has proven him wrong.

"Didn't I tell you," Jether says, "we are all circumcised, just like our forefather Ishmael."

"Well, in that case, you definitely have a special place in God's heart," concludes the priest. He embraces and kisses Jether on the cheeks and officially welcomes him into the fold of God's people. Lastly, the priest blesses him.

"Yahweh bless you and keep you! Yahweh make his face shine upon you and be gracious to you. Yahweh lift up his countenance to you and give you peace!"[25]

On hearing these words, Jether trembles with excitement and joy. This blessing is entirely his. It is as if God is personally speaking to him.

After the two friends have taken leave of the priest, they return to Ozem's house, where Ozem proudly tells his father what has happened. Then he asks, "Father, is it all right?"

Jether wonders what his friend is talking about. Although he knows him well, he can't guess what this is about.

Ozem's father nods his head in agreement, "Yes, my son, it is all right."

The old man has hardly finished his sentence, when Ozem grabs his friend by the shoulders and says, "You may come and live with us now."

Jether is overwhelmed by this generous offer. He has been so worried about his future, but it appears that God has already started to bless him. Being unable to continue living with his father, he and Ozem had tried very hard to find a solution as to where he should live. They had contemplated the idea of moving to Israel to learn to keep the laws. At first Jether hadn't been too thrilled about that plan, but after a while he had come to see that he would be able to honor his father better that way. The shame on his family would certainly be less poignant and yet he would be able to meet his father from time to time when he would come to Israel to trade. All this had helped him make the decision to move. The remaining question had been where he should live in Israel. Now this had been solved as well. Jether grabs his friend by the arm as he jumps up for joy. This is the best solution!

Ozem's father, Jesse, smiles and welcomes Jether.

Very soon Jether feels completely at home in this God-fearing family. He is now able to learn about serving Yahweh. Besides, Jesse doesn't make him work like a servant in order to earn his keep, but rather treats him like a son. In doing so he brings honor to Jether's tribe so that his father will not be completely rejected by the Ishmaelite sheikh.

Jether gets friendly with David, Ozem's youngest brother, and the two of them have long conversations. The young man has a strong faith in God, and Jether wants to learn to trust God in the same way.

Over time something develops in Jesse's household that often happens. Jether takes a special interest in Ozem's younger sister, Abigail. The affection turns out to be mutual and Jesse gives his permission for Jether to marry his daughter. Some of the people in Bethlehem criticize Jesse's decision but then he points out that his grandfather Boaz had a Moabite wife. If God himself accepts foreigners into his fold, who is he to refuse them?

Jether marries Abigail and because he has no relatives in Israel, he remains in the house of his father-in-law. Jesse builds them an extra room, just like he did for his older sons when they got married. Jether is a great asset to the family as he helps them with his knowledge about animals and his experience in trading. He happily works hard and the years fly by.

"The Israelites have decimated the inhabitants of the desert!" a young man calls out when he nears the gates of Bethlehem.

Jether is alarmed. *Is my family all right?*

Seated on the low benches at the city gates, the elders ask the man to tell them what happened. "You know how the tribes in Gilead have had frequent trouble with their neighbors?" he pants.

The elders nod. It is a well-known fact that the descendants of Reuben, Gad, and Manasseh in trans-Jordan are being harassed by the nomads every year in the dry season. In search of water and food for their flocks, a growing number of desert nomads encroach on Israelite land at that time and naturally, this is increasingly causing friction.

"The farmers in the region of the tribe of Gad challenged the Hagrites, because they blocked access to their well. Suddenly a fight broke out and soon others joined in the scuffle. The Ishmaelite tribes of Jetur and Naphish joined the Hagrites against the men of Gad, who were helped by Manasseh and Reuben. The Gadites and their allies were in the minority but there was no time to ask the king for help."

Again, the men at the gate nod. Everyone knows that King Saul is pre-occupied with the conflicts with the Philistines in the west.

"Then they called on the name of the Lord and they won the battle! They captured over a hundred thousand men! They also confiscated a lot of camels and sheep!"

"Praise Yahweh, the God of Abraham, Isaac and Jacob!" the men at the gate exclaim.

The words pierce Jether's heart. Even though he has become one with the Israelites, he still loves his own people and wants all of them to have peace with God as he has. He is about to say that the nomadic life is harsh and that it is very difficult to keep the animals healthy on the barren desert plains. At the same time, Jether knows very well that the Hagrites have acted wrongly by claiming the wells for themselves. He is embarrassed that some clans of his own people joined the Hagrites at the outset of the fighting. Silently, he prays for the Ishmaelites, "Oh Yahweh, God of Abraham, Isaac, and Ishmael, I beg you to unite my people with the Israelites and to teach them to live together in peace."

18 A Prophetic Song

During the years that follow, Jether has many adventures with his in-laws. Almost overnight, his brother-in-law, David, has become an international hero. He killed a Philistine giant while he himself was unarmed. He *did* have his sling, but what was that compared with Goliath's sword and spear? Jether realizes that David owed his success to God's miraculous intervention.

After that, David, the former shepherd boy, marries the king's daughter and from that day forward, the entire family is treated like royalty.

Then, at the very moment when Jether is able to build his own house, he and his wife and all her brothers have to flee their homes. King Saul has turned against David. David has disappeared too and chances are that the king will take revenge on David's family. Taking up his former life as a Bedouin, Jether goes back to living in a tent. He dwells among the Moabites, where he feels like a refugee. During this time, he often pleads with God to protect David.

Jether is aware of Saul's conspiracy to capture and kill David and it makes him doubt. Why doesn't God do something? David loves him so much; why does God withhold his blessings from him? Can he really trust Yahweh? Perhaps the Israelites' faith is not based on truth after all. Occasionally, Jether thinks back on the night he heard God's voice. *I must have dreamed it all. I should return to my own people. At least, there my life will not be in danger.* Jether feels conflicted as he waits for better times in Moab. Time and time again, he reminds himself of the wonderful things he has experienced ever since he started serving God wholeheartedly. During these times, his doubts disappear momentarily.

After a long while, there is finally some good news: King Saul is no longer a threat. He is dead. That means that Jether can return safely to Bethlehem. Fortunately, his house is still standing and although it is occupied by strangers, they move out as soon as the new king orders them to leave the premises. Now Jether can fully enjoy the peaceful life he has looked forward to.

A few years later, he moves again, but this time the reason is quite different it is for a joyous reason. The new king, David, his very own brother-in-law, has built a palace in Jerusalem and he has invited his entire family to live with him at the royal court. A time of prosperity has come upon the land and everyone is happy. Neighboring nations occasionally attack Israel, but David defeats each of them. The Philistines, the Edomites, the Moabites and the Ammonites are all overpowered by David's army and end up having to pay him tribute. Jether's duty at court is to mediate between the Ishmaelites and the Israelites. He encourages his people to be at peace with the king and advises them to ask for permission before they graze their flocks in Gilead or the other areas of David's realm.

Once again Jether prays, "Lord, have mercy on my people, and let them know and understand your love for them." Every time he utters these words, he is overwhelmed by a deep sense of peace, even though he doesn't see any visible change in the lives of his people. Although the Ishmaelites are faithful in doing their best to please God and to worship him as the Almighty, the Creator of heaven and earth, they do not realize that God desires to live among his people. He has even chosen to make his dwelling place among them in the Tent of Meeting which was built by Moses. Jether is sad. Whenever he has the opportunity, he speaks to them about his life with the Israelites. Though they accept him personally, especially now that he is the brother-in-law of the mighty King David, they don't really take his words seriously. At least, that is how it seems to Jether.

One day, many years later, Jether reflects on his life and all that he has gone through. He is an elderly man now and looks back in gratitude upon all the blessings he has received from God's hand; so many answered prayers. *In a way, I'm still an Ishmaelite,* he muses, *a real descendant of Ishmael, the man who carries the name, 'God hears'.*

Suddenly his nephew Obil bursts into the house. "Listen to this, Uncle Jether! The king has written a very strange song." He sounds frustrated.

"What is it about?"

"King David writes about his son Solomon. It is actually a beautiful prayer, just like the many poems he has written, but in this song he has gone too far. He suggests that Solomon will rule over all."

"You sound very agitated, but you haven't even told me what David exactly wrote. Besides, now that David has officially abdicated, his son Solomon *is* the rightful heir to the throne."

"Yes, yes, that's exactly what I'm talking about," says Obil impatiently, "David wrote about King Solomon. Listen to this," he continues. "May desert tribes bow down before him, and his enemies lick the dust."[26]

"Imagine that! Are we to lick the dust off the ground bowing down before his son? Even if Solomon is going to be the new king, I fully expect him to treat me with respect, especially since I have served his father faithfully all these years."

"Ahh, don't worry. It won't come to that."

"Easy for you to say. It won't affect you; you have become one of them, but I am an Ishmaelite and will remain one forever. I am proud of my people and I will never deny my roots."

Obil's words are unsettling and hurtful to Jether. It is true that he has changed his nationality and that he is now fully an Israelite, but he didn't do it out of cowardice. It had taken a lot of courage to cut all his earthly assurances and join the people of God. He had moved away voluntarily and thereby relinquished his right not only to his part of the inheritance, but also to any support from his family, if he should ever need it. If only he could have served Yahweh in his own country, properly following all the religious requirements of the law. Very few had understood that he hadn't betrayed his people, even though it had seemed so at the surface. Obil's words are a painful reminder of that time.

"You can't say you didn't do the same thing, nephew," Jether argues. "When the king was looking for an expert camel herder, you were quite pleased when I advised him to employ you. Since that time, you have fully enjoyed all the benefits of living at court."

Obil doesn't quite know how to respond. It's true, thanks to his uncle he had been given a golden opportunity. And even though he remained an Ishmaelite at heart, his family had seen his service to a foreign king as a betrayal.

"You know David as well as I do; he really appreciates and deeply trusts you." Jether pauses to allow his words to sink in. "Would he not tell his son to respect you as well?" Jether notices that his words affect Obil, for he doesn't reply immediately. He continues, "Who else does David mention in his song?"

Obil answers, "The Kings of Tarshish, Sheba, and Seba. As a matter of fact, he speaks about all the nations of the world. One line says, 'May all kings fall down before him, all nations serve him.'"[27]

Jether is amused but represses a smile, for he knows that would only wind his nephew up. The things David wishes for his son appeal to Jether, and he says in a matter-of-fact way, "Not bad really. What father would not want such blessings for his son?"

"Yet, I find that the king, eh… prince is going too far. Instead, he should be satisfied with the blessings that God has given the Israelites already. They dominate Edom, Moab and the Philistines. Do they want to rule over us as well?"

Jether thinks a moment and before he answers. "I can understand your concerns, Obil, but I don't want you to be upset for no reason. Let's talk about it some more after I have listened to the whole song."

Obil agrees and they continue to chat about different issues that affect their day-to-day lives.

Soon after the discussion with his nephew, Jether has a chance to visit David. It's the festival of the new moon and during this national holiday the entire family is invited for a lavish lunch. The beginning of the month is heralded with a day of rest; a day just like the Sabbath. Many centuries ago, God ordained this for the Israelites and David strictly keeps to the decree. Besides the mandatory burnt and sin offerings, he always provides several animals for a peace offering. The meat that remains after this last sacrifice will be prepared for the feast. The peace offerings remind the people of their peace with God. It also reminds them to live in peace with one another in the certainty that God loves them and accepts them as his people.

When Jether greets his brother-in-law, he notices how much David has aged and weakened. The lines in his forehead and the puffiness under his eyes betray deep anguish. David has been greatly affected by the recent trouble in his kingdom. Jether is aware of some of the problems. David's son, Adonijah, secretly has proclaimed himself king and it wasn't the first time that something like this had happened. A few years earlier, David's other son, Absalom, had attempted to dethrone his father as well. Because the highest military adviser had sided with Absalom, David had fled the capital and escaped with his life, just in time. This time, it's David's trusted general, Joab, who has betrayed him and joined forces with his son Adonijah.

As Jether lets his mind mull over the past, he feels anger mounting up inside him. Joab is such a treacherous coward! How could he have conspired to overthrow the rightful king and install Adonijah as the new monarch? Moreover, what Joab did to him personally a few years ago is still painfully raw. During the time when Absalom was killed and David returned from his exile, the king had appointed Jether's son, Amasa, as military leader. Not one week later, Joab had murdered him.

Jether turns to David and says, "If Amasa were still alive, we wouldn't have the current troubles."

"I know, Jether, but your son isn't there anymore. God will surely punish Joab for all his evildoing."

"Well, I hope so, for his hands are bathed in blood."

"I have given Solomon instructions on what to do about Joab. Come now, let us celebrate before our God. We will talk about this later," David concludes.

He calls two servants to help him stand up. Leaning heavily upon their shoulders, he hobbles to the dining hall where the table is prepared with large platters of steaming rice and a generous assortment of fresh and cooked vegetables, complemented by stacks of freshly baked flat bread. All the guests thoroughly enjoy the food, especially the tender roasted meat, which is served last. The wine David has chosen to complement the meal is much appreciated by the guests and all congratulate him on the excellent combination of food and drink. The feast culminates in a dessert table loaded with succulent fruit: tasty apples from the last harvest, sweet figs and dates and much more. It is a true royal banquet.

When everyone is satisfied, a servant goes around with a water jug for the guests to wash their hands. Then they retire to the guest hall where tea is being served. David reclines on the carefully arranged pillows and blankets at the very end of the room. When the servants have made him comfortable, he beckons Jether to come and sit next to him.

"Are you still writing poetry?" Jether asks.

"God continues to inspire me, my brother," David smiles. "Listen to my latest composition in honor of Solomon's coronation. It is a prayer for him." Because David's fingers are too arthritic to play the harp anymore, he calls the royal harpist to do it for him. After the prelude, he joins in with a powerful voice.

"Give the king your justice, O God,
and your righteousness to the royal son!
May he judge your people with righteousness,
and your poor with justice!"[28]

Jether really enjoys the beautiful hymn and softly hums along with the repeating melody.

"In his days may the righteous flourish,
and peace abound, till the moon be no more!
May he have dominion from sea to sea,
and from the River to the ends of the earth!
May desert tribes bow down before him,
and his enemies lick the dust!
May the kings of Tarshish and of the coastlands
render him tribute;
may the kings of Sheba and Seba bring gifts!
May all kings fall down before him,
all nations serve him."[29]

Tears well up in Jether's eyes. This is what he longs for. Instead of the cruelty of the nations' kings that surround them, Jether hopes for a king like David, one who serves the Lord with his whole heart. He silently prays, "Amen, may it ever be so, Lord. May your peace reign over all the earth."

"For he delivers the needy when he calls,
the poor and him who has no helper.
He has pity on the weak and the needy,

and saves the lives of the needy.
From oppression and violence he redeems their life,
and precious is their blood in his sight."[30]

This is what I have been praying for, Jether suddenly thinks, *that God will consider my fellow people, and that they will come to know him.*
Meanwhile, David continues to sing.

"Long may he live;
may gold of Sheba be given to him!
May prayer be made for him continually,
and blessings invoked for him all the day!
May there be abundance of grain in the land;
on the tops of the mountains may it wave;
may its fruit be like Lebanon;
and may people blossom in the cities
like the grass of the field!
May his name endure forever,
his fame continue as long as the sun!
May people be blessed in him,
all nations call him blessed!
Blessed be the Lord, the God of Israel,
who alone does wondrous things.
Blessed be his glorious name forever;
may the whole earth be filled with his glory!
Amen and Amen!"[31]

While the harpist plays the last few chords, Jether calls out, "Amen, may it be so. God be praised." His eyes are still moist when he looks at David and grabs his hand. "Thank you for this wonderful song. You have expressed the desire of my heart." Eyes beaming, David squeezes Jether's hand tightly. He has always appreciated Jether's genuine love for God, which he has seen grow over the years. "Thank you, my brother," he answers warmly.

That same evening, Obil stops by. He knows that Jether has heard the song now too. "What do you think of it?" he asks curiously. His tone betrays the turmoil in his heart and he hopes to gain his uncle's support.
"I was speechless," Jether responds, "it moved me deeply."
Obil sighs, he should have known. Jether has become an Israelite. Of course, he likes the song.
Jether senses his nephew's annoyance, but nevertheless he asks him, "Do you know what the song is about?"

"Of course, it's all about how under Solomon's powerful reign the Israelites will rule the entire world," Obil blurts out.

"I don't think so, Obil. I feel it is something much more profound. David's words reflect the heart of God."

"Yeah, and that means that we will bow down to the Israelites. Well, that's never going to happen," Obil replies fiercely. "Who do they think they are to put themselves above all the other peoples?"

Jether is saddened. He recognizes a harshness in Obil's voice that is mirrored by others who surround Israel, such as the Philistines and the Edomites. *God Almighty, why do the nations hate your chosen people?"* He quietly tries to explain, "It is not that the Israelites are better than any of the other people, Obil. It is God Almighty who, in his great wisdom, has chosen to make himself known to all people through them. He has chosen to work through their weaknesses, to make his grace known to all the nations."

Jether pauses to allow his words to sink in. He then continues, "It is not about a certain group of people, but rather about God himself. It is his desire that every man, woman and child on earth will know and worship him freely, willingly and joyfully. He has created man that he might love him with his whole heart. He is not looking for people who will submit fearfully and slavishly to him, nor for people who follow rituals. God invites us all to be reconciled to him. "

"I already have peace with God," Obil states emphatically. He tries to sound confident, but deep inside he realizes that Jether has something he lacks. He is jealous and has even considered becoming an Israelite himself several times. But fear of disapproval of his family and the shame he would bring to the entire tribe has hindered him. More than that, if he is truly honest with himself, those are not the main reasons. Above all, he is scared to let go of the security he feels in his life, in order to surrender to a God he cannot see.

"Anyhow," Jether concludes, "this song is a prayer of hope. One day peace will reign over all the world. That's what I am looking forward to." Then he looks straight into Obil's eyes. "And whoever will not bow down to him willingly, will one day be compelled to recognize him as the Almighty, just like Pharaoh in the time of the prophet Moses, when God struck Egypt with the ten plagues. I am hopeful that our families will submit themselves freely to him."

Obil knows this is the truth; there's nothing else he can say. His uncle's words have authority, but Obil is not quite ready to submit. Maybe later.

19 Sacks filled with Gold

To enter, one has to first pass through the outer gate where sentinels armed with shields, swords, and spears keep watch night and day. The large wooden doors only open to allow the occasional chariot in or out. Those who want to enter the palace grounds on foot must report to the sentry at the pedestrian entrance next to the main gate. Only trusted members of the court can come and go as they please, anyone else is questioned extensively about his family and about the business he has inside. On entering, visitors are escorted by a servant to the throne room. The way in to this room is at the end of a long pathway lined with an imposing colonnade of pillars that seem to reach to the heavens. Everything in the palace points to one approaching the mightiest man on earth: King Solomon.

A well-dressed man walks swiftly across the courtyard towards the throne room. He hastily climbs the steps that lead towards the entrance. One of the guards immediately opens the door for him and asks out of curiosity, "Is everything in order?" As usual, there is no response, but the expression in the man's eyes show there is trouble. Once inside, he hurries to the far end of the room. The king is conducting a hearing, whereby both parties have the opportunity to tell their side of the story.

The visitor whispers something into the ear of the king's nearest attendant, who in turn informs his master. Straightaway, the man is given permission to speak to the king. He respectfully bows down and then proceeds to tell him what he has seen out in the desert. "Oh King, a large company of armed men are approaching from the South!"

When King Solomon questions the man about the warriors' attire and the adornment of their camels, his eyes light up.

"They are the Queen of Sheba's soldiers," he explains. "They come in peace."

The man breathes a sigh of relief. *Incredible! We have never seen any soldiers from that distant nation, and yet the king knows exactly who they are. How wise he is!*

"Prepare a unit to ride out and welcome the queen," Solomon orders one of his army chiefs. After a little while, the enormous gates swing open and a large group of horses with their riders leave the palace.

A few days later, all of Jerusalem is in turmoil. The news has spread like wildfire. "Royal visitors from the ends of the earth!" The city is buzzing with excitement. "It's a woman!"

When the Queen of Sheba finally enters the city gates, crowds of people are waiting and see her seated majestically upon her royal palanquin and gaze in awe. They marvel at the retinue of foreign nationals. The children that line the road gape at the rich ornaments covered with precious stones that drape the camels' necks. There seems to be no end to the long procession accompanying the queen. What awe-inspiring visitors! Some of the spectators, however, are suspicious of seeing a foreign army within their city gates. *What if it is a ruse?* they wonder, but then they are reminded of Solomon's words. "The Queen comes in peace," he had proclaimed and whenever he makes a statement, they know it to be true. He is always right; there is no one as wise as he.

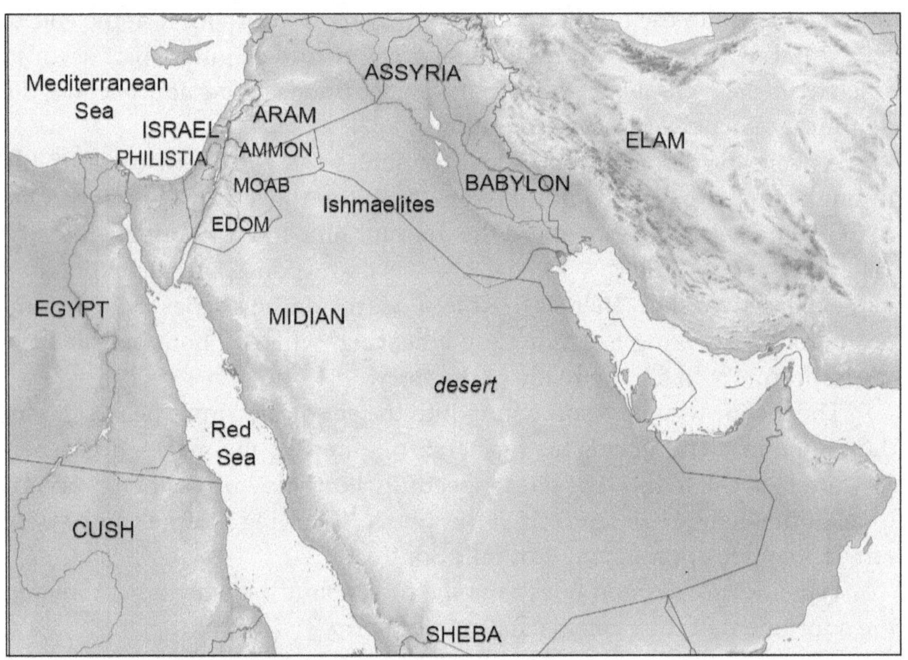

The kingdom of Sheba at the ends of the earth

In the palace courtyard, the empress descends from her litter to enter the throne room. Inside, she gasps as she observes the grandeur and splendor of the decor. Not only the walls, but also the ceilings are decorated with delicately carved cedar wood. The floors, rather than being just marble or stone are also overlaid with this expensive wood. She strides regally towards the golden throne at the far end of the room. Recognizing Solomon as superior to herself, she courteously bows down before ascending the steps to the throne. The King stands up and extends his royal staff to welcome her, inviting her to be seated on the imperial golden chair next to him.

Using a court interpreter, she asks him various questions. To her surprise he knows the answer to all of them. Whether she asks his opinion about nature, science or politics, there is simply no question too difficult for him. Furthermore, his speech is seasoned with wise sayings and proverbs. Sometimes the interpreter is at a loss to know how to appropriately render the meaning of these maxims, making for almost comical situations. Solomon is patient and laughs happily at the misunderstandings.

Then the queen picks up a word she has not heard before, and she asks her interpreter to repeat the phrase.

"The fear of Yahweh is the beginning of all knowledge,"[32] he says again.

"What is the meaning of Yahweh?" she asks. Once Solomon understands the question in Hebrew, he tells her some of the story of the Israelites. The queen listens attentively to the past events of God's personal involvement with Abraham; how He spoke with him and foretold that he would become a great nation but also about their four hundred years of slavery in Egypt.

"Did God free the slaves after that?" she asks.

"Yes, indeed, our God is always faithful to his promises," Solomon responds. "When the people called on God to free them from the oppression, He made himself known to a shepherd in the desert. This man had been saved and adopted by Pharaoh's daughter when he was an infant."

"Are you talking about Moses who ordered the ten plagues on the Egyptian people; the one who led his people right through the Red Sea?"

Solomon smiles and nods. "I wasn't aware you knew the story."

"When I was a child I heard about the God of Israel and his great power. I wondered for years whether the stories were really true or simply legends, so when I heard about your wisdom I decided to come and find out for myself. I want to know Yahweh more fully."

Deeply moved, Solomon looks at the woman who sits next to him. She has sacrificed a lot to get to know God. A proverb comes to mind and he decides to share it with her. "I, Wisdom, love those who love me, and those who seek me diligently find me."[33]

A reverent silence falls over the throne room. All present are mesmerized by these beautiful words. It is as if God himself is present. The queen finds Solomon's words inspiring and encouraging at the same time. The serene peace that surrounds her at that moment is something she has been yearning for as long as she can remember.

"God appeared to Moses," Solomon continues. "He spoke to him from a burning bush that was not consumed by the fire. When Moses asked God for his name, the Lord told him, 'I AM WHO I AM. I am Yahweh, the God of your forefather Abraham, the God of Isaac, and the God of Jacob. This is my name forever.'[34] "

If only He would be my God too, the queen thinks, but she doesn't voice her desire. "You are indeed fortunate, that God has chosen you and your people."

Due to the language barrier, Solomon misses some of the subtleties in her words, but her eyes and facial expression show that she has been deeply moved. For just a brief moment he feels a little embarrassed. Who is he that God has chosen him to be part of his people? Silently he prays for wisdom. Immediately he is reminded of the prayers during the dedication of the temple. Back then he had asked God, "When a foreigner, who is not of your people Israel, comes from a far country for your name's sake and prays toward this house, hear in heaven, your dwelling place, and do according to all for which the foreigner calls to you."[35]

God had then spoken to him very clearly, "I have heard your prayer and your plea, which you have made before me."[36]

Surely, God will hear the prayers of this woman as well. Solomon carefully crafts words to express his thoughts. "God wants to be Yahweh of all people on the earth."

When the translator gives the message to the queen, Solomon can see by her reaction that he is on the right track. She understands that Solomon is trying to reach out to her, yet she keeps her longings to herself. Instead, she asks a more general question, "Is the God of Israel, who has blessed you so much, willing to bless the whole world?"

"That's exactly what I am saying," Solomon replies emphatically. A passage from the Torah comes to mind and he continues, "This is what God promised our forefather Abraham. He told him, ' I will make of you a great nation, and I will bless you and make your name great, so that you will be a blessing. I will bless those who bless you, and him who dishonors you I will curse, and in you all the families of the earth shall be blessed.'[37] You can see for yourself that we have become a great nation."

"Indeed, your greatness has even been proclaimed all the way to Sheba," the queen laughs.

"God wants to bless all people, your people too."

"How can that happen? Do we have to become Israelites in order for him to bless us?"

"I don't believe so. My father has written a beautiful song about this. In it he clearly speaks of a time in which all people on earth will know and serve Yahweh."

The queen's curiosity has been aroused and asks when she can hear the song.

"I will make arrangements for the temple musicians to sing it tomorrow morning during the daily ceremony of burnt offerings."

"Would you allow me to see the words beforehand, so that my interpreter can translate it for me?"

Solomon has no objections and he arranges for one of the temple singers to dictate the song to the queen's interpreter.

Next, he consults quickly with the high priest, who is rather shocked when he hears what Solomon is suggesting. The king then reminds him of the words of the song and the priest understands that he really cannot have any objections. Solomon also tells him about the interest his royal guest has shown and says, "My father has taught us that God delights more in an obedient heart than in burnt offerings. Surely, He will not object."

"Well then," the priest decides, "I will allow it, solely on the condition that she is bathed and purified and not be unclean in her menstrual cycle."

That night the queen can't get to sleep. She is excited about the possibility of being close to Yahweh, the God who works miracles for his people. Although she is not part of the Israelites, Yahweh's chosen people, she has been given permission to enter the temple court. Tomorrow she will be able to observe the daily sacrifice. She is even more excited to hear the song. Never has she heard about people worshiping their god with songs and musical instruments. The gods of the people she is familiar with are fearsome, but this god, the God of Israel, dwells in the midst of his people and He invites them to enter joyfully into his presence. So many contradictions! His name is unique too: Yahweh; I AM.

Without realizing it she begins to pray, "Yahweh, I want to know You. I want to belong to You, Lord." While the queen whispers these the words in her heart, she dozes off and falls into a deep and peaceful sleep.

The next morning Solomon personally accompanies her to the temple court. He explains the meaning of the rituals which makes it easier for the queen to understand what is happening. She observes the priest laying his hand on the head of a one-year old lamb, which symbolizes God's reconciliation with his people. Then he slits the lamb's throat and catches its blood in a brass bowl. He sprinkles part of the blood on the altar. This symbolizes the cleansing of sins, which enables the people to be in God's presence. It reminds the queen of the stories that Solomon told about Moses and the Israelites. Just preceding their departure from Egypt, God had required them to slaughter lambs and paint the blood on their door frames. That blood had been a sign for the angel of death to pass over their house and their firstborn sons spared. Even back in the time of Abraham, God had provided a sacrificial animal to spare Isaac's life.

A little while later, the temple musicians begin to sing. Solomon nods at the queen, indicating this is the song she has been waiting for. The lyrics have been translated and written in elegant calligraphy on a papyrus scroll. While musicians praise the Lord with David's song, she follows the words on the scroll.

> "From you comes my praise in the great congregation;
> my vows I will perform before those who fear him.
> The afflicted shall eat and be satisfied;
> those who seek him shall praise the LORD!
> May your hearts live forever!"[38]

"Amen Lord, Yahweh, God of Israel. I seek You and I will praise You," the queen prays silently.

> "All the ends of the earth shall remember and turn to the LORD,
> and all the families of the nations shall worship before you."
> For kingship belongs to the LORD,
> and he rules over the nations."[39]

When the song has ended, Solomon kneels, together with all the Israelites that are with him. He then repeats the words of the priest who leads the congregation in prayer from a platform.

Following their example, the monarch prays in her heart, "Yahweh, here I am, I bow down before You; reign in my heart and reign in the hearts of my people."

At the end of the service, the priest lifts his hands up towards the heavens and blesses the congregation.

The queen is overwhelmed by a sense of peace. She feels so close to God that He seems to be in her heart. His holiness surrounds her and she feels secure in him.

Upon her return to the palace, she orders her servants to bring the gifts she has brought from her homeland. Solomon is amazed when he sees the enormous number of bags filled with gold and satchels full of precious stones. Many costly spices are displayed on the shiny cedar wood floor in front of his throne, and their scent permeates the entire hall.

"My people and I offer you these gifts," says the queen, "in honor of Yahweh, the God whom you serve wholeheartedly."

As Solomon looks at the abundance of expensive gifts, he is deeply moved. Gold from Sheba; his father sang about this. As he tries to remember the words of the song, they run through his head. "May the kings of Sheba and Seba bring gifts! ... Long may he live; may gold of Sheba be given to him!"[40]

This is happening now, right in front of my eyes, he suddenly realizes.

The queen continues, "Happy are your men! Happy are your servants, who continually stand before you and hear your wisdom! Blessed be the Lord your God, who has delighted in you and set you on the throne of Israel! Because the Lord loved Israel forever, he has made you king, that you may execute justice and righteousness."[41]

Then Solomon realizes that these words are exactly his father's prayer for him in that song. With a lump in his throat, he thanks his royal guest for all the precious gifts. "May Yahweh bless you and give you peace."

Solomon is not the only person in Jerusalem who realizes that David's prayers for his son have been answered. That same day the news about the treasures from Sheba spreads throughout the city. Even beyond the city gates, the people are talking about it. There is one old man, who upon hearing the news, also recalls the psalm David wrote so many years earlier. "Jether had been right all along", he mumbles to himself. "Even those who inhabit the ends of the earth are not being forced by military might, but they bow down freely before the son of David." He is sorry that Jether is no longer alive. He can no longer ask for his forgiveness for being so stubbornly critical about the David's song and for that, Obil is truly sorry.

In the years that follow, many more kings visit the royal palace in Jerusalem. They all pay their respect to Solomon and bring lavish presents. The rulers of the tribes of Ishmael travel to Jerusalem as well to pay their respects and bow down before the wise and mighty King of Israel.

When the king of his tribe goes to Jerusalem, Obil may join as a representative of the people. At his sovereign's side, he walks into the impressive throne room of Solomon. The richly adorned throne makes Obil gasp. Even the six steps that lead up to the royal seat are gold plated. As he approaches the throne itself, he is filled with a deep sense of awe and respect.

Then Obil does something he would have never thought he would do. He bows down before King Solomon; the son of his former master. As he prostrates himself, he shivers. It is as if God accepts him just as he is, and Obil experiences a deep sense of peace.

Sometime later, while reflecting upon what happened, Obil gains a new insight. In submitting himself to this earthly king, he has humbled himself before God Almighty. With this in mind, he begins to hum the melody to King David's song. The song that had caused him so much pain before now makes his heart overflow with joy. Before he knows it, he belts out the words of the now familiar Psalm,

"Blessed be the Lord, the God of Israel,
who alone does wondrous things.
Blessed be his glorious name forever;
may the whole earth be filled with his glory!
Amen and Amen!"[42]

20 Judgment of God?

"King Solomon, hear the Word of the Lord," a prophet cries out to the monarch who is on his way to the mountain facing Jerusalem. "Since this has been your practice and you have not kept my covenant and the statutes which I have commanded you, I will surely tear the kingdom from you and will give it to your servant. Yet for the sake of David your father I will not do it in your days, but I will tear it out of the hand of your son."[43]

Solomon pays no attention to the prophet and continues on his way to the high place where he plans to make a sacrifice to the god of the Moabites. His love for pagan women has induced him to worship their idols. Time and time again, he ignores the warnings of Yahweh, the God of his forefathers Abraham, Isaac, and Jacob. Although God gives him plenty of opportunities to repent and turn from his disobedience, Solomon disregards them and stubbornly persists in his rebellion.

After his death, Solomon's kingdom is split in two, just like the prophet foretold.

His son, Rehoboam, obstinately follows in his father's footsteps and worships foreign gods. When ten of the twelve tribes oppose his leadership and secede, Rehoboam continues to reign over just two tribes in the south and together they form the Southern Kingdom, called Judah. Jeroboam, one of Solomon's officials becomes king of the northern tribes, which retains the name Israel.

The glory days of King David and Solomon are over and the surrounding nations lose respect for the Israelites. After only five years on the throne, Rehoboam faces the Egyptian armies. The king goes to the temple and prays and pleads with God to be merciful, but God remains silent. The ruler of Egypt invades Jerusalem and plunders the city of all the treasures King Solomon had acquired over the years, both in the palace and in the temple. If only Rehoboam had listened to the prophets; if only he had listened to God.

Several generations later, when King Jehoshaphat reigns over the two southern tribes, the confrontation with enemies reaches a climax.

One evening, Jehoshaphat is enjoying the cool breeze on the palace roof terrace. The night is clear and the moon shines brightly, lighting up not only the city beneath him but also the surrounding mountains. The sound of a drum rises from the streets near the palace. Jehoshaphat turns to look in the direction of the revelry and notices a group of young men dancing in the street. From the windows of a nearby house arise the happy voices of women singing for a bride. The shrill sounds of their ululations and their enthusiastic clapping and the dancing maidens show their boundless joy.

The people are happy, Jehoshaphat muses as gratefulness fills his heart. He instinctively lifts up his eyes to the heavens and prays, "Thank you Lord, for your love and faithfulness to your people. You are good. Your compassion endures forever."

Behind those peaceful mountains, however, a man runs towards Jerusalem as fast as his legs will carry him. If only he could find a horse! Thanks to the full moon he can at least see well enough to avoid stumbling over loose rocks and dangerous potholes in the road. Just a little further and he will arrive at the city gates. *Hopefully, they will allow me to enter quickly.*

One of the guards high up on the city wall has already noticed him. He peers in the distance as he carefully studies the way the man is running. Then he calls out to the sentries below to open the door in the gate to allow the man inside. After that, he orders one of the palace guards to go and inform the king about the scout who just arrived.

"I have just come... from Hazazon-Tamar," gasps the messenger as he stands before the king, "I saw a huge army ... there. I saw tents, ... donkeys, and camels, ... as far as my eyes could see."

"Were you able to work out to which nations these armies belong?"

"The tents resembled those of the Ammonites ... and the Moabites, ... but I saw other tents ... that I didn't recognize. They might belong ... to the northern or eastern nations."

"Perhaps they are on their way to Egypt," one of the king's advisors suggests. "Didn't our informants in Ammon and Moab tell us that the kings were gathering their armies to attack the Egyptians?"

"According to the rumors, yes. Apparently, they have skirted round the south side of the Dead Sea," another counselor ventures.

The king looks worried. "Hazazon-Tamar is too far to the north for them to turn south again. This means they are preparing to attack us!"

He knows it is not uncommon for armies to cut across foreign territories to face a faraway enemy, but this is certainly not the case now.

He quickly calculates the distance between the enemy and Jerusalem. "Only three days!" he calls out.

"We won't be able to prepare our troops in such a short time," comments the first adviser anxiously.

"Either way, our army is no match for the forces of Ammon and Moab. "There isn't even enough time to ask the King of Israel for help," some of the others point out. Seized by panic, they all decide that it is going to be a lost cause.

"We must seek the Lord. He is our only hope," Jehoshaphat states and immediately declares a time of fasting and prayer. Messengers are sent out on the fastest royal horses to all the towns of Judah. All the people are called to seek the Lord and all able-bodied men must report to Jerusalem. A few spies are sent out to spy on the enemy's camp to try to discover their strategies.

The next morning, people from all over the tiny kingdom pour into Jerusalem. At every city gate servants of the king announce the special gathering. "All must meet this afternoon before the evening sacrifice at the temple court. The king will address the assembly!"

There is a gloomy atmosphere around the town. The day before, the people's mood had been jubilant, but now all is quiet. Usually, weddings last for several days, but the festivities have been stopped. While the fattened animals bleat plaintively in the courtyard of the groom's house, the good wines will remain in the storerooms for now.

In the late afternoon the spies return to the city on horseback. They immediately head for the palace. The serious look in their eyes betrays how severe the situation has become. The news is not good; everyone waits anxiously for the king's speech.

When the shadows lengthen and the waning sunlight casts a red glow over the buildings of the centuries-old city, King Jehoshaphat walks out onto the temple court. To the surprise of the people, he does not climb up to the royal platform. Instead, he takes his place among the people and steps onto a small podium. Some people find it strange for the king to lower himself in such a way, but others respect him even more and feel closely connected to him.

The priests ask for silence and Jehoshaphat lifts up his hands to the heavens. He begins to pray out loud, calling on the Lord by his personal name.

"Yahweh, God of our fathers, are you not God in heaven? You rule over all the kingdoms of the nations. In your hand are power and might, so that none is able to withstand you."[44]

Jehoshaphat's voice trembles as he says these words; thoughts of doubt assail him. *It's no use praying! Who are you fooling? Just surrender to the enemy; it's your only chance of survival.* The King of Judah has a battle raging in his heart but he bravely continues to beseech the Lord.

"Did you not, our God, drive out the inhabitants of this land before your people Israel, and give it forever to the descendants of Abraham your friend?"[45]

While he remembers God's faithfulness to Israel in the days of Moses, he feels strengthened. Resolutely, he continues to pray, "And now behold, the men of Ammon and Moab and Mount Seir, whom you would not let Israel invade when they came from the land of Egypt, and whom they avoided and did not destroy - behold, they reward us by coming to drive us out of your possession, which you have given us to inherit."[46]

The people shudder. So, this is the enemy's plan. The surrounding nations want to wipe them off the face of the earth. Some women begin to sob. The men try to maintain their composure as they put on brave faces, but inside they are paralyzed with fear.

Meanwhile, the king continues to pray. "O our God, will you not execute judgment on them? We are powerless against this great horde that is coming against us. We do not know what to do, but our eyes are on you."[47]

Jehoshaphat feels defeated. *Will God do anything?* he wonders. Hadn't God also said that if the people did keep his law, He would send them into exile?

Among the people in the court stands a temple servant from the tribe of Levi. He is a descendent of Asaph, one of King David's court composers. *Shall I sing now or shall I remain quiet,* Jahaziel wonders. That morning he had composed a new Psalm. It seems so applicable in this situation and so fitting following the king's prayer. And yet, he is nervous to start singing. He doesn't want to seem presumptuous in this grave crisis.

While he prayerfully considers what to do, the words 'do not fear' come to mind. Jahaziel recognizes that it is God's voice. *Lord, are you speaking to me or to the others?* Immediately another thought comes up. *Do not be dismayed at this great horde.* "What would you like me to do, Lord?' Jahaziel prays silently. *Say these words out loud,* is his next thought from deep inside. Now he is sure that he has a message from God for the people. He clears his throat and begins.

"Listen, all Judah and inhabitants of Jerusalem and King Jehoshaphat: Thus says the Lord to you, 'Do not be afraid and do not be dismayed at this great horde, for the battle is not yours but God's.'"[48]

As he slowly and emphatically pronounces the words, the next sentence enters his thoughts. Jahaziel surrenders to the prophetic message that wells up inside of him. "Tomorrow go down against them. Behold, they will come up by the ascent of Ziz. You will find them at the end of the valley, east of the wilderness of Jeruel. You will not need to fight in this battle. Stand firm, hold your position, and see the salvation of the Lord on your behalf, O Judah and Jerusalem. Do not be afraid and do not be dismayed. Tomorrow go out against them, and the Lord will be with you."[49]

Jehoshaphat drinks in the words. Calm replaces turmoil in his heart. He takes the inner peace as a confirmation that this is a message from God himself. Full of gratitude and renewed courage, he kneels reverently in the presence of the assembly, leaning on his elbows, until his forehead touches the ground. From the eldest man to the youngest girl, everyone present follows his example. After a few moments of silent prayer, Jehoshaphat stands up. The choir leader's eyes meet his, he nods, and immediately the temple singers lift up their voices in praise. One psalm follows another; harmonious sounds reverberate within the walls. Those who know the words join in the singing and the praises of God's people grow louder and louder. When the conductor of the temple choir starts the next psalm, the people are jubilant. Fear has given place to joy.

> "When the people of Israel left Egypt,
> when Jacob's descendants left that foreign land,
> Judah became the Lord's holy people,
> Israel became his own possession.
> The Red Sea looked and ran away;
> the Jordan River stopped flowing.
> The mountains skipped like goats;
> the hills jumped around like lambs.
> What happened, Sea, to make you run away?
> And you, O Jordan, why did you stop flowing?
> You mountains, why did you skip like goats?
> You hills, why did you jump around like lambs?
> Tremble, earth, at the Lord's coming,
> at the presence of the God of Jacob,
> who changes rocks into pools of water
> and solid cliffs into flowing springs."[50]

Everyone feels encouraged by the memories of the miracles in the past. As Jahaziel sings, he feels a warmth inside. *The Lord crushed the Egyptians at the Red Sea, without us having to fight them. What the Lord did then, He can do now too.*

The words of prophecy he has just spoken remind him of the words the Prophet Moses had uttered to the children of Israel when they faced Pharaoh's armies. Moses had boldly proclaimed in faith, "Fear not, stand firm, and see the salvation of the Lord, which he will work for you today. For the Egyptians whom you see today, you shall never see again."[51] He quickly concludes, *God is using me the way He used Moses!"* Humility and gratitude fill his heart as he silently voices his thankfulness to God.

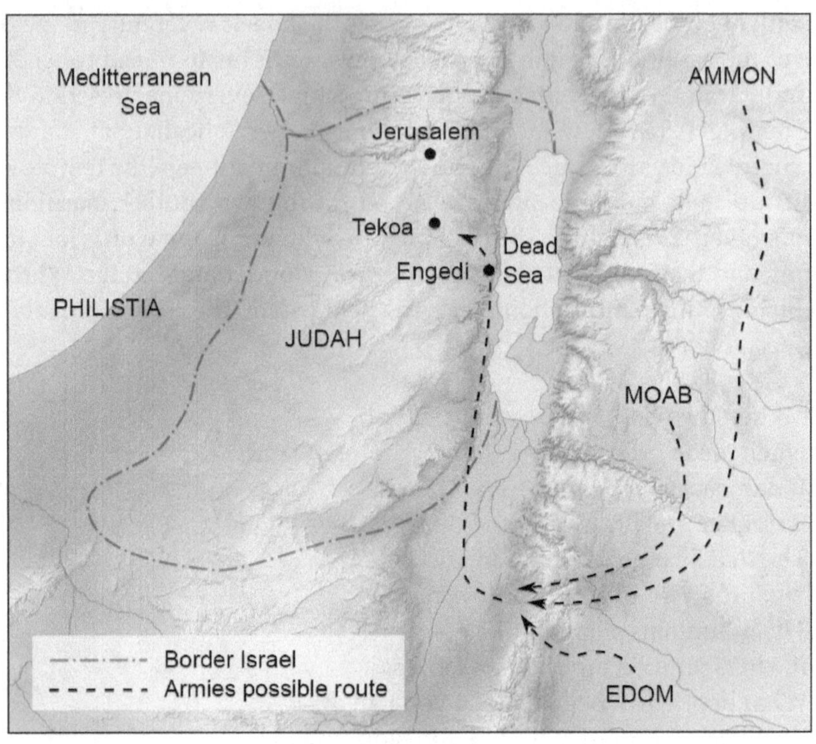

Possible route of the Ammonite, Moabite and Edomite armies

For an animation clip, go to
www.godlovesishmael.com/jehoshaphat

At last, Jehoshaphat orders silence and instructs the people what has to be done the following day. As the court slowly empties, Jahaziel tries to catch up with the king. As soon as Jehoshaphat notices him, he reaches out to him in a warm embrace and says, "Thank you for the words you have spoken today."

Jahaziel blushes at the king's approval. "They were not my words, O King, but the Lord's."

"I know, my son, but you spoke them in obedience to God."

Jahaziel is reassured and decides to tell the king about his new song.

Jehoshaphat is interested and allows Jahaziel to sing it right where they are. When he has finished, onlookers spontaneously burst into applause.

"Wonderful, Jahaziel, praise be to the Lord," says King Jehoshaphat, "I suggest that you practice it with the other musicians, so that tomorrow morning you can teach the people." The choir leader is excited as well and immediately directs all the singers to get together in the hall of the Levites. Jahaziel feels deeply honored and joyfully obeys the king's command.

Less than thirty kilometers from Jerusalem, the army chiefs of Moab, Ammon, and Edom are feasting. Wine is flowing abundantly as the men recount stories of valor of past battles. Silver goblets in hand, they also brag about the upcoming victory.

"In a little while, the land of milk and honey will be ours," says the Edomite chief.

"Yes, and we will make Jerusalem the capital of our nation," the Moabite chief adds.

"You mean our land, of course," laughs the Ammonite general.

The Edomites resent his comment. Their leader is clearly offended and says, "Jerusalem is ours."

"Why should it be? It is too far away from Edom to be its capital. After all, Jerusalem is really close to Moab; that makes it ours," contends one of their representatives.

The Ammonites disagree but decide to work it out later with their brothers.

"Actually, the land is rightfully ours," the Edomites argue. "After all, we are descended from Abraham, to whom God promised the land. You should be happy that we are willing to share the plunder. Jerusalem is ours."

"Whose idea was it to destroy Judah and take their land? Wasn't it our idea?" the Ammonites insist. "We will decide who gets what, including Jerusalem. Our forefather, Lot, was an inhabitant of this land."

The discussion heats up and as insults fly backwards and forwards between the tribal chiefs, the festive mood begins to change. Everyone knows that there is no easy solution for their argument so each of them secretly decides that they will never give up on what is rightfully theirs. Finally, they retire for the night to their own tents. Except for a few snoring men, the camp is blanketed by deep silence.

21 Nothing is Impossible for Him Who Believes

Slowly, the eastern sunlight chases away the darkness of the night. The splendid iridescence of morning becomes visible as black turns to blue and dark becomes light, followed by an orange glow that appears on the horizon. The watchmen in the city extinguish the oil lamps on the street corners and announce the break of dawn.

Jerusalem comes to life and when the first sunrays paint the sky red, people start to appear on the streets. A short while later, a long procession leaves the city through the Horse Gate towards the south. Dressed in sparkling white garments, the Levites are in front, while King Jehoshaphat and his army generals follow them on horseback. The foot soldiers the king has been able to muster over the past few days walk behind the horses. Bringing up the rear is a long trail of citizens following the soldiers. Most of them are unarmed but they trust that the Lord will come to their aid.

As King Jehoshaphat looks over his shoulder, he notices a few latecomers coming out of the gate. When the moment is right for some last-minute instructions to his subjects, he declares with a loud voice, "We will advance towards the enemy singing. The Levites will lead you in songs I have selected for this particular time. We will begin with Solomon's song for the dedication of the temple."

The Levites are ready and as soon as the conductor gives them the signal, they start singing loudly. "Give thanks to the Lord, for his steadfast love endures forever!"[52]

Some of the teachers of the law are tearful as some lyrics bring back to mind things that occurred many years ago. They picture how, in the days of Solomon, God sent down fire from a clear blue sky to set the altar ablaze. All this happened as the people sang this very song.

Jehoshaphat joins in the singing wholeheartedly. Now and again, when his thoughts wander and he thinks about the approaching armies, he cannot help but doubt. Feelings of insecurity and uncertainty plague him. *How can I expose my people to such danger? Shouldn't we return to the city, where it is a lot safer? We are walking into a death trap.* When he directs his attention towards God, the doubts melt away and he feels reassured that Yahweh will save his people today.

After marching for about half an hour, Jahaziel and the other temple musicians start to sing a new psalm.

"O God, do not keep silence;
do not hold your peace or be still, O God!
For behold, your enemies make an uproar;
those who hate you have raised their heads.
They lay crafty plans against your people;
they consult together against your treasured ones.
They say, "Come, let us wipe them out as a nation;
let the name of Israel be remembered no more!"

For they conspire with one accord;
against you they make a covenant—
the tents of Edom and the Ishmaelites,
Moab and the Hagrites,
Gebal and Ammon and Amalek,
Philistia with the inhabitants of Tyre;
Asshur also has joined them;
they are the strong arm of the children of Lot.

Do to them as you did to Midian,
as to Sisera and Jabin at the river Kishon,
who were destroyed at En-dor,
who became dung for the ground.
Make their nobles like Oreb and Zeeb,
all their princes like Zebah and Zalmunna,
who said, "Let us take possession for ourselves
of the pastures of God."

O my God, make them like whirling dust,
like chaff before the wind.
As fire consumes the forest,
as the flame sets the mountains ablaze,
so may you pursue them with your tempest
and terrify them with your hurricane!
Fill their faces with shame,
that they may seek your name, O Lord.
Let them be put to shame and dismayed forever;
let them perish in disgrace,
that they may know that you alone,
whose name is the Lord, are the Most High over all the earth."[53]

The whole procession listens attentively to the beautiful prayer prayed as a
psalm. When Jahaziel restarts the song, the men walking behind the Levites

join in. The memory of the victory over the Midianites strengthens them. *This is the God we serve,* they realize. After several more rehearsals, even the people at the rear of the procession have memorized the words and heartily sing along, their voices echoing far across the surrounding hills.

Before anyone realizes, they have travelled quite a distance. Passing Tekoa, they now march in the direction of the desert of Jeruel, nearing the place Jahaziel prophesied about.

Dust clouds in the distance announce the approach of men on horseback. Judging by the size of the group, Jehoshaphat concludes that it is relatively few. They must be the scouts that he sent ahead from Tekoa. Why are they so careless? They ride out in the open, visible to friend and enemy alike. Jehoshaphat is worried. Perhaps they carry bad tidings. Or… could it be that they bring good news? "Lord, I lay myself and my people in your hands once again. Save us, as You promised," he prays silently.

A little while later, the scouts come close enough for their markings and features to be distinguished. They are exuberant and wave their arms excitedly in the air, all the while cheering loudly. Jehoshaphat breathes a sigh of relief. "They come bearing good news!" he yells out to the people.

The first one to reach the king shouts, "Dead bodies are scattered all over the valley."

"As far as the eye can see, there are dead soldiers," another one adds.

"God has saved us!" a third scout calls out.

Before Jehoshaphat has the chance to spread the news, the people break out in jubilation. "We have been saved! Praise be to God!" The soldiers are ready to advance, but Jehoshaphat cautions them. Even though we trust God, and believe He cares for us, we must be careful not to blindly walk into what could be a trap."

The people recognize their king's wisdom and they heed his command. Shortly afterwards, at noon, they reach a lookout from which the entire valley can be surveyed. Indeed, the canyon floor is strewn with dead bodies in dried puddles of blood.

They all want to run down, but the king orders everyone to wait. He sends out scouts to check the surroundings for any possible enemy traps. As soon as the all-clear is sounded, the people rush down the hills into the lowlands. They quickly round up the stray donkeys and camels they find grazing between the corpses of the previous owners, and load them with all the goods – tents, weapons, food stocks, cooking pots and so on – left behind by the enemy.

Jehoshaphat smiles. *Even in David's day this did not happen.* He thinks again about Jahaziel's song. "Make their nobles like Oreb and Zeeb, all their princes like Zebah and Zalmunna, who said, 'Let us take possession for ourselves of the pastures of God.'"[54] *I now understand what Gideon must have experienced when on smashing clay jars his enemies attacked one another. Lord, You only are Yahweh, our God, the God of Abraham, Isaac, and Jacob. You will not allow any other people to take possession of the land You have promised to our forefathers.* Jehoshaphat decides that this psalm should be added to the collection of sacred temple songs.

As the Israelites bring in the spoils, it becomes clear who the enemy was. Most of the slain are Ammonites, Moabites, and Edomites, but there are also some they do not recognize. They look like typical desert raiders who travel around in small bands. These must be Amalekites, they conclude. There are no Syrians, Philistines or warriors from other nations among them.

Jehoshaphat is satisfied. Earlier, it had seemed that all foreign nations had turned against Israel, especially when the messenger had reported the presence of northern tribes. Fortunately, this turns out not to be the case. *Not everyone is against us,* Jehoshaphat thinks. Again, he reflects upon the words of Jahaziel's song.

"For they conspire with one accord;
against you they make a covenant—
the tents of Edom and the Ishmaelites,
Moab and the Hagrites,
Gebal and Ammon and Amalek,
Philistia with the inhabitants of Tyre;
Asshur also has joined them;
they are the strong arm of the children of Lot."[55]

Perhaps we should adapt the first few lines, Jehoshaphat considers, *they are not exactly accurate. We should really exclude Philistia, Tyre, and Asshur, and even the Ishmaelites and the Hagrites.* But as he reflects more on the Psalm, he changes his mind. Jahaziel spoke prophetically about the victory and it happened just as he foretold. That means that the rest of the words are prophetic as well. Jehoshaphat is reminded of several other psalms his ancestor David had written. There are many things he does not understand, and yet David was clearly inspired by God when he wrote them.

The following day the king tries to find out what exactly happened on the battlefield. One of the scouts brings him a few shepherd boys who have witnessed the entire event.

"About an hour after sunrise, they all started fighting amongst themselves," one of them says, "the armies of Ammon and Moab against the soldiers of Seir."

"Yes," another affirms, "and after that the Ammonites and the Moabites attacked one another."

Jehoshaphat's curiosity is aroused and he asks, "Are you sure about the time it began?"

"I swear by God, my King, that it was an hour after sunrise," the first boy exclaims emphatically.

Jehoshaphat looks at his army generals. His eyes tell them, "are you thinking what I am thinking?" The generals, however, don't notice anything. They are too busy thinking about the spoils.

The king attracts their attention when he asks, "At what time did we begin to praise God yesterday?"

"Hmmm, I think it was around the first hour," responds the man at Jehoshaphat's right-hand side. Then it hits him. "That's exactly the same time they started attacking one another!" he exclaims.

"Exactly!" Jehoshaphat confirms emphatically. "At the very time we praised Yahweh, our enemies turned against each other."

The men are lost for words. Not only are they deeply moved by God's power, but they have also learned a valuable lesson. Whoever honors and trusts God will not be ashamed.

The king turns once more to the shepherds. "Do you happen to know what made them fight one another?"

The boys shrug their shoulders. They have no idea.

Jehoshaphat thanks them for their information and then proceeds to give directions for burial of the dead to curb the stench of the now rapidly decaying corpses. He is hopeful that one day he will come to know the full story.

A few weeks later, a caravan of Ishmaelite merchants arrives in Jerusalem. Everywhere they go, they hear the story of God's victory over Ammon, Moab, and Edom. They have to smile. As far as they are concerned, it had not been that much of a miracle. Some of the Amalekites had escaped into the desert and told them exactly what had happened. It doesn't take long before the king finds out about the presence of the merchants in town. He wants to hear from them and invites them to his palace.

"What is the latest news from your land?" the king begins. "Can you tell me anything about the war?"

The eldest of the clan responds in detail. He explains that the army chiefs of the three nations began to argue about the division of the land they were about to conquer, particularly the city of Jerusalem. "Perhaps you can imagine, O King, how the Ammonites and the Moabites began to scheme together to annihilate the Edomites, to prevent them from laying claim to Jerusalem."

"But why would they attack one another after that?" Jehoshaphat inquires.

"Well, each nation both wanted Jerusalem for themselves. It is after all a pearl among the cities of the world. Who wouldn't want it?" the merchant answers.

Then Jehoshaphat speaks. He describes to them the impossible situation of the Israelites and their complete inability to even defend themselves in the face of such an onslaught. "It would have been much more intelligent for Moab, Ammon, and Edom, to conquer the land first, and then fight about the division of spoils."

The Ishmaelites have to admit the king is right. They are aware that the attack had been perfectly planned. The three enemy nations had been keen on spreading rumors about their impending raids into Egypt. As if true to their word to invade the land of Pharaoh, they subsequently marched their armies southwards along the eastern shores of the Dead Sea. Suddenly, they had changed direction and invaded Judah. It would have taken less than three days for them to completely wipe out Judah.

"Their arguments began as soon as we praised the name of Yahweh in the temple," Jehoshaphat continues, "and at the very moment we gave God all the glory, while on our way to battle, our enemies turned on each other and began to murder one another. Rest assured, my lords, that it was nothing but the hand of God that saved us."

The Ishmaelites cannot resist Jehoshaphat's clear logic as they stand in awe of Yahweh. "Indeed, there is no God, but Yahweh," one of them exclaims spontaneously.

At the end of their visit, Jehoshaphat warmly thanks his guests for their time.

And the Ishmaelites? They cannot wait to go home and be the first ones to tell this amazing story to their friends and relatives.

What have we discovered so far about the relationship between the Israelites and the Ishmaelites? Have they constantly been at odds with one another or was their interaction of a relatively positive nature?

In order to answer these questions, let us take one more look at the different historical events which occurred. In the list below, some references to Ishmael's descendants have been added that are part of the Biblical account.

a) References with positive connotations:

It did not take long for family ties between the two half-brothers to develop. Isaac's eldest son married Ishmael's eldest daughter. This becomes meaningful when we take a closer look at the customs of today's Arab nations in the Middle East. Up to this day, daughters are only given in marriage after both fathers of the future couple have formally met. The father of the bride wants to make sure that his daughter marries into a good family. That is why a groom that is a close relative, such as the son of an uncle and aunt of the bride, is often a preferable choice. The bond of marriage between the children of Isaac and Ishmael points to a solid relationship between both families.

At the very moment that Joseph's brothers plotted to murder him, a caravan of Ishmaelite merchants were on their way through the desert. This gave Judah, one of his brothers, the idea to sell him instead. Thanks to the presence of the Ishmaelites, Joseph's life was spared. As a result, Joseph was taken to Egypt, where he later became viceroy, eventually saving his father Jacob and his brothers from starvation.

Ishmael went on to live in the desert of Paran (Genesis 21:21). Several generations later, the Israelites dwelled in the same region, without being troubled by their half-brothers. (Numbers 10:12, 12:16, 13:3). This is in stark contrast to the actions of the descendants of Esau. The Amalekites attacked the Israelites in the desert, while the Edomites would not allow them safe passage through their own territory.

Centuries later, David would take refuge from King Saul in Paran (1 Samuel 25:1). Apparently, he felt safe amongst the Ishmaelites who lived there. Even the prophet Habakkuk speaks of Paran as the place from which God came to save Israel (Habakkuk 3:3).

Although Job's ancestry is not mentioned in Scripture, clearly he lived in the East, the area inhabited by the Ishmaelites. Not only is the Old Testament book that bears his name full of references to Bedouin life, but the names of his friends and enemies also point in that direction. It is therefore plausible that God-fearing Job was a direct descendant of Ishmael. To read more about this, go to www.godlovesishmael.com/prophet-job.

Even today, many marriages are carefully arranged to secure the preferred family tie and in many Arab nations, it is preferable to marry one's first cousin. Jesse certainly went against the traditions of his time when he gave permission to Jether to marry his daughter. In doing so, he professed great confidence in this descendant of Ishmael.

When David was King of Israel, he hired the Ishmaelite, Obil, as chief caretaker of his herd of camels, testifying to the same kind of trust and indicating that the two nations were on good terms with one another.

David's son, Absalom, went even further in appointing Amasa, Jether's son, commander-in-chief of his armies. After Absalom died, David appointed him as general, rather than his cousin Joab, who had faithfully served the royal family for many years.

Many Israelites named their children Ishmael.[56] As a rule, people name their children after someone they respect, not someone they despise. In the Middle East, it is still commonplace for parents to name their children after important leaders. Evidently, Ishmael was a popular name. Later, people started to use derivatives, such as Elishama, which means: 'my God has heard', or Shemaiah, which means: 'heard by God'.

It is also remarkable that the children of Basemath, Esau's Ishmaelite wife, were given more suitable names than the children of his Hittite wives, pointing to a positive influence of Basemath.

Lastly, King Solomon gave one of his daughters an Arabic name, Basemath.

In his book, *Ishmael in the Shadow of Israel*, Tony Maalouf, references additional positive examples of Ishmaelite men.[57] If this interests you, I recommend his book.

b) References with negative connotations:

During the time of the judges, the Midianites and the Amalekites and the people from the East rose up against Israel. This last group points to the Ishmaelites, who lived east of the Midianites. Since they were geographically a long way from Israel, it is unlikely that all of them joined the Midianites in their raids. Additionally, the overall history of Israel does not give any indication to assume that Ishmaelites were present in large numbers. Israel's conflicts were chiefly with their immediate neighbors. In fact, the book of Judges, as well as the rest of the Old Testament, speaks mainly about the Philistines, the Moabites, the Ammonites, the Edomites and the Amalekites. For a chart of the conflicts between Israel and the nations, see www.godlovesishmael.com/conflicts

When Saul was king over Israel, trouble broke out between the trans-Jordan tribes of Reuben, Dan, Manasseh and the Hagrites (1 Chronicles 5:10). The Hagrites, whose origins are unknown, brought about the conflict. Some suggest that they are the descendants of Hagar, who might have remarried after she left Abraham and Sarah.

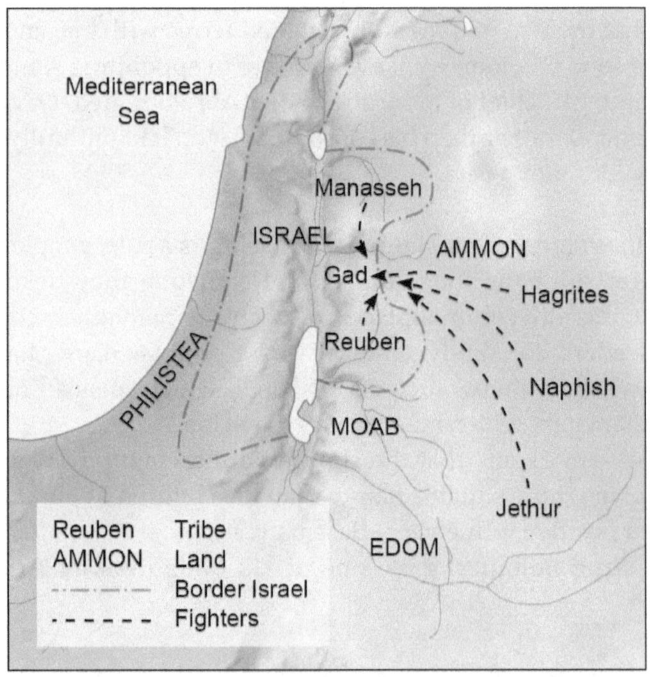

Conflict to the East of the Jordan

Furthermore, the descendants of two sons of Ishmael are mentioned by name: Jetur and Naphish (1 Chronicles 5:19-22). The bloody conflict eventually led to numerous casualties among the aggressors. It is worth mentioning that the Israelites living west of the Jordan did not come to the aid of their brothers. Apparently, the problems were of a rather local nature, which tribes would work out amongst themselves, instead of involving entire nations.

During the reign of King Jehoshaphat, vast enemy armies invaded the land. At first, the people thought the opponents were made up of different nations from east of the Dead Sea all the way to Syria (2 Chronicles 20:2). Later, the adversary turned out to be Moabites, Ammonites and Edomites, possibly accompanied by bands of mercenaries from other regions. Several Bible interpreters view Psalm 83 as a reference to this battle. It is no surprise that Ishmaelites are mentioned, because at first it was not at all clear what nations these troops belonged to. If indeed the Ishmaelites were involved in the attack on Judah, there were few of them, as the enemy is constantly referred to as only the three previously mentioned nations (2 Chronicles 20:1, 10, 22-23).

As we examine these negative examples closely, we realize that the Ishmaelites were never the initiators of any of the skirmishes with Israel. There is not a single story that supports the idea that all of Ishmael's descendants, meaning all twelve tribes, were involved in those conflicts. Furthermore, there are no Biblical references to skirmishes between the Ishmaelites and the neighboring nations. There is only mention of their collaboration, particularly with Edom, Moab, Midian, and Amalek.

There are two more points in which the Ishmaelites distinguish themselves from other nations:

Firstly, while the Bible speaks at length about the idolatry of the Ammonites, Moabites, Edomites and Philistines, even naming some of their idols by name, it remains silent about any idolatrous practices of the Ishmaelites.[58] Although this silence does not mean the Ishmaelites didn't worship idols, the Bible does seem to suggest that they served the God of their forefathers, Ishmael and Abraham.

Secondly, contrary to the other surrounding nations, they have never been accused of jealousy towards the offspring of Isaac and Israel. The Moabites, Ammonites, and Edomites coveted the land of milk and honey and attempted several times to conquer the Israelites who lived there.[59]

All of this points to the fact that the Ishmaelites were a God-fearing people, who willingly accepted their God-given place in the desert.

In conclusion, it is safe to assume that the relationship between the descendants of Ishmael and the descendants of Isaac was predominantly positive. The notion that Ishmael would always live in enmity with his neighbors, based on a loose interpretation of Genesis 16:12, is not supported by history.

On the contrary, the Bible points out a warm kinship. This does not mean that there have been no conflicts between Israelites and Ishmaelites. These conflicts, however, must be viewed in the larger context of the nations which surrounded Israel. Her immediate neighbors, the Ammonites, the Moabites, and the Philistines, were her real enemies. By far, the biggest trouble makers were the Edomites, the descendants of Esau, with the Amalekites surpassing them all with their evildoing. Therefore God ordered them to be annihilated. This sharply contrasts with the Ishmaelites who dwelled further east and south. Why did God inspire the writers of the Old Testament books to record all these historic events, giving us insight into the interrelations of the different people of the Middle East? Could it be that in doing so He is affirming his love for Ishmael? Could it be that He desires us to understand that He has a plan for the descendants of Ishmael?

It might have surprised you to encounter the Queen of Sheba in this part of the book, and perhaps you are wondering what her story has to do with the Ishmaelites. At the end of this book, it will become clear why she was brought into this narrative. God's promises of blessings extend all the way to the people at the Southern tip of the Arabian Peninsula.

Lastly, consider the following parallels between the families of Ishmael and Isaac.

1. God used the Ishmaelites at a crucial moment in Joseph's life: when his brothers were about to kill him. Indirectly, the Ishmaelites became an instrument in God's hands to save the Israelites from starvation. Many years later, God used Joseph, a descendant of Isaac, to save the Ishmaelites from a similar fate.
2. God provided a ram for Abraham as a substitute burnt offering for his son. Job, who was most likely an Ishmaelite, regularly made burnt offerings for his sons.
3. God ordered Job's friends to make a burnt offering to atone for their sins. Centuries later, God commanded the Israelites through Moses to bring burnt offerings to atone for their sins.
4. Even today both Jews and Arabs[60] circumcise their male children!

In the next part of this book we will consider the prophecies spoken by Israel's prophets. This will shed more light on the question whether God has a plan for the Ishmaelites or not.

God's plan for the Arabs

A fresh look at the Old Testament prophecies
with regards to the descendants of Ishmael
who are later called Arabs.

And Abraham said to God, "Oh that Ishmael might live before you!"
God replied, "As for Ishmael, I have heard you."
Genesis 17:18,20a

At the time of the birth of Jesus the Messiah

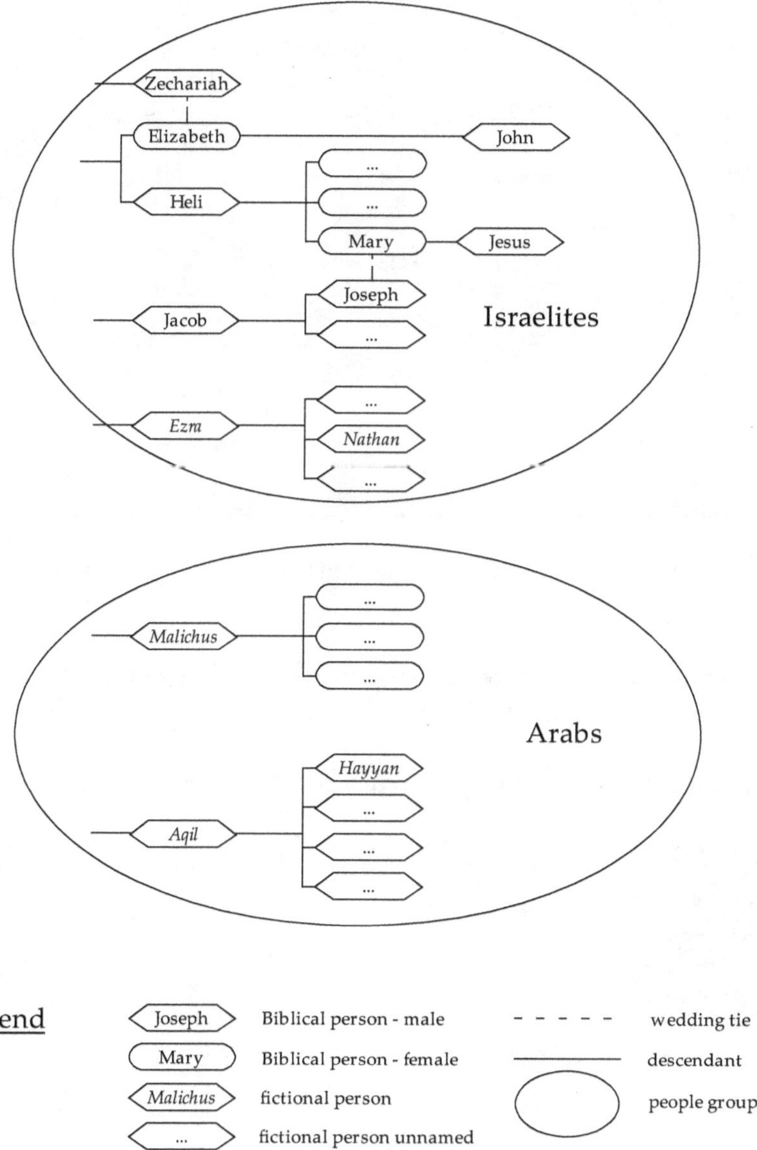

Legend

Joseph	Biblical person - male	- - - - - - wedding tie
Mary	Biblical person - female	descendant
Malichus	fictional person	people group
...	fictional person unnamed	

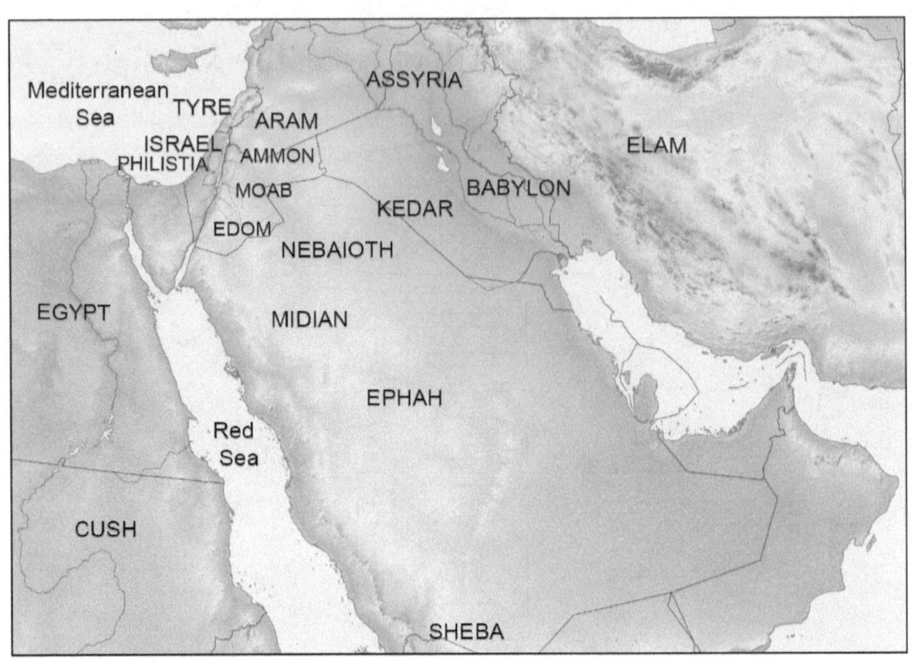

Some of the people groups named in Old Testament prophecies

Around the time of the birth of Jesus, the nations of Ammon, Moab, Edom and Philistia had ceased to exist.

For a short animation clip, go to www.godlovesishmael.com/promises.

800 years after the death of King Jehoshaphat;
shortly before the birth of Jesus the Messiah …

22 Blessings in Disguise

"Water, fresh water!" a man calls out, as he places a skin filled with the precious liquid on the ground. A clay cup in hand, he watches anxiously for thirsty customers. The noonday sun is beating down directly overhead and people are looking for ways to cool off. The town square is filled, and business is brisk. The weekly market never fails to attract merchants from far and near coming in hopes of selling or trading their goods. To the left, farmers have displayed their freshly harvested fruits and vegetables. "Dates! Freshly harvested from Sheba!" someone yells. To the right, vendors have set up stalls with all sorts of sewing paraphernalia for tent making and tailoring. From far across the square, the blacksmith noisily clangs iron upon iron making nails. Further down, a camel lazily circles a wooden olive press. The owner commends his product, "Extra virgin olive oil!" The clatter and pungent scents of the noisy marketplace blend in with the oppressive heat.

On the top floor of an imposing mansion on the square, two men recline on luxurious rugs. The lively bustle outside does not disturb them. The thick clay walls of the house offer perfect insulation against the noises and heat. But even without that, they are too engrossed in the documents spread out on the ground before them to notice the noises or heat.

"Look, I recently purchased this one in Jerusalem," Malichus says to his friend, as he holds up a papyrus scroll with silver embellishments around the edges of the artfully decorated wooden shafts.

"Show me," says Aqel curiously, as he stretches out his hand to grab it.

Malichus quickly pulls the scroll back. "I want to study it myself; after that you can take a look," he laughs.

"What's written on it?" asks Aqel.

A twinkle appears in Malichus' eyes. "Messages of a Jewish prophet."

"What's so special about that? Don't we have a lot of those already?"

"True, but this one contains messages about our people. It mentions Kedar."

"How is that news? We have seen earlier writings by one of the ancient prophets. What's his name again?"

"You mean Jonah?"

"No, not Jonah, there are no references about our people in the writings of Jonah. I remember now. Ezekiel. It was Ezekiel," recalls Aqel.

"That's true," Malichus agrees. "Although it really only speaks about our trade relations with Tyre. That message has nothing to do with us as a people."

"Are you sure about that?" Aqel asks. Without waiting for his friend to respond, he calls on one of his servants to fetch him something. A little later, the young man returns, carrying a large papyrus scroll. Aqel swiftly opens it and tries to find the spot he is looking for. In the meantime, Malichus begins to read his own precious copy.

"Here it is," Aqel says, breaking the silence and immediately begins to read aloud. "Arabia and all the princes of Kedar were your favored dealers in lambs, rams, and goats; in these they did business with you."[61]

"See! That is not a prophetic message!" his friend insists.

Aqel is annoyed. He does not want to admit his friend is right. Slowly, he unrolls the scroll until he reaches the opening words of Ezekiel's discourse. Suddenly, his eye catches an interesting phrase saying, 'sons of the East.' *Who could the prophet be referring to?* Immediately, it becomes clear. "Malichus, listen to this," he asserts enthusiastically as he reads him the passage.

"The word of the Lord came to me: 'Son of man, set your face toward the Ammonites and prophesy against them. Say to the Ammonites, Hear the word of the Lord God: Thus says the Lord God, Because you said, 'Aha!' over my sanctuary when it was profaned, and over the land of Israel when it was made desolate, and over the house of Judah when they went into exile, therefore behold, I am handing you over to the people of the East for a possession, and they shall set their encampments among you and make their dwellings in your midst. They shall eat your fruit, and they shall drink your milk.'"[62]

"This is about us," he goes on. "It has already come to pass, too."

"What makes you say that? Malichus asks. "The prophet Ezekiel lived in Babylon and he speaks about the East. We live to the west of Babylon."

"Look, it is true that Ezekiel said those words while he was in Babylon, but the message is addressed to the Ammonites, and so it speaks about the people who lived east of *them*, not east of Ezekiel."

"Why, I never looked at it that way," says his friend as he widens his eyes and leans back against the wall. "You might actually be right. Didn't some of our ancestors move to Ammon and Moab centuries ago after the powerful Babylonian King Nebuchadnezzar destroyed their cities?"

"That's exactly what it says here," Aqel says, as he stares reverently at the words in the scroll. "Listen to the rest."

"I will make Rabbah a pasture for camels and Ammon a fold for flocks. Then you will know that I am the Lord"[63]

"How is it possible that Ezekiel was able to foretell what was going to happen in such detail? Most of them still live there in their tents," Malichus wonders out loud.

"And even today they herd their camels amongst the ruins and their sheep, goats and donkeys."

"Exactly, Aqel. The Ammonites never took the land back from our ancestors."

"That's interesting! I think they don't even exist as a people anymore. Have you ever heard anyone talk about the Ammonites?"

"God be praised! He told his prophets exactly what would come to pass. There is no other god beside him."

For a moment, both men are silent. They need time to process what they have just understood. Then Malichus asks, "What about the Moabites? Didn't our forefathers occupy their land as well? Was that foretold too, or did they go into battle with the Moabites?"

Aqel finds the place where he left off and continues to read aloud.

"Therefore I will lay open the flank of Moab from the cities, from its cities on its frontier, the glory of the country, Beth-jeshimoth, Baal-meon, and Kiriathaim. I will give it along with the Ammonites to the people of the East as a possession, that the Ammonites may be remembered no more among the nations, and I will execute judgments upon Moab. Then they will know that I am the Lord."[64]

"Clearly, everything has happened exactly as it was foretold," Malichus concludes, lowering his voice in astonishment. "God is truly with us, Aqel. He promised to bless our forefather Ishmael, and continues to do so."

"Now, if you don't mind, I am curious to know what is written on the scroll you just bought. Who knows? There might even be promises for our children."

Malichus hears the hint in his friend's words. It is difficult for him to consider, but at the same time, it would be a shame to refuse a friend, so he graciously offers Aqel the scroll.

"Please, my friend, you be the first to read it. I am occupied with other things anyway." Silently he hopes that Aqel can discern from his tone of voice that he is just being polite, that he is not actually too busy.

"You don't have to do that," answers Aqel. He knows very well that Malichus is anxious to read the scroll first and he continues, "You haven't even read it yourself. I will borrow it when you're done."

"Really, you are my closest friend and I would really like you to read it first," Malichus repeats. To preserve his honor, he urges his friend to take the scroll and hands it to him.

Aqel then decides, "I would like to re-read Ezekiel while you study the new scroll; that way we will both bring something new to the table next time we meet."

Thankfully he's understood, Malichus thinks. Then he compliments his friend, "That's an excellent idea. As soon as I've finished, I will bring it to you."

Aqel is satisfied with the outcome; he can be patient for a few days. Next week his friend will come to town again for business on market day.

That night, Malichus pores over his new acquisition with the gleam of an oil lamp until the early hours. He is moved to tears when he reads,

"It shall come to pass in the latter days
that the mountain of the house of the Lord
shall be established as the highest of the mountains,
and shall be lifted up above the hills;
and all the nations shall flow to it,
and many peoples shall come, and say:
"Come, let us go up to the mountain of the Lord,
to the house of the God of Jacob,
that he may teach us his ways
and that we may walk in his paths."
For out of Zion shall go the law,
and the word of the Lord from Jerusalem.
He shall judge between the nations,
and shall decide disputes for many peoples;
and they shall beat their swords into plowshares,
and their spears into pruning hooks;
nation shall not lift up sword against nation,
neither shall they learn war anymore."[65]

"Oh, God, how my heart longs for that time. Let there be peace on earth," he prays silently. "You know that we don't want to quarrel with our neighboring nations. May they leave us in peace and then we can leave them in peace. Instruct all the nations your ways and allow us to live in freedom, just like You promised Hagar, the mother of our forefather Ishmael."

Over the next few days, the two men spend more time than usual studying the ancient writings. The enormous number of promises in the scroll of Isaiah amazes Malichus, but Aqel is disappointed. He is unable to find any other prophecies about his people in Ezekiel's writings. Except for the one passage he read earlier to his friend, nothing is said about the Arabs* at all, and the only ancestor mentioned by name is Kedar. Finally, the ancient name 'Ishmaelites' does not appear anywhere and neither does 'the sons of the East.'

Why are there so many prophecies about the about nations, and none about us? Aqel asks himself, puzzled. Suddenly, new understanding comes to him and his face lights up. The prophecies concerning the other nations are mainly about judgment, while the few words that are written about his people are of a more positive nature. He quickly unrolls the scroll until he arrives at the passage that speaks about different nations. He recognizes the piece he read with Malichus about Ammon and Moab, followed by a passage about Edom, the descendants of Esau. Then the talks about the Philistines and the empire of Tyre. As soon as Aqel starts to read that part, the length of the text devoted to this prosperous city takes him aback: there is column after column filled with predictions of judgment, interspersed with lamentations. Everything the prophet wrote down has come to pass. Indeed, only a few centuries earlier the Babylonians had come in, conquered, and totally destroyed the mighty city of Tyre.

Then Aqel turns his attention to some of the other nations Ezekiel wrote about. First, there is a short passage on Sidon, followed by a lengthy piece on Egypt.

That must be it, but to be sure, I'll read just a little more. Israel is mentioned in just a few lines, after which the text continues to talk about Edom. With growing amazement, his eyes peer over the words. This is really serious!

"Thus says the Lord God: Behold, I am against you, Mount Seir, and I will stretch out my hand against you, and I will make you a desolation and a waste. I will lay your cities waste, and you shall become a desolation, and you shall know that I am the Lord. Because you cherished perpetual enmity and gave over the people of Israel to the power of the sword at the time of their calamity, at the time of their final punishment, therefore, as I live, declares the Lord God, I will prepare you for blood, and blood shall pursue you; because you did not hate bloodshed, therefore blood shall pursue you. I will make Mount Seir a waste and a desolation, and I will cut off from it all who come and go. And I will fill its mountains with the slain. On your hills and in your valleys and in all your ravines those slain with the sword shall fall. I will make you a perpetual desolation, and your cities shall not be inhabited. Then you will know that I am the Lord."

---

* The first people to be called Arabs in the Bible are the descendants of Ishmael. For more information, see www.godlovesishmael.com/arabs.

"Because you said, 'These two nations and these two countries shall be mine, and we will take possession of them'—although the Lord was there— therefore, as I live, declares the Lord God, I will deal with you according to the anger and envy that you showed because of your hatred against them. And I will make myself known among them, when I judge you. And you shall know that I am the Lord."

"I have heard all the revilings that you uttered against the mountains of Israel, saying, 'They are laid desolate; they are given us to devour.' And you magnified yourselves against me with your mouth, and multiplied your words against me; I heard it. Thus says the Lord God: While the whole earth rejoices, I will make you desolate. As you rejoiced over the inheritance of the house of Israel, because it was desolate, so I will deal with you; you shall be desolate, Mount Seir, and all Edom, all of it. Then they will know that I am the Lord."[66]

What a terrible judgment! What have they done to deserve this? Aqel wonders. He re-reads the passage thoughtfully. Could it be that the answer to his question is right there? Using his index finger, he carefully traces the words on the papyrus. "Because you cherished perpetual enmity," he reads, and then, "because you did not hate bloodshed."

It is true, God never meant for us to harm one another. Thankfully, we are not so hateful, Aqel thinks with pride. He feels a warm glow inside. He is a true Arab, a direct descendant of Ishmael. His people do not despise the other nations, they don't seek their ruin, but rather they seek their well-being, especially of the tribes of their half-brother, Isaac.

What was it that Malichus said? "God is truly with us. He has promised to bless our forefather, Ishmael, and he continues to do so." Spontaneously a prayer of thanksgiving comes from Aqel's lips. "Lord, You are good to us. Praise be your name."

23 New Discoveries

"Welcome, welcome," Aqel greets his friend, kissing him on both cheeks. "How are you?"

"God be praised! How are you? And how are your sons?" Malichus asks in reply.

"They are well, praise be to God. How are your children?" Aqel purposely avoids the word 'daughters', even though Malichus has no sons. It is inappropriate for a man to ask about another man's female relatives. One can only do so indirectly.

"Praise be to God, they are all healthy." Then Malichus confides in his friend that he has found a suitable groom for his oldest daughter. Negotiations on the dowry are in full swing with his sister's husband, the father of the groom.

"May God grant them happiness," Aqel says.

A little while later, both men sit down on the plush rug in Aqel's guest room. A servant brings coffee and dates for Malichus, so that he can be refreshed from his travels. His journey wasn't tiring at all, but this is part of Middle Eastern hospitality.

The men are eager to continue their discoveries in the ancient Scriptures. The custom is, however, that they respect the hospitality traditions first. Aqel must first take care that his friend is comfortable. Malichus, for his part, asks about the events of the past week. As a judge, Aqel mediates many a family quarrel. He is an apt storyteller and articulates a couple of his experiences as a judge in such a humorous way that Malichus roars with laughter.

When the time is right, Aqel asks, "Have you learned anything interesting from the new scroll?"

"Let the wise hear and increase in learning, and the one who understands obtain guidance"[67], Malichus answers with a smile on his face.

"That's a wise saying; a truer word has not been spoken."

"I found it in a scroll containing proverbs from King Solomon. But that's not what I wanted to speak to you about today." Malichus takes another sip of his coffee and then pulls his precious possession out of a leather bag. He carefully unties the strap and opens up the scroll.

His curiosity aroused, Aqel watches anxiously.

"I found something that clearly refers to us. Listen," Malichus says as he begins to read.

"Let the desert and its cities lift up their voice,
the villages that Kedar inhabits;
let the inhabitants of the rock sing,
let them shout from the top of the mountains."[68]

"That sounds interesting, but what makes Kedar glad?"

"Let me tell you. Listen to what it says before." Malichus finds the beginning of the passage and reads,

"Behold my servant, whom I uphold,
my chosen, in whom my soul delights;
I have put my Spirit upon him;
he will bring forth justice to the nations.
He will not cry aloud or lift up his voice,
or make it heard in the street;
a bruised reed he will not break,
and a faintly burning wick he will not quench;
he will faithfully bring forth justice.
He will not grow faint or be discouraged
till he has established justice in the earth;
and the coastlands wait for his law."[69]

Deeply moved by these beautiful words, Aqel says, "What an intriguing prediction. I wonder who the servant is referring to?"

"I have no idea. I thought it might refer to one of the great kings of the past, but none of them fits this description."

"No, all world rulers were men of great violence. Nebuchadnezzar and the other Babylonian kings were brutal dictators, every single one of them."

"The Persian emperors were not much better," Malichus adds. "They were followed by Alexander the Great, another ruthless man, and not exactly a servant of the people."

"Who else is there?" Aqel wonders out loud. "The Seleucids who succeeded Alexander the Great were not any better. How about the Roman Emperor Augustus? Right now, he doesn't reign over all the earth, but who knows what might yet happen?"

"Well, do you really consider him to be a ruler who brings about justice?" Malichus asks.

"No, not exactly," Aqel laughs and then continues, "when did the prophet who wrote this actually live?"

"I found a complete conversation between him and the Jewish King Hezekiah, who lived about eight centuries ago."

"Well, in that case, perhaps the passage points to an Assyrian King. Their empire extended across large parts of the world."

"I am sorry to disappoint you, Aqel. This scroll describes in detail the attack of King Sennacherib on Judah. I cannot see any justice in that event. He was only looking to enlarge his empire. Besides, it seems to me that all kings of the past acted more or less in the same way."

"Yeah, I'm afraid you're right. And yet, this is a promise about a king who will reign in righteousness. Evidently, this king is still to come."

"That's exactly what I believe. Listen to what else it says." Malichus picks up the scroll, clears his throat, and continues,

"Thus says God, the Lord,
who created the heavens and stretched them out,
who spread out the earth and what comes from it,
who gives breath to the people on it
and spirit to those who walk in it:
"I am the Lord; I have called you in righteousness;
I will take you by the hand and keep you;
I will give you as a covenant for the people, a light for the nations,
to open the eyes that are blind,
to bring out the prisoners from the dungeon,
from the prison those who sit in darkness.
I am the Lord; that is my name;
my glory I give to no other, nor my praise to carved idols.
Behold, the former things have come to pass,
and new things I now declare;
before they spring forth I tell you of them.""[70]

"Wonderful! Just wonderful!" Aqel exclaims. "A king who sets innocent prisoners free and who brings light and joy wherever there is darkness and turmoil. What a wonderful time that will be."

"Indeed," Malichus affirms. "This is the reason why Kedar is to rejoice. This is the most awesome thing to look forward to: real peace, not only for us, but for all peoples of the earth." Malichus turns to the scroll once more and reads,

"Sing to the Lord a new song,
his praise from the end of the earth,
you who go down to the sea, and all that fills it,
the coastlands and their inhabitants."[71]

"If only we were still living when this will happen," Aqel sighs. "But there is no chance of that, especially when we see how Emperor Augustus is expanding his dominion."

"You're right. Things don't look good, but don't forget that God is sovereign over all the nations and peoples of the earth, even emperors. Listen to what else I read."

"Of course, go on."

Malichus carefully rolls the scroll toward the end. It takes a while before his eyes spot the passage he wants to read, but then he has finally found it.

"Arise, shine, for your light has come,
and the glory of the Lord has risen upon you.
For behold, darkness shall cover the earth,
and thick darkness the peoples;
but the Lord will arise upon you,
and his glory will be seen upon you.
And nations shall come to your light,
and kings to the brightness of your rising."[72]

Aqel interrupts his friend with a spontaneous prayer from an overflowing heart. "Dear God, please let this come to pass soon. Let your light shine in the darkness, so that the nations may see You."

"Amen," Malichus affirms; then he continues to read.

"Lift up your eyes all around, and see;
they all gather together, they come to you;
your sons shall come from afar,
and your daughters shall be carried on the hip.
Then you shall see and be radiant;
your heart shall thrill and exult,
because the abundance of the sea shall be turned to you,
the wealth of the nations shall come to you.
A multitude of camels shall cover you,
the young camels of Midian and Ephah;
all those from Sheba shall come.
They shall bring gold and frankincense,
and shall bring good news, the praises of the Lord.
All the flocks of Kedar shall be gathered to you;
 the rams of Nebaioth shall minister to you;
they shall come up with acceptance on my altar,
and I will beautify my beautiful house."[73]

When he finally puts down the scroll, Malichus asks Aqel, "What do you think?"

"This is so fitting with what you read earlier about the servant and it is only fair that we should all honor this righteous king," Aqel states.

"I wonder when he will appear. These quotes talk a lot about light. What do you suppose that means?"

"I really have no idea. I have studied the entire scroll of Ezekiel and haven't found a single clue. What about your scroll? What does it say about this light?" Aqel stares at his friend questioningly.

"Now that you mention it, I actually did notice something. Let's see, yes, right here," Malichus says enthusiastically.

"For Zion's sake I will not keep silent,
and for Jerusalem's sake I will not be quiet,
until her righteousness goes forth as brightness,
and her salvation as a burning torch.
The nations shall see your righteousness,
and all the kings your glory,
and you shall be called by a new name
 that the mouth of the Lord will give."[74]

"This speaks about the light of Jerusalem, which means it refers to a city and not a servant," Aqel observes.

"But then it says, 'The nations will see your righteousness,'" Malichus counters.

"Keep reading, perhaps we will then understand better what Isaiah was talking about."

Malichus agrees and continues,

"You shall be a crown of beauty in the hand of the Lord,
and a royal diadem in the hand of your God.
You shall no more be termed Forsaken,
and your land shall no more be termed Desolate,
but you shall be called My Delight Is in Her,
and your land Married;
for the Lord delights in you,
and your land shall be married."[75]

Then Malichus stops reading. He looks at his friend and says, "You're right, this is not about a person and it's more than a city; it's about a nation. But wait a minute; there is another piece in here." With great agility he turns the scroll the other way and reads,

"And now the Lord says,
he who formed me from the womb to be his servant,
to bring Jacob back to him;
and that Israel might be gathered to him—
for I am honored in the eyes of the Lord,
and my God has become my strength—
he says,
'It is too light a thing that you should be my servant
to raise up the tribes of Jacob
and to bring back the preserved of Israel;
I will make you as a light for the nations,
that my salvation may reach to the end of the earth'"[76]

"Right, this must be about the same servant. Fascinating, Malichus! You are a blessed man for obtaining this scroll of Isaiah during your last journey to Israel."

"Ah, it was mere coincidence, my friend. I wasn't exactly looking for it."

"All the more blessed you are! It appears that God ordained it!"

"I can't deny that," Malichus smiles, "God is always with us."

"You should be a teacher," remarks Aqel.

"If God wills, my friend," responds Malichus. At that moment, he smells the scent of freshly baked bread – a clear indication that the time for lunch is nearing.

"Forgive me, but I have to go. I need to return home now."

"Please join us for lunch, dear friend; there is plenty of food for you and your servants."

"Thank you, but I have a lot to do this afternoon and I do not want to burden you."

Aqel understands from this that his friend would not mind staying longer. This is exactly what Aqel had hoped for, for he would like to learn more about Isaiah's scroll. So he says, "It's no burden at all. On the contrary, I would be honored if you would share a meal with me."

"Very well," Malichus agrees and he gives instructions to his servants care for the animals and get ready for the meal.

About an hour later, the men are seated in a circle on the ground around bowls of steaming stew and rice. While the guests enjoy the delicious food, Aqel watches them carefully, making sure that there is enough food to go round. He directs his servants from time to time to refill the breadbaskets or bring the next dish. When all are satisfied, they relax and lean back against the wall. As they move, each of them mumbles, "Praise be to God. I am satisfied." Several can be heard belching loudly, indicating that the food was tasty. The host is reassured that he has fulfilled his obligations of generosity towards his guests.

All the dishes are stacked and carried away by Aqel's servants. They return with desert - trays overflowing with a selection of fresh fruit.

24 Not Everything is as It Should Be

Squatting on the ground, Malichus bends slightly forward to pick up a piece of fruit from the platter in front of him. Using his fingers, he gently presses the bottom of the rind to his teeth. Juice runs down his hands as he bites into the flesh; he savors its sweetness for a moment.

"This is the best mango I have ever tasted," he compliments his host.

"Really, it is just this season's produce," Aqel answers rather indifferently.

Malichus, however, knows that this is the best quality in the market and that Aqel has made an effort to send a servant to buy it. But it is not fitting for a God-fearing man to look for personal honor, even if he has done something well. For that reason, he replies fittingly, "Praise be to God who gives us all good things!"

"God is generous indeed!" Aqel responds. In the meantime, he reaches over to refill his friend's cup with sweet mint tea, but Malichus covers his cup with his right hand, indicating that he is satisfied.

Finally, it is time to pull the scrolls out once again.

"What have you learned since last week?" Malichus inquires with obvious interest. After everything he has told his friend this morning he is anxious to hear what Aqel has to say.

"To be quite honest, not a lot; I have not come across any more passages about our people." Suddenly Aqel remembers the new insight he had received. His face shows his excitement when he tells his friend in detail about how the Arabs and Ishmaelites are not mentioned in the judgments of God.

"That's really interesting! I'm glad you told me this," Malichus responds.

Aqel, sensing that this is more than just a commendation of his friend, asks him, "What do you think about it?"

Malichus remains silent. There is something he needs to tell Aqel, but he hesitates. It is all rather negative. However, out of respect for their relationship, he can't really withhold this from him. Aqel will find out sooner or later. Holding up Isaiah's scroll, he says, "I read about a severe judgment on our people in here."

"Really, what does it say?" Aqel asks surprised.

Carefully, Malichus opens the scroll; his eyes scan the columns as he searches for the prophecy. When he finds it, he reads aloud.

"A prophecy against Arabia:
You caravans of Dedanites, who camp in the thickets of Arabia,
bring water for the thirsty;
you who live in Tema, bring food for the fugitives.
They flee from the sword, from the drawn sword,
from the bent bow and from the heat of battle.
This is what the Lord says to me: 'Within one year, as a servant bound
by contract would count it, all the splendor of Kedar will come to an
end. The survivors of the archers, the warriors of Kedar, will be few.'
The LORD, the God of Israel, has spoken.'"[77]

"This is indeed quite serious," Aqel agrees when his friend has finished. But after reading all the encouraging passages that morning, Aqel looks at it in a more positive light. "I am quite sure, my friend, that these things have already come to pass a long time ago."

Malichus hadn't thought of that. He leans back into the cushions against the wall as he processes the idea.

"When could this have happened?" he asks himself out loud.

"Most likely during the time of King Nebuchadnezzar. He was the cruelest ruler ever and built the largest and most powerful empire known to man," Aqel reacts. "Many of our ancestors were murdered at that time?"

"That is impossible, for the prophecy clearly states: 'within a year'. These things must have occurred while the prophet was still alive. Isaiah lived during the reign of the Assyrian King Sennacherib."

"That's true and during that time our forefathers often resisted the Assyrian leaders. Apparently, the prophet warned them. I wonder though, what sins they committed to warrant such a severe punishment?"

"What do you mean?" Malichus asks.

"Well, when I read about the judgments of the various nations in the scroll of Ezekiel, their sins are usually mentioned. Why would it be different here?

"I like the way you think. It befits God's character to warn the people before He punishes them," says Malichus. "Here, please, read it for yourself," he asks his friend as he hands him the scrolls. Aqel is overjoyed to accommodate; breathing in deeply with anticipation and reverence he takes the prophetic book with both hands and starts reading the column in question.

"Strangely, it doesn't mention anything about their transgressions. Neither does it name the iniquities of any of the other nations. Look, the prophet speaks right here about Babylon and Edom, but doesn't mention their sins either."

"Perhaps God decided to only allow Ezekiel to speak about this and not Isaiah," Malichus reasons.

"That makes sense. And yet, I would like to know why our forefathers were being punished."

"Let us visit the leader of the Jewish Synagogue, near the Big Gate. Perhaps he can answer our questions."

Aqel immediately agrees with this idea and calls one of his servants to put the scrolls away. "Do you mind if I take my son Hayyan along?"

"On the contrary! A wise father teaches his sons about all things," Malichus praises his friend. Soon they are on their way.

Three men and a boy are sitting down in the study of the Jewish teacher of the law. After formal introductions and a cup of sweet tea, the host asks his guests how he can be of service.

"Rabbi Ezra," Aqel begins, "you know how we love to study the ancient scriptures."

The balding elderly man with a long white beard nods solemnly. He has known the judge for a long time and appreciates his wisdom and justice. It is not easy to refuse the large sums of money the rich often offer in exchange for a favorable verdict, and Aqel's reputation for not taking bribes is widely known.

"This is the case, Rabbi," Aqel continues. "For the last few weeks we have been examining the messages of the prophets Isaiah and Ezekiel and we have come across some promises regarding our people."

Somewhat astonished, the rabbi looks at him. The old familiar prophecies go round in his mind. He is used to concentrating on what is written about Israel, but knows there are also passages about the nations surrounding Israel and recalls a mention to do with the Arabs. "Could you give me an example?" he asks with genuine interest.

"In the scroll of Ezekiel it says that the land of Ammon and Moab will be an inheritance for the sons of the East," Aqel explains.

"That has already taken place in the time of King Nebuchadnezzar," Ezra points out.

"Isaiah speaks of a time when the people of Kedar will sing for joy and worship God in Jerusalem," Aqel continues.

"Kedar shall sing for joy … and worship God… in Jerusalem," repeats the rabbi slowly, as he skims the history of the Arab nations in his mind. "This hasn't happened yet." Carefully he concludes, "Apparently this is referring to a future event."

"That's exactly what we believe. We also have read that God will send his servant, who will reign in righteousness over all the earth."

"That's right," Ezra confirms. He sighs deeply and then spontaneously quotes a prophecy that comes to mind.

"The people who walked in darkness
have seen a great light;
those who dwelt in a land of deep darkness,
on them has light shone.
You have multiplied the nation;
you have increased its joy;
they rejoice before you
as with joy at the harvest,
as they are glad when they divide the spoil.
For the yoke of his burden,
and the staff for his shoulder,
the rod of his oppressor,
you have broken as on the day of Midian.
For every boot of the tramping warrior in battle tumult
and every garment rolled in blood
will be burned as fuel for the fire.
For to us a child is born,
to us a son is given;
and the government shall be upon his shoulder,
and his name shall be called
Wonderful Counselor, Mighty God,
Everlasting Father, Prince of Peace."[78]

As soon as Malichus hears the word 'light', he looks at his friend. Aqel has heard it, too, and immediately turns toward Malichus. Their eyes betray their thoughts. When the rabbi starts speaking about the child, their hearts begin to beat faster. This is exactly what they were talking about this morning.

That's strange, Malichus thinks, *these words sound familiar. Is this perhaps from Isaiah's scroll?* He waits until Ezra has finished before he asks, "Which prophet has spoken these words?"

The rabbi thinks for a moment. His thoughts linger on the wonderful promise of the Prince of Peace, whose coming he is longing for. Then he looks Malichus in the eye and says, "God gave this message to the prophet Isaiah."

Aqel is surprised. He cannot quite imagine that Malichus missed that. Is it perhaps on a different scroll? But when he looks at his friend, he notices that Malichus avoids eye contact with him. He seems to be a little flustered.

Indeed, Malichus feels embarrassed. How could he have overlooked such a beautiful prophecy? He quickly changes the subject back to the reason for their visit.

"We also read about judgments on our people, but we couldn't tell what the problem was that provoked the judgment."

Aqel adds, "This is curious, for whenever God judged a nation through his prophets, He gave them the reason for their punishment."

"Which books did you read that in?" the Jewish teacher of the law asks them.

"Isaiah and Ezekiel," Malichus replies.

"Let us open the book of Jeremiah," decides Ezra. "Many messages about the nations of the world are to be found there." He gets up from the floor, walks over to the built-in cabinet, and opens the wooden doors. Behind the doors, in an alcove in the wall, are dozens of carefully-stored scrolls. Aqel and Malichus stare in amazement at all the precious documents they would love to read for themselves, but they realize they cannot, for these are written in Hebrew and not in Aramaic.

Shortly, the rabbi joins them again on the floor and opens the scroll he took out of the wall cabinet. But before doing so, he holds the book out in front of him and kisses both parts of the felt covering. This is a new experience for the guests. The way the rabbi pays homage to the words of the prophet surprises them, but then they realize that these are not just any books; these writings contain the words of God Almighty.

After a while, the rabbi finds the passage he was looking for. "Let me translate this for you," he says, as he begins to read.

"Concerning Kedar and the kingdoms of Hazor that Nebuchadnezzar king of Babylon struck down. Thus says the Lord:

'Rise up, advance against Kedar!
Destroy the people of the east!
Their tents and their flocks shall be taken,
their curtains and all their goods;
their camels shall be led away from them,
and men shall cry to them: 'Terror on every side!'
Flee, wander far away, dwell in the depths,
O inhabitants of Hazor!
declares the Lord.
For Nebuchadnezzar king of Babylon
has made a plan against you
and formed a purpose against you.

Rise up, advance against a nation at ease,
that dwells securely,'
declares the Lord,

'that has no gates or bars,
that dwells alone.
Their camels shall become plunder,
their herds of livestock a spoil.
I will scatter to every wind
those who cut the corners of their hair,
and I will bring their calamity
from every side of them,'
declares the Lord."[79]

When the rabbi is finished, he carefully rolls up both sides of the scroll before he routinely wraps it in the dust cover. After placing the scroll on the table in front of him, he addresses his guests, and says, "Do you understand now what the sins of the Kedarites were?"

The two friends look one another in the eye, and then Aqel says cautiously, "The people imagined themselves safe at that time, even though King Nebuchadnezzar had already prepared his armies to attack them."

"Very good," agrees the rabbi. "Why did this grieve the Lord so much?" Neither Aqel nor Malichus can answer that question. They wonder what could be wrong with feeling safe.

"Let me rephrase the question," continues Ezra. "Who were they trusting in for their safety?"

Hayyan, who has been quietly listening to the conversation, taps his father on the shoulder. Aqel inclines his head and his son whispers something into his ear. He nods in agreement. The boy speaks politely and asks, "Honored Rabbi Ezra, they should have trusted in God, rather than in themselves, is that correct?"

Surprise registers on Ezra's face. Then he looks at him with approval in his eyes and says, "That's right, my son, very good indeed."

Hayyan sits up; it feels good to be treated like an adult by these wise men.

Ezra turns from the son to the father and says with a smile on his face, "You have a clever son, Judge Aqel. Surely, he will become a good successor to you."

"Thank you, Rabbi. Praise God, from whom all wisdom flows!"

Malichus wants to make sure he has understood the rabbi and asks, "Are you saying that our people have never caused significant problems for Israel?"

"I can assure you that the problems between my people and yours have always been of a trivial nature. Even the name 'Ishmael' has been popular with Jewish families over the years. This name also appears regularly in the Scriptures. Of course, there have been conflicts, but they cannot be compared with the suffering and problems that the Ammonites, Moabites, and Philistines have caused us throughout the centuries. From the Edomites, we would have expected differently, for they are closely related to us, but they caused us by far the most harm. Therefore, they have been punished most severely. That is the consequence of rebellion against God's will."

Malichus doesn't quite understand and asks the rabbi, "Can you please explain that?"

"Of course; God chose Jacob over Esau, just as He chose Isaac over Ishmael. One must accept this; it is the only way to have peace in this world."

Aqel is not happy with this answer. Hadn't God given the Israelites the best land, while his people had ended up in the desert? Then he remembers that God in the end gave them the land of the Moabites and the Ammonites. "How do you view the relationship between your people and us Arabs?"

Ezra understands the sensitivity of the subject for Aqel, so he reassuringly replies, "Excellent, otherwise I wouldn't be living here!"

The tension breaks and the three visitors laugh jovially. Still, Aqel is not quite satisfied with the answer and asks, "How do you see this in light of the Scriptures?"

The rabbi thinks back to the time it all began and says, "God blessed Ishmael for the sake of Abraham, his beloved friend. He made Ishmael into a great nation, just like the descendants of Isaac." As his mind travels back through history, another thought comes to mind. Ishmael and Isaac were the only two people who God named before they were born. This idea strengthens Ezra's next words, "God has chosen the Israelites to be the nation from which the Prince of Peace shall come; at the same time, He has a special purpose for the Ishmaelites. Just think of what the Prophet Isaiah said."

Aqel remembers the prophecies about Kedar and Nebaioth they read last week. They shall go up to Jerusalem together to worship God. Is that what the rabbi is talking about? Burning with curiosity, he asks, "What role does God want us to play?"

"Arabs shall lead the nations in true worship of God, when the Prince of Peace appears," replies Ezra. "God's blessings on the Jews, as well as on the Arabs, shall continue until the end of the ages. He wants to use you to make him known amongst the people." As Ezra speaks he is amazed at the words coming from his own lips. He has never understood it so clearly before. It is as if God himself is speaking through him.

Malichus and Aqel thoroughly enjoy everything they hear. They're speechless as they solemnly reflect on these marvelous new insights.

Finally Ezra asks, "Is there anything else, I can do for you, my honored friends?"

"Many thanks for your time. You have answered many of our questions." Malichus, the elder of the two friends, answers.

"If there is ever anything else, I should like to be of service. You are always welcome in my house."

Upon leaving the house, the rabbi warmly embraces both men.

"A thousand times thanks for everything," Aqel says again as he turns in the direction of the Big Gate.

"May the Lord keep you," the rabbi calls out after them.

Shortly afterwards, both men, preoccupied by their own thoughts, arrive at the square where Aqel lives. *When will we be able to talk of these wondrous things again?* they wonder.

25 Free Prisoners

No. Impossible! Aqel thinks. He has read many peculiar things before, but this… this is unbelievable. Frustrated, he rolls the book up and puts it away. *Time to go to sleep,* he tells himself. But first, he needs to find some way to relax a little. Confusing thoughts continue to churn around in his tired brain. He climbs the large uneven steps of the stone stairway that leads to the roof terrace. Once upstairs, he heads for his favorite spot on the wall along the edge of the roof.

As he looks up at the starry splendor that lights up the night sky, Aqel meditates on God's majesty. "Thank You, God for making everything so beautiful," he whispers.

At first the square below seems completely deserted. But then he notices the shadow of a man gliding past the houses and stores. Straining his eyes, Aqel tries to catch a glimpse of the man's face. *Aha, it is Nawfal. So, tonight he is the night watchman. He is very trustworthy and takes his job seriously. Great, that means those of us in town can enjoy a peaceful night.* Behind the mountain ridge that demarcates the valley where the town lies, a bright light slowly appears. The moon unhurriedly rises higher and higher in the sky. Its radiance dispels the darkness and Aqel can now see the desolate landscape outside the city walls.

Immediately his thoughts go back to what he read earlier. *Really impossible! Miracles like that don't happen! But what if it did happen? Wouldn't that be amazing? Doesn't everyone long for that?* Aqel pours out his heart to his Creator. "Please, Lord Almighty, teach me your ways. I don't understand much of this, but I really want to see this happen." There is no answer. Apart from the chirping noise of some crickets and the occasional screech of a passing bat, the world around him remains silent.

As usual, Malichus stops by on market day. As soon as he sees his friend, he notices that something is wrong. Hopefully it's nothing serious. But first, he asks Aqel in detail about his health and the health and well-being of his children and other relatives. Aqel tells him all is well with his family and his work.

"What are your thoughts on the book of Isaiah?" Malichus finally asks.

"It is absolutely wonderful," Aqel answers. "Thank you for letting me borrow it this week." Something in his voice betrays a lack of enthusiasm.

"I am curious to know whether you have learned something new," Malichus carefully probes.

For a moment, Aqel hesitates. *Should he tell his friend about the passage he struggles with, or should he just share some superficial thoughts?* He looks Malichus in the eye and decides to trust him. "Let me read you a passage," he decides as he opens the scroll.

"The desert and the parched land will be glad;
the wilderness will rejoice and blossom.
Like the crocus, it will burst into bloom;
it will rejoice greatly and shout for joy.
The glory of Lebanon will be given to it,
the splendor of Carmel and Sharon;
they will see the glory of the LORD,
the splendor of our God."[80]

Aqel skips a few lines and then continues,

"Water will gush forth in the wilderness
and streams in the desert.
The burning sand will become a pool,
the thirsty ground bubbling springs.
In the haunts where jackals once lay,
grass and reeds and papyrus will grow."[81]

When he has finished, Aqel looks at his friend and asks, "What do you think of that?"

Malichus grins broadly. "One day, my dear friend, we will be in Paradise, and then we will enjoy all the good things God has promised us."

"I know, but I don't believe this passage refers to life after death. It speaks specifically about Lebanon, Mount Carmel and the Hills of Sharon. It must be about this earth.

"Hmmm, you are right. I had not looked at it in that way. Even so, it is still beautiful, isn't it?"

"Yes, but just think about it. What if this was to happen, say, in our lifetime? Imagine going to the market and finding yourself riding your camel around several lakes instead of crossing the desert on dusty roads."

"Well, I wouldn't mind that at all," Malichus laughs.

"What about when the wadi becomes a fast-flowing river, year-round, and you can't cross it anymore?"

"If the delicate crocus bloomed in the desert, then surely fresh vegetables would grow there too. Then I wouldn't have to come all the way here to buy them at the market place."

"If… if… you keep saying 'if'." Aqel is somewhat irritated. "It doesn't say that it might happen; it says that it *will* happen!"

"What are you trying to say?"

"This is impossible. I just cannot imagine that something like this could ever happen."

"But who says this is about our desert." This is a Jewish book, with a message for the Jews. You just mentioned Sharon and Carmel. What else is written?"

"It's all very clear. Listen." Aqel continues to read.

"And a highway will be there;
it will be called the Way of Holiness;
it will be for those who walk on that Way.
The unclean will not journey on it;
wicked fools will not go about on it.
No lion will be there,
nor any ravenous beast;
they will not be found there.
But only the redeemed will walk there,
and those the LORD has rescued will return.
They will enter Zion with singing;
everlasting joy will crown their heads.
Gladness and joy will overtake them,
and sorrow and sighing will flee away."[82]

"Is that all?" Malichus asks thoughtfully. "I thought there's more in this passage."

"Yes, that's true. In the middle of the description on the changes that will take place in the desert, it says the following,

"Strengthen the feeble hands,
steady the knees that give way;
say to those with fearful hearts,
"Be strong, do not fear;
your God will come,
he will come with vengeance;
with divine retribution
he will come to save you."
Then will the eyes of the blind be opened
and the ears of the deaf unstopped.

> Then will the lame leap like a deer,
> and the mute tongue shout for joy."[83]

"Don't you see? This speaks about the God of Israel freeing his people," Malichus concludes. "This occurred a long time ago. The Persian King allowed all Jews who had been previously captured by the Babylonians, to return to their homes."

"I know that, but I'm quite sure they didn't walk straight through the desert. And even if they did; the desert wasn't exactly paradise on earth."

"So, this is still to happen," Malichus suddenly realizes.

"Exactly," Aqel re-affirms, "and I, for one, cannot fathom this."

"Yet, it is a beautiful promise," says Malichus, "the idea that the people of God will one day cross our land. Imagine that God will use us to pave the way for the salvation and liberation of the Jews? It reminds me of what I read earlier about the desert."

Immediately, Aqel hands his friend the scroll and when Malichus has found what he was thinking about, he begins to read aloud.

> "Till the Spirit is poured on us from on high,
> and the desert becomes a fertile field,
> and the fertile field seems like a forest.
> The LORD's justice will dwell in the desert,
> his righteousness live in the fertile field.
> The fruit of that righteousness will be peace;
> its effect will be quietness and confidence forever."[84]

"That sounds very similar like the passage I read earlier. Why don't you continue a little?" says Aqel, his curiosity aroused.

"Here it says, 'My people will live in peaceful dwelling places, in secure homes, in undisturbed places of rest.'"[85]

"This is also clearly about the nation of Israel and not about us," Aqel asserts.

Malichus, however, isn't convinced. He senses the narrative has something to do with the descendants of Ishmael. Aren't they the ones who have been living as nomads in the desert all their lives? Didn't even the rabbi say that they, the Ishmaelites, will have a role to play in the future? Then he takes another look at the preceding passage. "Listen to this now; doesn't this sound familiar to you?" he asks and reads aloud.

> "See, a king will reign in righteousness
> and rulers will rule with justice.
> Each one will be like a shelter from the wind

and a refuge from the storm,
like streams of water in the desert
and the shadow of a great rock in a thirsty land.
Then the eyes of those who see will no longer be closed,
and the ears of those who hear will listen.
The fearful heart will know and understand,
and the stammering tongue will be fluent and clear."[86]

"This is exactly the same thing that I read just now. It talked about the blind seeing, the deaf hearing, the lame walking, and… "

"… and the mute speaking," Malichus completes. "That's not what I mean. The theme of this passage is the righteous ruler. Thinking about our own people, who does that remind you of?"

Aqel remains in deep thought as he tries to remember in what context the prophet mentioned the Arabs or the Ishmaelites. The only thing that comes to mind is the judgments, but he doubts that is what Malichus is referring to. It must be a promise. "Are you thinking of the text that says that Nebaioth, Kedar, and Sheba shall worship in Jerusalem?"

"That has something to do with it, but I am actually thinking of another text about Kedar."

"I am sorry, I give up," says Aqel a bit disappointed.

"A while ago, we learned about the call for Kedar to rejoice over God's chosen servant, who will establish righteousness upon the earth."

"Oh yes, that's true, but I can't quite remember the exact words. Could we perhaps go back to it and read it again?"

"Good idea," Malichus answers, as he unrolls the handwritten page a little further.

Aqel is amazed at what he hears. "Behold my servant… I have put my Spirit upon him; he will bring forth justice to the nations…till he has established justice in the earth…I am the Lord; I have called you in righteousness… I will give you as a covenant for the people, a light for the nations, to open the eyes that are blind, to bring out the prisoners from the dungeon, from the prison those who sit in darkness… Behold, the former things have come to pass, and new things I declare; before they spring forth I tell you of them… Let the desert and its cities lift up their voice, the villages that Kedar inhabits; let the habitants of the rock sing for joy, let them shout from the top of the mountains."[87]

"Astonishing, Malichus! I still can hardly believe it, but it seems that our desert will actually come to life!" Aqel exclaims. "I have been acting like I am blind and deaf to God's plan."

"Oh Aqel, we are just ordinary people. Few are chosen to be prophets," Malichus answers him reassuringly.

In the meantime, all kinds of thoughts are running through Aqel's head. *Prisoners being set free; what does that mean?* "God, open my eyes; what do you want to make known to me?" he prays. Suddenly, he remembers something his father used to say, "You are destined to be free; let no one enslave you." *That had to do with our forefather, Ishmael. Though I live in freedom at the edge of the desert, I hardly feel free inside.* Aqel's wandering thoughts trouble him. *I am always worried about money, and thinking of ways to get richer. I work hard to keep my good reputation in the city, and I am always fighting the temptation to look lustfully after women. I really am a slave to myself.* Aqel would love to talk about his thoughts with his close friend, but perhaps these are a bit too personal. He remembers what the rabbi had explained. Judgment came upon Kedar because of its pride.

Malichus watches his friend and notices a deep frown in his forehead. "Don't take it so hard. God is merciful," he emphasizes encouragingly.

Aqel doesn't reply. He wonders how to put his thoughts into words. Then he decides to take the bull by the horns and asks, "What do you think about a person who constantly strives for his honor and tries to avoid or even cover up his shame; is such a person truly free?"

Malichus is a bit stumped by such a deep question and is silent for a while. Purposely trying to remain vague, he finally responds, "Perhaps not." Deep inside, he is aware that Aqel is right, but to admit that means that he is not truly free either. All his life he has been a proud Bedouin, fiercely protective of his independence.

Although Aqel is not fooled, he hesitates to respond. On the one hand, he doesn't want to cause his friend embarrassment. On the other hand, he senses the need to be completely honest. That requires that he sets an example. So he says softly, "I desire freedom in my heart; only then will I be able to rejoice over a blossoming desert."

Reluctantly Malichus whispers, "You are right. We are all prisoners of our own darkness."

Aqel appreciates the confirmation. Suddenly something dawns on him. "Malichus, God promised our forefather, Ishmael, freedom. Let us trust him, not only for our physical freedom of living in the desert, but also for inner freedom. I believe that God's servant will help us to achieve that."

Malichus is stunned by what he hears and doesn't quite know what to say. The only thing he can think of is, "Aqel, your name suits you perfectly; you are a wise man indeed."

"Thank you, my friend," says Aqel. "We should work together to discover more about this."

Malichus nods.

26 A Prophetic Star

An elderly man makes his camel kneel and then stretches out one limb towards the ground. Slowly, he slides off the saddle until his foot finds a stable, smooth cobblestone. Then he brings his other leg across the camel's back. Standing up straight, he untucks his robe from behind the ornamental belt. The rich fabric of his traditional garment falls in deep pleats to his feet and flutters in the gentle breeze. He carefully ties the camel to the metal ring in the wall of a house, then walks towards the ornate, handcrafted wooden door. With his rugged hand, the man lifts the heavy metal knocker and bangs it several times against the large nail in the door. The dull sound echoes between the bare walls of the stairway inside.

"Who?"* a woman's voice comes from within.

Without saying his name, the man replies, "It is I."

Thumping sounds on the stone staircase indicate someone is coming to the door. A fumbling noise is heard as the heavy wooden latch is slid open. Finally, the squeaky door swings open and a face appears from behind.

"Malichus, what a surprise! What brings you here today? It isn't even market day!" Aqel exclaims.

"I know, but last night I witnessed something very interesting! I wanted to tell you about it straightaway."

Aqel wonders what this is all about. *Last night, hmmm… so it was after dark.* Suddenly, his lips curl into a broad grin. "Have you perhaps discovered yet another star?" he asks smiling. He knows that Malichus is even more fascinated by astronomy than he is.

"Yes, you could say that! Except this one is much brighter than any of the others!"

"You are making me curious. We know all the big stars by heart, and now you are telling me that a new one has appeared?"

"I don't understand it myself. That's why I have come to see you. Then we can observe the stars together tonight."

"Good idea! I will invite Sami as well," Aqel suggests. "He knows a lot about the constellations and their significance." He cannot imagine a new star would suddenly appear, so if he can't convince Malichus, then Sami can help him.

Malichus follows Aqel up the stairs to the guest room where he spends the rest of the day mostly … waiting.

---

* This is what Arabs literally say.

The sun has almost set and dusk envelopes the valley in a dark blanket that is slowly rolled out. Soon, the constellations will visible enough for Malichus to point out the star he has noticed. Slight feelings of doubt begin to gnaw at him. What if he is wrong after all? He doesn't want to embarrass himself in front of his friends.

Leaning their backs against a wall on the flat roof, the men have made themselves comfortable on thick blankets, while their eyes are focused on the West, where Malichus' star can supposedly be seen.

Aqel's younger sons are engrossed in a game, huddled in a circle elsewhere on the rooftop. Their game consists of rows of light and dark pebbles with which they aim to block their opponent. They are having a lot of fun and when one of them makes a silly mistake, the others giggle loudly. Hayyan is more interested in the adult world and sits next to his father quietly listening to the conversations.

Speaking from experience, Sami says, "If we want to see this star we must wait until it is completely dark." He knows that the heavenly bodies are most clearly visible right before the new moon.

"I am certain that we will be able to see it tonight," Malichus insists once more as he searches at the sky.

After a few minutes the pink glow has disappeared from the horizon.

"Look! Over there!" Malichus calls out suddenly. "That's it!" The others scan the black expanse with their eyes, searching for the star he has seen. "Follow the line down, through the middle of Libra, and then look slightly to the right.

"There it is!" Sami exclaims. His well-trained eyes have followed what Malichus described. Shortly after, Aqel sees it, too. "That is really a bright star!" he agrees.

"Have any of you seen this one before?" Malichus asks eagerly.

Both men shake their heads. "No, this is remarkable *indeed*," Sami says. Then he adds laughing, "Pity I didn't see it first!"

In the meantime, Hayyan gently nudges his father and asks him, "Can you please show it to me, too?" Aqel point his finger in the direction of the star and Hayyan is amazed. "What a beautiful bright light, Father."

Sami, who has heard Hayyan, agrees with him. "It certainly is, young man." Hayyan beams at the compliment from this knowledgeable astronomer.

"What could this possibly mean?" Sami wonders aloud. "Such a bright star must be there for a reason."

Light, Malichus thinks. *There is something special about that word, but what?* Suddenly he remembers. "Aqel, do you recall what the rabbi said? Didn't he speak about a brilliant light that shines in the darkness?"

Aqel scratches his head. Then something dawns on him. "Yes! I remember when we spoke with him about the servant God would send, he immediately cited a prophecy."

"Yes, that's it, a prophecy from the scroll of Isaiah!"

"Let's look it up now," Aqel suggests. Malichus agrees and shortly explains to Sami what they have discovered lately in the Jewish scrolls. Immediately they get up and descend the stairway to make their way to the guest room, followed closely by Hayyan who finds it all very interesting.

"The people who walked in darkness have seen a great light;
those who dwelt in a land of deep darkness, on them has light shone."[88]

"It is indeed very applicable," Sami admits after Malichus finishes reading the passage. "A light shining in the darkness. This is exactly what we have seen this evening."

"Didn't I tell you before, that its brightness is visible even in the moonlight?" says Malichus.

But Sami is not easily convinced. "We are not exactly walking in the darkness, my friend. We always enjoy our well-deserved night's rest."

"Yes, literally perhaps; but what if we are to understand this figuratively?" Aqel asks his friend.

Sami remains quiet as he thinks of a fitting response.

"Let me read you a little more," Malichus suggests. "Maybe we will understand better." In the flickering light of the oil lamps, he continues,

"For to us a child is born,
to us a son is given;
and the government shall be upon his shoulder,
and his name shall be called
Wonderful Counselor, Mighty God,
Everlasting Father, Prince of Peace.
Of the increase of his government and of peace
there will be no end,
on the throne of David and over his kingdom,
to establish it and to uphold it
with justice and with righteousness
from this time forth and forevermore.
The zeal of the Lord of hosts will do this."[89]

As soon as Aqel hears him mention the 'son', he pricks up his ears. "Remember, when, only a short time ago, we talked about the darkness?" he asks Malichus animatedly.

"Yes, it was about prisoners," Malichus answers reluctantly. This is not a subject he enjoys talking about.

Because Sami has not been part of their previous conversation, he inquires, "What are you two talking about?"

Aqel responds enthusiastically, "This scroll describes *us*, the Kedarites, and our joy over God's servant who comes to free prisoners out of darkness and restore justice upon the earth."

"That sounds good for those that are held captive, but I fail to see what that has to do with our situation today." Sami remarks dryly.

"Well, Malichus and I were talking about how we, as Arabs, are literally free to go wherever we please."

As Sami listens he nods in agreement.

"Figuratively speaking, we are prisoners of all kinds of bad habits and sinful thoughts," Aqel continues. "One way or another, we all suffer from this problem. No exceptions!"

No need to emphasize it so, Sami thinks, but he realizes that Aqel is right. "Are you trying to say that God's servant will come to change men's minds and hearts?"

Sensing that Sami has a hard time accepting this idea, Aqel tries to express his thoughts in milder words. "The only thing I want to say is that God desires to give us complete freedom." For a few moments, he remains silent; then he adds, "This is what I long for."

Filled with admiration, Hayyan looks up at his father. He must be deeply moved, for Hayyan has rarely seen him this vulnerable.

"Now what?" says Sami. He is hesitant to commit himself to anything. "I can't deny that the star is indeed unique."

"I firmly believe that it is somehow connected to the passage we read in Isaiah," Malichus states. "The question is, 'How can we find out its significance for us'?"

"I have a suggestion. Let us go and ask Rabbi Ezra," suggests Aqel. The others concur, and they decide to pay a visit to the scribe the very next morning.

"May I please join you, Father?" Hayyan asks. Before Aqel can answer, Sami jumps in and says, "Of course, young man. You are a part of this adventure."

"All right then," consents Aqel, "as long as you finish tomorrow's morning chores in the afternoon."

"Of course I will, Father. Thank you so much," Hayyan reacts excitedly.

"Now to bed, son," decides his father. Hayyan understands and a little while later he is sound asleep, dreaming about discovering new constellations.

"You claim that you have seen a new star in the West, a star that shines brighter than all the other ones?" Rabbi Ezra repeats. "That is extraordinary indeed!"

"We are wondering about its meaning," Aqel explains. "We were thinking it might have something to do with the things you told us last time we visited with you."

Ezra's thoughts revert to the time when these Arab men visited him. It had been a pretty uncommon visit, not because he or any of the other Jews do not get along with them, but rather because their worlds are so far apart. Both communities prefer to keep themselves to themselves. "Yes, I remember telling you about the coming Prince of Peace, who will rule in righteousness over the whole earth."

"Indeed!" Aqel confirms his words. "Could it be that the appearance of this star has something to do with that?

Sami listens fascinated to the conversation. This is much more interesting than the things Aqel told him last night about God's servant. *A peaceful world, who doesn't want that?*

"A star and a prince," the teacher of the law muses. "That is a good question. I really need to think about that. Come back to me in two days and I will give you my answer."

Disappointed, the three men look at one another. It is especially difficult for Malichus to accept this delay, since he must go home and will not be able to return until the next market day. But there is nothing to be done.

Before leaving the rabbi's house, Aqel confirms the appointment. "So, in two days we will return, and you will have an answer for us."

"As surely as God lives, I will give you an answer," affirms the rabbi. He knows it is difficult for them to be patient and tries to lighten their disappointment. Then the men each go their separate ways.

Two days later, two men and a boy are on their way to the house of the Jewish Rabbi. Malichus is missing. However, Sami has decided to go along; he is becoming more and more curious about the new star.

"Shalom," comes the greeting from the teacher of the law when he opens the door for his guests.

Aqel feels honored. He knows it is a common Jewish greeting, but not usually shared with any of the non-Jewish citizens of the town. When Aqel's son looks at him questioningly, he explains, "Shalom means 'peace and well-being'."

"It sounds similar to our greeting, Father," says Hayyan. Overhearing the conversation between father and son, Rabbi Ezra, can't help but jump in. "It is the other way around, my boy. Your greeting sounds like Shalom."

Aqel is slightly annoyed by this statement and thinks, *Why do the Jews always think they are better than we are?* Although deep down, he understands what the rabbi means. Whenever he and his friends greet one another in Arabic, they say, 'peace and health'. The Jewish greeting, however, goes much deeper, as it not only expresses the wish for physical well-being, but also emotional and spiritual well-being. Resulting from centuries of sheer survival in the desert, Arabs are usually less concerned about those aspects of their fellow men. The Jews possess something Aqel and his people lack. He secretly admires them.

A little while later, they all sit on the floor of the scribe's study. An old, well-read scroll lies opened on the floor in front of them. Clearly, Rabbi Ezra has been expecting them.

With a twinkle in his eyes, he asks, "So, you want to know the meaning of the star?" The men nod eagerly. "I have good news for you," he continues. Aqel and Sami are anxious to hear the answer, but first the scribe covers his head with a shawl. Only when he is convinced that his head is properly covered, does he pick up the scroll. He kisses the top and begins to read.

"I see him, but not now; I behold him, but not near: a star shall come out of Jacob, and a scepter shall rise out of Israel."[90]

"Friends, this is your answer," he says finally as he carefully puts down the scroll.

Surprise registers in Aqel's eyes. *What does this have to do with God's servant?*

Ezra gives an explanation straightaway, without any further questions. "Jacob and Israel are the names for the same person, our forefather, from whom our nation derives its name. That means that the scepter and the star are one and the same as well. The only person who carries a scepter is a king. Thus the star is a reference to a ruler, who will be born out of the people of Israel.

"Could it be that the Prince of Peace has already been born?" Aqel asks.

"It is difficult to say. I have studied all my commentaries on the Scriptures, and the general consensus is that this prophecy has been fulfilled by the reign of our King David."

Aqel has a hard time accepting this. He does not believe it is pure coincidence that they have been learning so much about the righteous leader lately. That is why he asks, "Are there other sources, perhaps other experts on these ancient writings, who agree with our ideas?"

"There are," accedes the scribe, but they are few in number. As teachers of the law, we need to be careful. Better to err on the side of caution."

Aqel decides to let the matter rest for the time being, and changes the subject to the latest town news, but he feels confused. Should he believe this rabbi who knows the Jewish Scriptures inside out? Or should he follow his heart that believes that the brightly shining star announces the birth of the Prince of Peace? If only he could speak to Malichus at the moment. He understands exactly what is going on in his mind. *Just be patient a little longer,* he consoles himself. *In a few days it will be market day again.*

27 In Search of the King

"Where is the newborn King of the Jews?" Aqel asks.

The innkeeper looks at the foreigner in amazement. "What are you talking about? No king has been born!"

Another man butts into the conversation and says with a smile on his face, "King Herod is an old codger, only in his dreams could he have more children!" When Aqel leaves, the man thinks to himself, *that guy is crazy.*

Aqel doesn't fare much better at the local market place, where he quickly gets laughed at. "A newborn king? The heir to the throne is already a grown man. You are a little late, my friend."

The merchant of an antique shop explains that Herod is not really a Jew, but actually a descendant of the Edomites.*

Time and time again, the answer remains the same. No one has heard about a royal child being born.

As the group of foreigners scours the streets and alleys of Jerusalem for news of a royal birth, they feel more and more discouraged and begin to wonder whether they have just imagined things.

Aqel clearly remembers the words of Rabbi Ezra. "Most commentators believe this prophecy has been fulfilled with King David. It is always better to err on the side of caution." How he wishes the doubts would stop, but no, they continue to haunt him. The more people mock him, the more he doubts.

Malichus fares even worse. He was the one who had been so strongly convinced that the Prince of Peace had been born. He was the one who had persuaded everyone to go on this journey to try to find the newborn king. The others had been heavily influenced by the rabbi's explanation, but not Malichus. No, the moment he heard about the star of Jacob, he had known in his heart: this is it. But now, even Malichus begins to think he might have been mistaken. He remembers how much he had wanted it to be true. He had been the one to see the star first of all! After a long and arduous journey, they had arrived in Jerusalem a few days ago. Sami and some other God-fearing friends had joined them. Had it all been for nothing?

At the end of the day, the group returns to the inn utterly exhausted and disillusioned. After dinner, they discuss their next move and then decide to stay one more day in Jerusalem. Some of them want to explore the city.

---

* For more information, see www.godlovesishmael.com/herod

Others are thinking about finding a Jewish teacher of the law who might be able to help them, since Jerusalem is the center of Jewish learning and the place where Ezra obtained his scrolls.

After much deliberation, Malichus suggests a prayer of thanksgiving to God. After all, this is all about him. He is the reason that they are here.

"God of heaven and earth, we thank You for the life You have given us. We glorify You as our Maker and ask You to lead us in your ways. If it be your will, please show us the way to the royal child. We cannot do it ourselves. We praise your name. Amen."

For a while, Malichus feels at peace, but soon doubts begin to plague him again. When he is ready to settle down for the night, he tries to shake off the negative thoughts. *I should let it rest until the morning; then I will give it some more thought.* After what seems like hours of wrestling with his disappointment and fear, he finally falls asleep.

The following day, the friends split into two groups. In hopes of gaining some clarity, Malichus and Aqel decide to visit the temple. They would really like to enter the inner court and witness one of the daily burnt offerings to God, but it will not be easy to actually do that. As they near the gate, they notice several men in foreign attire go in. "Let us slip between the crowds," Malichus suggests. Aqel agrees and together they join in with the throng of people trying to enter the temple court.

Then, a young Levite gatekeeper notices the two foreigners, approaches them and says, "Forbidden for non-Jews."

"We worship the God of Abraham, Isaac, and Ishmael," answers Malichus.

"Have you converted to Judaism?"

"Ehh ... no... not officially, but we do believe in God the Creator and we worship him."

"I am sorry, but you are not allowed to enter," the young man says.

Though he is disappointed, Malichus doesn't want to argue with him and turns away. "Apparently, there is no place for us in God's house," he concludes. Aqel is not put off that easily and asks where they might find a teacher of the law. The Levite is willing to help and tells them to wait for him outside the gate.

While the friends are waiting around the corner from the gate in the burning sun, they hear someone reading aloud. Unfortunately, they cannot understand the language.

When the temple service is finished, the crowd leaves again through the gate. Finally, a man approaches them. "You wanted to see me?" he asks.

Aqel explains the reason why they have come to Jerusalem and tells him about the star and their subsequent search for the royal child.

"It is true that we live in expectation of the righteous Prince of Peace, but he hasn't been born yet," the man answers. "It is about time," he adds softly, "for we are more than tired of the Roman domination. It is because of them that we are limited in our freedom to worship God according to the law."

"What exactly does God's law dictate?"

"First of all, every baby boy must be circumcised on the eighth day," the teacher of the law explains. Malichus and Aqel smile at each other, for they were circumcised as children.

"Furthermore, one must keep the Law of Moses," the man continues. He then tells them about the Ten Commandments God gave to Moses on two stone tablets.

"We kept those from the time of our youth," Aqel reacts confidently.

The Jewish man doesn't seem impressed and proceeds to explain about the various ceremonial laws and constraints.

So many rules. Malichus is frustrated. *It's impossible to keep them all.* Besides, Malichus feels that this teacher of the law talks down to them and he finds the tone of his voice demeaning. Yet, Malichus remains courteous and at the end of their conversation, he thanks the man politely.

Before they go, however, Aqel asks the teacher what was being read in the temple court.

"It was a passage from the book of the Prophet Hosea," replies the man. "Beautiful words, by the way, they fit your question about the coming Prince of Peace."

"Could you perhaps translate it for us?"

The teacher is eager to oblige and he quotes, "Therefore, behold, I will allure her, and bring her into the wilderness, and speak tenderly to her."[91]

As he hears the word 'wilderness', Malichus' interest is aroused. "What does this prophet say about the desert?"

From what the Jewish scholar tells them next, Malichus understands that this is not about the Ishmaelites but rather about the Israelites. Suddenly, something the teacher of the law says catches his attention. "And I will abolish the bow, the sword, and war from the land, and I will make you lie down in safety."[92]

It sounds a lot like the reign of peace Isaiah spoke about, Malichus thinks happily.

"Israel, I will betroth you to me forever. I will betroth you to me in righteousness and in justice, in steadfast love and in mercy. I will betroth you to me in faithfulness. And you shall know the Lord."[93]

The emphasis on the nation of Israel dampens Malichus' enthusiasm.

Does this refer only to the Israelites, or does God have something for me and my people as well?

"And in that day I will answer, declares the Lord, I will answer the heavens, and they shall answer the earth, and the earth shall answer the grain, the wine, and the oil, and they shall answer Jezreel, and I will sow her for myself in the land."[94]

Now Malichus is even more confused. Thoughts spin round in his head. *How can the desert blossom like a rose? Isn't the search for water in the desert an on-going struggle? Is God speaking to Israel from the wilderness, our dwelling place? Will there be a role for us as descendants of Ishmael? Is that perhaps the time when peace will reign and when the desert places will become fruitful with an abundance of wheat and fruit trees?*

While Malichus thinks anxiously about it all, the scribe continues quoting the Scriptures. "And I will have mercy on No Mercy, and I will say to Not My People, 'You are my people'; and he shall say, 'You are my God.'"[95]

What? Is God going to accept us in the end, next to Israelites, as his own people? flashes through Malichus' mind. *Right now, we are not his people, yet we are the closest of kin to the Jews, rabbi Ezra laid out so clearly for us.*

Although Malichus would love to ask the scholar more questions, he is put off by the man's attitude. He prefers to wait and ask Ezra, who is not as haughty.

After lunch, the friends return to the inn to take a nap. When the sun is at its height the shops and businesses all close down for a few hours and there is little else to do.

"What have you found out?" Sami asks curiously. He hadn't been able to join them that morning, for it had been his turn to watch over the company's valuables. The expression on the men's faces already tells him the answer.

Aqel's disappointment is obvious; he recounts that they are none the wiser. "Even the teacher of the law at the temple wasn't much help." After exchanging a few more words, the men lay down to rest while Sami goes out to find a bite to eat.

"Tap, tap." Aqel wakes up to a gentle knocking sound on the door and immediately calls out, "Who?" *Could it be Sami or one of the others? No, they never knock but simply say "Open up!"*

"Some visitors are asking for you all," comes the reply from the other side of the wooden door. Malichus is still dozing, but as soon as he hears the word 'visitors', he is wide-awake.

"Are you expecting someone?" he asks his roommate, even though he already knows the answer.

Aqel shakes his head and calls back, "I will be right down!" Then he turns to Malichus and says, "That's odd, I think they want to talk to both of us, as he said, 'you all.'"

"Or perhaps they want to see the others. In any case let's go and find out," Malichus replies.

In the inn's reception room, two well-dressed Jewish men come towards them. After exchanging the customary greetings, they explain the reason for their call. "The king wants to see you," one of them says.

Alarmed, the friends look at one another. *What have they done wrong? Is one of the others in some kind of trouble?* "What is it, is it serious?" asks Aqel.

"No, no, not at all," says the king's spokesman reassuringly. "It is urgent though; please come with us immediately."

Since it appears that they have no choice, Malichus and Aqel ready themselves to follow the two men. At the same moment, Sami returns from his lunch. Since his presence is not requested, he stays behind to look after their possessions.

As Malichus and Aqel walk through the streets, accompanied by the king's servants, they feel very uneasy and out of place. That same morning, people had given them strange looks and even laughed at them because of their questions regarding the royal child, and now this!

When they arrive at the gate in the wall around the government buildings, Malichus is reminded of a royal encounter he read about. *Could it be that the Queen of Sheba used this very gate when she entered the city with her entourage?* He knows she came to Jerusalem for an audience with the famous Jewish King Solomon. And now, he is here with Aqel, also in Jerusalem, about to meet another Jewish King. He may not be the king they are looking for, but if there is anyone who might be able to tell them about a newborn king, it is he. Who knows, perhaps now they will find out how all the pieces of the puzzle fit together.

Contrary to their expectations, the messengers take them through a side entrance straight into one of the private apartments of the king, rather than into the large public audience room. There they warmly welcomed with tea and delectable sweets. A few moments later, King Herod enters the room; he greets them affably and appears to be a friendly man. The ruler inquires kindly after their families and their nation. Malichus is happy to fill him in with the latest political developments in their region of Arabia.

Eventually, the king asks them, "Are you the ones who are looking for the newborn king?"

Malichus feels completely at ease now and tells him about the star and the texts they read in the ancient scrolls. Finally, he also voices his frustration about not being able to find the child.

"I have good news for you," the king says eagerly. "I know where you may find the royal child."

Malichus can hardly believe his ears.

Herod notices the incredulous look on his visitor's face and continues, "In the scroll of the Prophet Micah, it says, 'But you, O Bethlehem Ephrathah, who are too little to be among the clans of Judah, from you shall come forth for me one who is to be ruler in Israel, whose coming forth is from of old, from ancient days.'[96] I believe you will find the king in Bethlehem."

Overjoyed, Malichus expresses his gladness by calling out, "Praise be to God. All thanks to the God of heaven and earth."

King Herod appears delighted as well. With a smile on his face he says, "When you have found the child, please, let me know. I want to go and worship him too."

"Of course, we will certainly do that," Malichus and Aqel answer as one.

The king's messengers accompany the friends to the inn where the others have been waiting for them anxiously. When they see the Malichus' and Aqel's cheerful faces, they sigh with relief.

"We know where he is," Malichus explains ecstatically. He swallows hard as he feels tears coming. The bottled-up tension from the last few days spill out. Aqel takes over and tells the others about the pleasant exchange with the king. "He pointed out to us that we will find the Prince of Peace in Bethlehem. Once we have found and worshiped him, he wants to go, too."

When Malichus hears his friend say these words, he suddenly realizes something and says, "We will precede the Jewish King in paying homage to the Prince of Peace."

"Ha! We will precede all the Jews," Sami adds amused.

"Well, let's not think too highly of ourselves," Aqel responds, "Pride comes before a fall."

"Aqel, you bring honor to your name again," Malichus quips. Then turning to the others, he says, "The journey to Bethlehem will take about an hour. If we leave now, we can get there before sunset, before the city gates close. Then, early tomorrow morning we will go and find the royal child."

Everyone agrees with the plan and they begin their preparations for the next part of their journey.

28 The Miracle Child

Green hills, dotted with olive trees stretch as far as the eye can see. A wide road scarred with ruts in its sandy bed, winds through the landscape in a southern direction. Stacked boulders line the sides of this much-traveled trade route. It is easy to work out where to go, and for a change there is no need for the men to ask for directions. As the camels trudge forward at a lumbering pace, the men swing backwards and forwards on their heavily packed humps. Occasionally, a few tents with a Roman flag fluttering on one of the longer tent poles come in sight.

"Yet another checkpoint," Aqel sighs.

"So far, they haven't been too much of a problem," Malichus reminds him. Suddenly, he bursts out laughing.

"What's up?" Aqel asks.

"When the Prince of Peace becomes the ruler, such obstacles will be gone forever."

"Not in our lifetime," laughs Aqel. "That would take at least twenty years."

"You never know," Malichus smiles and winks at Sami who is riding next to Aqel, "As far as I can tell, you will be the lucky one, Sami. You and Hayyan will be there to enjoy the reign of peace," he adds.

A soldier stops the travelers and wants to know where they are coming from and where they are going and from which people and tribe they are. The men are tired of answering the same questions over and over again, but they do understand these are turbulent times. The Jews regularly rebel against the Roman domination and the Romans are trying to suppress any kind of insurrection. *If someone was planning a revolt, surely he would not be using the main road. Maybe they aren't clever enough to realize that,* thinks Aqel.

"What is your business in Bethlehem?" the soldier asks gruffly.

"We are coming to see the new...," Malichus stops mid-sentence. It's not very wise to tell him that they are about to worship a new king. Quickly, he thinks up another story, and continues, "...trade partners in Bethlehem."

The Roman soldier seems to accept the story, but before he lets them pass, he wants to search their packs. On finding incense and myrrh, he is satisfied and holds his hand out. Malichus understands all too well what this gesture means. He sighs deeply as he takes two pieces of incense from his travel sack and hands them to the soldier. Without as much as a 'thank you' he puts them in his pockets and waves them through. The small trading caravan sets off for the final leg of their journey.

"How do you think we will find this child?" Sami wants to know. "There must be a lot of new babies in a city this size."

The king told us that the Prince of Peace would be a descendant of the line of the renowned King David," Malichus explains. "He even quoted Isaiah, saying, 'Then a throne will be established in steadfast love, and on it will sit in faithfulness in the tent of David; one who judges and seeks justice and is swift to do righteousness.'"[97]

"Is that the same King David, who, as a young boy, defeated a giant?" Sami asks. He has often heard his father tell the story as an example of courage and faith in God.

"Exactly," confirms Malichus, "and on top of that, he subjugated all the surrounding nations during his reign: the Moabites and the Ammonites, the Philistines and the Edomites; even the Aramaic people!"

"Seems fitting then, for the Prince of Peace to be his descendant."

"I agree. As soon as we get to Bethlehem, we will ask the town elders. I imagine they are descendants of David as well."

"But what if there are several families with newborns? How will we know which one is the Prince of Peace?" asks Sami. He is not at all sure that it will be that easy.

"Yes, I have thought about that too," says Malichus, "King Herod asked me when exactly I saw the star. Aqel and I were able to work out on precisely what day that was, so we have an idea as to when the baby was born. But most of all, we should trust God that He will help us. After all, He directed us to the right town already."

Reassured, Sami turns his camel and continues the journey alongside a different companion.

Having followed the conversation from a distance, Aqel spurs his camel to come alongside Malichus. "When you recited the Prophet Isaiah just now, I was reminded of what Ezra told us."

Malichus turns to face his friend. "Tell me, what do you mean?"

"When the prophet spoke about the coming Prince of Peace, he mentioned that David's throne has been established on his Kingdom. The passage begins with, 'Of the increase of his government and of peace there will be no end.'"

"Oh yes, indeed!" Malichus calls out and immediately cites the rest. "On the throne of David and over his kingdom, to establish it and to uphold it with justice and with righteousness from this time forth and forevermore."[98] Looking at his close friend, Malichus sees Aqel's face beaming. He knows exactly why. One day there will be no more corruption!

While talking about these things, the group moves along slowly but steadily across the rolling landscape between Jerusalem and Bethlehem. From the top of a hill, they can see the city of David in the distance. The setting sun caps the brown city walls in a reddish hue. *A peaceful sight, a perfectly suitable birthplace for the Prince of Peace,* Malichus thinks. To the left of him an eagle takes to the air, gracefully gliding on its majestic wings. Unwittingly, Malichus' eyes trace the movements of the bird circling above him, higher and higher. Fascinated by the eagle, Malichus strains his eyes until he suddenly notices something out of the ordinary in the clear blue sky. "Aqel, look at that!" he calls out in amazement. "Look up there; to the left!"

Aqel looks up and sees the soaring eagle. Then his eyes catch what Malichus has pointed out: a powerful light, shining brighter than the most brilliant star, Sirius. "This looks like the same one we were watching at home!" he calls out.

By now the others curiously look up at the sky as well. Their trained eyes have little trouble detecting the unusual star.

As Malichus turns his attention to the road again, he notices something else. "It is pointing in the direction of Bethlehem!" he exclaims with excitement. "It must be the same star! God be praised!"

"Look!" says Aqel, "it seems to hover straight above the town!"

Immediately, the astronomers begin a heated discussion. Although each one tries to come up with an interpretation of the presence of the star, no one is able to give a clear explanation as to why it is there.

"It has to be a supernatural occurrence," says Sami.

Immediately, Aqel remembers a passage from Isaiah and quotes the prophet's words reverently. "The people who walked in darkness have seen a great light; those who dwelt in a land of deep darkness, on them light has shone."[99]

The friends conclude that they are the witnesses of a miracle. God, the Creator of all things, who spoke in the beginning and said, "Let there be light", is lighting their path to the Miracle Child.

Filled with an even greater anticipation, the men press on. Their minds brim with joy as they urge their camels into a brisk trot. Elderly, graying Malichus is as happy as a child. His cries of joy cause other travelers to look up warily and then jump out of the way of this raucous group of Arabs. The swirling dust clouds in their wake don't go unnoticed, and the sentries at the Roman checkpoint just outside the city boundary have spotted the Bedouins from afar. They quickly summon some of the other guards and when the travelers approach their post, they put them through a thorough search. After an exhausting interrogation, the men are finally allowed through. In the meantime, the sun has nearly set. Very soon it will be dark.

Sami is the first to notice. "Look! The star has moved!" he calls.

"Are you sure?" asks Malichus doubtfully. He is still annoyed at the delay caused by the Roman soldiers.

"Absolutely!" Sami maintains. At first, it was above the middle of the city, but now it has moved a little to the right.

Some agree with Sami, but others side with Malichus, who does not quite believe the star has changed its position. And since Malichus is the eldest of the company, he has the final word. Sami has no choice but to concede. As soon as they enter the city gates though, Malichus admits that Sami was right after all. *Follow the star to the royal child*, is what comes to his mind instinctively. Or is it more than just a thought? Could it be a voice speaking within him? Malichus doesn't know but decides to follow the light. To his surprise, they are being led into the poorest part of town.

"Are you sure we are supposed to be here? Isn't this child of royal descent?" Aqel asks.

"I don't understand it either, but the star is pointing us straight ahead." If Malichus hadn't been convinced of the fact that the star was showing them the way, he would have turned around and gone into the rich part of town. But now he is ready to go by what he feels and lets the supernatural star show him the way.

The streets are too narrow to ride side by side and the Bedouins are forced to go in single file. Finally, they arrive at a tiny square wedged between squatty single-story houses. The star has come to a halt and Malichus waves to his friends to stop. Then he orders Sami to knock at one of the modest dwellings to ask if any of the residents of this neighborhood are from the line of King David.

"The people who live next door are David's descendants," says the man who has appeared in the doorway. He then asks his son to take Sami next door. Barefooted, the little boy runs to the neighbors and calls out, "Mister Joseph! You have visitors!"

A little while later, the door opens and the face of a slender young girl appears at the door opening. "Who is it, Andrew?" she asks gently. When she peers over the boy's shoulder, she notices the stranger and, instinctively cautious, she closes the door to a crack, which she peers through with one eye. *What does this man want with Joseph?*

Trying to save the situation, Sami quickly explains to her why he and his friends have come.

"I cannot help you. When my husband returns, he will speak to you," the young woman says politely as she closes the door. Sami hears her put the latch back in place and realizes they cannot do anything but wait.

After what seems like an eternity, a plainly dressed man walks into the square. He looks up curiously, as he notices all the camels lying there. Then he notices the rich foreigners with them. *What are they doing here? Looking for slaves perhaps?* As soon as he reaches the door of his house, one of the men walks up to him. Joseph reacts cautiously. This man might have evil intentions.

"Good evening, are you Joseph?" Sami asks politely.

"Good evening to you," Joseph greets reservedly. "Yes, I am Joseph. Can I help you?"

Malichus joins them and tries to reassure Joseph. Earlier, while they were still waiting, many of the children from the neighborhood had come and gawked at the colorful travelers. Some of the children had been quite eager to tell them about Mary's miraculous pregnancy and about the angels who had appeared to the shepherds as they were watching over their flocks by night and how these angels had announced the birth of the Savior in the town of David. It is from them that Malichus learned about an old man who had approached Joseph and Mary in Jerusalem, knowing that their baby was the promised Messiah. Malichus now also knows that the child's name is Jesus, which means, "Yahweh saves." No doubt this child is the Prince of Peace! Quickly, Malichus tells Joseph why he and his companions have come.

Meanwhile, Mary has opened the door again and her husband, now confident that these men do not wish them harm, asks the strangers to come in. Hastily, he spreads out some blankets on the bare clay floor. "Welcome to my humble home," he says shyly.

Water simmers in a metal pot above a tiny smoldering fire of thorn branches in one corner of the room. A little oil lamp is suspended on a bent stick in the wall.

By the faint glow of the flame, Malichus distinguishes in another corner of the room a rolled-up blanket from which a tiny head protrudes. *This is He!* Reverently, he speaks the words he now knows by heart, "Wonderful Counselor, Mighty God, Everlasting Father, Prince of Peace."[100] Then he kneels down spontaneously and presses his forehead to the ground. The others follow his example.

Mary and Joseph watch in amazement. How extraordinary is this child; even royal visitors from afar come to worship him!

Malichus then leads the group in a prayer of thanksgiving to God Almighty, the Creator of Heaven and Earth, who has guided them to the Righteous Ruler. Overwhelmed at meeting the royal child, he begins to weep. While tears of joy and wonder flow freely, Malichus can hardly speak. Finishing his prayer, he says, "God in Heaven, may the eternal kingdom of this Prince of Peace be established soon; may his will be done in this world, so that all the nations will worship You. Amen."

The others echo his 'amen.'

Shortly afterwards, the men are sitting in a circle on the ground sipping the hot tea Mary has prepared for them. It is tea without sugar, for the young couple cannot afford such luxuries, but the men don't care. They have come to see the wondrous child and are completely satisfied.

Then Malichus instructs the youngest of the group, "Bring out the gifts." Immediately, two of the men step outside and promptly return with several chests. The modest one-room house hardly offers enough space to put everything down. Everyone huddles close to one another to make room for all the gifts.

Joseph and Mary watch in amazement when Aqel lifts the cover of the first chest. It is filled to the brim with gold! A real king's treasure! Joseph had only been able to afford two thin gold bracelets for Mary's dowry. This is enough gold to purchase dozens ... no, even hundreds of bracelets!

When the second treasure chest is opened, the pungent but pleasant fragrance of incense permeates the room. Joseph and Mary realize that this is an expensive gift as well. The last time they were able to burn incense had been during their wedding and it had been of the cheapest quality. *This is a superior type, probably the kind that is used in the temple,* Joseph muses. *I must tell Zechariah about it; he knows about this sort of thing.*

Finally, Aqel lifts the cover of the last chest. The aroma that emanates from this chest is even more pungent than the one before. "Myrrh," Joseph whispers to Mary, who is seated right behind him. This herb is commonly used for the embalming of dead bodies, Mary realizes suddenly. The thought sends shivers down her spine. Along with the happiness she feels, she cannot help but have a sense of foreboding. *What is the meaning of all of this?*
The baby, who is almost one year old,* awakens and looks around the room with his big brown eyes.

"Jesus," Malichus says softly. Right away, the child turns his head towards him. "God saves," Malichus mumbles reverently. The room is too dark to really be sure, but it seems to Malichus that Jesus smiles at him. This is the most beautiful gift he can imagine. He feels a deep connection with the child. "God be praised," he says softly.

When he and the other men have finished their tea, Malichus announces it is time for them to go. "We must let this young couple have their rest," he says.

"Please, stay with us for the night," Joseph invites. Although he would

---

* For information about Jesus' age, see www.godlovesishmael.com/jesus-age.

be unable to host the whole group, surely the neighbors would help putting up these important men.

"Thank you, but we have made reservations at the inn," answers Malichus. Fortunately, they had sent Sami earlier to inquire about available rooms. *How kind and generous of Joseph to offer us his place for the night,* Malichus thinks.

After the honored visitors have left, Joseph and Mary talk for hours about this unusual event. "Mary, what wealth!" Joseph has tears in his eyes as he speaks. "Now we will be able to build our own house. And I will be able to buy new tools." Mary just smiles. She does not want to disappoint her husband, but these gifts have been given to Jesus. "Let's ask God for wisdom about this, " she suggests.

"You are a wise woman, " Joseph says as he kisses her on the cheek. "What do you think about what happened here tonight?"

"I don't really understand. So many people have already come to see Jesus. The night he was born, the shepherds visited us and when we went to the temple to dedicate Jesus, the old man, Simeon, and Anna, the prophetess, came to us. All of them received a revelation from Yahweh about who Jesus is, yet, none of them knelt down before him. Now these foreign Arab men from the East have traveled for weeks to come and bow down before him to worship him."

"And they brought him all these precious gifts, befitting the child of a king," Joseph adds.

Looking her husband in the eyes, Mary says, "You know, Joseph, I have a sense that God has a special purpose for what has happened this evening."

Joseph knows his wife well enough to understand how sensitive she is towards the things of God. To him, things are not always as clear-cut and that's why he says, "Time will tell."

Mary does want to emphasize what she believes to be true and says decisively, "God has something special for the Arabs."

The Bible is filled with direct and indirect promises with regards to the descendants of Ishmael. It appears that among all the peoples of the Middle East, they really mattered to God.

Acknowledging the Arabs and other eastern people, as descendants of Ishmael might be a novel idea to you. And yet, based on the Scriptures, as well as supported by non-scriptural historical sources, we may conclude this to be accurate. A detailed study about the origins of the Arabs can be found at www.godlovesishmael.com/arabs.

a) Prophecies

Let us review the various prophecies we have come across in this part of the novel. They will be discussed in the same order of appearance in the book.

In Ezekiel 25:1-10, we read that Ammon and Moab would be an inheritance for the sons of the East. This covers the area east of the Dead Sea. That means God gave land not only to the children of Israel, but also to the Ishmaelites.

Isaiah 42:1-13 describes God's servant, who, filled with the Spirit of God, will bring righteousness on earth and be a light to the nations. The Kedarites, who are the largest Ishmaelite tribe, are encouraged to trust that this event will take place and to express their thankfulness joyfully. The desert of Kedar is being called upon to lift up her voice. One could suggest that this promise has at least partially been fulfilled with the appearance of the wise men from the east at the time of the birth of Christ, but Isaiah describes a fairly large area. This suggests that some of these things have yet to take place.

Ezekiel 35:3-15 speaks of a severe judgment over Edom, the descendants of Esau. This is justified by the many times the Edomites entered into conflict with the Israelites, as we have seen in the previous part of this book. By contrast, such severe judgments have not been recorded concerning the Ishmaelites.

Isaiah 60:1-7 states that the descendants of Kedar and Nebaioth will worship God in Jerusalem. Here a role has also been reserved for the nation of Sheba, whose God-fearing queen we have become familiar with during the reign of King Solomon. Furthermore, the Scriptures make mention of the people of Midian and Ephah.

There are commentators who draw parallels between this portion of Scripture and the adulation of Jesus by the wise men from the East, because they brought him gold and incense. Since these men came from the East rather than from the South, it is unlikely that they originated from Sheba. However, it is very likely that the wise men purchased their gifts from traders from Sheba. So, it is entirely possible that their visit to the newborn Jesus was an early fulfillment of God's word through the mouth of Isaiah. A much broader fulfillment, however, is yet to come. The prophecy indicates that all aforementioned nations, who now inhabit the Arabian Peninsula, will one day bring their gifts to the God of Israel.

In Isaiah 21:13-17 we read about God's judgment on Kedar, mentioned here as a part of Arabia. It is specifically mentioned, that this affliction was to take place in the timeframe of a year. So, this prophecy does not point to an event in the future, but was fulfilled during those days.

To find out why God chastised the Kedarites, we must search the Scriptures in depth. The only verse that sheds light on this issue is found in Jeremiah 49:28-33 where it is written that Kedar acted out of pride. When the Babylonian armies swept over and took possession of all the nations of the then known world, including Israel, the Arabs looked on smugly from the safety of the desert. Yet, God told them they would not be spared either. As He did with the Israelites, God also broke the pride of the Kedarites, teaching them that He alone is God Almighty.

Many people like the idea of a blooming desert. Western Christians are inclined to look at these verses from a Jewish perspective. One might think of the Judean and Negeb deserts, which even today mainly consist of bare rock formations and large sandy plains. Yet, when we apply the passages in Isaiah 32:1-4, 15-18, and 35:1-10 to the Arabs we immediately picture the much larger deserts in Jordan and Saudi Arabia.

It is generally believed that the Jewish exiles that the Persian King, Cyrus the Great, permitted to return to their land, did not travel straight through the Iraqi and Jordanian deserts. If they did, many would have perished from thirst. No, they returned to Israel the same way they had gone into exile, via the northern mountain ranges where they would have found enough drinking water for all the men, women, and children. This indicates that the verses in Isaiah have not yet been fulfilled.

Could it be then, that God is going to use the Arabs to prepare the way for the Jews to come to Christ in large numbers? This seems to be Hosea's message in chapter 2:13 where God says that He will call his beloved nation into the desert to speak to her heart. It seems that God has ordained a plan for the inhabitants of the deserts, the Arabs, to speak to the hearts of the Israelites.

Hosea 2:22 supports this idea. God promises to make a people that were not his people, into his people. The God who rejected Ishmael as the son of the promise, accepts his descendants, the Ishmaelites, as his people. This, too, is fitting with God's character. The fifth part of this book examines this theme more closely.

b) The descendants of Ishmael and Isaac

In the previous part of this book we looked at the relationship between the Israelites and the Ishmaelites. The Bible also tells us about different inter-actions between the Israelites and the Arabs. To get a complete picture of the relationship between these two peoples, we would like to briefly look at them. The following references address occasions in which the Arabs are mentioned.

2 Chronicles 9:14 – All the kings of Arabia paid tribute to King Solomon. This narrative follows the story of the Queen of Sheba. There is no mention anywhere that any of these nations were under Solomon's control. Therefore we can safely assume that the Arabian kings voluntarily paid their tribute to Solomon to honor him, just like the Queen of Sheba did.

2 Chronicles 17:11 – Some Arabs brought offerings of rams and goats to King Jehoshaphat. According to the previous verse, the fear of the Lord had come upon the surrounding nations so that they did not make war against this Israelite King. It seems that the Arabs gave up some of their wealth freely, in acknowledgement of the power of the God of Israel.

2 Chronicles 21:16 – Jehoshaphat's successor, his son Jehoram, did not walk with God. Consequently, the Lord stirred up his southwestern neighbors against him. Not only the Philistines, but also the Arabs attacked him. During this time the conflict was ongoing between them, until Jehoram was succeeded by his son Ahaziah. (2Chronicles 22:1). It can be noted that only the Arabs who were living near the Cushites were involved. The Arab tribes east of Judah were not involved in this conflict.

2 Chronicles 26:7 – The God-fearing King Uzziah fought the Arabs who dwelled in Gur-Baal, and in doing so he received God's help. This passage indicates that the conflict with the Arabs who lived southwest of Judah con-

tinued not only throughout Jehoram's reign, but also throughout the reigns of several of his successors.

Nehemiah 2:19 – Three men opposed Nehemiah in the rebuilding of the walls of Jerusalem. They were the Sanballat, the Moabite, Tobias, the Ammonite, and Geshem, the Arab. This last one may have been a descendant of Ishmael.

Over the centuries, it has become common practice to use the label "Arab" in identifying many different people groups. Today, even the people who inhabit North Africa are generally called "Arabs," while most of them aren't or don't want to be identified as such. It is therefore very possible that at the time of Nehemiah, several people groups would have been classified under that same heading. It is also striking that no reference can be found about the Edomites in either the book of Nehemiah or the book of his contemporary, Ezra. That suggests that Geshem may well have been a descendant of Esau.

All in all, although the relationship between the Israelites and the Arabs was at times marked by adversity, most of the time the two peoples were on good terms with one another. And whenever there were conflicts between them, only a small part of the Ishmaelites would take part in the skirmishes, while the majority left Israel alone.

This fact supports the conclusion in part two of the book. Isaac's descendants were generally on friendly terms with Ishmael's descendants.

c) Parallels

We conclude this review with a short overview of parallels between the descendants of Ishmael and the descendants Isaac.

1) Solomon's wisdom surpassed the wisdom of all the people of the East and all the wisdom of Egypt (1Kings 4:30). This comparison indicates that the people from the East, together with the Egyptians, were among the wisest people on earth. In Jeremiah 49:28 the Kedarites, descendants of Ishmael, are identified as people of the East. So, very wise men came from both peoples.
2) The Wise Men from the East were the first ones to actually worship Jesus. None of the Israelites who had visited baby Jesus prior to the arrival of these descendants of Ishmael; neither the shepherds, nor Simeon, nor Anna, had worshiped him. It wasn't until much later that the Jews also began to worship him, starting with simple fisher-

men, and later some scholarly men as well, such as Nicodemus and Joseph of Arimathea. These two peoples were the first to acknowledge Jesus as King of Kings, with the Arabs even preceding the Jews.

3) Both peoples received land from God, according to his promise to their forefather Abraham. The Israelites took possession of Canaan after God had pronounced judgment on the people who were living there at the time. The Ishmaelites received Moab as well as Ammon as their inheritance after God had pronounced judgment on both of those nations.

4) God punished both peoples because of their pride. Jeremiah 49:28-33 describes the pride of the Kedarites and refers to them as synonymous with the tribes of Ishmael in the East; the pride of the Israelites has been chronicled in Isaiah 9:8 as well as in other passages.

5) The desert will bloom. It is quite possible that we are still awaiting a literal fulfillment of this prophecy. In a spiritual sense, the prophecy reveals that the Ishmaelites will lead their half-brothers and prepare the way for the Israelites to return to God. In this sense, God's blessing is being revealed in both the lives of the Ishmaelites and the Israelites (see Isaiah 32:1-4, 15-18; 35:3-6; 43:19-21; 51:3).

In this part of the book, we have seen several prophecies with regards to the descendants of Ishmael that have not yet come to pass. One day, they will worship God freely in Jerusalem. In addition, it seems that these desert dwellers will play a special role as forerunners for their half-brothers, the Israelites, to point them to the Father. The Wise Men from the East can be seen then as harbingers of the fulfillment of these marvelous prophesies.

What became of the Arabs in the time of Jesus and the early church? We will consider this in the next section.

Part 4

God Hears the Arabs – the Descendants of Ishmael

During the Life of the Lord Jesus Christ
and the Apostle Paul

His Name will be Ishmael – God Hears
According to Genesis 16:11

At the time of Jesus the Messiah

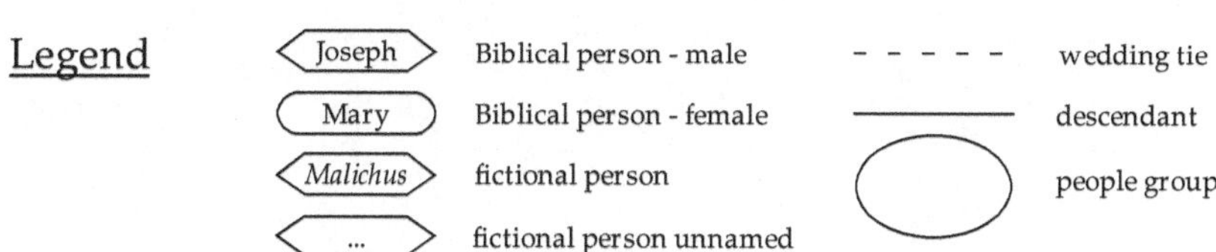

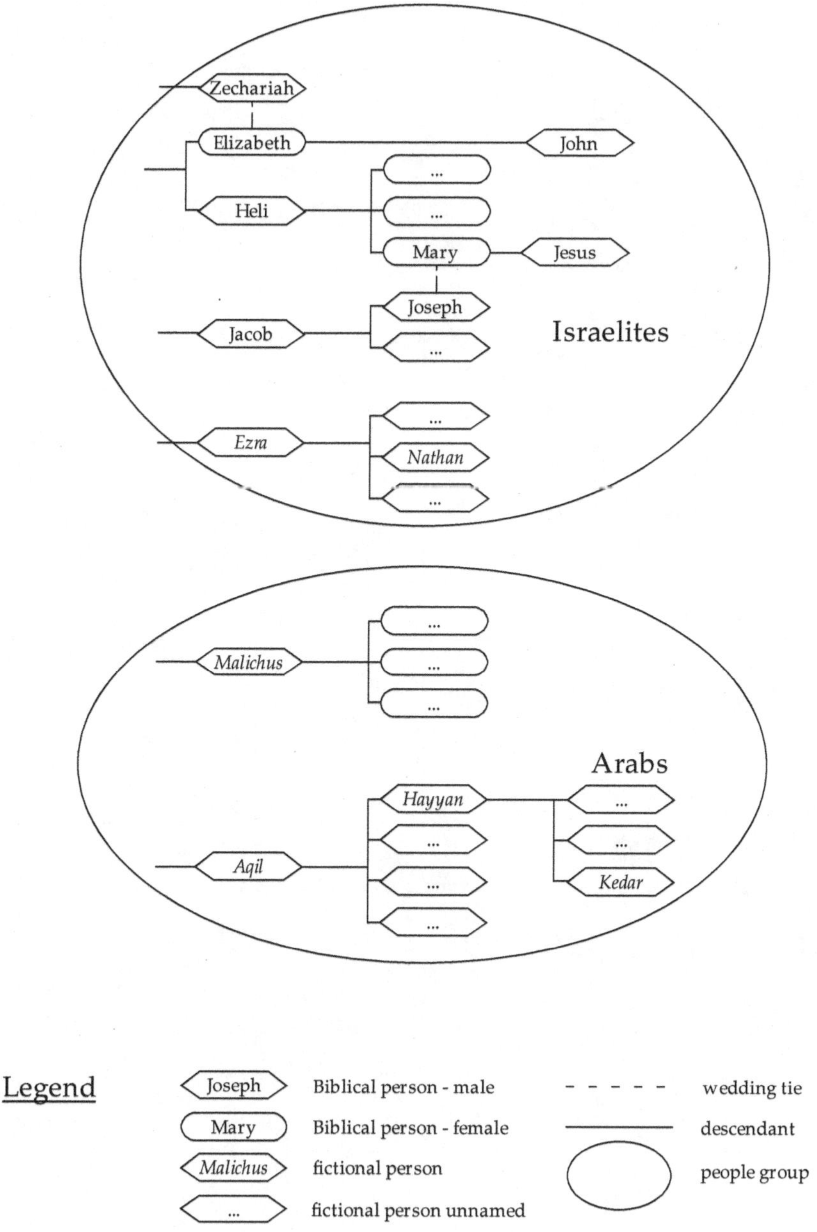

After the wise men from the east worshiped Jesus in Bethlehem

29 On the Brink of Death

Two young men happily walk hand in hand down the street. No one pays attention to them. It had been different for the newly-wed neighbor who had taken his wife by the hand. His shameful act had offended the decency of the townsfolk, who had reprimanded him severely, warning him to only show his affection for the opposite sex in privacy. But for the two boys, the handholding shows the depth of their friendship in a respectful way. Suddenly, one of them hears his name being called.

"Hayyan, come here!"

The boy looks over his shoulder and notices an elderly man by a shop, gesturing to him. "Peace be on you," he greets the man politely. Then he recognizes his father's friend.

"And peace be on you," replies the man. "Has your father returned from his travels?"

"No, not yet," Hayyan answers slightly irritated. He tries to hide his annoyance with the question that so many people have asked him lately. *Why do people continue to bother me with these queries?*

"When will we see him again?"

How am I supposed to know, Hayyan thinks, but he answers the man in the same way he has heard his father speak, "God knows."

"There is no God, but God," says the man, before he turns around to continue his conversation with the shopkeeper.

Having no specific purpose in mind, Hayyan and his friend continue to stroll. "Let's go to the West Gate," Nathan suggests. "Perhaps we can find out the latest news."

A broad grin spreads over Hayyan's face. He enjoys spending time with his inquisitive Jewish friend. Because they are kindred spirits, their friendship is strong.

"Excellent!" he replies, "Let's see who will get there first!" Immediately he lets go of Nathan's hand and takes off running.

Nathan is at his heels straightaway but as he speeds through the city streets, he can hear his father saying, "Always conduct yourself honorably in the presence of others. We must set a good example in town." *If only I were the son in an ordinary family; I would have so much more freedom,* Nathan thinks. But his father is the head of the local synagogue.

Hayyan, as the son of the judge, must deal with the same issues and so, just before they turn the last corner leading up to the gate, they slow down to a more decent pace. Still somewhat out of breath, they arrive at the place where the town elders are seated.

"Look who's coming!" one of them exclaims. For a moment, Hayyan thinks the man is speaking about them, but then he looks up and immediately recognizes the caravan in the distance. No longer caring about the staring eyes of the elders, he pulls Nathan's arm and together they set off running towards the travelers.

Moments later, the caravan enters the city gates. Hayyan is mounted on his father's camel. "How was it, Father? Did you get to see the royal child? What did he look like?" Hayyan is full of questions. With one strong arm around the boy, Aqel calms his son down. "Tonight I will tell you everything, my son."

"After we saw the baby king Jesus, we talked about our experiences until the early morning," recounts Aqel, "Sami went outside a few times to look for the star, but it had disappeared."

With his mouth open, Hayyan listens to his father's amazing stories.

"That night I had a nightmare. On our way back to Jerusalem, one of our camels stumbled and died for no apparent reason. After that, robbers came, beat us up and stripped us of all our belongings. I was lying in a pool of blood, when I suddenly woke up."

"That sounds like a warning from God," says Hayyan.

"Absolutely," Aqel confirms, "and the funny thing is that the other men had similar dreams. One of them saw the face of King Herod in his dream, as if he had something to do with it."

"What did you do, Father?" Hayyan asks inquisitively.

"We had to make a difficult decision. After deliberating for ages, we finally decided not to go back to King Herod. "

"But you always taught me that if you give someone your word, you must keep it."

"That is true, my son." Aqel looks him in the eyes and with a serious tone he says, "Breaking a promise is a great shame, especially breaking a promise to a king. But in the end, we were thoroughly convinced that the dreams came from God, which is why we decide to follow him rather than the king."

Hayyan is confused. "How can God go against his own rules? Aren't we supposed to be truthful?"

"I do not quite understand it myself, my son, but deep down inside, I am convinced we did the right thing."

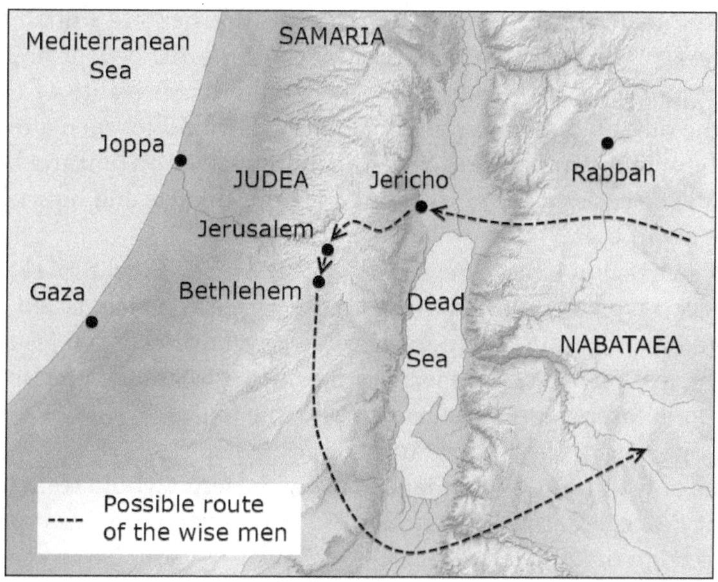

The visit of the wise men

A few months later, Aqel hears some awful news. "Are you absolutely sure? Did King Herod really order all infants and toddlers in his realm to be killed?"

The merchant swears by God that he is speaking the truth, but Aqel can't believe him. The news worries him and he just can't stop thinking about it. *What could have motivated the king to commit such evil? That would only cause the people to rise up and revolt.* Suddenly, it dawns on him that Jesus must have been killed as well. This tells him decisively that the rumor cannot be true.

The next market day, Malichus pays another visit to his friend. "Did you hear?" he asks.

"Yes, I did, but I don't believe it at all," says Aqel and he explains why.

"Well, not all infants in the entire nation were murdered, only those in Bethlehem and surroundings," Malichus informs him.

"Why would he do such a thing though?" Aqel wonders out loud. "Didn't he tell us explicitly that he wanted to go and worship the royal child?"

"Perhaps it was a ruse. To be honest, I thought it was strange of him to ask us when exactly we had noticed the star. Why would a prominent Jew not know about the birth of the Prince of Peace?"

"Are you saying you think he killed Jesus?" Aqel blurts out, as tears begin to well up in his eyes. He had intensely longed for a new reign of peace. Would it all be over now, before it even started?

"I fear that was the purpose of the mass murder, but I don't think he was successful." Doubt resonates in Malichus' words; he is trying hard to convince himself. On the one hand, there's the harsh reality of the news, but on the other hand, he cannot imagine God would let such a thing happen without intervening. Suddenly, something dawns on him and he smiles. "That's it!" he exclaims. "Do you remember our dreams and how perplexed we were about them?"

"Of course, but what difference does that make?" Aqel asks skeptically.

"Well, if we had returned to the king's palace as he had asked us to do, he would have sent out his troops right away and surely slain Jesus," Malichus explains. "While he was waiting for us to tell him the precise location of the infant, Joseph and Mary had ample time to flee."

"I hope you're right," says Aqel.

"The only thing I don't understand is why Herod would want to kill the Prince of Peace," Malichus continues. "Doesn't everybody want peace and justice to reign on this earth?"

"I understand Herod's father was an Edomite. Their people have clashed with the Israelites for centuries."

"But Herod explicitly told us he and his family had become Jews, so he is different," Malichus counters. He tries to adopt a more positive approach.

Aqel shrugs his shoulders. "There are many people who, while outwardly appearing to be devout, are full of hatred and envy on the inside."

Malichus cannot deny that. He prays quietly in his heart, "Almighty God, protect Jesus, your Son." Suddenly, he becomes alarmed by what he just prayed. *God does not have a son. Jesus is the son of Mary!* Yet, the words came straight from his heart. "God, forgive me, for speaking so," Malichus prays as a silent after-thought. Although no answer comes, he senses all is well.

Aqel notices his friend's preoccupation and asks, "Is something wrong?"

Malichus looks at his friend and swallows deeply. The words are on the tip of his tongue, but he decides to keep his thoughts to himself for now. "I just cannot get over Herod murdering all those innocent infants," he answers.

"Neither can I," Aqel agrees. Then, something comes to his mind. "Do you think there is a prophecy that speaks about this?"

The question makes Malichus excited. "That could very well be so," he says. "After all, the prophecies about the location of the birth of the Prince of Peace were very precise." Thinking about this gives both friends renewed hope; together they decide to pay another visit to Ezra, the scribe.

"Mary," the whisper comes in a gentle voice.

No reaction.

"Mary!" Joseph persists, hoping he won't wake the infant boy.

Mary doesn't even move.

Then, Joseph gently shakes his wife, until she finally opens her eyes and asks sleepily, "What?"

"I dreamed an angel came to warn us. He said we have to leave this place."

On hearing the word 'angel', Mary wakes completely. "What did he look like?" she asks with a whisper.

When Joseph describes the supernatural being to her, Mary recognizes him as a messenger from God. "What did he tell you?"

"He said to me, 'Rise, take the child and his mother, and flee to Egypt, and remain there until I tell you, for Herod is about to search for the child, to destroy him.'[101] What do you think about this?"

Now wide-awake, Mary needs no more convincing and she says, "Clearly, this is a warning from God; we must leave immediately."

Joseph struggles with conflicting thoughts. He had been looking forward to returning to his work as a carpenter. With all the gifts they had been given, he would finally be able to make all his dreams come true. At the same time, he carries the responsibility for his family. On asking God for wisdom, a popular proverb from King Solomon comes to mind. "Trust in the Lord with all your heart, and do not lean on your own understanding. In all your ways acknowledge him, and he will make straight your paths."[102] Now he knows exactly what to do. He is not willing to take any risks and decides to heed the dream. A devoted husband and father, he gets up immediately and makes the arrangements for their departure. Packing up does not take long, their meager possessions fit on one donkey. There is only one problem. Joseph does not own a donkey.

It is in the middle of the night. Surrounded by darkness with just enough light from the crescent moon, Joseph goes over to his neighbor's house and softly knocks on the door. Fortunately, the neighbor is willing to sell him his donkey for a nugget of gold. The donkey is not worth that much money, but under the circumstances, Joseph has no other choice.

Two hours later, the small family is ready to head out. Before sunrise, they leave their house and take to the road. The little boy, Jesus, is delighted to be seated up high on the packed donkey. It is the first time that he's going on a journey and he takes in his surroundings with childlike fascination.

Mary, who is seated behind him, looks ahead silently. With a heavy heart, Joseph walks next to them, through the narrow streets towards the city gate. As Mary turns her head to take one last glance at the square where they spent their first happy months as a married couple, big tears roll down her cheeks. *What will the future bring?*

Once they arrive at the gate, they must wait patiently for sunrise, when the gatekeeper comes to lift the heavy bars and open the large wooden doors. And so, at the crack of dawn, the young family leaves the safety and protection of the town behind and set their faces towards a foreign land, with a foreign language and foreign customs.

"Are you all right, Joseph?" Mary asks concerned. With bent shoulders, her husband trudges along the bleak desert road, occasionally kicking at the loose gravel. He seems lost in his thoughts.

What should I tell her? Life is full of struggles. And it all began when Mary came back from a visit to her cousin – expecting a baby!

The shame is etched in his memory. At first, everyone had thought he had secretly lain with Mary. Since it had not been true, he had vehemently denied it. He had assumed that Mary had been unfaithful to him. If the angel of the Lord had not spoken to him in a dream, he would have quietly divorced her. However, Yahweh's message had been perfectly clear.

After the harassments by the people of Nazareth had diminished, Joseph had been quite content. He had felt greatly honored in the knowledge that God had chosen him out of all the young men in Israel to raise the promised Messiah. But the compulsory census by Caesar Augustus had complicated everything. He had been looking forward to begin family life with his betrothed, but that dream had been shattered when they were forced to travel all the way to Bethlehem, the birthplace of his ancestor, King David. To make matters worse, they had not been able to find a suitable place to lodge. If Mary had not been expecting a baby, they could have traveled so much faster and would have been able to find a guest room with their distant relatives, but they had had to settle for a room at the very bottom of a house, right next to all the livestock.

"Please, tell me what is wrong, my beloved," Mary nudges gently with her soft, warm voice. "I am listening." Her words convince him to voice his apprehensions and as he begins to spout his frustrations, Mary listens patiently.

"After all of our problems, now we have to flee, too," Joseph sighs. "My last dream has been crushed as well. We can only hope King Herod does not decide to send his armies after us."

Mary sympathizes with her husband for whom this has been so hard. Things have not been easy for her either, but the encounter with the angel and the miracle of her supernatural conception have given her a profound awareness of the greatness and presence of God. As a result, she has been able to let go of her worries. "Lord, please show Joseph your presence and your abiding love," she prays silently. Having done so, she is able to be more positive and cheerfully says, "Thanks to the generous gifts we have received we have the privilege of visiting Egypt."

Joseph cannot help but laugh. His friends in Nazareth would probably envy him, because many of them would love to see the ancient pyramids, the palaces of the pharaohs of old and the majestic Nile River. "You are an amazing woman," he says to Mary as he smiles at her, "but if it were up to me, I would have preferred to build us a house first."

As the words tumble out of his mouth, Joseph senses they are not pleasing to God. He gives it a little more thought and then remembers the Scripture reading on Sabbath. "My dear love," he addresses Mary, "last Sabbath day, the rabbi spoke from the book of Habakkuk concerning the text: 'The righteous shall live by his faith.'[103] We will trust the Lord our God for all our needs."

Mary gazes fondly at her beloved husband, her heart overflowing with emotion. She reflects how much she loves and esteems this serious and honest man. "Amen," she replies and then adds with a smile, "He has even used Arabs to provide for us."

30 Who is the Promised One?

"Are you asking me whether there is a prophecy regarding to the death of the Prince of Peace? Of course not!" Ezra exclaims. "How could he then reign forever? How did you come up with that idea?"

"Haven't you heard about King Herod killing all boys under the age of two in Judah?" Aqel asks.

Of course Ezra knows about that awful event. How is it even possible for someone to do such an evil thing?

"We are afraid that the child, Jesus, may have been murdered as well," the judge continues. He can follow Ezra's train of thought; it is quite likely that Jesus is still alive. On the other hand, the facts beg to differ.

"Do you know of any other prophecies with regards to Bethlehem?" asks Malichus.

Ezra shakes his head. "No; the only obvious promise is the one I have told you about before. This is how you knew the Messiah would be born there." He notices the look of disappointment in the faces of these God-fearing men. Their dedication to the Prince of Peace is an example to everyone, and he would love encourage them somehow. "Would you like me to read it to you again?" he asks.

They do not have to think long about that. Looking around the circle of men, Ezra sees them nodding eagerly as they look expectantly at him. Young Hayyan, who is seated to his right, leans forward attentively. Next to him is Nathan, who doesn't seem very interested. *Thanks be to God for his friendship with Hayyan*, Ezra thinks, *that boy has a good influence on my son*.

On the left are Malichus and Aqel, seated next to each other like brothers.

Life can be such a mystery. Just a few years ago, the only friends I had in this city were Jews, Ezra muses. Since the first visit from these two Arab men, his view of the world has been radically changed. He has started to value their true love for God, the Creator. Even though they do not follow all the statutes of the Torah like converts to Judaism do, they unmistakably seek to please God wholeheartedly. Ezra wonders how the Lord will look upon them on the Day of Judgment. Would God reject them simply because they do not celebrate the Jewish feasts or do not bring him the prescribed burnt offerings? According to the teachers of the law and the Pharisees, only those who strictly adhere to the Law of Moses will be saved. But God said about himself that He is "merciful and gracious, slow to anger, and abounding in steadfast love and faithfulness."[104]

"Nathan, bring me the scroll of Micah," Ezra charges his son. "Look for the small one with the acacia wooden handles and the red velvet cover." The boy gets up immediately and rummages through the book cabinet for the scroll in question. For the last few years, he has been allowed to study his father's books on his own and he is now quite familiar with the five books of Moses, the Torah. He doesn't know a lot about the books of the prophets yet; they are much harder to understand. Watching his son, Ezra has an idea. It is the perfect opportunity for him to read some of the passages publicly. *This way I will be able to focus on translation.*

Ezra takes the scroll from his son and asks him to take a seat next to him. After kissing the scroll, he opens it carefully and searches for the appropriate passage. Then, he points with his index finger to the line where he wants Nathan to begin reading, and says, "Start here, my son, and continue until the word 'earth'."

The sounds of the Hebrew words enthrall the listeners. Some of them are recognizable, as they are similar to their own Aramaic language, but it is not enough to be able to understand the message well. They are grateful for Ezra's translation of the passage.

> "But you, O Bethlehem Ephratah,
> who are too little to be among the clans of Judah,
> from you shall come forth for me
> one who is to be ruler in Israel,
> whose coming forth is from of old,
> from ancient days.
> Therefore he shall give them up until the time
> when she who is in labor has given birth;
> then the rest of his brothers shall return
> to the people of Israel.
> And he shall stand and shepherd his flock in the strength of the Lord,
> in the majesty of the name of the Lord his God.
> And they shall dwell secure, for now he shall be great
> to the ends of the earth."[105]

When he has finished translating, Ezra asks his visitors, "What do you think about this?"

"On the basis of this prediction, we can assume that the Prince of Peace is still alive. It clearly states that he will reign over all the earth," replies Malichus. Still, he is plagued with doubts and not yet fully convinced.

As far as Ezra is concerned the answer is unambiguous, but how can he show that to these men? "Sometimes it is difficult to know whether we can really trust God's Word," he begins, "therefore it is good to remind ourselves of the words God spoke through the mouth of Balaam."

"Balaam? Was he not the one who predicted that a star would rise from Judah?" Aqel asks.

"His precise words were, 'a star shall come out of Jacob'. But you are right, I am talking about the same Balaam," the rabbi confirms. Thoroughly enjoying the inquisitiveness of his fellow townsman, he makes a radical decision. Rather than letting Nathan read from the book of Numbers, he hands the scroll to Malichus. It is an odd feeling to put these holy Scriptures into the hands of a Gentile, but Ezra feels the Lord is leading him to do so and it is good.

Malichus is surprised by this sudden gesture of the Jewish scholar. He is very different from the man he and Aqel encountered near the temple court in Jerusalem. Then with a deep voice he begins to recite Balaam's prophetic message in Aramaic.

> "God is not man, that he should lie,
> or a son of man, that he should change his mind.
> Has he said, and will he not do it?
> Or has he spoken, and will he not fulfill it?"[106]

Towards the end of the passage tears well up in Malichus' eyes. This is the answer to all his questions. There have been so many things he does not understand, and the older he gets, the worse it becomes. But God is not man; He doesn't lie, nor does he deceive. He fulfilled his own promise about the star through this Gentile Balaam. Now all things will be done according to his good Word. Malichus is confident that Jesus is alive! When he looks up from the scroll, his eyes meet Ezra's.

The scribe's eyes are wet too, as he is deeply touched by how God's Spirit is working in the heart of this Arab man. Here is an Arab, far removed from the promises of God as a non-Jew and yet so closely related to him by virtue of their common ancestor, the patriarch Abraham.

In the weeks and months that follow, the Arab friends lean heavily on the passages of Scripture they have learned from Ezra. Here lies their greatest hope. In the meantime, they keep an eye out for news. Malichus is getting older and rarely makes the journey to Israel. During those times, he always inquires about Jesus Bin Joseph. Unfortunately, each time he returns home disappointed. Most people have never even heard of him, and those that claim to know a Jesus Bin Joseph always refer to another; a younger or an older Jesus. One day, Malichus decides to go to Bethlehem to visit Joseph's relatives, but even they have no news. They only remember that during those awful days, Joseph fled with his wife and young son in the middle of the night. This is a small consolation, but it is all Malichus has. At least, he knows for sure that Herod did not assassinate Jesus.

A few years later, Malichus passes away. Though he never saw the Prince of Peace again, the God-fearing man leaves this life fully trusting that God will do all that He has promised through the prophets.

Aqel goes to visit his friend's family and, as custom demands, sits for seven days in mourning with them. All male relatives meet together in a large tent. Everyone is saddened by the departure of this beloved man. Stories of bygone years are told; there is even some occasional laughter to lighten the somber mood. These little distractions, as well as the time spent in close proximity with one another, bring comfort and a sense of kinship to the mourners. When the moment is right, Aqel asks one of his friend's sons-in-law, "How was he in his last moments?"

"My mother-in-law was there and she told us he went peacefully," replies the young man. "He was not afraid of dying at all."

Relieved, Aqel sighs. *Malichus did not lose hope in the Prince of Peace.* At the end of the seventh day, Aqel returns home.

Every time travelers return from Israel, he asks them if they have heard of Jesus Bin Joseph. Every time, the answer is the same. "No."

The years go by, and finally, Aqel becomes an old man who seldom ventures out.

"He is back. He is back!" Hayyan shouts, as he runs up the stairs. Tears roll down his cheeks. This is the best news he could ever bring his father.

Aqel sits quietly in a corner of the living room, staring into space. He has heard his son's voice, but cannot quite make out what he is saying. Most likely, he is talking to his one of his other sons, or perhaps to his grandchildren.

A moment later, Hayyan dashes into the living room, completely out of breath. "Father! He is back! The Messiah is back!"

Finally, Aqel understands what his son is saying. Incredulously, he looks him in the eyes. There have been several freedom fighters claiming to want to overthrow the Roman regime. Every time they had wondered whether one of them could be Jesus, but they had only been rebels who tried to intimidate the Romans with their swords. Their actions did not agree with the words in the ancient scrolls written down by the prophets of old.

"Why do you think that this one really is the Messiah?" Aqel's voice croaks as he asks the question.

"This man has no sword; he has never even used one. The entire time he is speaking of the kingdom of God and he says that the people have to repent."

Aqel's face lights up. *This man is different.* "What else do you know about him?"

"He lives a very simple life in the desert," says Hayyan, "and I heard that he is a man of humble character, without any sign of pride."

Aqel's heart skips a few beats. Could it be true? Jesus did come from a poor family. "Did you get his name?"

"I couldn't quite work that out. It seems he has more than one name," Hayyan replies. "Some say that he is Elijah, some say he is the prophet, while others think he is the Messiah."

"Have you heard anyone call him Jesus?" Aqel remains skeptical. The fact that they are calling him the Messiah does not necessarily mean anything. In the past, there have been scores of freedom fighters that people referred to as 'messiahs'.

"I haven't," confesses Hayyan and then suggests, "Perhaps Elijah is another name for him."

That's hard to believe, thinks Aqel. But then he has second thoughts and says, "You could be right, because Elijah means, 'my God is Yahweh', and Jesus means, 'Yahweh saves'. As far as the names go, they are closely related."

"True! And wasn't our forefather named Abram before he became Abraham?" Filled with excitement, his father adds, "And Jacob was renamed ..." but before he can finish, Hayyan gleefully completes his sentence, and both simultaneously exclaim, "Israel!" The men burst out laughing. Aqel extends his hand palm up towards his son who amicably slaps his hand. It is their way of saying, "I understand and completely agree with you."

Still not entirely convinced yet that this Elijah is truly Jesus, he asks his son, "How old is he?"

"They say he is around thirty years old."

"It's got to be him, my boy," Aqel decides. "It has been about thirty years, since I worshiped Jesus in Bethlehem. He was but a young child then."

Spontaneously, Hayyan kisses his father on the forehead. Then he embraces the fragile, old man carefully. They are both overjoyed.

Some days later, Hayyan undertakes the long journey westward. His father is too old to travel, but he encourages his son to go and see Elijah. Rumor has it that the prophet preaches in the rugged desert of Judah. Hayyan realizes he might have a difficult time finding Elijah, but he fully trusts God will be by his side to help him. After all, in the past, God helped his father to find the Messiah, who was then only a toddler.

To his surprise, before he has even reached the mountainous regions of the Judean wilderness, Hayyan notices a large crowd gathered near a shallow part of the Jordan River. Right in the middle and high up on a huge rock, a man dressed in a simple robe made of camel hair, addresses the crowd.

"Is this the prophet, Elijah?" he asks one of the spectators.

"Everyone says he is," the man replies.

Hayyan's heart begins to race with excitement. *This is the Messiah. The promised Prince of Peace!*

After dismounting his camel, he tries to get a little closer, but the crowds press in on him from all sides and all he can do is to pick up the words of the preacher.

"Whoever has two tunics is to share with him who has none, and whoever has food is to do likewise."[107]

That's fair, thinks Hayyan, *if everyone would do that, there would be no poverty in the world.*

Then a couple of soldiers ask the man a question. Hayyan is not able to catch what is asked but the prophet's answer comes loud and clear, "Do not extort money from anyone by threats or by false accusation, and be content with your wages."[108]

Thinking of his own work as a judge, he remembers now how his father always impressed on him never to accept bribes from anyone. Since the other judges in town don't hesitate to accept little incentives, Hayyan is not looked upon favorably by most of the wealthy people. *If only everyone would do as this prophet is teaching, life would be so much better*, he muses.

A group of Jewish teachers of the law draws close to the throng of people. Hayyan recognizes them, because they dress just like his friend, Nathan. Respectfully, the people step aside to allow the dignitaries in their richly adorned and flowing robes through. They head straight for the man on the rock and shower him with questions. The crowd becomes silent, and Hayyan is now able to follow the exchange easier.

"Are you the Christ?" the eldest of the group asks. Hayyan is elated; it is exactly what he would have wanted to ask him. Now he will get the confirmation he has been looking for straight from Elijah's own mouth.

"No, I am not the Christ," the answer comes firmly. Hayyan gasps. *Perhaps I did not understand correctly*, he reasons, *or maybe the question was unclear.*

The scholar continues his questioning, and asks, "Are you Elijah?" The man denies this, too.

"Are you the prophet then?" Again he shakes his head.

Finally, the rabbi asks the question that has been burning inside Hayyan's heart, "Who are you then?"

"My name is John," the man answers. "I am the voice of one crying out in the wilderness, 'Make straight the way of the Lord,' as the prophet Isaiah said."[109]

Hayyan no longer follows the conversation. Deeply disappointed, he turns around and walks away. He is not the Messiah after all. There is no reason for him to stay any longer. With a heavy heart he mounts his camel and starts on the long journey home.

If he had only stayed one day longer, Hayyan would have made a fascinating discovery.

31 He is Alive

Two men are seated comfortably in the guestroom, enjoying one another's company. They are undisturbed by the children who run to and fro. This is their way of life, many times until late at night. At one end of the room, a four-year old boy sleeps on the floor. The other children pay no attention to him, but only to their game. It is not unusual for little ones, overcome by tiredness, to fall asleep just about anywhere in the house. Completely absorbed in their game of 'soldiers', the older boys swing their wooden sticks about that serve as weapons. Their younger sisters watch them quietly, while the older ones help their mother in the kitchen. Occasionally, the boys glance at their grandfather or father, and sometimes one of them even sneaks onto Grandfather's lap. That child is immediately cuddled and kissed on the forehead, after which he quickly returns to playing. The men, in the meantime, are engaged in a heated discussion.

"Is it John, you said?" Aqel asks again. "The name sounds familiar. He thinks back to a meeting long ago. Slowly, the memories of that conversation return to his foggy brain, and Aqel continues, "Jesus had a cousin named 'John'."

Hayyan eyes his father expectantly. "What do you know about him?"

"I will tell you," says Aqel and then he begins to explain who John is. "His father was a Jewish priest. One day, while he was attending to his duties in the holy place of the temple, a man appeared to him. Zechariah was greatly troubled and worried the man might hurt him."

Hayyan nods. He understands what the priest's trepidation must have been like. He would not like to be alone in a closed room, with a sturdy stranger appearing out of nowhere.

"As it turned out, the man was a messenger from God," Aqel continues. "He told the priest that his prayers for a son had been heard by God. Just imagine, Zechariah and his wife were childless, and she was past childbearing age.

"That's incredible!" exclaims Hayyan. "It reminds me of the story of our forefather Abraham, whom God also gave a son through Sarah in their old age."

"You're right," says Aqel. "For this child too, God had a special plan. From the time of his birth, he was not allowed to drink wine or any strong drink; he was being set apart for the service of God."

Hayyan leans back as he thinks about what he has just heard from his father. He enjoys a good cup of wine once in a while, but the town drunks set a bad example for the young people. If you truly want to serve God, you should never be drunk and the best way not to become drunk is to never drink any alcohol.

"God would use him to bring many Israelites to repentance."

"How so? I thought the Messiah would do that."

"I never quite understood it myself. It had something to do with preparing a righteous people for the arrival of the Lord."

"Really? That reminds me of something John said when I heard him speak. He told the people that he was the voice in the desert, preparing the way of the Lord, making his paths straight."

Aqel looks up surprised. Suddenly, a discussion he had with Malichus long ago comes to mind. They had talked about the divine promise of a blooming desert. "My son, I believe your journey has not been in vain."

This time it is Hayyan who looks up surprised. As far as he was concerned, it had all been a waste of time, but now his father seems to think there is more to it after all.

"Let's see. I believe it is the scroll of the Prophet Isaiah that speaks about the desert." The deep frown in Aqel's forehead betrays his earnest attempt to remember the precise words. "'The wilderness and the dry land shall be glad; And a highway shall be there, and it shall be called the Way of Holiness; the unclean shall not pass over it.'[110] One way, or another, it must have something to do with the appearance of John," Aqel concludes. He has no explanation for it, but in his heart it feels right. "When I used to discuss these things with my friend, Malichus, we could never figure out whether this was a prophecy for Israel or for us."

"If I understand correctly, John is the one who will prepare the straight way for the Lord. He exhorts people to righteous living for God," Hayyan asserts.

"I believe that, too, my son. Do you know what that means?"

As Hayyan contemplates the significance of his father's words, he tries to analyze the events one by one. According to his father, God would use John, the messenger, to bring people closer to himself. John tells the people that he is not the Messiah, but only the one who comes to prepare the way. Furthermore, John is Jesus' cousin. Hayyan carefully comes to a conclusion. "That means John prepares the way for the Prince of Peace?"

"This is exactly what I believe to be true," says Aqel, grinning from ear to ear. "As a matter of fact, we do not have any reason to doubt that Jesus is still alive. God is all-powerful and absolutely able to makes his plans come to pass. It was his hand that kept King Herod from killing the Messiah."

Encouraged by this thought, Hayyan sits up. He remembers something of the conversation between the prophet and the teachers of the law. "Now that you mention it, I heard John speak of someone who was supposed to come after him and who was, in fact, standing among them, even at that very moment. That person had even been before him already![111] It was all very confusing to me."

When he hears what his son says, Aqel's eyes light up. "This fits completely with the miraculous birth of Jesus. His mother told us explicitly that her pregnancy was not a normal pregnancy, but by God's power."

Hayyan doesn't follow his father's train of thought. What does he mean?

Aqel notices the puzzled look in his son's eyes, and says, "Do you remember what I told you about Mary and her child right after I returned from worshiping him in Bethlehem? She was betrothed to Joseph, when a messenger from God appeared to her telling her she would be with child. He explained that the Holy Spirit would come upon her and the power of the Most High would overshadow her."

"Are you telling me that Jesus the Messiah is half man and half God?" Hayyan asks somewhat stupefied.

"My son, it is a mystery," replies the old man, "but now I do understand why John said that the one who would come after him, had been before him, too. Somehow, Jesus must have been in heaven before he came to earth as a man. He took upon himself the form of a man."

While he is speaking, Aqel thinks back with fresh understanding. "You know, the mother of our forefather, Ishmael, once had an encounter with a strange man. He spoke to her with such authority as only God himself would. I am beginning to believe that it was Jesus who appeared to her in the wilderness."

Hayyan has been listening attentively to his father. This is going too far! Centuries ago, Jesus appears to Hagar, and now just a mere thirty years ago, Mary gives birth to a baby Jesus! It is simply impossible! Out of respect for the elderly, he keeps quiet, but he finds the whole idea preposterous and disturbing. For a moment, he wonders if his father is losing his mind. The only thing that is not incomprehensible to him is that Jesus is still alive, and John is aware of that. "Perhaps I should go back and try to talk to John," he thinks out loud.

"I would most certainly do that, my son." Aqel encourages him.

As soon as Hayyan's duties allow, he takes to the road again. To his great delight, he finds John at the exact same location near the ford in the Jordan River. Again, throngs of people crowd around the preacher, making it difficult for Hayyan to get near to him.

"Welcome, foreigner!" someone calls out. Hayyan turns in the direction of the voice and finds a friendly-looking man standing behind him with an outstretched hand. Courteously, he greets the Jewish man with the word, 'Shalom', just like his father taught him to do.

"What brings you here?" the man asks warmly.

"I have come to listen to the preacher, John," Hayyan replies. He does not want to tell this stranger the real reason for his visit, at least not before he knows what his reaction will be.

The man looks at him and continues, "Have I not seen you here before, a couple of weeks ago, perhaps?"

"It's quite possible," Hayyan replies coolly. He wants to be careful.

The friendly man notices that Hayyan is a high-ranking Arab and would like to do him a favor, so he says, "Would you like to speak to the prophet?"

Although this is the main reason Hayyan has come here again, it would be impolite and contrary to local customs to accept the invitation with any measure of eagerness. So, he hides his excitement and responds with some reservation, "It is really not necessary. He seems very occupied and I do not wish to burden him."

"It is no trouble at all, my friend," John's follower answers jovially. "On the contrary, my master would be honored to meet you."

Moments later, Hayyan is introduced to John. Soon the conversation turns to his father's encounter with the Prince of Peace. When John learns about the men who traveled from the East to come and worship the King, his darkened, suntanned face beams with delight. Hayyan senses an inexplicable link with this man, whom he hardly knows. As he pours out his heart, something stirs deep inside of him.

"Of course, Jesus, the Messiah, is alive," John points out with a smile. "God always keeps his promises, *always!*"

Now Hayyan can hardly contain his eagerness to meet him too. "Where can I find him," he asks.

"A few weeks ago, he was right here with me," John replies, "but I haven't seen him since. No one knows where he is staying at the moment."

Excitement turns to disappointment. Now what?

"Don't worry, my friend. God will lead you to him," John reassures him.

"If I may be so bold, how did you know that you were not the promised Messiah, while everyone thought you were?" Hayyan gently inquires.

The question makes John laugh. "Many people have asked me the same thing. If they would only study the Scriptures and believe the things God has told them through the prophets."

Then John begins to explain to the young man how God himself made a blood sacrifice in Paradise to make coverings for Adam and Eve. He also explains how the sacrificial lamb God provided at the very moment Abraham was about to offer up his son, Isaac, serves as an example of God's substitute to save a human life. During the conversation Hayyan responds from time to time with the appropriate Scriptures his father has taught him over the years. This Arab, who has so much knowledge of the Torah and other scrolls, impresses John greatly.

"Therefore only a perfect sacrifice can atone for sin, and since the Messiah is born of God, He alone is perfect," John asserts. "That is why I was aware from a very young age that he is the Messiah."

"And you actually met him only a few weeks ago?"

"That's right. While I was baptizing people, my cousin, Jesus, came to me. Suddenly, God made it clear to me that he was indeed the Lamb of God. He asked me to baptize him as well. Even though I was hesitant at first, I could do nothing but obey. Straightaway, as Jesus came up from the water, the heavens opened up and a radiant white bird, like a dove, came to rest on him. Immediately, I knew that it was the Holy Spirit of God, visible to all, descending on Jesus."

Hayyan is fascinated by the things he has just heard. The Spirit of God, descending on Jesus like a dove from heaven… it is a wondrous thing indeed. *This is too good to be true,* he suddenly thinks. Though he tries to rid himself of the thought, the doubts remain. Finally, he voices them and asks, "Are you sure that what you saw was not just any ordinary bird on which the sunlight reflected?"

"Absolutely sure." John laughs. "God revealed to me beforehand that this was going to happen. And when Jesus stepped out of the water, the dove stayed on his shoulder. Even as he walked towards the foothills in the direction of the desert, the bird did not fly away. Moreover, immediately following the baptism, I heard a voice coming from heaven who said, 'You are my beloved Son; with you I am well pleased.'"[112]

"Really? A voice from heaven?" Hayyan has great difficulty believing that. But then, what about the stories he heard about his forefather Ishmael? Didn't he also hear the voice of God?

John looks lovingly at this young Arab man as he repeats, "Yes, a voice from heaven; even the patriarchs experienced this; and not only Abraham and Isaac on Mount Moriah, but also Hagar and Ishmael at the well."

"I would love to hear the voice of God myself," Hayyan blurts out. As soon as the words tumble out of his mouth, he regrets them. What a childish thing to say for a man his age and stature! And yet, the words he spoke came straight from his heart.

"Perhaps, one day, you will," John says, and then he adds, "Jesus the Messiah will baptize with the Holy Spirit and fire!"[113]

"How will I know when this happens?"

"Unfortunately, I have no answer to that, my dear friend," the prophet admits. "Maybe, one of these days, you can ask him yourself," he says cheerfully.

At the end of their conversation, a teary-eyed Hayyan thanks his new friend for taking the time to speak with him and with his heart overflowing with the abundance of wonderful things he has heard and seen, he returns home.

"The Messiah is really alive; I just did not meet him yet," Hayyan finishes recounting his latest journey. Aqel cannot get enough of it. He recognizes in his son the same zeal for the Prince of Peace he used to have while he was young. "Thank you, God, for your faithfulness and love to my offspring," he prays silently. Focusing his full attention on Hayyan, he says, "My son, you will see the kingdom of peace."

As he considers the events of his last journey, Hayyan feels a deep sense of peace growing in him; he knows that everything is going to be all right.

A few days later, Aqel passes away peacefully; satisfied with his life. He has come home.

32 A Meeting with the Living Word

"No! Missed it again!" the little boy sighs with exasperation. Stick in hand, he tries to catch an ant, darting across the hot desert sand, but the insect is too fast for him. The boy's mother, holding her baby daughter in her arms, squats next to him. While she nurses her little girl, she tirelessly swats away the annoying flies that try to land on the baby's eyes and runny nose. Meanwhile, she listens with fascination to the man on the hill. *I wish I were a man,* she thinks, *then I could have found a spot much closer to the speaker.* But he is surrounded by men who think very highly of themselves. Fortunately, she woke up early this morning; so at least she is not right at the back of the crowd.

Every day, great throngs of people, thousands of men, women, and children, have been coming to this location. They all want to be as close as possible to the man in a sparkling white robe.

Hayyan and Nathan are somewhere in the crowd as well. Hayyan is pleased that his best Jewish friend has been able to see the Messiah during the last Passover celebration in Jerusalem. And he is glad he convinced Nathan to join him on this special journey. As a result, they are together here, on this green hillside in the northern part of Israel. They listen spell-bound to the teacher, who is sitting on a boulder amidst the crowd.

"You have heard that it was said, 'You shall love your neighbor and hate your enemy.' But I say to you, love your enemies and pray for those who persecute you, so that you may be sons of your Father who is in heaven. For He makes his sun rise on the evil and on the good, and sends rain on the just and on the unjust. For if you love those who love you, what reward do you have? Do not even the tax collectors do the same? And if you greet only your brothers, what more are you doing than others? Do not even the Gentiles do the same? You therefore must be perfect, as your heavenly Father is perfect."[114]

While listening to the teacher, Hayyan tries to make sense of everything. The people are saying that this man, clothed in a linen robe, is the Messiah. So, this is Jesus Bin Joseph; the one who his father worshipped while he was yet an infant. Hayyan is struggling to believe that he is that same person. The Prince of Peace has not met his expectations. Where is the distinguished personality, dressed in expensive and ornate garments? Where are his foot soldiers and menservants? Where is the imposing palace? This Messiah is but a simple man, surrounded by farmers and fishermen, women and children. And yet, the tone of his voice touches Hayyan to the core. He speaks with such authority. Hayyan is confused. Could he really be the promised King?

Suddenly, a man squeezes through the crowd. He carries a little girl in his arms; her legs hang down limply.

She is paralyzed, just like my own little boy, Kedar, Hayyan realizes with a shock.

The father walks towards Jesus and when the Messiah looks at him, he says, "Lord, please, be merciful to her."

Hayyan is curious to see what will happen next. It has been said that Jesus is able to heal all diseases, even those that have baffled the doctors. But can he make the lame walk? There is no known remedy for this disability. Hayyan knows this all too well, due to his own son. He has not spared himself money and effort but no physician has been able to help him. Some of the town's people told him, "It is God's judgment." Hayyan feels hurt by the gossip. He only wants to follow Yahweh and has renounced all idol worship. Still, God the Creator has not blessed him in everything. His little Kedar remains paralyzed and for as long as he lives, he will need special care. Hayyan loves his son passionately. While his thoughts are still on his youngest son, the impossible happens right in front of his eyes.

After Jesus speaks to the girl, her father carefully lowers her to the ground. She then stretches out her legs all on her own and stands up. When her father lets go, her knees do not buckle, neither does she fall over. A moment later, she starts running around! The crowd cheers, "God be praised! A thousand thanks to the Most High God!" Jesus spoke only a word and the girl was healed.

Hayyan feels happy and sad at the same time. *The rumors are true. Jesus heals all those who come to him. Oh, if only he would heal my son, but it's impossible for Kedar to make the long journey to Israel.*

On the way back home, the friends discuss in detail all they have heard and seen.

"What do you think? Is he really the Prince of Peace?" Hayyan asks.

"To be honest, just like you, I was expecting someone entirely different," replies Nathan. "I did enjoy his teachings. Did you hear him say, "You have heard that it was said, 'An eye for an eye and a tooth for a tooth.' But I say to you, Do not resist the one who is evil. But if anyone slaps you on the right cheek, turn to him the other also.' "[115]

"Yes, I did, but I find that teaching difficult," Hayyan admits, "I mean… I like the idea of not repaying evil with evil. But to do the exact opposite, to allow yourself to be shamed voluntarily when someone insults you; I think that is going too far."

"Well, I don't think you should be taking it literally," Nathan reassures him. "It is a typical way for us, Jewish people, to express ourselves. Remember what he said about looking at women with lustful intent?"

"Hmmm, yeah, I didn't understand that either. If we were to take that seriously, no man on earth would have two eyes left. In no time, we would all be stone-blind."

"Exactly," Nathan laughs. "He certainly didn't mean that we should actually rip out our eye after looking lustfully at a woman. What he meant is that we should not ignore our sinful thoughts, but instead, deal with them right away."

Surprised by his friend's keen insight, Hayyan looks at him and says, "Amazing! If we all did that, there would be no more arguments."

"Neither would there be any more wars," adds Nathan.

"There would finally be peace on earth!" Hayyan exclaims happily. "That's the best teaching I have ever heard!"

Nathan looks a little perplexed, almost as if he wants to say: *What about me? Am I not a good teacher?* However, he wisely keeps his mouth shut. After all, his friend is not talking about just any teacher of the law, but about the Anointed of God, the Prince of Peace.

In any case, their trip has served its purpose. Both men know now with absolute certainty that this Jesus is the Messiah, promised by God through the prophets. All they must do now is wait until he comes to power and overthrows the Roman oppressors. They will be among the first to crown him as the new and rightful king. There is nothing they look forward to more.

In the years that follow, there is often news about miracles performed by the Messiah. He has even raised people from the dead. His followers are becoming more numerous each day.

Not long now, Hayyan thinks, *and there will be enough followers for him to set himself up as king.* He secretly hopes that one day, Jesus will come to Arabia; maybe he could even heal Kedar. He has thought about borrowing a cart from someone to take Kedar to Jesus. But his great responsibilities as a judge, as well as the daily issues he must deal with, prevent him from turning his wishes into a reality.

One day however, it may simply be too late.

"I don't understand at all," Nathan whispers hoarsely. He sits hunched down with his hands in his hair. He hasn't washed himself, nor put clean clothes on. "It simply does not add up. All the people bowed down before him, they threw their cloaks on the road, and called out, "Blessed is the King who comes in the name of the Lord! Peace in heaven and glory in the highest!"[116] Nathan swallows a couple of times as he tries to hold back his tears, while he continues to go over what he knows. "He smiled at the people who surrounded him. After entering the city, he went straight to the temple to throw out the unscrupulous sellers and those hypocritical moneychangers doing their ugly business inside the court. The people were jubilant and applauded him. They all seemed so happy that finally someone had come to rid them from these greedy men who pretended to act in the name of the Lord. It was the perfect moment for Jesus to proclaim himself the new king." Again, Nathan chokes up.

"And then?" Hayyan asks invitingly. "What happened next?"

"A few days went by and Jesus continued to teach about the kingdom of God to those who came to the temple. In the meantime, we were glad to see how he put some of the religious leaders, who cared about nothing but themselves, in their place. We were thinking that he might be waiting until the Passover, when the city is filled with Jews from surrounding nations. But then…" Nathan swallows heavily, attempting to control his tears and finish the story.

Hayyan looks with compassion at his friend. They have both nurtured big dreams since the first time they saw the Messiah. Both were looking forward to the coming reign of peace. Before his death, Hayyan's father had told him that it would be established during his lifetime. From what Nathan is telling him, it must not have been far off. Hayyan listens carefully as his friend continues to relate the story in bits and pieces.

"When I arrived at the temple on the preparation day for the feast, I noticed there was almost no one there. My first thought was that the Messiah must have gone elsewhere in the city and I assumed he had finally taken up his place as the rightful king. Then, I walked up to the residence of the Roman ruler. After the temple, this seemed to me the most obvious place for the Prince of Peace to assume his kingship. And there, you are not going to believe it, there he was … crowned …"

Hayyan bites his tongue. He wants to shout out, "This is marvelous!" But the anguish on his friend's face clearly shows him there is more to this story and he knows he needs to listen now.

"… with a crown of thorns."

Hayyan immediately brushes off what Nathan says, for he must have been mistaken, but again he doesn't voice his skepticism.

Nathan's face is wet with tears when he repeats, "A crown of thorns on his head; *this* is what they put on him. And they beat him with a whip, thirty-nine floggings, which is the lawful punishment for a criminal!"

"How is that possible?" Hayyan is now indignant. "He has never hurt anyone, not a single person. On the contrary, he was always ready to help anyone who needed it!"

"I know," Nathan nods sadly, "It is all because of those corrupt, hypocritical high priests. They arrested him and accused him of whatever they could think of."

"How could God allow this to happen?" Hayyan objects.

Nathan shrugs his shoulders and then tells him the rest. "That's not all. They took him to this place outside the city wall to crucify him."

Furiously, Hayyan pounds the ground with his fists and shouts, "They are the worst of the worst, how dare they do that to someone who they know full well will not defend himself!"

"As a matter of fact, until the very end, he acted as he had said," Nathan adds, "I didn't hear him scream or curse, not even a single time."

"What then? How did it end?"

"I have no words for this, Hayyan. There were two other men being crucified with him. They resisted being crucified and several soldiers needed to hold them down, but not Jesus." For a moment, Nathan silently relives the excruciating moments he personally witnessed there at the Hill of the Skull. Then he begins again, "He laid himself down on the wood and, before the soldiers could command him to do so, stretched his arms out wide."

"He was a perfectly good man," Hayyan remarks. Suddenly, with dismay, he says, "It almost sounds like this is what he wanted to do!"

"Didn't I tell you? I can't understand it!" Nathan answers. "Suddenly, it became pitch dark, even though it was in the middle of the day. It was a heavy, frightening darkness, as if the gates of hell were opened. A few hours later, around the time of the afternoon prayers, the darkness lifted. Shortly after that, Jesus died."

Hayyan is deeply disturbed. What can he do now? If it had been anyone else telling this alarming story, he wouldn't have believed it. But he has known Nathan since childhood. His best friend would not make these things up. *It appears that my father was wrong after all. Even though he was convinced that Jesus was the Prince of Peace, the promised Messiah, this Jesus is dead.* Then, reassuring thoughts come to mind. *No, no, no, all that the prophets foretold has come to pass in the life of this Jesus. Right from the very start, when he was conceived without any sexual contact and growing in the womb of a virgin. A clear miracle of God.* These thoughts keep circling in Hayyan's head.

"I stayed in Jerusalem for the seven days of the feast," Nathan continues, "but I had lost all sense of joy."

Hayyan nods. He admires his friend for his faithfulness. He himself would not have stayed longer. Of course, he is not a Jew, and the three yearly feasts, when all Israelite men have to gather in Jerusalem to celebrate, don't mean much to him.

"Now, towards the end of the week, I began to hear rumors that Jesus was alive again. But that is impossible."

"Why would you think that?" Hayyan asks with lips slightly curling up. He feels a glimmer of hope. "I remember Jesus once raised a man from the dead who had been in the grave for four days."

"Are you talking about Lazarus? That's true," confirms Nathan, "but now Jesus himself is dead; there is no one to raise him from the dead."

That is a dilemma Hayyan has no answer for.

"The Jewish religious leaders are saying that is it nothing but gossip and a trick by Jesus' disciples. According to them, his followers secretly stole the body out of the grave and then told everyone that he was raised from the dead, so that the people believe that he is indeed the Prince of Peace."

"I am disappointed to hear that," says Hayyan. "These followers really should know better to say something like that, after all that they learned from Jesus."

"It's not so hard to understand how people, whose dreams are crushed, sometimes act in strange ways." Nathan ends.

33 Fire that does not Consume

The streets of the old inner city buzz with excitement; people from all over are milling about. The time of the annual harvest festival has arrived, and the mood is joyful. This is one of the three times a year, when God-fearing Jews from all over the world flock to Jerusalem for a pilgrimage to worship their God in the holy temple.

The sweet-smelling aroma of freshly baked bread sweeps through an alleyway. A man, dripping with sweat, tosses a couple of round, flattened pieces of dough onto a wooden board. Smiling, he gingerly shoves them into the brick oven. He is pleased as business is brisk these days.

"Two loaves!" one of the customers calls out.

The baker hands him two warm pieces straightaway. He can tell the man is a foreigner as his accent is thick. He grins and says, "Welcome to Jerusalem! A blessed feast!"

The man smiles and returns the greeting. "To you, too, a blessed feast!" He pays the baker who then continues his work, humming a merry tune. The foreigner saunters away towards a tea shop, where he relaxes on one of the straw mats spread out on the ground. Whenever he comes to the city, he likes to take his breakfast here – a cup of sweetened tea with freshly baked bread. Munching on his savory roll, he watches the passers-by who lazily stroll through the alleyway, engaging in animated conversation. *What is going through their minds?* he wonders. *Are any of them as grief-stricken as I am?*

He, Nathan, cannot shake off the memories of the last feast in Jerusalem. Passover was only seven weeks ago. It was then that the Messiah had been crucified. Now he has returned to Jerusalem for the Feast of Harvest.* Then the believers bring a part of the first fruits of their harvest and livestock as sacrifices to God. Those without a farm, bring an offering of money to thank the Lord for his blessings.

Inadvertently, Nathan reaches for the money pouch under his cloak. Fortunately, it is still there. You never know. He would not be the first foreigner to be robbed during the busy days of the feast.

When a beggar girl approaches the tea house, he gives her the last piece of his bread and buys her a cup of tea. Afterwards, he walks towards the temple, where he spends the rest of the day meditating and discussing religious matters with other synagogue leaders. Tomorrow, during the festive assembly, he will bring his offering.

---

* For more information, go to www.godlovesishmael.com/harvest-feast.

The next morning, Nathan rises with a heavy heart. Normally, he would have gone earlier to the temple to bring his offering, but this time he can hardly get himself moving. The grief over the death of the Prince of Peace is still very raw. If his love for God was not so strong, he would not even have come to Jerusalem this time; he would much rather have stayed at home. Ever so slowly, he pushes through the crowded streets and alleys towards the temple. Suddenly, there is the sound of a storm right above him. Shortly after, he sees crowds of people trying to squeeze into one of the side streets. Curiously, he hurries after them until he reaches a square. That is where he sees something amazing: a group of men with flames of fire on their heads. He can't understand why anyone would do such a thing. *Have they gone insane? Who in his right mind sets fire to his own hair?* When he takes a closer look, he notices that the flames are not burning their hair. Only then, do the words they speak begin to penetrate his confused mind.

"Blessed be the Lord God of Israel, for He has visited and redeemed his people, and has raised up a horn of salvation for us in the house of his servant David,
as He spoke by the mouth of his holy prophets from of old. Grace to you and peace from God our Father and the Lord Jesus Christ, who gave himself for our sins to deliver us from the present evil age, according to the will of our God and Father. And his mercy is for those who fear him, from generation to generation, to Abraham and to his offspring forever."[117]

How is this possible? Am I hearing right? It seems these men are speaking in Arabic. For a moment, Nathan thinks he's dreaming, but when he feels the warmth of the sun on his face and smells the sweaty bodies of the men around him, he knows it's not a dream. *This is incredible! These men look like Galileans, and yet they speak fluent Arabic without a hint of an accent.* Then he hears another from the group address the crowd in Aramaic. This time Nathan can clearly tell the man is a Galilean. What an amazing event! With growing wonder he listens to the speech.

"Men of Judea and all who dwell in Jerusalem, let this be known to you, and give ear to my words. For these people are not drunk, as you suppose, since it is only the third hour of the day. But this is what was uttered through the prophet Joel:

'And in the last days it shall be, God declares,
that I will pour out my Spirit on all flesh,
and your sons and your daughters shall prophesy,
and your young men shall see visions,
and your old men shall dream dreams;
even on my male servants and female servants
in those days I will pour out my Spirit, and they shall prophesy.

And I will show wonders in the heavens above
and signs on the earth below,
blood, and fire, and vapor of smoke;
the sun shall be turned to darkness
and the moon to blood,
before the day of the Lord comes, the great and magnificent day.
And it shall come to pass that everyone who calls upon the name of
the Lord shall be saved.'"[118]

Nathan knows the words of the prophet Joel well enough to silently mouth the last few verses. In the meantime, he wonders if this is what the prophet meant. God will show wonders in the heavens above and signs on the earth below. This is a clear sign: the flames of fire on the heads of these men. Nathan is relieved. Reassured that this is an indication of God's love for his people he listens attentively to what these men are saying. "Men of Israel, hear these words: Jesus of Nazareth was sent by God. The mighty works and wonders and signs that God did through him attest to that. With your own eyes you have seen them. This Jesus was delivered up into the hands of unbelievers, according to the definite plan and foreknowledge of God. You crucified and killed him by the hands of the lawless Romans."[119]

On hearing these words, Nathan's grief threatens to overwhelm him again. In his mind, he pictures Jesus, wearing a crown of thorns on his head, being beaten and whipped, mocked and spit upon, and finally nailed to a cross. What is this man saying? Is he saying that God planned this beforehand? That seems unbelievable. Why would God cause his own prophet to suffer so cruelly? But then Nathan remembers the prophet Job. Hadn't God ordained his suffering too? For Job, however, things had ended well, but not so for Jesus.

"However, God delivered him from the clutches of death and raised him up from the dead. The prophet David already spoke about Jesus when he said, 'I saw the Lord always before me, for he is at my right hand that I may not be shaken; therefore my heart was glad, and my tongue rejoiced; my flesh also will dwell in hope. For You will not abandon my soul to Hades, or let your Holy One see corruption. You have made known to me the paths of life; You will make me full of gladness with your presence.'"[120]

Though Nathan is still confused, his heart begins to fill with joy. The things he hears now tie in perfectly with the events surrounding the life and death of Jesus. Perhaps he is not dead after all; perhaps he has really risen from the dead and really did appear to his followers. But his common sense tells him something different. *Don't interpret David's Psalm in this way. Jesus' followers are purposely trying to mislead you and the rest of their audience.*

The speaker hasn't finished. In a booming voice he continues, "Brothers, the patriarch David died and was buried, and his tomb is with us to this day. Being therefore a prophet, and knowing that God had sworn with an oath to him that he would set one of his descendants on his throne, he foresaw and spoke about the resurrection of the Christ, that he was not abandoned to Hades, nor did his flesh see corruption. This Jesus God raised up. We saw him several times with our own eyes."[121]

The eleven men standing next to the preacher nod as one, confirming that they too have seen Jesus.

The leader still hasn't finished and continues, "God exalted Jesus by placing him at his right hand and gave him the promised Holy Spirit. Today Jesus has poured the Spirit over us. That is what you are seeing and hearing. For David did not ascend into the heavens, but he himself says, 'The Lord said to my Lord, Sit at my right hand, until I make your enemies your footstool.'"[122]

God has raised the Messiah from the dead and placed him on the throne, the place of honor, at the right hand of God… the words echo in his head … *until his enemies have been made his footstool.* Processing all that he has heard, Nathan concludes that Jesus must be the promised Prince of Peace after all; and while he holds all power not only on earth but also in heaven, his kingdom is not of this earth but of heaven. As ruler over all, he has authority over all the evil spirits and demonic powers. He proved that while he was still on earth; then he already held the power to free people who were possessed by evil spirits.

Finally, the Galilean calls out with a loud voice, "Let all the house of Israel therefore know for certain that God has made him both Lord and Christ, this Jesus whom you crucified."[123]

Many in the audience are troubled and ask, "What shall we do?"

"Repent and be baptized every one of you in the name of Jesus Christ," the speaker responds, "then your sins will be forgiven and you will receive the gift of the Holy Spirit just like we have. For the promise of God's Spirit is for all of you; God desires to pour out his Spirit, not only on you, but also on your children and for all who are far off, everyone whom the Lord our God calls to himself."[124]

For a moment, Nathan thinks of his best friend at home. What would he think of this? The idea that God wants to pour out his Spirit on all people is something new to him. Just imagine, that Hayyan too would be called upon by God to receive his Spirit; that would be wonderful.

I had better take another look at the prophecies when I get home, the Jewish teacher thinks. His mood is visibly improved as he sets off for home.

Although Hayyan's neighbors are used to seeing the Jew and the Arab embrace one another with a kiss on the cheek and the shoulder, they continue to think it's odd. The two close friends, however, do not care what anyone thinks. They are happy to see each other again.

"Praise God for your safe travels!" Hayyan exclaims as soon as he sees Nathan.

His friend answers, "God protect you."

Hayyan takes his friend by the hand as he leads him into his house. It doesn't take long before they are deep in conversation. The Arab man's jaw drops when Nathan tells him that Jesus' followers have all seen him with their own eyes after he had died and been buried.

"They all confirmed that he has risen from the dead and that he appeared to them afterwards," Nathan emphasizes. "And not only once, but several times and in different locations too. A few weeks later, some of them saw him ascend into the heavens. It happened while he was still talking with them, that he was suddenly lifted up and finally disappeared into the clouds."

"It almost looks like history is repeating itself!" Hayyan asserts.

"What do you mean?"

"My father often told me, "Hayyan, God loves our people. He spoke to Ishmael and Hagar from a cloud, before He saved them from certain death. Always remember this!"

"Now that you mention it, I believe my forefather Abraham experienced something similar when he was about to sacrifice his only son, Isaac," Nathan replies. "It's as if he heard the voice of the Messiah then."

"You mean to say: *our* forefather Abraham," Hayyan laughs.

With a smile, Nathan accepts the mild rebuke of his friend.

"What else can you tell me? Did anything else happen?" Hayyan questions his friend curiously.

In great detail, Nathan shares the new explanation of the Scriptures. "I would like to search the Scriptures for myself, before I accept his teaching as truth, though," he says as he finishes. Hayyan understands. As the spiritual leader of his people, Nathan carries the responsibility for the entire Jewish community in the city. Even though, there is little oversight from Jerusalem and Nathan is given free reign, he feels a firm calling not only to properly expound the Scriptures, but also to walk in the ways of the Lord, before the Jewish congregation. "There is something I almost forgot to tell you," he suddenly remembers. "The disciples had flames on their heads and their hair wasn't singed by the fire."

"That's impossible," says Hayyan. "They must have tricked you. Perhaps they had pouches filled with oil on their heads."

"It made me wonder too, but then one of their leaders spoke about a promise of God through the prophet Joel."

"What did he say?"

"I would like to look it up before I share it with you."

"Come now, I'm your friend. If it doesn't make sense, I will not tell anyone," Hayyan promises facetiously. "It will remain our secret." He manages to convince his friend, and Nathan continues, "God will pour out his Spirit on all people; there will be a sign of blood, fire and columns of smoke."

"I get it!" Hayyan exclaims enthusiastically.

Puzzled, Nathan looks at his him. How can his friend, a non-Jew, know what this means, while he, the Jewish teacher of the law, still has not been able to figure everything out?

"It reminds me of something the prophet John once told me," Hayyan adds. "He said that Jesus the Messiah will baptize with the Holy Spirit and with fire. John could not fully explain it to me then, but now I understand."

Nathan cannot quite follow his friend and looks at him baffled.

"It's like this: while I was still a young man, my father allowed me to join him when he visited a Jewish rabbi."

"Do you mean *my* father, in *our* home?"

Hayyan laughs and clicking his tongue, he confirms his friend's words. Then he continues, "I will never forget it. My father spoke with him about a passage in the scroll of Isaiah that talks about our people, the Kedarites. There is a prediction that we will rejoice in the servant of God."

Nathan eyes his friend curiously. He has never heard his friend speak about this.

"I believe it says, 'Behold my servant. I have put my Spirit upon him; and a faintly burning wick he will not quench; he will faithfully bring forth justice; till he has established justice in the earth.'[125] The fire is symbolic for God's holy presence. Jesus, the Messiah, shall strengthen the weak fire of God within the believers, while at the same time he shall consume the unrighteous with his fire."

"Really!" exclaims Nathan. "I have never looked at it like that before." He appreciates his friend's insight, but deep in his heart he is a little embarrassed about his own ignorance. *How can this Arab man precede me in understanding the things of God? I must go back to studying the scrolls!*

34 Innocent Blood

Their heads covered out of respect for the Most High God, a group of men sit in a large circle on colorful woven rugs. After a while, one of them gets up and the others follow suit. Solemnly, the man walks over to a small recess in the wall and with a steady hand slides the intricately embroidered curtain open. Two doors, decorated with exquisite woodcarvings, are revealed. The ark, as the alcove is aptly named, hides dozens of scrolls of Scripture. After a moment of silent contemplation, the bearded man chooses one of them. Then he walks over to the square platform in the middle of the hall and climbs up the three steps. Reverently, he kisses the scroll and undoes the cover. He turns his face towards the ark on the western wall, in the direction of Jerusalem, and begins to sing. As he follows the text on the scroll, his words echo around the bare, white walls of the house of prayer.

> "Behold, my servant shall act wisely;
> he shall be high and lifted up,
> and shall be exalted.
> As many were astonished at you—
> his appearance was so marred, beyond human semblance,
> and his form beyond that of the children of mankind—
> so shall he sprinkle many nations;
> kings shall shut their mouths because of him;
> for that which has not been told them they see,
> and that which they have not heard they understand."[126]

The word 'servant' reminds Nathan of a conversation he had with his friend, Hayyan. They still see each other regularly and recently they discussed in detail this 'servant of God' who was supposed to bring peace on earth. It has been quite a few years since Jesus Christ was raised from the dead and still no reign of peace has been established anywhere. Is it a mere coincidence that precisely today's Sabbath reading is about the 'servant'? Fascinated, Nathan continues to listen.

> "Surely he has borne our griefs
> and carried our sorrows;
> yet we esteemed him stricken,
> smitten by God, and afflicted.
> But he was pierced for our transgressions;

he was crushed for our iniquities;
upon him was the chastisement that brought us peace,
and with his wounds we are healed.
All we like sheep have gone astray;
we have turned—every one—to his own way;
and the Lord has laid on him
the iniquity of us all.
he was oppressed, and he was afflicted,
yet he opened not his mouth;
like a lamb that is led to the slaughter,
and like a sheep that before its shearers is silent,
so he opened not his mouth.
By oppression and judgment he was taken away;
and as for his generation, who considered
that he was cut off out of the land of the living,
stricken for the transgression of my people?
And they made his grave with the wicked
and with a rich man in his death,
although he had done no violence,
and there was no deceit in his mouth."[127]

How interesting, Nathan thinks, *this servant sounds exactly like Jesus.* He remembers seeing the wounds from the lashing on Jesus' back, the crown of thorns on his head, the mocking and mistreatment by the soldiers. Jesus did not defend himself. The death sentence had been completely unjustified, and he died with two common criminals either side of him.

"Yet it was the will of the Lord to crush him;
he has put him to grief;
when his soul makes an offering for guilt,
he shall see his offspring; he shall prolong his days;
the will of the Lord shall prosper in his hand.
Out of the anguish of his soul he shall see and be satisfied;
by his knowledge shall the righteous one, my servant,
make many to be accounted righteous,
and he shall bear their iniquities.
Therefore I will divide him a portion with the many,
and he shall divide the spoil with the strong,
because he poured out his soul to death
and was numbered with the transgressors;
yet he bore the sin of many,
and makes intercession for the transgressors."[128]

After the Scripture reading, the scroll is placed back into the ark and the men take their seats on the floor again. Normally, it would have been Nathan's turn to expound the passage, but this morning a teacher of the law is visiting them. Having a guest speaker can be an enriching experience and this rabbi has an excellent reputation as a dedicated follower of the Law of Moses.

"Brothers, I have good news for you," the lecturer begins, "the servant Isaiah prophesied about, has come."

Astonished, the listeners look round the circle. What does this preacher from Tarsus mean? "Surely, you have heard of Jesus of Nazareth, who performed signs and wonders and announced that the kingdom of God was at hand," Rabbi Paul continues. "You also know that he was crucified by the Romans." Several men nod their head in agreement. "This same Jesus conquered death and was resurrected from the grave, after which he returned to the Father in heaven as his disciples were watching."

As the preacher testifies to his convictions, the mood in the synagogue changes noticeably. "Jesus of Nazareth was just a regular prophet!" a man with a furrowed brow exclaims. "No one has ever risen from the dead!" Several others assent and mumble in agreement, "Indeed!" and "Amen!".

Not surprised by their reaction, Paul reassures his listeners. "I was just like you. I had heard and believed the rumors about the disciples stealing his body and subsequently claiming he had been raised from the dead. But I can assure you that those rumors were not true."

The men relax a little; apparently this rabbi knows what he is talking about and doesn't believe the rumors.

"I devoted myself to putting a stop to the teachings of Jesus. To do this, I even traveled to Damascus to put the people of the Way in prison," Paul explains. "As I neared Damascus, suddenly, a light from heaven shone around me and I heard a voice saying, 'Saul, Saul, why are you persecuting me?' In fear, I fell to the ground, and asked, 'Who are you, Lord?' and he said, 'I am Jesus, whom you are persecuting.'"[129]

At the mention of the name of Jesus, the tension rises again in the meeting hall. Several of the men laugh at the notion that Paul personally met Jesus. "He is making this up. He was probably suffering from heat exhaustion and couldn't think straight," they whisper among each other.

Even so, some are curious about this supernatural experience. Nathan is one of them. He is transfixed by Paul's words. In his mind he goes back over the conversations with Hayyan. *Again, a voice from heaven; this time the speaker even made himself known.* It is clear to him that this really took place.

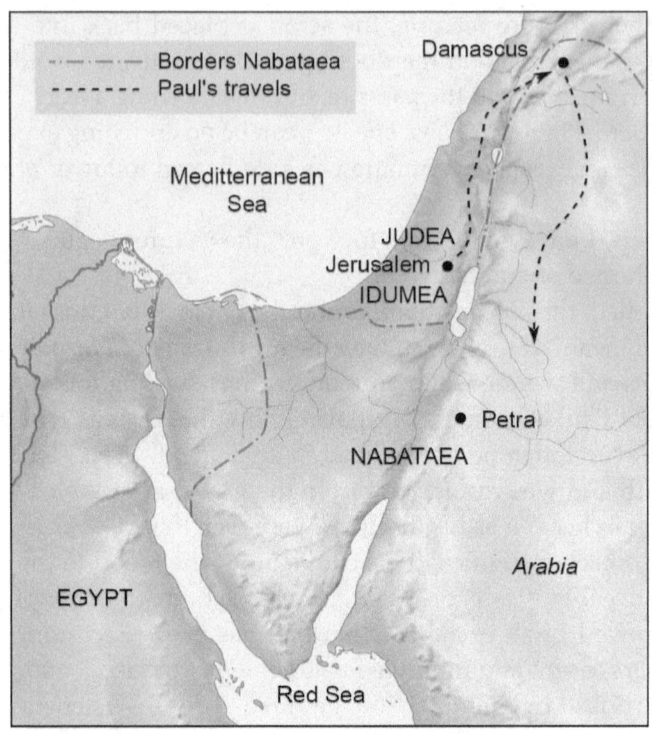

Paul's probable journey in the Nabataean kingdom of Aretas IV

In the meantime, Paul describes what happened to him after he arrived in Damascus. He had been completely blinded by the light, but a Jewish follower of the Messiah had prayed for him in the name of Jesus. "Immediately, my sight was returned to me," Paul says. "Thus, I can tell you with certainty that Jesus the Messiah is alive."

Some of the men now frown angrily and motion to Nathan that he should stop Paul from speaking. As rabbi of the synagogue, he must make sure the teaching is sound. While Nathan feels the pressure from the members of the Jewish community, deep in his heart he is full of joy at the words of their guest. Therefore, he decides to ignore the angry glares and allows Paul to continue.

"Today, we read about the servant of God," Paul resumes. "The prophet Isaiah predicted his suffering. This has been fulfilled in the life of our Lord Jesus Christ; he suffered at the hands of his fellow citizens in Jerusalem. We thought God was punishing him, when he was crucified, and indeed this is true."

On hearing these last words, the men quieten down again. They are aware that Jesus had told the High Priest he was the Son of God. That meant he had equated himself, a man of flesh and blood, with the Most High God.

This is the worst sin imaginable: a mere man making himself equal to God! He had obviously deserved to die.

"God did not punish him though for reasons we thought he should be punished," Paul asserts. "Jesus the Messiah lived a sinless life and did not deserve punishment. Even the Roman prefect, Pilate, said that he was a righteous man. Jesus kept not only the Law of Moses, but also adhered to the Roman mandates."

While listening, Nathan wonders: *Why did God punish an innocent man?* Fortunately, he does not have to wait long for the answer.

Paul explains, "The reason why Jesus suffered innocently is found in the words of the Prophet Isaiah: 'But he was pierced for our transgressions; he was crushed for our iniquities; upon him was the chastisement that brought us peace, and with his wounds we are healed.'"[130]

While still speaking, Paul looks around the circle of men. He can tell they do not fully understand and so he decides to use some illustrations from Scripture to clarify his claims. "Throughout history, God has given us many examples of innocent suffering on behalf of humanity. Think about the way God cared for Adam and Eve after they fell into sin. He made them garments of animal skins to cover their shame. God took some of the beautiful animals He had created and sacrificed them to make coverings for the first man and woman. God gave them the best of what He had."

Paul pauses for a moment to let his words sink in and then continues, "After that, God gave our forefather Abraham an innocent ram to take the place of Isaac. A few centuries after that, in preparation for the Exodus from Egypt, the firstborn sons of Israel were saved from the angel of death, through the blood of the Passover lamb our ancestors sprinkled on their doorposts. Even to this day, our countrymen daily bring burnt offerings to the temple in Jerusalem as atonement for their sins. These sacrifices point to the perfectly innocent Lamb of God: Jesus, the Messiah. Because of our sins, Jesus' hands and feet were pierced as he was nailed to the cross. Because of our transgressions, his soul was crushed. He was punished so that we might have peace; he was wounded so that we might be healed. Because of his atonement, we can be reconciled to God."
Now everything falls into place for Nathan. With his whole being, he knows this is the truth and he thanks God for this wonderful news.

At the end of their meeting, Nathan has to suffer the scorn of some of his fellow Jews, but for now it doesn't bother him. No opposition can take away the peace and rest in his heart.

He invites Paul to have lunch with him and tells his oldest son to take a message to his best friend's house.

35 Free At Last

"Yes, his sacrifice was for everyone; that is why he *is* the Prince of Peace," Paul emphasizes. He looks at those gathered around him in Nathan's house. A number of members of the Jewish community have come to hear more about the Messiah. They are seated on floor cushions along the walls of the guest room, with Paul and Nathan at the far end. Not all of them are Jews, however. In their midst is an Arab man who listens intently, soaking up every word from the Jewish scholar.

Several scrolls are spread out on the floor. Although Paul can quote the text by heart, he prefers to show these studious men directly from the source. After he finishes explaining the significance of the suffering servant, Paul returns to the same scroll to read another passage.

"For to us a child is born, to us a son is given; and the government shall be upon his shoulder, and his name shall be called Wonderful Counselor, Mighty God, Everlasting Father, Prince of Peace. Of the increase of his government and of peace there will be no end, on the throne of David and over his kingdom, to establish it and to uphold it with justice and with righteousness from this time forth and forevermore. The zeal of the Lord of hosts will do this."[131]

"My father used to speak about this," says Nathan as he swallows the lump in his throat. He remembers the dozens of times he heard these same words from the mouth of Ezra. "This is what he was looking forward to." Then he looks down and adds wistfully, "but he did not get to see it happen."

Filled with compassion, Paul looks at him. "Many looked forward eagerly to the coming King, yet they did not see his Kingdom established. But God is abounding in grace and mercy, and He will reward each one according to their works in faith."

Hayyan suddenly thinks of another prophecy from Isaiah's scroll he had heard about. "My father would often speak of the Arabs praising God because of his servant. What about that?"

It takes some time before Paul finds the exact verses about the sons of Ishmael, but then he reads aloud, "Then you shall see and be radiant; your heart shall thrill and exult, because the abundance of the sea shall be turned to you, the wealth of the nations shall come to you. A multitude of camels shall cover you, the young camels of Midian and Ephah; all those from Sheba shall come. They shall bring gold and frankincense, and shall bring good news, the praises of the Lord. All the flocks of Kedar shall be gathered to you; the rams of Nebaioth shall minister to you; they shall come up with acceptance on my altar, and I will beautify my beautiful house."[132]

Astounded, Hayyan exclaims, "That's incredible! I had completely forgotten about this passage, but now I remember because my father used to speak about this one as well. What I am talking about, however, is the part that speaks specifically about the desert."

Paul needs no further clues; he knows exactly which text Hayyan is referring to. He rolls back the scroll a little until he reaches that passage.

"Let the desert and its cities lift up their voice,
the villages that Kedar inhabits;
let the inhabitants of the rock sing,
let them shout from the top of the mountains."[133]

"Yes, this is it!" Hayyan calls out excitedly.

In the meantime, Paul studies the sections preceding and following the text in order to explain the passage correctly to this Arab lover of God. His eyes then catch the words, 'God's Servant'. This expression has been given a completely new meaning since his unexpected encounter with Jesus. Immediately, he starts to read, "Behold my servant, whom I uphold, my chosen, in whom my soul delights; I have put my Spirit upon him; he will bring forth justice to the nations. He will not cry aloud or lift up his voice, or make it heard in the street; a bruised reed he will not break, and a faintly burning wick he will not quench; he will faithfully bring forth justice. He will not grow faint or be discouraged till he has established justice in the earth; and the coastlands wait for his law."[134]

Tears well up in Hayyan's eyes. He is reminded of the words of the Prophet John, who told him about the dove that landed upon Jesus' shoulder and remained there afterwards. Clearly, it was prophesied centuries ago that God would fill his servant with his Spirit. That servant led a perfect, sinless life to be an unblemished sacrifice, for the forgiveness of the sins of the entire world. To Hayyan, this seems more than enough reason for the tribe of Kedar to break out in exultation.

The discussions between the men go on for a long time. Nathan and Hayyan are deeply moved. Everything they went through and all the Scripture passages they know have come together; it all makes sense now. Paul recognizes the power of God at work in the hearts of these men. Then he feels the Holy Spirit nudging him to say, "Call these men to repentance and to be baptized." *Are those really God's words?* he wonders. The voice speaks again. "Ask Hayyan about Kedar." Trusting the inspiration of God's Spirit, he addresses the Arab man seated across from him and asks, "How is Kedar?"

Hayyan is really surprised. How does this stranger know his son's name? Could it be that Nathan told him? He politely answers, "God be praised. He is doing well."

Paul can hear hesitation in his voice, which prompts him to repeat the question.

Again, Hayyan indicates that his son is doing well. Even after the third time, he answers, "God be praised. He cares for us." Hayyan has learned not to complain about the difficulties in his life. God has ordained it and if you do not accept that, you are, in fact, rebelling against him. But when Paul continues to gently prod a little further, Hayyan finally tells him the whole story. "Kedar has been paralyzed since infancy, when he had a serious fall. I would have liked to take him to Jesus for healing, but before I could work out the details of how to get there, Jesus had been crucified."

While Paul listens to the story, he prays quietly to God, "Lord, what is your will?" After Hayyan finishes, Paul can feel his heart pounding in his chest. He has a strong conviction that God is going to heal this little boy. At the same time, doubts run through his mind. *What if I pray and nothing happens? Then these men might start to doubt my message. Then again, I just proclaimed to them that Jesus' stripes bring us healing, and he healed all who came to him?* Paul doesn't hesitate any longer and asks to see Kedar.

A lot of curious children turn up at the Arab's house. They have come to see the stranger. Not only Hayyan's children, but also the sons and daughters of his brothers who live nearby, press in around him. They are used to walking in and out of their uncle's house freely and are quick to seize the opportunity to meet someone new. This time, however, Hayyan sends all out, except his own children. He only wants Kedar's brothers and sisters to be present when the Jewish man prays for their disabled brother.

Nathan has come too. As Paul's host, he wants to make sure that his fellow teacher of the law is treated well. Besides, he is aware that the Jewish community has certain expectations of him as their rabbi. He must see to it that nothing erratic or bizarre occurs. Above all, he is extremely curious to see for himself what is going to happen here. He knows that Jesus, the Messiah, was able to heal people; he saw it with his own eyes. Would Paul, a mere man, be able to do that too?

Paul speaks with authority as he holds the child's hand, "In the Name of Jesus the Messiah, stand up!" His father has been holding Kedar's limp body upright on his lap. Suddenly, the boy begins to stretch out his left leg and then his right. As he slowly slips off his father's lap, he turns over on his knees and pushes his upper body up with his arms. And then he stands up straight, without any support, for the first time in his life!

Tears of joy roll down Hayyan's face. This is the miracle he has prayed for so often, though he had given up hope. Awe-struck he says, "God be praised! Thank you, Jesus!" Hayyan is startled by his own words. *I am talking to Jesus and he is not even here.* At the same time, he feels a holy presence in the room, as if God himself is with them. He looks at Nathan and when their eyes meet, he senses that his friend is experiencing the same.

Indeed, Nathan also has an inexplicable awareness of God's supernatural presence. Something new dawns in his heart: it was not Paul who healed the boy, but God! Overwhelmed by the miracle of God's grace, he responds to Hayyan's words with a resounding "Amen!"

In the meantime, Hayyan's other children clasp their little brother's hand. Laughing noisily, they dance and jump around the room with joy. Kedar, grinning from ear to ear, allows them to pull him into their fun. He is speechless due to what has just happened to him.

Then the door opens and Hayyan sees the face of his twelve-year-old daughter appear around the corner. She has reached an age when it is no longer appropriate to be present when there are male visitors, but she wants to transmit a message to her father from her mother. Hayyan smiles. Of course, his wife wants to know what has happened. Immediately, he tells his other children to allow Kedar to go with his daughter to the women's quarters.

The neighboring women have joined Hayyan's wife out of curiosity. When their sons had returned home with stories about the strange Jewish visitor at Uncle Hayyan's house, they immediately went over to visit their sister-in-law. As soon as they see Kedar walk into the room, they cry out with joy. Never have they seen anything like this. There aren't even any stories of such miracles in the traditions of their parents and grandparents. It is simply impossible. And yet, it happened right here.

At the same moment, Hayyan realizes something very important: Jesus truly lives and reigns! Never before has a man been raised from the dead and ascended into heaven. Hayyan senses the same holy presence he felt when he heard Jesus speak in Galilee. He is aware of his own sinfulness and confesses to Paul, "I am a sinful man and do not deserve God's favor. I am not worthy of his blessing."

Paul looks at him with compassion and confirms Hayyan. "But," he continues, "this is exactly the reason for which Jesus came; to save and bless sinners."

Nathan thinks about a statement he and his friend had heard from Jesus' own mouth and he repeats the words. "It is not the healthy who need a doctor, but the sick."[135]

"I am in need of this doctor," says Hayyan with conviction. He looks at Paul and asks, "What should I do?"

Paul realizes that God has been working in the heart of this Arab man for a long time. Besides, that same afternoon Hayyan heard the Good News in Nathan's house. A short explanation about conversion and baptism will be all that is needed. He then explains that immersion in water is symbolic for death and resurrection, the end of living for oneself and the beginning of living with Jesus. Nathan listens carefully and senses a stirring in his heart. He wants that too. He wants to live for the One who died for him on the cross.

"Is it not necessary for me to keep all the Jewish laws and traditions then?" Hayyan wants to be sure. In the past, he had considered converting to Judaism, but there had been a certain resistance in his heart to that idea.

"Not at all," says Paul. "You become part of God's kingdom solely by confessing with your mouth that Jesus the Messiah is Lord, and believing in your heart that God raised him from the dead. This is the way to salvation."

That same afternoon, Paul takes Nathan and Hayyan to a large round cistern just outside the city. It is a place where rainwater from the surrounding hills is collected through a system of channels and ditches. Rocky, uneven steps have been carved out in the side of the enormous crater. Usually, it's only women that come here, as they fill their jugs with water for domestic use. But now, three men are going down the steps toward the water.

At the water's edge, Paul asks them a few questions. "Do you confess that you were born in sin and that you do not deserve eternal life with God? Do you believe that Jesus the Messiah died for you, in order to save you? Are you prepared to stop living for yourself? Are you ready to start living for God, the Father, and obey him?"

Both men answer affirmatively, "Yes!" Then Paul takes Nathan by the shoulder and as he pushes him gently under water for a moment, he proclaims, "I baptize you in the Name of the Father, of the Son, and of the Holy Spirit." After that, it is Hayyan's turn.

Following the baptism, the men climb the stairway in the wall of the crater. Their faces are beaming and their hearts run over with joy. On their way up the large steps, the two friends cry out, "Praise be to God! All honor to God Almighty!" They continue glorifying God with new words that spontaneously come up.

Upon reaching the edge of the crater, Nathan notices something strange. *Did I hear correctly?* he wonders. He tries to focus on what Hayyan is saying and then he shouts, "Hayyan! You were speaking in Hebrew!"

His friend stops praising God and with a puzzled look on his face, he responds, "What did you say?"

"You were speaking Hebrew fluently," Nathan repeats.

Hayyan doesn't understand and says, "I have never learned Hebrew!"

Then Nathan remembers the simple fisherman who he had heard speak Arabic a few years before. Now it seems, the same thing is happening to his friend. As he climbs over the edge of the reservoir he says, "Hayyan, I saw this in Jerusalem. Do you remember me telling you about it?"

"I do, but what does that have to do with me?" Hayyan responds hesitantly. He has great confidence in his friend, but now he is starting to question his sanity.

"Well, God has promised to pour out his Spirit on all people," explains the Jewish man, "not only on the Jews. This was predicted by the prophet Joel."

"So, I have been filled with the Spirit too?" Hayyan asks in wonder. He moves his hand over his head, but then pulls back quickly, fearing he might get burned. A little dazed, he asks, "Do I have fire on my head?"

"No, you don't," laughs Nathan, "but I do believe you have been filled with the Holy Spirit."

Paul laughs too and adds, "Visible fire is no longer necessary. But the fact that you spoke in a foreign language is an unmistakable indication that you are filled with the Holy Spirit." A passage from the book of Isaiah comes to mind and he quotes, "Until the Spirit is poured upon us from on high, and the wilderness becomes a fruitful field, and the fruitful field is deemed a forest. Then justice will dwell in the wilderness, and righteousness abide in the fruitful field. And the effect of righteousness will be peace, and the result of righteousness, quietness and trust forever."[136]

As Paul looks at Nathan and Hayyan's joyful faces, he is surprised at the words he just spoke. The desert will become a fertile field. Apparently, this is not meant only for Israel, but also for Arabia. All physically and spiritually dry areas will come to life!

Before they return to the city, the two close friends embrace each other warmly. With a radiant face, Paul says, "You are brothers now." He has just come to understand that Christ removed the dividing wall between Jew and non-Jew, and that the half-brothers, Isaac and Ishmael, are now united as brothers in the Lord.

In the weeks that follow, Nathan must pay a big price for his faith. Some of the elders in the synagogue have come together to try to force him out of his position as rabbi. Thankfully, his friend Hayyan offers to help him, supporting him until he has found other work. One thing, however, no one can take away from either of them – the peace and the freedom the two friends have now found in Christ Jesus.

Isn't it intriguing that Paul went to Arabia so soon after his conversion? In a letter to the believers in Galatia, he wrote, "I went away into Arabia, and returned again to Damascus. Then after three years I went up to Jerusalem" (Galatians 1:17b-18a).

During his supernatural encounter with Jesus on the road to Damascus, Paul was appointed to be his witness (Acts 26:15-18) and he immediately obeyed on his arrival in the city (Acts 9:19-20). Therefore, it is most likely that Paul has gone to the synagogue during his stay in Arabia to testify about the Servant of God.

On his return to Damascus, the governor under King Aretas had guards waiting to seize Paul (2 Corinthians 11:32-33). The very mention of the Arabian King of the Nabataeans is significant in that it shows Paul was not only wanted by the governor but by the king himself. This, in and of itself, indicates that Paul did more than just stay in Arabia to meditate, as some Bible expositors claim. We can assume that Paul shared the Gospel with both Jews and Arabs in accordance with his calling. In this way, the descendants of Ishmael were the first non-Jews to hear the Good News. Coincidence or divine providence?

According to Genesis 16:10 and 17:20, the Ishmaelites became the first people to receive an unconditional blessing from God. Furthermore, Isaiah 60:6-7 mentions the descendants of Ishmael as the first ones to come to Jerusalem to bring their offerings to God. Many see a first fulfillment of this prophecy though the Arabs who came to worship the child Jesus.* These things point towards God's ordained plan for the Arabs that He is fulfilling.

Let us take a moment to examine the life of John the Baptist, whom we have encountered at the beginning of this section of the book. There are some interesting similarities between him and Ishmael.

1) Both men received their name from God before birth.
2) Both men were thought of as the promised one. At first, Abraham and Sarah thought Ishmael was the son through whom the entire world would be blessed. Similarly, many Jews were under the

---

* For an extensive study about the fulfillment, see www.godlovesishmael.com/wise-men.

impression that John the Baptist was the Messiah, through whom the world would be blessed.

3) A messenger from God supernaturally announced the birth of both men. Hagar did not know at the time whether she was pregnant with a boy or a girl. But the Angel of the Lord revealed to her that she was carrying a son. The Angel Gabriel paid an unexpected visit to Zachariah and told him he would become the father of John.

4) Both Ishmael and John lived in the desert; Ishmael in the desert of Paran and John in the wilderness of Judah.

5) Ishmael became the first one to be set apart through circumcision. As part of the Old Covenant, circumcision served as a sign of being set apart by God. John became the first man to be filled with the Holy Spirit from before his birth. He was set apart as well and was not allowed to drink wine or any strong drink. The indwelling of the Holy Spirit is a sign that someone belongs to God and has received the promise of the New Covenant (2 Corinthians 1:22 and 5:5, Ephesians 1:13).

One should not consider these similarities mere coincidences. God is clearly showing us the unfolding of a mystery.

Let us now go one step further and consider the four people in Scripture who received their names from God before birth. Here too, a compelling connection between what seem like unrelated events is evident.

1) Both Ishmael and Isaac received their names from God through the Angel of the Lord; John the Baptist and Jesus received their names from the mouth of the Angel Gabriel.

2) Ishmael and Isaac both faced death during their teenage years; yet both were saved from an untimely demise. Both John the Baptist and Jesus died a violent death in their early thirties.

3) Ishmael preceded Isaac in receiving the blessing of a great people. Other than these two half-brothers, no one ever received a similar promise from God. John the Baptist preceded Jesus in that he received the Holy Spirit while he was still in his mother's womb. No other person received the indwelling of the Holy Spirit before birth.

4) The descendants of both Ishmael and Isaac received land as an inheritance here on earth, with Isaac receiving the greatest share.* John

---

* Review chapter 22 and the summary of part 3 about Ezekiel 25:4,10 to gain more insight about the area of land Ishmael received. A more detailed study about the division of land God promised to Abraham can be found at www.godlovesishmael.com/land-arabs.

the Baptist received an inheritance as well: the people who repented and were baptized because of his preaching (Luke 1:16). It was Jesus, however, who received all believers as his possession (John 10:27-29, Hebrews 2:13b).

5) Ishmael can be considered the greatest among all the half-brothers of Isaac. The Bible esteems him and his offspring higher than the descendants of Keturah. He also obtained greater blessings than the descendants of Abraham's brothers, like the Moabites and the Ammonites, who descended from Lot, Abraham's nephew. Furthermore, the Ishmaelites overshadow the Edomites, who are the descendants of Isaac's son, Esau. Parallel to this is Luke 1:15 and Matthew 11:11 which state that there is no one greater than John the Baptist, born of a woman.

A careful study of these examples clearly establishes parallels between Ishmael as the forerunner of Isaac and John the Baptist as the forerunner of Jesus. Overall, we can safely assume the following:

Ishmael was the forerunner of Isaac in the emergence of these two peoples who received unique blessings from God.

John the Baptist was the forerunner of Jesus in calling the people to repentance and preparing the way for the Messiah.

In the Bible there are several promises that point unmistakably to a mass repentance of the Jews in the end times. Could it be that the Arabs will be the forerunners in this for the Jews?

Discover the answer to this important question in the next part of the book.

Part 5

God's Plan for the Arabs Within Sight

God's promises for Ishmael and his descendants
as seen through the eyes of
today's Christians and a Muslim.

Through Israel's fall salvation has come to the Gentiles,
in order to provoke the Jews to jealousy,
until the fullness of the Gentiles has come in.
Then all of Israel will be saved.
(According to Romans 11:11, 25-26a).

2000 years later

36 Difficult Questions

Peace2012: Hello, I would like to ask a question.

A short beep announces an incoming chat message. Youssef looks up from his homework to check the message. *Hmmm, 'Peace2012'. Not a familiar name.* For almost two years now he has been active in a chat room to engage Muslims in conversations about faith. Youssef is a Christian and people often contact him about his beliefs. Sometimes, Muslims use expletives and call him an infidel. Other times they openly ridicule the Christian faith. But once in a while, someone posts a serious question. It grieves Youssef to see people attack Christianity. He would like to openly share his faith, but for now it is much safer to do that from home than to preach the Gospel in the streets of Amman. Because he was born into a Christian family, he is free to attend church. But he is well aware that he belongs to a minority group. Also, being a Palestinian refugee is not at all conducive to becoming a respected member of Jordanian society. He quickly responds to the message.

Welcome111: Hello! Please, go ahead.
Peace2012: Why do you Christians believe in three gods? Allah is one.

Youssef reads the question on the screen and sighs deeply. *How is it that Muslims are so stuck in their thinking? They all seem to think that we believe in three gods, but that is not true at all.*

He asks God for wisdom in responding. *Lord, You already know this man. You know his heart and his reason for approaching me in the chat room. What do You want me to answer him?*

Youssef then thinks through different illustrations he has used before to explain the unity of God. The image of man being spirit, soul, and body did not seem to resonate with anyone. Neither did the picture of water, as it appears in a solid, liquid, or gaseous state. And the illustration of the sun as a star which emits light and warmth at the same time seemed inapt as an example too, as no one really caught on. To Youssef, these illustrations had been quite logical and yet none of the Muslim chat room visitors has ever understood them.

Suddenly, Youssef thinks of an egg. Promptly, he types his reply.

Ahmed peers at his computer screen in hopes of receiving a satisfactory answer. *Will this person have anything meaningful to say?* Finally, something appears.

Welcome111: Think of an egg. An egg consists of three parts, the egg white, the yolk and the shell. But which part is the egg?

Ahmed is disappointed. At school he learned that the Christians worship God, Mary, and Jesus. These three have nothing to do with an egg. Ahmed thinks it is a weird comparison. *Why is nobody able to come up with a viable answer?* Then he remembers something else he learned at school: Christians have strayed from the truth. This is why Allah sent the Prophet Mohammed, so that people in the whole world would know how to live. Even the Prophet Jesus himself said that a messenger would come after him. And yet, Ahmed would like to understand how it is that two billion people in the world follow the Christian teachings.

Frustrated, he types, "You Christians are blinded and reject the teachings of Allah and…" Suddenly he stops. *I should respond in a respectful manner; after all, our Prophet Mohammed dealt respectfully with the Jews in his time, even when they rejected him.*

Ahmed deletes the sentence he just typed and begins again, "It is blasphemous to compare God to an egg."

He smiles as he presses the 'enter' key. *If the imam* knew what I wrote, he would be proud of me.*

When Youssef reads the reply, he feels discouraged. *I did feel inspired when I wrote those words.* Right away he takes his thoughts to the Lord in prayer. *"Lord, I do not understand why this person could not just answer my question, but I trust You to work in his life. Please, make yourself known to him."*

For a few seconds, he considers explaining the egg metaphor one more time, but then rejects that idea. *Wait, is this from God, or is the enemy trying to keep me from presenting the truth?* Again, he turns to God. *"Lord, what do you want me to do?"* Even before he finishes pleading with his Lord, Youssef realizes that the quiet impression to leave things be, had entered his heart immediately following his earlier prayer. *This must be God's answer then.*

And yet, something doesn't sit right with him. *How will this person ever know the truth?*

Youssef is in conflict; still he decides to leave the example of the 'egg' for the moment. Deep within his heart, he hears, "Trust Me." This is enough confirmation; he can now respond with confidence.

---

* The word 'imam' is derived from the verb, 'to lead', as in 'to lead the way' or 'to lead by example'. The imam is the equivalent of a preacher/pastor of a church or a rabbi of a synagogue. The Arabic preposition 'amam' means 'before'. The imam leads the believers in their prayers by standing in front of them while facing Mecca.

A little while later Ahmed stares at the lines on the screen.

> Welcome111: I respect your fear of Allah. Unfortunately, as people we are limited in our knowledge of the Creator. That is why is it so difficult to understand that God the Father, the Son and the Holy Spirit, is one God. While Jesus walked on the earth, Peter, one of his followers, confessed, that He, Jesus, was indeed the Son of God. Jesus then explained to him that this was revealed to him by God the Father and not by flesh and blood.[137] It is only possible for us to know God as He chooses to reveal himself to us.

Ahmed is surprised. This Christian has great faith. His conviction of God's power and might speaks to that. Ahmed has always harbored different ideas about the People of the Book.* His imam regularly warns them that the People of the Book have been brainwashed, and yet, this Arab Christian has a solid faith and trust in God that he, Ahmed, lacks.

Alarmed at his own thoughts, he resolves to no not concern himself with questions about the Christian faith any longer. Besides, he is a little worried that his father or brothers will find out what he has been doing. If that were to happen, he would really be in trouble. One final, polite line from him will close this chat nicely.

Anxiously, Youssef waits for the visitor's reaction to his answer. The words had come straight from his heart. He doesn't have to wait long. Within minutes a new message appears on the screen.

> Peace2012: Thank you for your reply. I will pray for you that you learn the way of Islam and follow the Prophet Mohammed (peace be upon him).

Youssef is very discouraged. He can't understand why people are not more open. *Why am I still doing this? I am wasting my time. Why not do something fun instead. It hurts too much when Muslims start praying for me while it is my greatest desire to see them know the Lord Jesus as their Savior.*

With a heavy heart, Youssef logs off, but not before he writes one more short line. Then, he closes the chat box and, hoping for a message from his favorite cousin, opens his email. Noura is a real optimist and knows exactly how to encourage him. She also empathizes with him as he seeks to dialogue with Muslims. When she left for the United States, she promised him, "I will pray for you every day." He had been a little jealous of her getting the

---

* The Quran calls Christians and Jews 'People of the Book'.

opportunity to study in America, while he had to stay in Jordan. His father's business was not doing as well as his uncle's, so he must be satisfied attending the University of Jordan.

Sadly, there is no word from Noura. *Maybe tomorrow*, he thinks wishfully as he types one last line before he turns the computer off.

Welcome111: Just in case you have any other questions, do not hesitate to ask me.

As Ahmed reads Youssef's last response, his curiosity is aroused again. *That man has a really strong faith. How can he be so misled and so convicted at the same time, while I, a follower of the true religion, feel so restless?*

A few days later, Ahmed searches his browsing history for a website he visited earlier that week. As he scrolls through the myriad of sites, his eye catches the chat room where he met the Christian.

Although, he feels the man never gave him a satisfactory answer, he still has so many other questions. He clicks on the link. The little green dot indicates that 'Welcome111' is online. Now would be the perfect time to ask why the Christians claim that the prophet Jesus died. He has all but forgotten about what he was searching for in the first place and begins to type.

Youssef hears a beep.

Peace2012: Hello.

Someone is trying to contact him in the chat room. The sender's screen name rings a bell. 'Peace2012'. *Hmmm, a familiar name.* After quickly perusing his chat history, Youssef finds the conversation he had with the Muslim man who was going to pray for him. He's both glad and fearful at the same time. On the one hand, he is happy that the man has contacted him again. On the other hand, he's still sad at their last conversation. He doesn't want to be disappointed again. Then Youssef remembers what Noura wrote to him a couple of days ago. "Continue to pray and respond faithfully to their questions, and leave it to God to work in their hearts." Now is a good time to put this advice into action.

Welcome111: Hello, welcome back.
Peace2012: How are you?
Welcome111: God be praised, and you?
Peace2012: God be praised, all is well. I have another question.

Youssef is surprised. Usually it is a good sign when people ask more questions.

Welcome111: Go ahead.

A few minutes later, the familiar beep signals a new message.

Peace2012: Why do you Christians believe that Jesus (peace be upon him) died on the cross?

Youssef's face clouds over. How many times have people asked him this question? He knows the Muslims' thoughts on this subject. They always say that Allah would never allow one of his prophets to suffer and die like that. Some point out to him that if Jesus were indeed God, he could not have died, for God cannot die. It is a convincing argument. Hoping to stimulate them to think deeper, Youssef is usually a little evasive in his answers.

Welcome111: Both the Holy Book* and the Qur'an speak of Jesus' death; so it is only natural to believe this.

The reply appears after a few minutes.

Peace2012: According to Islam, Jesus will die, but only at the end of time, on his return, and not before as you claim.

Youssef had been expecting this answer, and does not even have to think about what he writes next.

Welcome111: In *Surah*** 3, *ayat**** 55 it is written: "God said, 'O Jesus! Verily, I shall cause thee to die, and shall exalt thee unto Me.'"[138] Clearly, God himself said that He caused Jesus to die after which He made him to ascend to heaven. This is exactly what it says in the Holy Book. Why don't you believe your own book?

Ahmed is angry. *How dare he assume to know what our book says? Even ordinary Muslims are not able to interpret the Qur'an; only Muslim scholars who have memorized the entire Qur'an and have gained a solid understanding of the ancient*

---

* The Bible is called 'the Holy Book' in Arabic

** A chapter of the Quran is called a *Surah*, while the Arabic word for a chapter in the Bible is *Ishaah*.

*** A *Surah* does not consist of verses but rather *ayat*, which means 'miracle'.

Arabic language are capable of doing so. Let alone a kafir who uses the Qur'an; this is haram.*** He can't help but shoot back sharply.

> Peace2012: You Christians are misled and do not know the truth! Allah did not allow his prophet to suffer!

As soon as Youssef had sent his reply, he felt uneasy. Perhaps he should not have asked whether 'Peace2012' believes his own book. The question had been harsh. When he reads the reaction of the Muslim, he realizes he has been out of line by replying in frustration rather than with gentleness. Immediately, Youssef confesses his sinful act and prays, "Father in Heaven, I am sorry for answering thoughtlessly. I was angry with this man's offer to pray for me. Please, Lord, forgive me."

As soon as he has finished praying, the feeling of uneasiness is lifted and peace returns to his heart. Then he continues and says, "Thank you, Lord Jesus, for dying on the cross for my sins and for cleansing me from all unrighteousness."

Youssef lifts up his eyes and pictures the indignant man's reaction again. "Lord, please, give me wisdom to respond in a way that is pleasing to You," he prays. Then a thought strikes him. *Write to him what you just confessed to me.* Now it is Youssef's turn to be confused and annoyed. *What? Do I really have to do that?* Straight away he tries to reason within himself. *This is utter nonsense. Why should I apologize to a complete stranger? Besides, the guy was more rude. I restrained myself and did not even tell him that it is he who is misled and not me.*

Youssef's mind swings between humility and self-defense. For one reason or another, the thought that he should apologize remains at the forefront in his mind. Common sense tells him, "Don't be silly!" But then there is that other voice, "Didn't you want this man to know Me?" Youssef is convicted.

Meanwhile, Ahmed has found the site he had initially been searching for. He is completely engrossed in one of the articles on the website, when a familiar beep signals an incoming message on chat. At first, he tries to ignore it, but finally his curiosity wins out.

---

* *Kafir* is the Arabic word for an unbeliever, someone who denies the existence of God. The term is also used by some groups of Muslims for Christians, Jews, and other Muslims who believe differently.

** According to the teachings of Islam, *haram* is the Arabic word for 'unlawful' or 'not permitted'.

Welcome111: I want to apologize; what I wrote to you was not pleasing to God.

Ahmed is taken aback and thinks, *what does he mean?* He immediately types in his question. A few seconds later, the reply appears.

Welcome111: I did not write to you in love and respect. Jesus asks us to love one another. That is why I apologize for the way in which I answered your question.

For a moment, Ahmed is touched; he has never even met anything like that before, but then he remembers something his father and his uncles used to tell him, "See, the Christians are weak. They do not stand up for what they believe."

Truth be told, Ahmed thinks the Christian did owe him an apology; after all, he had used the Qur'an to reprimand him about his faith: an unacceptable offense. And yet, something makes him uncomfortable. Admitting one's own weakness can also be a sign of great strength. Saudis, however, rarely do so; he knows that only too well. Ahmed senses that 'Welcome111' is sincere.

Peace2012: No problem.

Then he asks a serious question, straight from his heart.

Downhearted, Youssef leans back in front of the monitor as he waits for a reply. He is ashamed over his own weakness. *At least he cannot see me; it would have made things worse.* Finally, another message comes through. Youssef's heart skips a beat.

37 The Forbidden Book

Youssef can hardly believe his eyes when he reads the incoming message.

Peace2012: What does the Book* say about the death of Jesus? And what are your thoughts on this?

He re-reads the message, just to make sure he is not imagining things. It seems this man really wants to know what the Christian faith is all about. Besides, he is asking specifically what the Bible says. Youssef asks God for wisdom before he begins to write. Once the message is sent, he smiles. He looks forward to the Muslim's reply.

This is unimaginable! I cannot believe it! Ahmed is speechless. *Could this really be true? Could there really be more than three hundred prophecies about the Messiah in the Book?* A small voice inside his head warns him, "See? They have changed the Scriptures." Of course! Now he understands how Christians can make such outrageous claims. Straightaway, he puts his thought into a message and presses the "Send" button.

Peace2012: It is because you Christians have changed the *injil*.**

Welcome111: I'm not talking about the New Testament but about the Old Testament. This part of the Bible was written by the Jews and was in existence before there were any Christians.

Ahmed doesn't understand. He has never even heard about an Old or a New Testament, but it doesn't really matter. For all he knows, the Jews changed their books as well. Ahmed writes down his thoughts and clicks 'send'. Shortly afterwards, a new message appears on his screen.

Welcome111: The Old Testament is the name for all Bible books written before the Messiah was born, namely the Torah, the Psalms of David, and the books of the Prophets. Just like Muslims would not allow anyone to change the Qur'an, Jews would never permit someone to rewrite

---

* In the Quran, the Bible is referred to as "the Book"

** *Injil* is the Arabic word for the New Testament. For information about the misunderstanding that it would have been changed, see www.godlovesishmael.com/injil

the Torah or any of the other books, neither would the Christians allow the Jews to alter the injil. God himself protects his books.

Ahmed has to admit that the Christian has made a valid point. The Qur'an says that God preserves his books and that no one can change his word.[139] But the imam explained that too: only the books in heaven have remained unchanged. Ahmed fingers fly across the keyboard as he formulates his response.

Peace2012: That is why God sent us the last prophet and made sure the final book, the Qur'an, would not be changed.

Welcome111: Does this mean you believe that God was not capable of preserving the laws of Moses on earth?

The question startles Ahmed. *Of course I believe God can do this; He is God Almighty!* He doesn't want to put that in writing though, because it would look like he's admitting that the Christian is right. Instead, he asks him for some examples of prophecies about the Messiah.

With increasing interest he examines the texts from the Psalms and other books in the Bible the Christian sends him. Following each passage is a section from the *injil*, confirming the fulfillment of the prophecies in the life of Jesus, the Messiah. *It is indeed a miracle of God!*

Then he reads the next message from Welcome111. "The prophet Isaiah spoke very clearly about the suffering of God's Servant. He bore our sins."

Ahmed knows that this is impossible. No one can carry the iniquities and sins of another. On the Day of Judgment, everyone has to account for his or her own deeds. He decides to write that to the Christian.

Youssef was expecting a response along those lines and proceeds to explain why he believes the Servant of God bore the sins of all people. First, he mentions Adam and Eve, who were expelled from Paradise, after committing just one offense. Then he writes:

Welcome111: The Torah describes how God immediately helped them to lighten the resulting burden of their sin. He sacrificed an animal and clothed them with its skin. In this way, an innocent creature suffered in order to cover up their shame. God then promised Eve that someone would come from her offspring who would crush the serpent's head. But first, that snake would hurt him.

Curious to see what the Muslim thinks about this, Youssef ends his message with a question.

Ahmed reads the comments in the chat box with fascination. He tries to think of an article he read online not so long ago. Before that, he had never given the story of Adam and Eve much thought. *Whatever it was they did, it does not have much to do with us, except that it had been their fault we don't live in Paradise anymore,* he had always reasoned. But the article had addressed the fact that many diseases, such as diabetes, AIDS, and even color-blindness, are passed on from parents to their children. The writer of the article explained that, much in the same way, the children of Adam and Eve inherited their sinful inclinations from their parents. Cain, their son, even committed the first murder. Ultimately, all of humanity has been infected by sin, which caused mankind to be separated from God.

Ahmed comes back to the message about the animal God sacrificed and the snake that would hurt the offspring of the woman. These concepts are difficult, so very different from the Qur'an where things are described more simply, more clearly. The theology of Islam is easy to explain to unbelievers*, but the things he is reading sound very complicated. Strangely, Ahmed feels like he wants to know more. At the end of the message there is a question.

Welcome111: Who do you think 'the offspring of the woman' refers to?

The first thing that comes to mind is the prophet Jesus, who is born from the virgin Mary. He tries to think of other possibilities, but can't bring one to mind.

Peace2012: It must be about Jesus (peace be upon him).

Youssef, meanwhile, prays. "Lord, open his eyes to the Good News. You truly died and rose from the dead for every Muslim in the whole world, also for 'Peace2012'." He would like to know the man's real name and decides to ask him.

At first Ahmed hesitates, but then he realizes there are thousands of other men in the world with the same name, so why not give his real name.

Peace2012: Ahmed. And what is your name?
Welcome111: Youssef.

---

* See www.godlovesishmael.com/doctrines

Now that the ice is broken and the chat feels a little more personal, Ahmed asks about what happened between the woman and the snake. A few minutes later, Youssef's answer appears.

Welcome111: Jesus is indeed the offspring of the woman. At the end of time, the Messiah will settle the score with Satan. But before that, he had to suffer at the hand of the archenemy of God.

This is similar to the teaching of Islam. Ahmed can hardly contain his excitement as he writes back.

Peace2012: At the end of time, the Messiah will return to kill the antichrist. He, just like all the other prophets, has suffered many injustices in the world.

After Ahmed reads Youssef's next message, he is disappointed.

Welcome111: The Messiah suffered because he went to the cross willingly, laid down his life willingly, and died a martyr's death willingly. Because He, an innocent man, died in our place, God forgives us our sins.

How is it possible for Christians to continue to see these things so differently, after we have received the last revelation from Allah in the Qur'an? And yet, they are deeply convinced. A well-known text from the Qur'an comes to Ahmed's mind: "You will surely find the most intense of the people in animosity toward the believers [to be] the Jews and those who associate others with Allah; and you will find the nearest of them in affection to the believers those who say, "We are Christians." That is because among them are priests and monks and because they are not arrogant."[140]

Ahmed comes to the conclusion that of all religions, the Christians are indeed closest to Islam – closer than the Jews and idol worshippers.

On the one hand, his curiosity about the Christian faith lingers, but on the other hand, he finds their religion too confusing. The Qur'an clearly states that Jesus did not die on the cross.[141] Ahmed would prefer to forget about the whole thing.

"Allahu Akbááár!"* The call to prayer resounds throughout the city, echoing between the walls and the houses. Ahmed turns his computer off, walks over to the bathroom and washes his head, hands, and feet according to

---

* Arabic for "God is greater," the beginning of the Islamic call to prayer

the tenets of Islam. Moments later, he picks up his prayer rug and unrolls it routinely in the direction of Mecca. Barefoot, he steps from the soft carpet onto the small rug to start his evening prayers. He habitually recites the first chapter of the Qur'an. "… It is You we worship and You we ask for help. Guide us to the straight path."[142]

As he softly mumbles the words, he suddenly realizes what he is asking for. *I really want this!* In the meantime, he mutters the last part of the chapter, "the path of those upon whom You have bestowed favor, not of those who have evoked your anger or of those who are astray."[143]

Because of his exchanges with Youssef, he starts to see these things in a new light. *Why do so many Muslims fight one another, while the Christian nations in Europe and America are at peace with each other? Why do many Islamic nations hate the West, even though they are taking in Arabs, fleeing from our wars? And why is our own county so dependent upon western technology? What is the reason that we, the Arabs, have not invented anything? We do not even produce our own cars or planes.* Ahmed is startled. *It seems like the Christians have received greater favor from God than us Muslims!*

Then he remembers the imam had also explained this, "The Western nations are only rich and successful because they have robbed us. During the colonial days they plundered our land, and nowadays they send their armies to try to take our oil. In this world the *kuffaar** thrive, but in the afterlife, God will judge them for their immorality. God will bless us because we have used the oil profits to bring the whole world under Islam." Ahmed fully agrees with the Imam's words. *What happens when the oil runs out though? What then?* He cannot get the thought out of his head. Doubt and feelings of restlessness fill his heart.

As he continues to ponder that question, he suddenly pictures himself again as a twelve-year-old boy in front of his Qur'an teacher. "God's wrath rests upon the Jews and the Christians who have gone astray. God has bestowed his favor upon us Muslims." Then it had been as clear as daylight, but now this explanation seems inadequate. *If America is really that evil, why does everyone want to live there? Why does his own uncle have an American passport and why does he prefer to do business with Westerners rather than with Arabs?* Suddenly, Ahmed has an idea. On finishing his mandatory prayers, he puts the rug away and returns to his computer.

Boy, that is an interesting question! I have never had it before. Youssef is happily surprised by what Ahmed has asked. But how should he answer?

As he focuses on what the Bible says about God's favor, he tries to recollect a familiar verse he used to know by heart. After searching for a while

---

* Plural of *kafir* – the Arabic word for unbeliever

on the internet, one verse in particular jumps out at him. "The steadfast love of the Lord never ceases; his mercies never come to an end."[144] Thinking it might be an appropriate verse to answer Ahmed's query, Youssef copies and pastes it into the chat box. He then reads the next few verses. "The Lord is good to those who wait for him, to the soul who seeks him. It is good that one should wait quietly for the salvation of the Lord."[145] Youssef smiles. *How timely and fitting is God's word, not only for Ahmed, but also for me. He may know that God is good to those who earnestly seek him, and I may wait patiently on the Lord for Ahmed's salvation.*

Before hitting the 'send' button, Youssef reads the question one more time. It says, "What do you think is the meaning of, 'The path of those upon whom You have bestowed favor'?" *The word 'bestowed' means that something beautiful has been given, something you do not deserve. It is grace,* Youssef concludes. *And grace is all about Jesus.*

Suddenly he remembers something he read that very morning. *Where was it?* He scours his Arabic Bible program, finds the verse he is looking for and adds it to his initial reply. After writing a few more words, he closes with, "God bless you, your friend Youssef."

Ahmed's eyes dart across the screen. When he gets to the bottom, he remains fixated on the words he reads.

Welcome111: "For from his fullness we have all received, grace upon grace. For the law was given through Moses; grace and truth came through Jesus Christ."[146]

Ahmed is really touched. Before he continues reading, he takes a deep breath.

Welcome111: God's grace is sufficient for all, but only those who accept Jesus Christ as their Savior can experience his grace. All who believe that Jesus died in their place receive forgiveness of sin solely on the basis of Jesus' sacrifice. That is grace! You receive something you do not deserve.

How Ahmed longs for this! For such a long time, he has been feeling an inexplicable emptiness in his heart. No matter how faithfully he fulfills his Islamic duties, God always seems far away. In the words he just read he tastes something of a God who desires to be near him, without him having to perform good works to earn his favor. *Could this really be true?* As Ahmed reads on, he is struck by the words again.

Welcome111: If you ever have the chance, please read the Gospel of
John. And ask God to reveal the truth to you.

*This is incredible! This is just what I purposely asked God for when I was
saying my Islamic prayers.* Excitedly, Ahmed opens a new internet page. His
hands become sweaty from the tension he feels and his fingers stick to the
keys as he types, 'the Holy Book' in the search box. For the first time in his
life, he is about to read in the book of the Christians. *What would the Imam
say if he knew? What would my family think?* A Qur'anic verse comes to mind.
"So if you are in doubt, [O Muhammad], about that which We have revealed
to you, then ask those who have been reading the Scripture before you. The
truth has certainly come to you from your Lord, so never be among the
doubters."[147] *I do not want to be a doubter,* Ahmed realizes and he concludes it
is a good thing to read the Holy Book.

Several links to the Arabic Bible appear on the screen. Ahmed opens
the top one, but now he is confused. How is he supposed to find the Gospel
of John? He cannot locate 'John', or 'Gospel of John' or even *'Surah* John',
just the words: 'choose the *sifr'.* Ahmed has no clue what that means. Underneath, he notices the option to do a word search. He types, 'grace', and
immediately a long list of Bible references appears. Ahmed begins to scan
the list enthusiastically, but soon gets lost. Not wanting to give up, he opens
a dictionary and starts to look for the meaning of the word *sifr. Aha, 'part of
a book'. So that is how I will find the Gospel of John.*

A little while later, a Bible verse pops up on his screen. Ahmed reads,
"In the beginning was the Word, and the Word was with God, and the Word
was God."[148]

Interesting. The Qur'an calls Jesus the Word of God. Immediately, the *aya* in
question comes to mind as clear as day. "Christ Jesus the son of Mary was
(no more than) a messenger of Allah, and his Word, which He bestowed on
Mary, and a spirit proceeding from Him."[149]

"What are you doing?" an angry voice sounds.

Startled, Ahmed quickly turns around. His oldest brother is standing
behind him, reading the lines on the computer screen over his shoulder. As
Ahmed feels the blood drain from his face, little droplets of sweat start to
bead on his forehead. Since the shutters are closed to block out the heat of
the day, he hopes the room's dimness will keep his brother from noticing his
flushed cheeks.

"I, eh, I am trying to convert a Christian to Islam," Ahmed splutters. He
tries hard to sound convincing but he feels very insecure.

"No need to read the book of those infidels for that!" his brother retorts
sharply. "You will bring shame on our family!"

Without batting an eye, Ahmed says, "I am studying their lies in order to better convince them of the truth of Islam." *How long has he been standing there? Was he right here, looking over my shoulder while I was still chatting with Youssef?* As he tries to calm down, he remembers checking whether the door was closed before he opened the Bible program. *Phew! He doesn't know about my chat.*

But as his brother scans the screen, his attention is drawn to the icon of the open chat program in the bottom bar.

"Let me see! What have you told this Christian dog?" he says as he grabs the mouse to open up the chat box.

38 A Special Appointment

"No, I have not heard back from Ahmed yet," Youssef says, as he talks with his cousin on Skype.

Noura detects disappointment in his voice and tries to encourage her cousin. "I pray for him every day," she responds.

As far as I'm concerned, it's not making any difference, Youssef thinks, but he is careful to keep his thoughts to himself. *If Noura is convicted to keep praying for Ahmed, let her do so. Even if nothing happens, it won't do any harm either.*

"I recently went to a fascinating lecture by a speaker from Lebanon," Noura continues. "He pointed out that God has a unique plan for the Arabs."

"Really?" Youssef responds with indifference. After all the setbacks, he has nearly given up hope that any Arab Muslim will ever come to accept Jesus Christ as their Lord and Savior. He thinks back to the last time he chatted with Ahmed. He had seemed open, but then he had suddenly stopped communicating. Apparently, he too, had not been interested after all.

"You know God promised Hagar that Ishmael would be a wild donkey of a man. We have always regarded this as something negative," Noura asserts. "According to that man it is actually a positive thing."

Youssef is familiar with the verse and has always found it difficult to understand. Now with piqued interest, he sits up straight in his chair. "What exactly did he say?"

"The speaker read to us from the book of Job, where the wild donkey is portrayed as an animal that lives in freedom. In that sense, it is quite the opposite of the domesticated donkeys that work like slaves for their masters.

Youssef thinks about the donkeys of his Bedouin relatives in the south of the country. Sometimes his great-uncle jokes about them, saying they are his other 'pick-up trucks'. The poor creatures always must obey. Even though, at times they can be stubborn beasts, the master always wins, and in the end, the donkeys do as they are told.

"Which verses was he referring to?" Youssef asks. His voice betrays his curiosity. After Noura gives him the Bible reference, Youssef deftly enters it in his Bible program. When the passage appears, he reads,

"Who has let the wild donkey go free?
Who has loosed the bonds of the swift donkey,
to whom I have given the arid plain for his home
and the salt land for his dwelling place?

He scorns the tumult of the city;
he hears not the shouts of the driver.
He ranges the mountains as his pasture,
and he searches after every green thing."[150]

"It is true; the wild donkey lives in freedom," Youssef agrees, "but what does that have to do with Ishmael?"

"Look for the parallels," Noura urges carefully. She is eager to explain everything she has recently learned to her cousin, but she does not want to appear pedantic in any way, shape, or form. It's not suitable for women to flaunt their knowledge at the expense of their male relatives. Therefore, she is content to give Youssef small hints and allow him to discover the connection for himself.

Not wanting to appear ignorant, Youssef tries his hardest to understand what Noura is referring to. "Mmm, the donkey dwells in the desert and so did Ishmael."

"Exactly, and what other similarities do you notice?" Noura affirms his findings enthusiastically.

"Ishmael must have searched for 'everything green' for his flocks, just like our Bedouin ancestors had to do."

"I believe so, too," Noura responds, "but there is something even more beautiful."

For a minute, Youssef remains silent. Then he gives up. Reluctantly, he says, "I don't see any other parallels."

"Hagar was a slave girl," Noura explains, "just like a domesticated donkey."

"Oh, now I see!" exclaims Youssef. "Ishmael became free!" Right away, his mood lifts. This understanding changes everything. It had always bothered him that the Bible seemed to speak rather negatively about his ancestor. "The picture of a wild donkey actually gives us a positive image then."

"Yes, and not only about Ishmael; this is about his descendants too, even the Arabs of today," adds Noura.

"What do you mean?" Youssef asks puzzled. He thinks about all the men named Abdallah, Abdul-Salaam, Abdul-Aziz,* and others he has gotten to know in the chat room. "Most Arabs are not free at all. Many Muslim names reflect their relationship with God, as in being 'slaves of Allah', and they are proud of it." As Youssef shares his thoughts with Noura, there is sadness in his voice again.

"Yet, this is a prophetic promise for the Arabs," Noura insists, as she

---

* The Arabic word Abd or Abdul means slave (of) or servant (of). When used in a compound name, such as mentioned here, the second part refers to one of the 99 names of God.

proceeds to tell him some of the other things she recently learned. Not only things that demonstrate God's love for Ishmael but also about unfulfilled prophecies of Isaiah and other prophets. She talks about prophecies with regards to the descendants of Ishmael, like Kedar and Nebaioth, and about how God used Arab men to bless Jesus while he was still very young.

Youssef continues to be amazed. "How is it possible that we've never seen this before?"

"I was wondering the same thing. Then the speaker explained it so clearly," Noura continues. "He pointed out that we, as Christians, have started to apply all God's promises for Israel, to ourselves. For centuries now, we have been seeing ourselves as the spiritual Israel."

Youssef agrees. Just a few weeks ago, the pastor preached about that. He said that the promises for Israel have been fulfilled in God's spiritual people: the Christians. He emphasized how beautiful it is that Jews and Arabs can be part of it too. Isn't this why he, Youssef, is so determined to tell the Muslims about Jesus?

But Noura hasn't finished. "Since the founding of the State of Israel, things have started to change, however. After that, more and more Christians have started to read the prophecies of the Old Testament in a different light and have come to believe they primarily refer to today's Jews."

Youssef is fully aware of these developments. Hardly a day goes by that he doesn't still feel pain over what happened in 1948. During the war, his grandfather had had to flee, leaving behind his land and farm in Palestine. The Jews took over and since that time they, the Palestinians, have been forced to live as second-class citizens in the neighboring countries. Filled with bitterness, he responds, "Thanks to the political and material support of the Christians in America and Europe, the Jews are able to do as they please with our land, while we have to live in exile in Amman."

Noura senses the pain in her cousin's words. She, too, knows the stories about Grandfather's flight. But since she moved away from the Middle East, she has been able to be more objective about the situation and she is convinced that both sides are responsible for the Palestinian refugee debacle. However, telling her cousin that would not help him now. "It's a difficult issue," she concedes, "but that is why I am so encouraged by what this professor taught us."

"Really?" Youssef remains skeptical. "What exactly did he say?"

"Well, just like God has a plan for the Jews, He also has a plan for us Arabs, descendants of Ishmael. Think about all the promises to the prophets we just talked about."

Youssef's thoughts go back to what Noura explained earlier about Kedar, Nebaioth and Sheba. It all sounds very plausible.

Noura continues, and says, "Look up Romans 9 and read verses 25 and 26."

Truth be told, Youssef does not really feel like continuing this conversation, but he does not want to hurt his cousin's feelings, so he takes his mouse and clicks on the Bible program. Within seconds, the text appears on his screen:

"Those who were not my people I will call 'my people',
and her who was not beloved I will call 'beloved.'
And in the very place where it was said to them, 'You are not my people,'
there they will be called 'sons of the living God.'"[151]

After he finishes reading the short passage, Youssef says, "See, now we, the Christians, are God's people; the new Israel."

"I used to see it that way too," Noura affirms, "but there is another way to understand these verses."

"How?"

"At first, Ishmael's descendants were not God's chosen people, but there comes a time they will be God's people. Imagine, Youssef, most Christians in the world do not exactly consider the Arabs loved ones, but God says he will call us 'his beloved'."

Youssef likes that idea. After giving it a little more thought, he asks, "Do you think the same thing goes for the Muslim Arabs?"

"Why don't you read chapter 10, verses 19 to 21?" Noura says encouragingly.

Moments later, Youssef reads out loud,

"But I ask, did Israel not understand? First Moses says,
'I will make you jealous of those who are not a nation;
With a foolish nation I will make you angry.'
Then Isaiah is so bold as to say,
'I have been found by those who did not seek me;
I have shown myself to those who did not ask for me.'
But of Israel he says, 'All day long I have held out my hands to a disobedient and contrary people.'"[152]

The first part about jealousy does not really speak to Youssef, but the rest resonates with him. "This is peculiar," he says, surprised, "God allows people who don't know him to find him?" As he lets the words sink in, the truth behind them suddenly becomes clear. "I had always thought that this was something to do with the past. So..." Youssef chokes, searching for the right words. "So then, God still reveals himself to people who reject the Messiah as their Savior?"

"Yes, isn't that wonderful?" his cousin affirms warmly. "Imagine, God revealing himself to Ahmed, without him contacting you ever again."

That thought strikes a chord in Youssef's heart and tears well up in his eyes. Could it be true? Would God really reveal himself to Ahmed? And to all the others with whom he has shared the Gospel? Would Jesus reveal himself to people who do not ask for him? Youssef remembers hearing people testify to such things. He knows about Muslims who had visions or dreams in which they saw Jesus. As he tells Noura his thoughts, she surprises him with her answer.

"This is exactly what I believe. I am convinced that God is at work, even now," she says firmly. "Think about what I told you concerning the encounter between Hagar and the angel. The professor explained that the angel was a manifestation of Jesus before he was born on earth. Hagar didn't look for God and yet He revealed himself to her through Jesus."

Overwhelmed by a joy that overrides his skepticism, Youssef exclaims, "God be praised! How great is our God! How loving and gracious! Noura, this is almost too good to be true."

"I thought just that at first," his cousin admits, "but it is all stated so clearly. And you know, this text shows that God has a special purpose in mind."

"Really? And what is that?" Youssef asks curiously.

"God wants to use us to make the Jews jealous."

"I don't understand."

"Well, didn't you just read about God holding out his hands to a disobedient people?"

Youssef reads the text again. It makes him think about the tensions between them and his own people, the Palestinians. "It is certainly true that the Jews are disobedient and rebellious," he concurs.

"One of the ways in which God wants to extend his hands to them is through us," Noura explains. "He wants to use Ishmael's descendants to make Isaac's descendants jealous."

The idea sounds interesting to Youssef. For the past fifty years they have looked on the nation of Israel with envy as it has been helped by the greatest powers in the world in every possible way. "It would be nice if the roles were reversed and, for a change, we were blessed more than the Jews," he states.

"That's not what I mean," Noura says quickly, "This is about spiritual blessings, rather than material blessings. Look at Romans 11:11."

Pressing a few short-cut keys, Youssef finds the verse in a flash and reads, "So I ask, did they stumble in order that they might fall? By no means!

Rather through their trespasses salvation has come to the Gentiles, so as to make Israel jealous."[153]

Carefully, he asks, "Are you implying that the Jews are to become jealous of the Arabs being saved?"

"Exactly! The church has had little success in this domain over the past two thousand years," Noura answers, "and now God wants to specifically use the Arabs to accomplish his purposes, even Ahmed and all the others you have been in touch with."

Her last words give Youssef some relief. Perhaps all his praying and witnessing has not been in vain. At the same time, it's strange to read these verses in a different way, for this explanation doesn't agree with church doctrine or what he has experienced. "I still don't completely follow," he sighs.

Noura continues, "What do you think would make the Jews really jealous?"

After thinking about that for a few seconds, Youssef begins to grin. "Suppose the Lord would bless their enemies, they probably wouldn't know what to do," he says jokingly. In his mind's eye, he can just picture it: Muslim extremists who start to follow Jesus begging the Jews for forgiveness for having wanted to wipe them off the map. A bizarre picture indeed!

"Precisely!" Noura affirms. The tone of her voice is dead serious. "Don't forget that the Arabs and the Jews are, in fact, half-brothers. The time has come during which God allows himself to be found by people who are not seeking him, including Muslim extremists. If God blesses them with a personal relationship with Jesus, they will experience true peace and stop fighting for the Palestinian land. You can bet your life that the Jews will become jealous."

Silence follows. As Youssef tries to let the words sink in, a question comes to mind. "Why does God want the Jews to become jealous? Does He want to punish them?"

"You will find the answer a little further down," his cousin replies. "Have a look at verses 25 and 26."

Promptly, Youssef scrolls to the twenty-fifth verse and reads, "A partial hardening has come upon Israel, until the fullness of the Gentiles has come in."[154]

He tries hard to process what it says. For a while, the Jews will refuse to bow down to Jesus, but when the fullness of the Gentiles has entered the kingdom of God, their hearts will change. When he reads the word 'Gentiles', the millions upon millions of Muslims come to mind. As of yet, they are outside God's Kingdom, even though they think they are pleasing God with what they believe are good works. *So, this is really going to happen then? Many Arabs are going to accept Jesus Christ as their Savior!*

Going on to the next verse, Youssef reads, "And in this way all Israel will be saved, as it is written, 'The Deliverer will come from Zion, he will banish ungodliness from Jacob.'"[155]

Youssef is shocked. *This cannot be true.* Anger surges in his heart. "All of Israel will be saved? That's impossible!" he exclaims. "God cannot and *should not* just wipe away all the injustices that they have made us suffer over the years. Isn't He a righteous God? Appalled by the idea and without giving Noura a chance to reply, he adds, "This cannot be applied literally to the Jewish people."

Noura understands it is painful for her cousin to accept this as God's plan. She too experienced personal rejection while she was living in Jordan. Not only was she bullied by her peers, but the teachers would discriminate against her, solely because she was a Palestinian refugee. It was all founded on the State of Israel being on their land! It's not surprising that her church in the Middle East teaches that these verses concern all the spiritual descendants of Abraham.

Because of her contact with students in the United States, she has gained a greater understanding of the other side. The Jews have been oppressed through the centuries, especially during World War II. They suffered immeasurably, like no other people on earth. Above all, Noura realizes that she is no better than they are. If God had not opened her eyes and her heart to his great love for her, she would have been lost as well. It is only by his grace that, in the midst of many temptations, she can remain faithful to him. And only by his grace is she able to forgive those who have hurt her. That is the reason that she, a Palestinian woman, is able to love the Jews as God's people. After all, Scripture is very clear. There is no doubt about it. Softly, almost whispering, she replies, "God's ways are mysterious and his love is everlasting."

For Youssef, this is going too far. He had some doubts early on in their conversation, but now… this beats it all. The tone of his voice is sharp, when he says to her, "You had better watch out, Noura! You are being brainwashed in America. So many Christians there are pro-Israel and do not understand the suffering of the Palestinian people. They blindly support the Jewish cause because they believe the Jews are God's chosen people."

Noura feels misunderstood and lonely. She had hoped her conversation with her cousin would have been encouraging to both of them, but now the distance between them seems larger than ever. "The things I am telling you… I didn't learn these from Americans, but from a Lebanese man, who clearly understands the Middle Eastern dynamics," Noura says defensively.

"In that case, he is just as blinded as the rest of them," Youssef curtly replies.

Noura tries to save the situation by pleading with her cousin to re-read the verses prayerfully.

"You want me to be brainwashed as well? That's not going to happen!" Youssef has made up his mind. When Noura returns home for summer break, he will take her to his pastor. Surely, he will be able to talk sense into her.

A few minutes later, they say 'goodbye'. Both feel the pain of emotional distance in their hearts.

Noura prays for her cousin, "Oh Lord, please, make him understand Your unique plan for the Arabs as well as for the Jews. In Jesus' name. Amen."

In the meantime, Youssef stares at the screen, with a deep frown on his face. He is worried about his cousin. *She has gone crazy. She has become one of those insane fanatics!*

Musing a little about this and that, he suddenly hears a beeping sound. Someone is sending him a chat message. Although he is not exactly in the mood right now, he dutifully clicks on the blinking bar on his screen. There he reads, 'New message from User136'. Someone new is trying to contact him. He does not need this now and clicks 'cancel' without a further thought.

Two days later, as Youssef opens the chat program on his computer, there is another incoming message from that unfamiliar contact.

User136: Hello, Youssef!

This alerts him. *How does this new person know my name? Is someone watching me? Could it be a government spy or perhaps an informant from one of the Islamic fundamentalist groups?* He seriously considers blocking the contact, but then his curiosity gets the better of him and he decides to write a short reply.

Welcome111: Hello, who are you?
User 136: I have missed you.

Youssef wonders who would write such a thing, but he can't think who it could be.

Welcome111: Who are you?
User136: I am your friend from the south. I need to speak with you. It is urgent.

My friend from the south? Youssef feels uncomfortable. That sounds suspicious. He automatically jumps to the conclusion: *Of course! It's a spy who works for the security forces and is acting as if I know him.* Amidst growing feelings of doubt and fear, Youssef doesn't really know what to say. He has been threatened before in the chat room. Clearly, not everyone is pleased with what he does. "God, please, protect me," he prays softly. Peace fills his heart and he decides not to block this user after all, but talking to him goes too far. He never gives out his phone number to strangers. You never know whether someone might be trying to set him up as he is actively involved in sharing the Gospel online.

Welcome111: What do you want from me?
User136: I cannot speak about it now, but I will soon be coming to your country for a vacation and want to meet you.

Puzzled by the perseverance of this stranger, Youssef would really prefer to ignore him. But when he focuses on the Lord, he feels a certain calmness, despite all his doubts. He realizes he must be dealing with someone from another country, a foreigner, and that thought helps him to make his decision. He gives him his mobile phone number. It is something he would have never done for a Jordanian.

User136: A thousand times thank you! Hope to see you soon!
Welcome111: With peace.
User136: With peace.

Youssef stares at the words. *In sha Allah.**

---

* *In sha Allah* means God willing. Arabs often use it to express their hope or desire.

A cacophony of honking cars and loud motorcycles rings from the large roundabout.

Youssef doesn't notice, as he is used to the noises of the city. The screeching tires of impatient drivers on the oily asphalt don't bother him either. The black tarmac, that drinks in the sweltering heat of the sun every day, is richly decorated with stripes of rubber from the cars and trucks. White taxis constantly come and go.

As Youssef watches the constant stream of people moving around like ants on an anthill, he wonders what they all might be thinking about? Men, dressed in smart three-piece suits and briefcases in hand, hurry to work. Women, clothed according to the latest fashion and with fancy handbags neatly tucked under their arms, disappear into the shops, only to reappear after a few minutes. An old woman, hunched over with scoliosis, shuffles along the narrow sidewalk. The crumpled plastic bag in her hand tells Youssef she is on her way to the bakery for freshly baked bread.

A little while later, a woman, covered in black from head to toe turns in his direction. Carrying an infant on her left arm and holding a small boy with her right hand, she lazily strolls through the park gate where Youssef is sitting on a bench. As the dark figure passes him, Youssef begins to feel unsettled. Just like that woman, hidden behind her veil, the stranger who he has agreed to meet with, remain a mystery. All he can do is wait for the man who he gave his phone number to and who called him yesterday, to meet up with him.

Feeling his heart pounding in his chest, Youssef traces little circles with his foot in the dusty gravel. *Thankfully, Noura is praying for me now. Hopefully she didn't not forget.* "Please, Lord, protect me. Whoever this Ahmed is, and whatever his intentions may be, I pray that You work in his heart. I commit myself to you and lay this meeting in your hand, o God."

For the umpteenth time, Youssef nervously checks the time on his watch. It is past ten o'clock. *We had agreed to meet at nine. Perhaps he is not coming after all. I will give it a few more minutes and then I will go home. Maybe God did not want me to meet him after all.*

A yellow taxi comes to a halt right in front of the park entrance. These ones do not follow a fixed route through the city, like the cheaper white ones that Youssef always uses. He wishes he had the means to use these private taxis. It would save him the hassle of changing from one route to another, and he would never have to be crammed into the back seat with two or three other passengers. Youssef tries to see who is in the yellow cab. *He must be a wealthy man.*

As the door opens, a tall man, dressed in a spotless white robe, reaching his ankles, gets out of the car. His head is covered with a red and white-checkered cloth, which is kept in place by a black cord. His eyes are hidden behind a pair of designer sunglasses. Youssef immediately recognizes him as a Saudi. *Could it be him?* The park rarely attracts tourists this early in the morning. That is why he had picked this place. He wanted to limit the chances of approaching the wrong person.

Trying to be inconspicuous, the man wanders aimlessly into the park. Turning his head this way and that, he checks out the surroundings. Then Youssef gets up, walks towards the stranger and greets him, "Peace be with you! Can I help you?"

The Saudi man looks him in the eyes and asks softly, "Youssef?"

"Yes, I am he," Youssef confirms and then he asks, "Who are you?" He purposely avoids asking him whether he is the man from the south to make sure he is indeed the man he has agreed to meet.

Maintaining his guard, the stranger replies, "I am the one who called you yesterday."

Youssef is not reassured, but decides to take a risk. Though the man's voice is different from when he spoke with him on the phone, he unmistakably recognizes the same Saudi accent. "Welcome to Amman," he says amicably and offers him his hand.

Instead of just shaking his hand, the tall Saudi man pulls Youssef towards him and kisses him on the cheek and shoulder. After this warm greeting, he takes Youssef's other hand, and together they enter the park. "Where can we talk quietly?" he asks.

Youssef now faces a dilemma. If they isolate themselves, this stranger could easily overpower and hurt him. But if he wants to share his faith with this man, they had better find a location where no one can hear them talk. In a flash, he decides on a place where they will be visible to the public, but out of earshot. "Come, this way," he replies, as he leads his guest to a park bench at a safe distance from prying eyes and ears.

Thousands of miles away, on the other side a world, a woman has difficulty falling asleep. She gets up, kneels by her bed, and prays, "Father, please protect Youssef today and give him the words to say. I am asking you in Jesus' name." Finally, convinced that God has heard her prayers, she falls into a peaceful sleep.

Meanwhile, the man tells Youssef, "One day, I awoke, and when I opened the shutters, suddenly a bright light shone into my room. It was so much brighter than the sun, even lighting up the wall opposite the window. When I looked outside, I noticed something that resembled a man's face, but his countenance was so radiant I couldn't bear to look at it for long."

Youssef can hardly believe his ears. He tenses the muscles in his feet to make sure he is not dreaming. Sitting next to him is Ahmed! The man he chatted with a few months ago, has suddenly turned up out of nowhere. As he listens to him, he cannot help but think: *Is he telling the truth, or is this a trap? Perhaps Ahmed is playing a game trying to catch me. And yet, why would he go through so much trouble to come and see me all the way in Jordan? Hmmm... didn't Paul also go all the way to Damascus to persecute the Christians? I should probably expect the same zeal from an Islamic extremist.*

"Then I heard a voice through the window saying, "Follow Me!" I didn't know what was happening and closed my eyes. When I opened them, the man had disappeared. Since my room is on the second floor, I right away threw my window wide open to check if there wasn't a ladder, but I didn't see anything unusual. I didn't dare speak to anyone about this, but I have been greatly troubled for weeks now. I thought of you and was hoping you would be able to help me out. Who do you think it could have been?"

When Youssef looks at him he only sees his own reflection in the man's sunglasses. But he feels as if the eyes behind those shades are piercing him to the bone and it makes him feel uneasy. After a quick, silent prayer for wisdom, a Bible verse Noura pointed out to him recently, comes to mind: "I have been found by those who did not seek me; I have shown myself to those who did not ask for me."[156]

Now I understand, Youssef thinks and he answers, "It was Jesus who appeared to you."

"Do you mean the Prophet Jesus?" Ahmed asks puzzled. "That is quite impossible, isn't it? Why would he reveal himself to me, an ordinary Muslim? These kinds of things happened only to the prophets."

Compassion replaces the fear in Youssef's heart. Once again, he realizes how difficult it must be for a Muslim to see God and faith in a different light from the teaching they have received all their lives at the mosques. Suddenly, he thinks about Paul's conversion and he just knows he has to tell Ahmed the story. "Once there was a zealous man who was convinced he was doing God's work by imprisoning and killing the followers of Jesus. One day, however, while he was on his way to Damascus, a blinding light shone around him. He was forced to stop, fell to the ground, and heard a voice saying, 'I am Jesus.' Even though Paul's hands were drenched in innocent blood, Jesus chose to appear to him."

"So, you really believe that the man outside my window was Jesus?" Ahmed asks with growing amazement.

"I'm absolutely sure!" Youssef grins emphatically. "There's something else. When he still lived on the earth, Jesus the Messiah would often say to people, 'Follow me,' just like he did to you!"

"God be praised!" Ahmed exclaims happily. "I have seen *Isa al-Masih.**" Startled by his own words, he quickly looks around. Someone might have heard. He should really be more careful. It is not wise for a man like him, an Arab from the country that carries the responsibility of protecting Islam, to say such a thing. He continues softly, "How can I do that? I mean, how can I follow Jesus?"

Youssef barely contains his excitement. For the first time in his life, he has been approached by a Muslim who openly dares to ask him this question. Has he not been dreaming about this moment? Many times he has thought about how to answer this question and so he immediately replies, "Jesus said, 'If you love me, you will keep my commandments.' Following Jesus, means doing what he says."

Ahmed understands. As a Muslim he is used to following the decrees of the Prophet who he is named for.** The problem is that he has no idea what the commandments of Jesus are. The Qur'an says very little about his teachings.

"You should be able to read about it in the *injil,*" Youssef continues.

Ahmed's mood drops. His short-lived joy is threatened by disappointment. "That's impossible," he reacts despondently.

Youssef pities the man sitting next to him. For a long time, he had doubted his sincerity, but now it seems he has been allowed to look into his heart. *Perhaps we are closer than I could have ever dreamed.* Again, he is reminded of a Bible verse, "… until all of God's non-Jewish people are included."[157] Even though Christians and Muslims have lived in their own separate worlds for centuries, they have something in common: both are non-Jews. *Interestingly, I have always considered myself part of a spiritual Israel, while I actually belong to the non-Jews. Perhaps, Paul's letter to the Romans does speak about a physical Israel. Maybe Noura is right after all.*

After these musings, Youssef refocuses on their conversation and he asks Ahmed, "Why is that not possible?"

Ahmed decides to tell him the whole story. "No one knows this about me," he emphasizes. "You are the first one with whom I've shared it."

Youssef is honored to have gained Ahmed's trust. He knows how un-

---

* *Isa al-Masih* is the Islamic Arabic wording for Jesus the Messiah

** The names Ahmed, Hamed, Hameed, Hamoud and Mahmoud, have all been derived from the name Mohammed

usual it is in his culture to confide in someone. It would make you vulnerable and you always want people to think you are in control. You might possibly share your deepest thoughts and feelings with a close friend but never with your family and most certainly not with strangers.

Ahmed then confides to Youssef about how his brother had unexpectedly entered his room while he was chatting with a Christian and how his brother had found out what their conversations were about.

"That same evening, he told my father about it," Ahmed tells him. "My father was livid and threatened to take my phone and my computer away and, if necessary, lock me in my room if I ever dared contact the Christian again. No matter the implications, the honor of Islam must be upheld at any cost. Because of my doubts and my questions, my father was fearful that I would bring shame on our entire family."

Youssef nods. He understands the situation well. He is familiar with many cases where father or brothers have ostracized or even killed their closest relatives for wanting to follow the Messiah.

"That is when I decided to no longer chat with you," Ahmed continues, "but then came the uncanny appearance at my window and I simply *had* to talk to someone about it. I couldn't think of anyone but you."

Deeply moved, Youssef is at a loss for words. *That's why Ahmed stopped chatting to him.* Suddenly, it all becomes clear: why Ahmed approached him under a different username and why he acted so secretively. *I know from experience how challenging it is to live as a Christian in the Middle East. It must be infinitely more difficult for someone like Ahmed.* Any lingering doubts about Ahmed's sincerity melt away and instead, Youssef's heart is filled with empathy for this fellow-Arab. *There must be a way for Ahmed to read the Bible. God wouldn't leave him in the dark, would He?*

'Allahu Akbar! Allahu Akbar!' The words of the muezzin in countless minarets around town echo between the high-rise buildings next to the park. The melodious chant of the familiar call to prayer interrupts the conversation. Startled, Ahmed realizes it is time for the afternoon prayer. He hasn't finished talking with Youssef, but duty calls. Quickly, he excuses himself from his new friend. Moments later, he leaves the park and turns towards the mosque across from the roundabout.

Mesmerized by this unusual meeting, Youssef follows the Saudi man with his eyes. What a privilege! Though he didn't get to see the eyes of this Arab Muslim, he was allowed a peek into his heart. There are still many questions, yet Youssef thanks God for this turn of events.

Thank you, Lord, for revealing yourself to Ahmed, Youssef prays in his heart. *Please, complete the work You have begun in his life.* He has barely finished when he hears a still, small voice, "Do not be afraid, trust in Me. I will accomplish this." Youssef feels encouraged, though at the same time sadness is in his heart. Finally, here is someone who really wants to learn from him, yet he seems so out of reach. *Will I ever see him again?*

"You see?" Noura exclaims enthusiastically, "it's exactly the way it is written in the Bible!"

Yousef thinks his cousin is a bit too pedantic. Now that he has allowed the passages of Scripture in Romans to sink into his heart, he is no longer upset with his cousin. But to claim his *one* meeting with just *one* Muslim as such strong evidence for her position goes too far. "Ahmed is just one of millions, Noura," he protests over their Skype connection.

His cousin, however, doesn't give up so easily. "One in a million as far as you know," she says laughingly. Lately, Noura has recently been delving into Scripture and now, she is convinced more than ever that God is going to save many Muslims.

"Why don't you tell me then how many you know of that have come to Christ?" Youssef asks defensively.

That's a hard one. Noura doesn't personally know any, but then she says with wisdom, "The most important thing is that God knows."

Her answer doesn't satisfy Youssef, and he declares with firmness, "Talk is easy! If it were really true, we should be able to see some fruit."

Noura has no desire to give in just yet. "I know Palestinian Muslims who have had the same experience. One of them even used to be a terrorist."

"What? And you're telling me this now?" Youssef exclaims with surprise.

A little less eagerly, Noura admits she does not actually know them personally. "But I heard about them. I even read the life story of Tass Saada in his book, *Once an Arafat Man.*"

"You shouldn't believe everything that people write," Youssef retorts.

"I completely agree with you there," Noura concurs. "My teachers often point this out to us. I was curious about this Saada and looked him up online. What I found there seemed reliable enough. Whatever the story is, I firmly believe that it is within God's plan to redeem many millions of Muslims and your friend, Ahmed, is one of them."

Youssef cannot deny that last part. It has been nothing less than amazing to see how Jesus revealed himself to Ahmed and how Ahmed now wants to accept him as Lord. Thinking about all this, he remembers a question he had wanted to ask his cousin earlier. "Do you have any thoughts on the passage in Galatians where Paul writes about Ishmael and Isaac? It says that the son of the bondswoman persecuted the son of the free woman, which clearly puts Ishmael in an unfavorable light, don't you think?"

"Funny that you mention this," Noura laughs "Just last week I spent some time going over those verses."

"And? What is your conclusion?"

"Wait just a second while I get my notes."

Youssef hears some shuffling and rustling sounds through the loud-speakers on his computer. While he waits for Noura to come back to the screen, he opens another web browser to search for Tass Saada. As he googles his name, a long list with a host of websites appears. To his surprise, Youssef reads that Saada has his own organization.

Immediately, he clicks on that website and reads what the Palestinian ex-terrorist envisions: "Our heart is to reconcile Muslims to the Father and then to all people through the Gospel of Jesus Christ."[158]

Wow! There are entire organizations dedicated to this. Perhaps Noura has been right all along. Perhaps God has been doing a lot more than I realize.

"Okay, I am back," the familiar voice calls out. "Let me see. Well, to begin with, this is not at all about Ishmael."

"What do you …?" Youssef interrupts her.

Noura, ignoring him, continues, "It's only an illustration about life under the law versus life under grace."

"Yes, but Ishmael is clearly mentioned by name here," Youssef interjects.

Noura begins to laugh. "Perhaps the Lord has a sense of humor. If you look closely, you will see that Ishmael refers to the Jews here, while Isaac represents the Greek Galatians. The normal references have been switched."

Youssef is quite lost. "Wasn't Ishmael the son of the bondswoman and Isaac the son of the free woman?"

"Yes, but here, the Jews who maintained the pre-eminence of the Mosaic Law are being called slaves, while the non-Jews, the Gentiles, who put their trust in Jesus Christ are considered free, as living under grace."

"Wow! I have never seen it in this way before!" Youssef exclaims. "That does sound plausible."

Pleased that her cousin is so receptive to this interpretation, Noura takes it a step further. "There are so many beautiful parallels for us Arabs in this book. For example, in Galatians 3:13 it says that Christ has redeemed us. Does that not remind you of a passage in the book of Job, something we talked about before?"

For a moment, Youssef is silent. Then, cautiously, he says, "Do you mean, 'God sets the wild donkey free'?" As the words tumble out of his mouth, he suddenly makes an interesting discovery. "Noura!" he says loudly, "It's truly remarkable that God said to Job that the wild donkeys were not free at first, but that they had been freed later on!"

"Hey, no need to shout, cousin! You will break my speakers!" Noura says mildly irritated.

"Just turn the volume down then," Youssef says with a laugh, but he does tone his voice down a little.

"What was it that you said just now?" Noura asks.
Youssef repeats his observation and continues, "I have never heard of wild sheep or cows. God did say to Job, however, that He set the wild donkeys free. Apparently, they had not been free before; they must have been domesticated animals that were subject to their masters."

Now, it is Noura's turn to be surprised. She can see the parallel between Ishmael, the wild donkey of a man, whom God freed from his fate as the son of a bondswoman and the underlying reference to all Arabs who are still slaves to a religious system of rules and regulations. "Wow, Youssef! This is beautiful! I would like to discuss these things with my Lebanese lecturer. I am curious to see what he has to say about it; I think I will e-mail him immediately."

Youssef is excited. Flattered by what his cousin has said, he wonders if he has discovered something no other Bible scholar has noticed before. While Noura is typing away on her keyboard, Youssef allows his thoughts to go back to the passage about Ishmael and Isaac in Galatians. He looks up the verse in question and reads, "He who was born according to the flesh persecuted him who was born according to the Spirit."[159] Youssef cannot help but being drawn to the word 'persecuted' and the happiness over his discovery fades away. It is such a strong word. He asks Noura if she can explain.

"It is a tricky point indeed," she concedes. "You must understand that this is not the same word that is used in Genesis. The Hebrew word literally means, 'laugh, play, or mock'. It definitely does not have the same negative connotation as 'persecute'.

"Okay, I understand that, but why did Paul then say to the Galatians that Ishmael 'persecuted' his little brother?"

After checking her notes, Noura answers, "Actually, Paul used a Greek word with several possible meanings. That word can sometimes be translated as 'persecute', but also can mean simply 'follow' or 'pursue', without any hint of violence."*

"That's interesting!" But why would the Bible translators have chosen to use the word 'persecute', instead of 'follow', which as you said earlier would be more in line with the translation of the Hebrew 'play' in Genesis.

"According to some traditions, Ishmael threatened Isaac with a bow and arrow," Noura explains. "This, together with the things Arabs have commit-

---

* For more information, please consult www.godlovesishmael.com/galatians4

ted in the name of Islam, have influenced the Bible translators to choose the word 'persecute' as the proper interpretation of the original Greek.

"If I understand correctly, this passage in Galatians does not necessarily put us in a bad light?" Youssef concludes thoughtfully. "But… what was Paul trying to say then?"

"This entire epistle addresses the fact that doing good works according to the Law of Moses cannot get you into heaven. The Law is like a mirror, showing us our inability to keep it. Without Christ, we become slaves to its rules and regulations. Instead, we are to believe the promise of God that in Christ we receive forgiveness for all our bad deeds," Noura states, "and yet there were Jewish believers who mixed grace with the law and taught that people should continue to keep certain commandments of the law in order to be saved. Paul used this particular example to make it clear that people are saved by grace, not by keeping the law. For the same reason, God told Abraham, many centuries ago, to do what Sarah asked in sending Ishmael and his mother Hagar away."

"Wait a minute. That sounds as if God did not really want to send Ishmael away," Youssef observes.

Noura smiles. She delights in her cousin's sharp mind. "True, nowhere is it written that God ordered Abraham to send Ishmael away. Only when Sarah complained, and Abraham asked God to help him in that situation, did He say anything."

"That makes the whole thing Sarah's fault then," Youssef states. "If only she would have kept her mouth shut, we would never have been rejected as we are by Western Christians who now take side with the Jews."

Noura has no ready answer for this, but then she remembers something the Lebanese speaker, had said during one of his lectures. She scans her notes. "Ah, here it is! Professor Maalouf explained that God allowed Sarah's wishes to be fulfilled because He wanted to use these circumstances to accomplish his purposes."

"For me, that doesn't fit," Youssef replies. "If Sarah had not been so jealous in the first place, Ishmael could have stayed and continued to enjoy his father's love as well as the blessings God gave to Abraham."

"I don't know. Perhaps Abraham showed so much love to Ishmael that Sarah became frightened he would proclaim his first-born to be his heir, instead of her son Isaac." As Noura thinks about what she just said, something else comes to mind. "Or maybe, Abraham would have given Isaac the greater share of the inheritance and Ishmael would have tried to take it from him?"

"Hmmm, that would actually make sense," says Youssef. "Even nowadays Muslims are trying to do the same thing. The extremists want nothing more than to wipe the entire Jewish nation off the map."

"That is exactly what the Edomites tried to do in the past," Noura adds. "For centuries they have been attempting to conquer the land of the Israelites."

While Noura is still speaking, Youssef hears a familiar beep. Someone is trying to contact him through the chat room. Routinely, he opens it and notices a message from 'User136'. Youssef interrupts his cousin, "Noura, Ahmed is online and wants to chat with me. Let's continue our conversation another time."

Noura understands and ends the Skype conversation with, "I will pray for both of you."

Immediately, Youssef types a greeting to his new friend.

After the customary exchanges of pleasantries, Ahmed tells Youssef he is afraid of going online to read and study the Bible.

Welcome 111: After what you told me about your brother and your father, I completely understand your dilemma. I do have a Bible program on my computer I could forward to you. That way you will not have to go online.

User136: It won't make any difference, because my whole family has access to my computer.

Welcome111: Can't you set up your own user password?

User136: No. They would know right away that I have something to hide. They will think I am into pornography, forbidden politics, or Christianity.

Welcome111: What about a program for your smartphone or your iPad?

User136: My friends and I often share our devices to exchange the latest music, so even that is too risky for me.

Welcome111: Ok, a small pocket Bible then? One you can easily hide in your room?

User136: Hiding it is not the problem. The hard part is to find a place where I can read it without being seen."

Youssef is out of ideas. *Maybe it simply isn't possible for Ahmed to have access to the Word of God. And yet, there must be a way for him to be able to study the Bible. What else is there? Oh, yes, there are a host of Christian programs on satellite television these days.*

Welcome111: Can you receive the signal of Hotbird?

User136: Possibly, but if we position our dish in the direction of that particular satellite, we will get into serious trouble. They broadcast some pretty dubious programs as well. Neighbors are able to see our dish from their roofs; they would start gossiping about our family.

Youssef understands this all too well. He must be careful as well to protect his own family's honor. To shame one's family is the worst thing one can do. But now, Youssef has completely run out of ideas to help his friend study the Bible without attracting attention. Youssef has two thoughts running through his mind. On one hand, he knows that Jesus said we should not worry if we are persecuted and that the Holy Spirit will give us the right words to say. On the other hand, Ahmed's faith in Jesus is still so very new. Youssef worries he will not be able to stand if his family and friends were to pressure him to return to Islam. He is reminded of a parable Jesus told his disciples. A farmer went out to sow, and some of the seeds fell on rocky ground, where the birds came and ate it up. *Couldn't the enemy rob Ahmed of the truth in his heart in the same way? That must not happen.*

In the end, Youssef tries to find a middle ground as he composes his response to Ahmed and he types, "Trust God to protect you. He did it before, when your brother discovered you were chatting with me and nothing serious came from it." Before he sends it, Youssef re-reads what he has just written. *No, that's a poor example. They might not have carried out their threats against Ahmed, but only because he continued to live as a Muslim.* He deletes everything and replaces it with a short, simple sentence.

Welcome111: I will pray for you.

User 136: Thank you, brother.

Youssef feels happy and sad at the same time. Ahmed has called him 'brother'. No one has ever done that through the chat room. *But how will he fare? Will the Islamists be able to crush the new life that has sprouted in Ahmed's heart?* These are questions Youssef has no answer for.

41 If Hamas Forgives the Jews

"To the side," the young man in the back seat calls out. The driver quickly maneuvers his white taxi through the heavy daytime traffic and stops at the curb. The man hands him a few coins before getting out of the ramshackle car. After adjusting his jacket, he walks towards the large building in front of him and climbs the stairs. As soon as he opens the door, cool air welcomes him. He breathes in deeply. After the ride inside the cramped and musty smelling taxi, rambling through the busy streets in the burning sun, it is a great relief to enter the spacious, air-conditioned hall.

Due to the bright sunlight outside, the inside of the building appears to be very dark and it takes a few minutes for his eyes to adjust to this dimly lit space. The business-like interior with its dark and somber color scheme gives a dreary feeling. This is not a nice place to be, but it does not bother him. He has only one goal in mind. Will he be successful?

After finding a computer which is free, he quickly types the name of the author into the search engine. *Nothing!* Even a search by title does not yield any results. Just to be sure, he goes over to the shelves and searches several rows of dusty books. Unfortunately, there is nothing to be found there either. Visibly disappointed, Youssef makes his way to the exit. Moments later, he squeezes into the backseat of another white taxi, next to two sweaty men.

During the ride home, Youssef appears lost in thought. It was to be expected they wouldn't have the book. *Such a pity that Christians cannot be more open about their faith in our country! No wonder Noura enjoys being in America. The Muslims there are a minority and cannot exert any real political pressure like they do here.* Youssef considers ordering the book by mail, but he doubts it will ever arrive. Back to the Internet it is, where he can access information from all over the world.

That night, Youssef eagerly looks for online material about Tony Maalouf and his points of view regarding the descendants of Ishmael. As a university student at the College of Foreign Languages, English is not a problem for him. A few seconds later, an exhaustive list appears on the screen. Youssef clicks on the first link and finds all kinds of information about the professor, but no articles by him. On the second link, he has more success. He finds a report of Maalouf's guest lectures at a university. Youssef quickly scans the document, and the further he reads, the faster his heart beats. The Proverbs 31 woman, Caleb the spy, Job, the Rechabites during the time of Jeremiah, the Wise Men from the East, ... according to Maalouf all of them were

Arabs.[160] *The Bible really does have a lot to say about Ishmael and his offspring!*

Youssef then drags the mouse over to the next page and reads, "Wild donkeys are nomadic and admirably free, a positive symbol in Bedouin and ancient near eastern culture."[161] Youssef could not agree more. Suddenly, he realizes: *Maalouf understands. He is an Arab, too.* Youssef no longer regards Noura with skepticism and he continues to read the text with an open mind.

At the end of the article, Youssef reads, "We hear a lot, too much in fact, about how evangelicals (especially of the dispensationalist flavor) are uncritically pro-Israel because of a numinous admiration for this unique Biblical people."[162]

Indeed! Youssef thinks. *This man hits the nail right on the head.* He excitedly reads the rest.

"What if evangelicals saw some of what Maalouf sees, and began thinking of Arabs with a similar sense of awe and fascination? God saw Hagar and heard Ishmael, and has watched over the Arab peoples, the other children of Abraham, all this time. Mass Arab conversion to Christ is hard to imagine these days, but so is the kind of mass Jewish conversion envisioned by the book of Revelation. Tony Maalouf is persuaded that the two belong together."[163]

Youssef is impressed. *Finally, someone knows how to balance the two. God has a plan with both the Jews and the Arabs.* He cannot wait to talk to Noura. He had been worried that she was being brainwashed in the United States, but now he understands why she reacted so enthusiastically to this Lebanese scholar. Unfortunately, she's not online, so Youssef decides to spend some time in prayer for the Muslims, especially for Ahmed.

About nine hundred miles to the south, two enormous steel doors of a massive compound swing open at the click of a button. A brand-new silver-gray Mercedes S Class Coupe slowly rolls out through the gate and turns onto the road. Behind the wheel is a man dressed in a sparkling white robe, his head covered with a traditional red and white headdress, and a pair of designer sunglasses perched on his nose. From the outside, he looks like any other wealthy Saudi businessman. But what about on the inside? He glances at the sharp peaks of the minarets that grace the mosque in his street and cannot help but wonder who God really is. "Maker of Heaven and Earth," he mutters softly, "If You truly are the God of the Christians, please reveal yourself to me, but if You are the God of Islam, please, then make that clear to me as well, for it is You I want to follow."

Nothing happens. The appearance of the man at his window is still fresh in his memory, as is his visit with Youssef a couple of weeks ago. *But what now? I have nowhere to read the Bible without being disturbed.*

Ahmed cannot think of a solution. Trying to distract his thoughts from this dilemma, he turns on the radio. Several stations offer Qur'anic recitations. Though the familiar chanting still sounds beautiful to him, he feels emotionally detached from them. Other stations air news about the royal family and praise the commitments of government officials who are not only committed to the well-being of the citizens, but also to the promotion of the Islamic religion. Bored with the meaningless babble, he pushes the search button again. There is nothing on FM that interests him. Even though the AM band usually has poor reception, Ahmed tries to find something there. Shifting through several static filled broadcasts, he suddenly hears something that catches his attention.

"To… we …ead from … ospel of Ma…. These … words … o… Messiah." *What is this? A program about the Messiah? On the radio?* As soon as he spots a parking place along the road, he swiftly pulls over. The reception is still very poor, so Ahmed must really focus to hear what is being said. To eliminate any distracting sounds he switches the air conditioning to low.

"… have heard that it was said … shall love your neighb … hate your enemy. But I … love your enemies and pray for those who persecute you, …. sons of your Father who is in heaven. For He … sun rise on the evil … the good, and sends rain on …."

Bah, I wish I could understand it better! Ahmed tweaks the radio a little in hopes of getting a clearer reception, but all he hears is static. He quickly goes back to the original wavelength and tries to concentrate on the broadcast.

"…not even the tax collectors … you greet only your brothers … more … than others? Do not … Gentiles … same? You therefore … perfect, as… heavenly Father …"[164]

Then the message is followed by music, so Ahmed turns it off and puts his car in gear. Little beads of perspiration have appeared on his forehead and he wipes his face with his headscarf.

A little later, he wonders if he started sweating because of the words on the broadcast or because the blazing sun has caused the temperature in the car to increase. Whatever the case may be, some of the words are etched in his memory, and he can't stop thinking about them. "Love your enemies and pray for those who persecute you." *Such profound words! Are they really Jesus' words?*

Ahmed thinks of his brother. Ever since he caught him chatting with Youssef online, Ahmed has been avoiding him. In his heart, he even cursed his brother. *Such a busybody! Why he cannot just leave me alone? Because of his meddling, I dare no longer look for Christian websites. Is Jesus asking me to pray for him? I cannot do that!*

Filled with mixed emotions, Ahmed continues down the road. He is delighted by his discovery of the Christian radio program, but frustrated by that one sentence that speaks to him so deeply.

"Well, how is Ahmed?" Noura asks with interest.

"He would like to learn from the Book," Youssef replies, "but he cannot do that."

"Why not?"

"His family is watching his every move. He doesn't dare keep a Bible in his house, not even a digital version on his computer or on his phone."

Noura sighs deeply. She has picked up on the disappointment in her cousin's voice. Such a contrast with the freedom she enjoys in the United States. At first, she had been amazed that she could come and go wherever and whenever she pleased, without worrying whether neighbors or the secret police were monitoring her, but now she has got used to it. Of course, she is careful not to bring too much attention to herself, because every fellow student from the Middle East is a potential informant for her country. She doesn't want to cause problems for her family; they could be harassed by the secret police as well, and in the worst-case scenario she would be blacklisted and thus prevented from ever returning to her home and family in Jordan.

"In any case, I'm happy you were able to speak with him," she encourages her cousin, "I will pray specifically for Ahmed to gain access to a Bible."

"Thank you, Noura. I really appreciate that." Youssef feels relieved. It's good to talk with his cousin. She always knows how to encourage him when he is down. After his meeting with Ahmed, Youssef needed her support more than ever; he has other friends, but it sometimes can be difficult to know who to trust.

Because he tries his best to share his faith with Muslims, some of his Christian friends have started to call him a fanatic. Others would probably avoid him altogether if they knew he is openly talking with a Saudi man and has even met him. They are afraid of Muslim fundamentalists that they will find out and cause problems for the Christians in Jordan; hence the reason why he keeps quiet about his contacts through the chat program.

He then says to Noura, "By the way, I read some stuff about Tony Maalouf, the guy you talked about several times."

"And?" Noura asks.

"I am impressed. He clearly shows the pro-Israel people in the US that God loves the Arabs, too."

Noura sighs with relief. "Oh, I am so glad you see that too." She wants to say more, but holds back. *If I say too much, he might get annoyed and close himself off again.*

"While we're on the subject, I am also curious to know what you wanted to tell me about the Edomites the last time we spoke."

Noura tries to think back to their last conversation, but she cannot recall what Youssef is referring to. "Remind me, please; what exactly did we talk about?"

"I had said that Muslims want to take away everything from the Jews."

"Oh yes, that's it," Noura remembers, "they are acting just like the Edomites of old."

"Really?" Youssef is surprised and adds, "I never knew that!"

"Have you ever read the story of King Jehoshaphat? God gave him the victory over Israel's enemies, who had gathered to attack. Those people were the Edomites, the Moabites, and the Ammonites."

"Indeed! I knew that God gave Jehoshaphat the victory but I never thought about who the enemy was. But..." Youssef objects, "that happened only once."

"Not really, dear cousin, the whole book of Obadiah deals with the Edomites. God judged them because they rejoiced over their brothers, the Jews, being taking into exile."

"Interesting. Say, Noura, weren't the Edomites the ones who during the time of Moses prevented the Israelites from going through their country on their way to the Promised Land?"

"That's true," Noura confirms. "The book of Ezekiel describes it even more clearly. Listen." Looking for the passage she has in mind, she quickly flips through the pages of her Arabic Bible. "In chapter 35, Ezekiel describes the judgment on Edom for their attempts to take the land God had given to Israel and Judah. Here, in verse 10 and 11 it says, "Because you said, 'These two nations and these two countries shall be mine, and we will take possession of them'—although the LORD was there—therefore, as I live, declares the Lord GOD, I will deal with you according to the anger and envy that you showed because of your hatred against them. And I will make myself known among them, when I judge you."[165]

"Wow, such similarity to what the Muslim extremists want to achieve!" exclaims Youssef. "It is as if the spirit of Esau continues to live in our countrymen who hate Israel." He is impressed with the new perspective, as it provides an explanation for the suicide attacks committed by the Islamists. *But what about Ishmael?* Youssef tries to recall some of the thoughts his cousin had shared with him in their previous conversations. "Noura, didn't you tell me that the Ishmaelites were rather peaceful in their dealings with the descendants of Isaac, while the Ammonites, Moabites and Philistines were among those who caused most of Israel's problems?"

"That's right, and the Amalekites surpassed them all. Without any provocation, they attacked the Israelites in the desert after having left Egypt."

"And they were the descendants of Esau," Youssef adds excitedly. "One might then conclude that violent Muslims follow the example of Esau, while peace-loving Muslims tread in the footsteps of Ishmael."

"That is an interesting thought, cousin," Noura says admiringly. "Here in America, so many Evangelicals think that the Arabs are violent Islamists. Perhaps they have an inkling about the presence of Arabic Christians, but the idea that most Muslims want to live a normal life, just like them…" Noura falters. Then she sobs.

"What's the matter, my dear cousin?"

"How different this world would be if … if all Christians truly followed Jesus' example," Noura stammers.

Youssef knows his cousin quite well, but at present he cannot follow her train of thought. "What do you mean?"

"Well, Jesus gave his life for sinners: for criminals, murderers, terrorists, for everyone."

These are familiar words to Youssef, which he's heard many, many times before. That's why he doesn't understand what Noura is getting at.

"Youssef, just imagine, if all Christians were to love Muslims from the depths of their hearts and seek their well-being," Noura's voice comes softly. "Then the walls between them could be broken down. Then many would come to faith, just like God has promised. And then…" Once again Noura chokes, her emotions threaten to overwhelm her. Youssef waits patiently as she regains her voice. "… then these Muslims will start treating the Jews in the same way."

A tear rolls down Youssef's cheek. In his mind, he pictures the leaders of Hamas and Hezbollah publicly forgiving the Jewish occupiers. *Oh, if only that would happen. Who knows? That could even cause their attitude to change and perhaps one day, I would be able to return to the land of my grandfather.*

That same evening, Ahmed finally has an opportunity to go online without having to worry about someone looking over his shoulder. His older brother is away from home, while the others are entertaining some of their friends. His mother and sisters are in the women's quarters watching their favorite television show. They won't be bothering him for the moment.

Fortunately, 'welcome111' is online. Ahmed would like to speak on the phone with Youssef, but since the phone lines in his country are regularly tapped that would be too risky. He types, "Hello" and waits for the reply.

Welcome111: Hello, how are you?
User136: God be praised, and how are you?
Welcome111: I am fine. How is your family?
User136: God be praised, and your family?

Welcome111: Everyone is well.
User136: What about your family in America?

Ahmed politely avoids asking directly about Youssef's cousin. Though he is curious to know how she is doing, custom forbids him from asking about female relatives. Youssef has told him that she prays for him. It touches him that she would do that, and he is strangely attracted to her. He secretly hopes to meet her one day, but he doesn't dare to ask for her Facebook name. What if he upset her and she stopped praying for him? Then he would lose what little he has.

Welcome111: My cousin is doing well. She continues to pray for you, my friend.
User136: Please, thank her for me, and, please, tell her not to stop.
Welcome111: Why? Did something happen?

Youssef realizes a sense of urgency in Ahmed's question.
In a few words Ahmed describes his experiences of the past few days to his Christian friend.

User136: Then I heard him say, "Pray for those who persecute you." I just cannot get it out of my mind. I would have loved to hear the rest, but the reception was very poor.

Youssef is filled with joy, realizing that God has answered his prayers. He has provided Ahmed with an opportunity to learn from the Bible. Clearly, the Lord is at work in Ahmed's life. Youssef responds enthusiastically.

Welcome111: You heard part of Jesus' teachings to his followers. It can be found in the Gospel of Matthew.

Ahmed breathes a sigh of relief. He was hoping his Jordanian friend would be able to help him out.

User136: Could you maybe forward me the entire passage?

Youssef wonders why Ahmed does not search an online Bible program for himself, but respecting the wishes of his Muslim friend, he copies and pastes the verses in question.

Welcome111: "You have heard that it was said, 'You shall love your neighbor and hate your enemy.' But I say to you, Love your enemies and pray for those who persecute you, so that you may be sons of your Father who is in heaven. For he makes his sun rise on the evil and on the good, and sends rain on the just and on the unjust. For if you love those who love you, what reward do you have? Do not even the tax collectors do the same? And if you greet only your brothers, what more are you doing than others? Do not even the Gentiles do the same? You therefore must be perfect, as your heavenly Father is perfect."[166]

Ahmed feels an inner resistance to these words. His palms become moist with sweat. *Does God really want me to forgive my enemies? That is not right. God commanded, "an eye for an eye, and tooth for a tooth."* [167] *That is justice!*

After the flush from his initial anger subsides, Ahmed allows himself to hope that there is another explanation.

User136: Who were the tax collectors?

Welcome111: They were Jewish government officials employed by the Romans to collect taxes for the Roman Empire. They routinely overcharged their fellow men and pocketed the difference. In the eyes of the Jews they were the most corrupt people in society.

On reading the reply, Ahmed smiles. *It seems like Jesus was talking about my country. We have an abundance of corruption too.*

Then Jesus' words wash over him again. *So, he wants us to pray not only for our royal family who primarily line their own pockets, but also for the religious policemen who make my sisters' lives so difficult.* He recognizes that those same people often treat each other well. According to Jesus, however, being nice to your friends isn't enough. In his heart, Ahmed senses the validity of Jesus' words, but the task seems impossible. His heart sinks.

User136: No man can love his enemies.

Youssef completely understands Ahmed's response. Has he not struggled himself over the hateful messages he receives from Muslims in the chat room? Humanly speaking, it is indeed impossible to love those fundamentalists who continuously pressure the Christian minority which he is part of, and yet, this is what God commands.

Welcome111: Yes, in and of ourselves it would be impossible to do so. There is only one way: ask God to give you the strength. He will do it!

User136: How do I know for sure that God will do this?

Youssef tries to think of an appropriate passage of Scripture to send to his friend, but nothing comes to mind.

Welcome111: Just read the Bible. God himself will guide you and speak to your heart.

Whilst typing, Youssef remembers again that Ahmed doesn't have the freedom to read the Bible. Suddenly he gets an idea and his eyes light up.

Welcome111: When you're driving, you could perhaps use an MP3 player to listen to the Bible.

Ahmed is surprised. *Why didn't I think of that myself?* As a male member of society, he has complete freedom of movement. He can come and go as he pleases and his own vehicle gives him a lot of privacy. Glad he has finally found a way to learn more about the Bible in a safe and unrestricted way, he sends his friend a closing message.

User136: Thank you for your advice, my friend.
Welcome111: You are most welcome, my brother, any time.

Relieved, Youssef prays silently, *Thank you, Lord, for helping me and giving me wisdom.*

42 A Radical Request

What could have happened? I haven't heard from him for months. Youssef often worries about his Saudi friend. All sorts of things could have gone wrong. Perhaps his brother caught him with a Bible. Or maybe Jesus' teaching was too hard, and he just gave up. Did the enemy come and destroy the seed planted? Or…

Whichever way he looks at it, it's a fact that he hasn't spoken with Ahmed for over eleven months. At first, Youssef regularly checked the chat program to see if 'User136' was online, but after a few months he stopped. Now, he hardly even prays for him anymore. There are so many others who have contacted him and need his attention. Yet, it's painful whenever he thinks of Ahmed.

He had had a wonderful time catching up with Noura over the summer. Together, they had prayed passionately for Ahmed and Youssef can still see them in his mind seated on his uncle's flat rooftop. Noura had been sent up there to fetch the dry laundry and Youssef had offered to help her. The white sheets had been fluttering in the wind while he and Noura lifted Ahmed in prayer before the throne of God. Youssef had been encouraged and hopeful because Noura reminded him of the words of the apostle, Paul, "And I am sure of this, that he who began a good work in you will bring it to completion at the day of Jesus Christ."[168]

Beautiful words, but can they be applied to just anyone? As if everyone will be saved! But then again, Jesus clearly revealed himself to Ahmed. He must have begun a good work in him? Youssef cannot stop thinking about it. He has not completely given up, but the unshakeable confidence in God's plan for Ahmed is no longer there. Even after all he has learned about God's love for Ishmael and the Arabs, he is just not sure that anything will ever change. *It was probably easy for Paul to have such confidence, but the Islamic world of today is quite different from the Arabs of his time.* And yet, deep inside, Youssef knows God wants him to hold fast to the truths of the Bible without being fazed by the circumstances.

The sonorous hum of an Arabic worship chant interrupts the conversations of the students in the university lounge. It's Youssef's ringtone and he picks up his mobile phone to check the call. There is no name, just an international number. He recognizes the Saudi country code. *Could it really be him? Maybe his brother is using his phone to try to trap me.* The only way to find out is to answer the call. Reluctantly, he presses the green answer button on his phone. He takes a deep breath before answering.

"Hello."

"Hello, how are you, "says a voice at the other end.

"Good, and you?" Youssef answers politely. In the meantime, he tries to recognize the male voice. *He sounds like Ahmed, But, of course, his brother might sound the same.*

"God be praised. I'm so glad to speak to you again.'

Youssef acts as if he doesn't know who he is talking to and asks, "Who's speaking?"

"It's Ahmed, of course. Don't you remember me?"

Youssef feels embarrassed. It's not nice to respond to your friend like this, but how could he have known for sure it was Ahmed? From a very early age he has learned never to trust a Muslim. How often has his father been cheated? He tries to be light-hearted when he says, "Hello, Ahmed, I am so happy to hear from you again!"

Ahmed doesn't beat around the bush. "I am in Amman and I need to see you as soon as possible. Can we meet tonight in the same park?"

That is bad timing for Youssef. Every Thursday night he goes to his church's youth group and tonight is his turn to lead the Bible study. Now he has a dilemma. *What should I do? If I say 'no' to Ahmed, he will feel discouraged, maybe even rejected. He might never contact me again.* That thought helps Youssef to decide and he replies, "Ok, straight after *Maghreb*."*

"Excellent. I will see you then."

After the line is disconnected, Youssef stares at the phone in his hand. Overwhelmed by emotion, he hardly notices the buzz of students talking around him. *Ahmed is here. I will meet him again tonight.* He's not sure whether he should be happy or worried. Ahmed had sounded exuberant enough, but that doesn't necessarily mean he is doing well. As Youssef processes the short conversation, he senses God's peace fill his heart. It's as if God is saying to him, "Didn't I promise you? Trust Me."

As soon as Youssef gets home, he turns his computer on. He desperately wants to speak with Noura. She's probably not online at the moment, as it's morning in the US and most likely she is attending her first lecture. *Maybe she is sick or a lecture was cancelled.* Sadly, her name doesn't appear in the list of people who are online.

Then Youssef calls the youth leader to apologize for his absence that night. Fortunately, the man understands. He tells him not to worry at all

---

* Maghreb means sunset. It indicates one of the five Islamic prayer times.
  See www.godlovesishmael.com/prayertimes

and wishes him God's blessing. Youssef certainly needs that blessing to-night.

The hustle and bustle of the traffic navigating the roundabout is unending. Soot-covered buses puff out clouds of black smoke and tiny beat-up cars zigzag in between larger luxury vehicles, all competing for a space on the crowded roads. Here and there, a brave, or perhaps foolish, pedestrian tries to cross the street, dashing and darting, narrowly avoiding the insanity of downtown Amman traffic. The sun is setting in the western sky and neon advertisement panels, one larger than the next, light up the sky, all clamoring for attention. Colorful garlands of flashing lights decorate the entrance to the park. Groups of students walk in and out, merrily laughing with each other or talking on their phone. Street vendors attempt to draw the attention of passers-by, hoping to sell some of their wares. Spread out on small tables or carpets are the toys, computer games, perfumes, and clothes, all waiting for new owners.

A tall, olive-skinned Saudi man in a three-piece suit is seated near the entrance. He taps his fingers. *Will he come? He sounded a bit hesitant earlier on the phone.* Fortunately, he has a sharp memory and he can easily picture Youssef's face.

In the meantime, Youssef checks his watch anxiously. He has been waiting for a white taxi for twenty minutes. Eight have passed him by, all fully oc-cupied. That's not uncommon for this time of day. It's rush hour and people are either returning home from work or going shopping downtown. Since he doesn't have a lot of money, he has no choice but to wait for one of these. Finally, a white cab stops near where Youssef is waiting and an elderly pas-senger gets out. He quickly jumps in, but almost every traffic light turns red and there is gridlock everywhere; the journey seems interminable. On top of that, the taxi driver must make many stops to allow people to get on and get off. When Youssef finally arrives at the roundabout in front of the park, it is dark outside and almost time for the last evening prayer. One hour has passed since *Maghreb*. He wonders if Ahmed will still be there.

A little later, Youssef disappears into the crowd at the entrance of the park. He looks around for a tall man in a white robe and a checkered head-scarf. Though he has noticed several Arabs that fit the description, all are either with their wife and children or with friends. Slightly apprehensive, Youssef looks around to see whether there is anyone by himself.

Suddenly, he feels a tap on his shoulder. Startled, he turns around to see a man with a smile on his face.

"Hello, Youssef," the man says, grinning from ear to ear. His dark eyes reflect the dimly flickering light of the park lanterns.

"Welcome, Ahmed," Youssef says timidly. The imposing figure in front of him looks so different from the last time they met. "Er… sorry to be so late."

"It doesn't matter. I am happy to see you," Ahmed reassures him. Then he pulls Youssef into an embrace and heartily kisses him on both cheeks. The men walk to the same park bench as eleven months ago and Youssef invites Ahmed to sit down.

Soon, Ahmed voices his burning question. "Can you take me to church? I want to be baptized!"

Youssef almost falls over in surprise. *Am I hearing things?* For a moment, he doesn't know what to think. He is pretty sure his pastor would not agree to this. He always says, "We are a minority here, Youssef. It's important for us to stay on good terms with the Muslims." Youssef understands why he says that but his pastor's views do not seem consistent with the teaching of the New Testament. *Weren't Peter and the other apostles a minority too? Yet, they preached the Gospel and publicly baptized those who came to Christ. They suffered persecution, but Jesus had warned them about that in advance.*

Before he answers, Youssef wants to know how Ahmed came to this decision.

"Your idea about listening to the Book while driving was brilliant," Ahmed explains. "I took every opportunity I had to download Bible books and then listened to them whenever I was alone in my car. Sometimes, I would go for a drive around town, just to listen," he grins.

Youssef laughs too, thankful that Ahmed had found a way to get to know the Word of God after all.

"At home, people were watching my every move," Ahmed continues. It was as if my family knew what I was doing. That's why I couldn't take the risk of writing to you again."

Youssef nods empathetically, yet, he has a nagging question. "How come you did openly contact Christians online at first?"

"Well, let me tell you. As a Muslim I felt free to look for answers to my questions about your faith. But after the appearance at my window, and especially after my first meeting with you, I felt I had become more vulnerable. Deep in my heart, I had become convicted of the truth about Jesus the Messiah and was no longer able to say I was a Muslim."

"So then, you were changed when God touched your heart. From that time on, you were an underground believer," Youssef concludes.

Ahmed looks at Youssef with surprise. "What does that mean? Is it like the secret police?" Suddenly alarmed, he carefully scans his surroundings, checking for anything out of the ordinary. Then he whispers, "You know, in my country some of the beggars work undercover for the intelligence service. Some go as far as pretending to be mentally ill, just to gain information on unsuspecting citizens."

Youssef nods knowingly. He often feels the walls have ears and he always has to be on guard. Smiling, he says softly, "This has nothing to do with the secret police. Underground believers are people who cannot publicly declare their faith in Jesus Christ; they worship and follow him in secret.

Now Ahmed understands. Getting back to his purpose of meeting Youssef, he whispers, "Jesus said that we should not *just* listen to what he says, but we should also *do* what he says. He was baptized too, and so..." Ahmed feels a lump in his throat. He realizes only too well the risks of what he is about to undertake. However, if Jesus truly gave his life for him, Ahmed wants to withhold nothing and dedicate his life to his Savior. He looks at his friend expectantly.

Youssef is happy yet frustrated at the same time. He would like to shout for joy due to Ahmed's dedication to Jesus. At the same time, he very much doubts his pastor will grant his friend's request for baptism. Like most other Christians in Jordan, he lives in fear of Muslim retaliation and not without reason. But if he is not willing to pursue Ahmed's request, who will?

"Aren't you going to church tomorrow morning?" Ahmed continues. "If possible, I would like to be baptized then and return home straightaway. I don't want my family to become suspicious because of my prolonged absence."

Youssef understands now why Ahmed had been in such a hurry to meet him. Thankfully, he had been able to cancel the Bible study, but putting together a baptism service for the next morning is a different matter. That looks impossible.

"I will do my best, my friend, I promise. But it is short notice," Youssef explains.

"Don't you want to do what Jesus says?" Ahmed is taken aback by his friend's seeming lack of enthusiasm. "Doesn't it say in the *injil* that Philip baptized the man from Ethiopia as soon as they saw water?"

Astonished by his friend's familiarity with the Bible, Youssef is torn. If only he could be as radical as his new brother. "Lord God, why are we Christians so easily frightened and intimidated. Why can't we just trust You?" he prays silently.

Later that evening, Youssef turns his computer on again to Skype Noura. Sadly, she's not online. He decides to send her an e-mail instead. In carefully chosen words he tells her what has happened. At the end of his message, he pleads with her, "Please, pray for wisdom. We *have* to help him."

Melodious chanting pierces the early dawn's fresh air. Emanating from large loudspeakers high atop the minarets, the words of the *Shahada** resound throughout the valleys of Amman. "God is greater. I bear witness that there is no god except God. I bear witness that Muhammad is the messenger of God."

Usually, Youssef sleeps right through the call to prayer, but this time the words slowly wake him up.

"Come to prayer! Come to success! Prayer is better than sleep!"** As he awakens, the fog lifts from his brain. The first thing he thinks about is his meeting with Ahmed the previous night. Do these Qur'anic words still hold the same meaning for him? Does he still feel obliged to perform the ritual prayers, even after he has put his trust in God's grace?

Lying in bed, with his eyes still closed, Youssef prays silently, "Father in Heaven, please help Ahmed to realize that he no longer has to slavishly follow all these rules, but that You love him as a father loves his son. Help Ahmed not to be afraid of You but only to trust in your grace."

Ten minutes later, the last mosque falls silent. Youssef turns over on his side in the hope of getting more sleep, but he can't stop thinking about his friend's situation. *Perhaps Ahmed will be baptized today. What would Noura think about this? I hope she has read my email.* Unable to contain his curiosity any longer, he jumps out of bed and turns his computer on. He is thrilled to find an email from his cousin, but when he opens it, he is less than pleased with its content. It says, "Be careful, Youssef. So many Muslims come to church saying, 'I want to be baptized,' while they aren't sincere. They use it as a pretext to get a visa to the United States."

Feelings of loneliness flood Youssef. His closest companion, the only person with whom he has shared so much about Ahmed, is now discouraging him to help a believer from an Islamic background to be baptized. Disappointed, he reads the rest of her letter. "Some even go as far as to tell naïve Christians wonderful testimonies of conversion, stories they have heard or read about. Gullible Christians take them blindly at their word, only to get into great trouble later on." *She thinks I am being a fool. Wasn't she the one who*

---

tried to convince me that millions of Muslims will be coming to faith in Christ? How preposterous!

Youssef begins to feel annoyed at her. The moment he needs her encouragement the most, she lets him down.

"I'm not saying you should not allow it, but I do want to ask you to proceed with caution. I don't want you to inadvertently destroy your ministry."

What a pessimist! Whatever happened to her optimism?! Youssef looks down to the end of the e-mail.

"As usual, I pray for you; also, for Ahmed.
Love,
Noura."

Thinking about her caution, Youssef has to admit that what she said has indeed happened before. *But what if someone has really come to faith? You cannot simply reject him or her, can you?* Doubt then creeps into Youssef's heart. *Is Ahmed's faith real? That first time we met, he did hide his eyes from me. Although he did look like Ahmed, it could have been his brother. If his brother read all our chat conversations, he would know exactly what we have spoken about and he would be able to pretend to be him. Imagine that!* In desperation, Youssef turns to God. "Lord, You know exactly what is going on in Ahmed's life. This is your work, not mine. May your will be done, in heaven and on earth, today, here in Amman."

Youssef feels at peace now and he thinks of an idea. He will ask someone else to baptize Ahmed. If that person refuses, Youssef will not be responsible for Ahmed's disappointment. He doesn't want to hurt his friend's feelings and he senses that this is an option they both can live with.

Several hours later, the two friends take their seats on one of the narrow wooden benches inside the church. Ahmed is dressed smartly in his Italian three-piece suit. He prefers to dress in his traditional Arab garb after work and on the weekends, but he wouldn't have dared to show up in church in his white robe. Jordanian Christians don't wear them, and he would stand out like a sore thumb. Attracting undue attention from even one Muslim could get him into serious trouble with the secret police. The curious and suspicious looks from the regular churchgoers cause him enough stress as it is. If he had been alone, he would probably have turned around and left. In fact, he would not even have dared entering the church building.

From the pulpit, someone announces a song to the congregation and a pianist begins to play the introduction. Youssef opens a songbook and points to the lyrics. Ahmed doesn't even notice what Youssef is indicating as he is so taken aback by what he is experiencing. The sound of the people singing praises to God lifts his spirit. Mesmerized, he takes in the words of the hymn.

> My soul and all that is within me, bless the Lord.
> Bless his name, his holy name.
> Do not forget the great things He has done.
> The One who forgives your sins, all of your sins.
> The One who heals your diseases, all of your diseases.[169]

Ahmed clearly senses God's presence. It is as if the heavens have opened to him. He ponders the words in his heart. *The One who forgives your sins, all of your sins.* Then he thinks back to a radio broadcast about forgiveness. He remembers very well what the presenter had said. "Jesus took upon himself the punishment for *all* sins, past, present, and future, of *all* people." It had really disturbed him then. Islam teaches that those who make the Hajj will be forgiven of all their past sins.* But for God to forgive you for future sins, would mean you can do as you like, because you have been forgiven anyway!

Ahmed is beginning to understand the mystery. Two thousand years ago, Jesus underwent the punishment for the sins of all of mankind. Of course, that would mean not only past sins, but also future sins. If we believe that Jesus truly died on the cross for our sins and we ask him to forgive us, we are indeed forgiven. Even though he hasn't fully grasped it yet, Ahmed does believe, wholeheartedly.

After a few more hymns, the preacher announces, "The reading for today is from Isaiah 35. We will read the verses one through ten."

Someone gets up from the congregation, walks over to the microphone under the pulpit, opens his Bible and begins to read,

> "The desert and the parched land will be glad;
> the wilderness will rejoice and blossom.
> Like the crocus, it will burst into bloom;
> it will rejoice greatly and shout for joy.
> The glory of Lebanon will be given to it,
> the splendor of Carmel and Sharon;
> they will see the glory of the Lord,
> the splendor of our God."[170]

---

* For more information about this teaching, see www.godlovesishmael.com/pilgrimage.

Ahmed feels overwhelmed. This is too good to be true! In his mind's eye, he pictures the desolate outskirts of Riyadh and imagines himself driving out of town, surrounded by colorful flowers and lush green fields, instead of the usual shriveled up brambles, bare rocks and endless sand dunes. No more funnel-shaped clouds of dust, but instead dancing blades of grass and fruit trees swaying in the gentle breeze. The arid desert landscape of his home would indeed rejoice. *God be praised,* he says under his breath.

Youssef's heart skips a beat. Through the conversations with Noura, he has begun to see everything in a new light. He doesn't see these verses just figuratively, but now applies them literally to the desert outside of Amman. One day, that desert will rejoice. As Youssef tries to imagine what that will be like, he pictures Bedouins dancing for joy in front of their tents. Suddenly, he understands the connection between their joy and God's glory. *They will rejoice because they have seen God's majesty. The same must be true for the Muslims in the large deserts of the Arabian Peninsula! God will reveal himself to them and then they too will rejoice in him. Ahmed, who is sitting right next to me, has – quite literally   experienced this when he saw Jesus face to face!* Greatly encouraged, Youssef listens to the rest of the Scripture reading.

"Strengthen the feeble hands,
steady the knees that give way;
say to those with fearful hearts,
'Be strong, do not fear;
your God will come,
he will come with vengeance;
with divine retribution
he will come to save you.'"[171]

Youssef listens with growing amazement. Here he is, feeling anxious about bringing Ahmad to church and about the baptism, and Ahmad probably is as well. How appropriate these words of Isaiah are for them. *God is encouraging us both to be strong and not fear. He will save us from trouble.* For Youssef, this is enough confirmation that he is doing the right thing. Perhaps some will disapprove, but he is sure now that it was God's will for him to bring his new brother to church. Youssef quickly glances at his neighbor, but Ahmad doesn't respond. He is concentrating on the reading.

"Then will the eyes of the blind be opened
and the ears of the deaf unstopped.
Then will the lame leap like a deer,
and the mute tongue shout for joy."[172]

Jesus did all of those things, Ahmed realizes. He remembers the stories he's heard while driving his car. Jesus healed the blind, the deaf, the lame, the mute and even the lepers. He simply healed everyone. *Hey, we just sang about that too.* Ahmed's heart leaps for joy and spontaneously, he prays in his heart, "Lord, my soul blesses You!" Shortly after, the teachings of the imam pop into his head. *You cannot bless God, He is the Creator.* Yet, Ahmed feels a peace in his heart that he hasn't known before. So he pushes those thoughts aside and focuses on the worship service.

In the meantime, Youssef's thoughts have taken a different direction altogether. He thinks of those who are spiritually blind, those who proclaim daily through the mosques' loudspeakers that Jesus is not the Son of God. They cannot see God for who He really is. They are like the deaf who cannot hear the soft, gentle voice of God's Holy Spirit in their hearts. He thinks of sincere Muslims who have been paralyzed by their fear of God's judgment and do not dare walk in the joyous faith that Jesus has died for their sins. He thinks of those who seem muted, afraid to confess to their relatives and friends that Jesus has conquered all the powers of darkness and that he is Lord of all creation.

> "Water will gush forth in the wilderness
> and streams in the desert.
> The burning sand will become a pool,
> the thirsty ground bubbling springs.
> In the haunts where jackals once lay,
> grass and reeds and papyrus will grow."[173]

Again, Ahmed pictures the desert. The few times it rains, the *wadis-*quickly overflow and the resulting flashfloods carve deep crevasses into the arid wastelands. One day, all that water will no longer flow into the sea, but instead create beautiful glassy lakes. *How interesting that the Book speaks of this!*

The next few verses, although they sound fascinating, do not hold as much meaning for Ahmed.

> "And a highway will be there;
> it will be called the Way of Holiness;
> it will be for those who walk on that Way.
> The unclean will not journey on it;
> wicked fools will not go about on it.
> No lion will be there,

---

* Plural of *wadi,* a dry riverbed

nor any ravenous beast;
they will not be found there.
But only the redeemed will walk there,
and those the Lord has rescued will return.
They will enter Zion with singing;
everlasting joy will crown their heads.
Gladness and joy will overtake them,
and sorrow and sighing will flee away."[174]

For Youssef there is great hope in these words. One day, all suffering will cease. Zion makes him think of the new, heavenly Jerusalem in Paradise. He imagines himself dancing for joy on the golden streets, hand in hand with Ahmed ... and with Noura, on their way to the center of the city where they will see their Lord, Jesus Christ, face to face. For a second, Youssef feels ashamed. *I'm not supposed to hold my cousin's hand in public. But then again, in Heaven, we will all be brothers and sisters.*

"Beloved in the Lord Jesus Christ," the preacher begins his sermon. "About 700 years before the Messiah, the prophet Isaiah foretold the jubilant return of the Israelites from exile. This came to pass when the Jewish exiles were permitted to return to their homeland, after 70 years of captivity in Babylon. Jesus Christ himself provided a deeper fulfillment of this prophecy than that. He made known to us the beauty of the Father. He said, "Whoever has seen Me, has seen the Father."[175] Jesus opened the way to the Father. Through him we have access to God. He came to set us free from the burden of sin, the yoke of slavery. All who put their trust in him as their Savior, will receive power to break away from bad habits, and when we allow Christ to reign in our hearts, he will transform our inner dryness into fruitful soil. Then we will bear much fruit. Together with all believers worldwide, we rejoice in the inner peace God gives us when we enter into his rest. We are his people and for as long as we are living on this earth we look forward to the heavenly Jerusalem where we will adore him and worship him, where we will be forever in God's presence, worshiping and adoring him."

Youssef swallows a couple of times. Although he really likes what his pastor is saying and mainly agrees with him, in light of all that he has recently learned, he firmly believes that there is yet another message here – a prophetic message for both the descendants of Ishmael as well as for the Jewish people. He feels like standing up and calling out, "Pastor, the blossoming desert refers to the Arabs who will come to faith in Jesus. The spiritually barren regions will come to life through God's Holy Spirit. And then they will prepare the way for the Jews, just like John the Baptist prepared the way in the desert for the Lord Jesus Christ. When the Muslims come to faith in Jesus, they will no longer hate the Jews or seek their destruction; instead they will point them to Christ. Then the Jews will also come to faith in the Lord Jesus." Youssef stirs uncomfortably as tension rises in him; it takes real effort to control himself and keep quiet.

Then the pastor cites another verse about a way that is being prepared. He reads, "In that day there will be a highway from Egypt to Assyria, and Assyria will come into Egypt, and Egypt into Assyria, and the Egyptians will worship with the Assyrians. In that day, Israel will be the third with Egypt and Assyria, a blessing in the midst of the earth, whom the Lord of hosts has blessed, saying, 'Blessed be Egypt my people, and Assyria the work of my hands, and Israel my inheritance.'"[176]

He continues preaching from the text, "What is this 'highway' but Christ himself, who gave himself to the believers as a safe way, where the unclean do not go, but where only the saints are found. Why is the phrase 'in that day' repeated about five times in the verses 18 to 25? Does that not point to the fullness of time in which the Lord Jesus came to bring us these blessings? He came in person as "the Way" in which the nations come together to enjoy the spiritual unity and abundance of blessing. The unity of Egypt and Assyria and Israel is a symbol of the universal Church, in which former enemies are joined together in a spirit of love and unity. Through the coming of Christ all become members of one church that will enjoy his divine work."[177]

Youssef nervously picks at his fingernails. He is taken up by a whirlwind of thoughts. *See? Those nations are specifically mentioned by name. These verses are not only meant for those who already belong to God's Kingdom, but also for the Egyptians, the Jews and the Syrians.* Youssef prays silently, "*Oh Lord, please help the preacher to clearly see that you also love the Muslims; that You want to touch them too.* Then Youssef looks at Ahmed. *I wonder what he is thinking?*

Ahmed is relishing the pastor's words. This is the best day of his life. He senses the presence of God like never before. Most of what the preacher is saying is beyond his comprehension, but it doesn't faze him because God is present.

"When will the desert blossom?" the preacher asks the congregation rhetorically and continues, "Let us read Isaiah chapter 32, verses 15 to 18:

> "Until the Spirit is poured upon us from on high,
> and the wilderness becomes a fruitful field,
> and the fruitful field is deemed a forest.
> Then justice will dwell in the wilderness,
> and righteousness abide in the fruitful field.
> And the effect of righteousness will be peace,

and the result of righteousness, quietness and trust forever.
My people will abide in a peaceful habitation,
in secure dwellings, and in quiet resting places."

"As I said before, the phrase 'My people' refers to us. We are God's people and as such we suffer injustice and persecution in this world, but God will vindicate us. One day, we will be able to live in peace and harmony and we will no longer be harmed by anyone."

Several church members nod their heads in agreement. As a small Christian minority, they are hard pressed from all sides. At school, their children learn Islamic history and memorize entire passages from the Qur'an. Christian political parties are not allowed and the churches don't receive any government subsidies to repair or restore their buildings. On the contrary, the pastor sometimes even receives threatening phone calls from antagonistic Muslims.

Youssef too, understands what the preacher is talking about. He frequently faces discrimination at university and other places, just because he is a Christian. But now he sees these Bible passages from a whole new perspective. If many Muslims come to repentance and are born again, they will no longer disadvantage the Christians and other minority groups. Then he and the other Christians will no longer have to live in fear and under threat from the Islamists. On the contrary, then justice will prevail in the barren land and their emotional desert will turn into an oasis. And if the Arabs begin to take care of their environment, the dry desert might quite literally become a green paradise.

"Finally, let us give some thought to the streams of water that shall break forth in the desert," the pastor says, as he draws near to the end of his sermon.

Ahmed, who is fascinated by this topic, listens attentively to every word the pastor utters.

"The Lord Jesus said that rivers of living water would flow out of the hearts of the believers," the man continues. "He was talking about the Holy Spirit who would be poured out upon them."

Ahmed recalls a well-known Qur'anic verse that says, "Christ Jesus the son of Mary was a messenger of Allah, and His Word, which He bestowed on Mary, and a spirit proceeding from Him."[178] Immediately, he begins to question what he just learned. *How can a prophet, Jesus, a man, be poured out like a spirit on the believer? Is this preacher claiming that God consists of three gods?* Yet, Ahmed experiences an undeniable sense of peace through the words of the pastor. He decides to follow the voice in his heart, for this is the kind of peace he has been searching for all these years.

The words of the preacher trigger a very different response in Youssef. He must think about the outpouring of the Holy Spirit at Pentecost. *What promise did the Apostle Peter cite then?* Effortlessly, he flips through the pages of his Bible to the beginning of the Book of Acts. He lets his finger slide across the wafer-thin pages until he arrives at the verse he had in mind.

"In the last days, God says,
I will pour out my Spirit on all people.
Your sons and daughters will prophesy,
your young men will see visions,
your old men will dream dreams.
Even on my servants, both men and women,
I will pour out my Spirit in those days,
and they will prophesy."[179]

Youssef's mind races from one thought to the next. *God pours out his spirit on all people… then that includes the Muslims too.* Overjoyed at the thought, he realizes what God is doing. *This is what has happened to Ahmed. He saw a vision! And when God suddenly pours out his Spirit on the Muslim world, millions upon millions could come to faith.* Youssef looks at his friend and their eyes meet. Ahmed's eyes are brimming with tears, betraying his deep, emotional state. Youssef fixes his eyes on him, letting Ahmed know he senses a deep kinship with him.

"When God's Spirit is poured out in the human heart, his spiritual drought changes into a well of life. His barren soul will begin to blossom and bear fruit for eternity," the pastor continues.

Youssef has a hard time focusing on the rest of the sermon. The message he is receiving from these verses is so much more powerful, so much more beautiful. Then his thoughts drift again to his burning question for the pastor. *What will he say, when I share Ahmed's request with him?*

44 *The Beginning of a Great Harvest*

After the closing hymn, the pastor returns to the middle of the podium and announces, "Receive now the Lord's blessing."

Ahmed wants that blessing with his whole heart. When the congregation rises, he jumps up in anticipation of what will come next. The pastor stretches out his arms over the attendees as he pronounces the blessing and Ahmed soaks up his words.

"The grace of our Lord Jesus Christ and the love of God and the fellowship of the Holy Spirit be with you all. Amen."[180]

Straightaway, the pews come alive with the sounds of scuffling and murmuring. Shaking hands, the church members greet one another and wish each other God's blessings. Youssef notices the curious looks his friend is attracting and, attempting to avoid awkward questions, he quickly grabs Ahmed's hand and leads him away. Together they go forward to meet the pastor, who is talking to another church member.

As he follows Youssef, Ahmed still basks in the afterglow of the tremendous experience. He feels so close to God; it's as if God's presence is all around him. By chance he glances outside through the open church door and notices a man in the distance in a familiar, long white robe. Immediately, he's shocked back to reality. *What am I doing here? I don't belong here! I should get out of here. Right now!* Doubt and fear creep into his soul. *Baptism? Don't be so stupid! My family will kill me. Don't believe the lies of the Christians!* His anxious thoughts seem to be whirling out of control. *They have altered the Bible. These Christians will lead you astray! Return to Islam before it is too late.*

The voices in Ahmed's head wage a fierce battle as he stands next to Youssef patiently waiting for the pastor to speak with them. He tries to understand what is happening. At first, he had been full of joy, but now he has been robbed of his happiness and he feels nothing but fear and anxiety. He tries to re-focus his thoughts on God and his promises. A Bible verse comes to mind, which he heard before on the radio. "The thief comes only to steal and kill and destroy. I came that they may have life and have it abundantly."[181]

"Oh, Lord, that is what I want!" Ahmed prays desperately in his heart. "I want life!"

As soon as the pastor has finished the conversation, he turns to Youssef and Ahmed, greets them cordially and asks, "What can I do for you, gentlemen?"

"I have a special request," replies Yousef. "May we speak with you in private?"

Slightly apprehensive, Ahmed takes a seat on a well-worn leather armchair in the tiny church office. Suspended from the ceiling, an old rusty fan wobbles and squeaks rhythmically. It doesn't give much relief from the stuffy heat, but instead plenty of stale air and dust move around the room. The threadbare rug on the tile floor has clearly seen better days. There is an obsolete computer monitor on the desk that looks like it is from the Stone Age. The rest of the lackluster room is filled with shelves containing books with discolored covers and faded pictures of children. A single wooden plaque with the words, "The Lord is my Shepherd" in tasteful Arabic calligraphic lettering, hangs on the wall directly across from Ahmed.

Youssef sits down on one of the other chairs while the pastor pulls up his desk chair to formally greet the guest.

It looks like this leader doesn't spend much church money on himself, but instead supports those who are really in need, Ahmed muses. He already admires this man who so selflessly cares for others. The pastor eyes him kindly and Ahmed senses a warmth flowing from him, such as he has never felt from any of the Islamic religious leaders he knows. *These Christians have something we Muslims don't have,* he realizes. *I want that, too.*

A little while later, there is a light knock at the door; a lady enters holding a tray with three cups of tea. Ahmed notices how the pastor thanks his wife lovingly and again he is touched. *Our women are never thanked for what they do. After all, it is their duty to serve the men.* The smile on the pastor's wife's face speaks volumes. She is happily married to her husband. Ahmed's own mother never smiles like that. His father is the boss at home and sometimes even threatens to beat her if she resists his will. It's not that they do not love each other, but the affection on display here is noticeably absent in his own family.

After the lady has left the office, Ahmed says, "Youssef has helped me a lot to find the way. I was blind but now I see the truth. I know that God sent Jesus the Messiah to forgive my sins."

Youssef beams. As he listens to Ahmed's story, he understands more and more how God has used him in the life of this Saudi man and his heart overflows with gratitude to God.

Pastor Majed is deeply impressed by everything that Ahmed tells him. The story about the vision of Jesus especially captures his attention. God has revealed himself to Ahmed without human intervention. At the same time, he has his doubts. *Could it be a trap, after all? What if this man made up the whole story, only to catch us Christians in the act of trying to convert Muslims? The secret police do not understand that true conversion is a change of heart, something that cannot be achieved through man's effort but is the sovereign work of God. They will never believe that I don't try to convert anyone.* At the same time, Majed is convinced of Youssef's integrity; otherwise he wouldn't have even started this conversation.

Then Ahmed voices his request. "I want to obey Jesus and be baptized."

The pastor has seen this question coming and he answers, "I would love to help you, but I will not be able to give you a baptism certificate."

When Youssef sees that Ahmed doesn't understand what the pastor means, he briefly explains it to him.

"Oh, I don't really need that," Ahmed exclaims. "That would only cause problems for me. Besides, did Philip and Paul ever give such a document to the people they baptized?"

Youssef laughs heartily. *This man's faith is really sincere. No need for ceremony, just simply following what the Bible says.*

The pastor laughs, too, at Ahmed's innocent, almost childish remarks. *Indeed, this is what Jesus meant when he said we must become like children.*

"Pastor Majed, is it possible for Ahmed to be baptized this afternoon?" Youssef asks politely.

The pastor frowns. Usually, he allows for several weeks for preparation. First, the person who wants to be baptized must understand clearly what he is about to do and take time to think through the implications. In short, he must be sure. Furthermore, the elders of the church must agree, and there cannot be any opposition from the church members either. These things take time.

Youssef understands his pastor's reasoning and so he adds, "Pastor, this is an exception. Ahmed is not going to be a church member who will be coming to church every Sunday." At the risk of sounding facetious, Youssef queries, "What do you think John the Baptist would have done?"

Ahmed and Youssef wait anxiously for the older man on the simple desk chair to respond. Majed, however, doesn't want to answer immediately. This is a real dilemma and he would prefer to talk it over with someone else. "Please, give me a moment," he excuses himself as he gets up to go and find his wife. Sometimes, she intuitively knows what the right thing is to do; while he remains stuck in his thoughts between arguments for and against. In a few sentences he explains his predicament to her and she immediately responds, saying, "Youssef is right. You should baptize this man."

With his heart beating, Majed returns to his office where the young men are engaged in an animated discussion about the sermon.

"Alright," he sighs. His throat is tight and he has to make an effort to continue. What if someone hears what he is about to do? Perhaps they would ask him to leave his post as pastor of the church. "I will baptize you," he says finally.

"God be praised! Thank you so much!" Ahmed replies happily.

"But I cannot do it here in the church," Majed continues.

Ahmed is surprised and looks at his friend. Didn't he tell him earlier that the church has a built-in basin for the purpose of baptisms?

Youssef feels ill at ease. On the one hand, he would like his Arab friend to be baptized in the church, like any other believer, but on the other hand, he understands Pastor Majed's misgivings about it. Together, they try to come up with a solution. The luxury hotels have swimming pools, but no privacy. Another option would be to drive to the Jordan River, but that is at least an hour away.

"The only other possibility is a bath tub," Majed resolves. "The only problem is that I do not have one." He looks at Youssef quizzically.

What would my father say if I were to bring Ahmed home? Probably he would be quite upset. Youssef ardently searches his brain for another solution for the baptism, but he can't think of anywhere. Reluctantly he says. "I will ask my father."

Majed reassures him when he says, "If your father agrees, that will be a confirmation from the Lord."

Ahmed cannot understand them at all. *Why is this so difficult? Isn't this what Jesus asks his followers to do? Shouldn't we then just obey him?*

Youssef promises that he will ask his father immediately, agreeing that if his father gives his consent, the men will meet at his house around *Asr*.*

That evening, Youssef once again opens Skype to talk to Noura.

"Listen to this!" He can hardly contain his excitement. "He took a bath!" He carefully omits any direct references to Ahmed's baptism. One can never be too careful of who might be listening in on these communications. The Jordanian secret police is very alert to any activities that might undermine the authority of the government.

Noura is not sure how to react. She is happy to hear her cousin's story of how everything worked out that afternoon, but at the same time he hadn't heeded her warnings. *I just hope it turns out well.*

When she finally says, "That's nice," Youssef detects coolness in her voice, but tries to ignore it. He continues, "You know, God has blessed this act in a much greater way then I could have ever anticipated."

"Really? In what way?" Noura remains skeptical.

"Well, in the first place, it was a courageous act of Pastor Majed to do what is written in the Bible rather than following the church rules."

Noura cannot deny this. She had not expected him to do that. The pastor is a nice enough man, but he strongly abides by the orthodox traditions and customs of the church. When a teenager, she would have liked to sing modern worship songs during the services, but that was never a subject for discussion. Leaving her thoughts aside, she asks, "What happened after that?"

---

* Arabic timestamp for mid-afternoon. For more information, see www.godlovesishmael.com/ prayertimes.

"In the second place, my father agreed to have it in our house."

"Really? You're crazy!" Noura blurts out. With a calmer tone she continues, "Don't you realize what could happen if the neighbors or even passers-by find out what took place?"

Youssef feels annoyed. "God is doing miracles here, Noura! You were the one who pointed this out to me before! I fully trust that if we obey him, He will also protect us."

"Was your father present?" Noura asks, obviously still concerned.

"No, unfortunately, my family decided to visit friends this afternoon." Youssef replies.

Noura sighs with relief. At least if problems were to arise later, her uncle could say that he was not aware of anything. "What happened after that?"

Youssef relates to her how he was touched to the core by what occurred next. "After Ahmed dried himself and changed his clothes, he suddenly said, 'I feel there is a barrier between God and me. He wants me to let go of my anger towards my brother and bless him instead.' That was such an awesome moment." While Youssef is still speaking, he feels overwhelmed again and tears come to his eyes. This was such clear evidence of God's Spirit at work in a man's heart. Youssef continues, "We then prayed together and he asked God to forgive him his anger. After that, Ahmad pronounced a blessing on his brother."

Now it is Noura's turn to be tearful and she says in a choked voice, "Truly, this is what Jesus has accomplished on the cross; reconciliation between God and man, which leads to reconciliation between people as well."

With a broad smile on his face, Youssef says, "Exactly. God does not want anyone to perish, but everyone to come to repentance."[182]

Noura thinks of a conversation she had with Youssef earlier. She still hopes her cousin will accept her point of view and says, "Do you remember when we spoke about God's plan for the Arabs?"

"Of course, He will cause many of them to come to faith," Youssef responds happily.

"Indeed! And what will happen after they accept Jesus Christ as Lord and Savior?"

"The Jewish people will become jealous of them, right?" Youssef says somewhat hesitantly.

"Yes, but that's not all! Do you remember what it says in Romans 11 verse 26?"

Youssef doesn't, at least not now, so Noura answers her own question. "It says all of Israel will be saved!"

Youssef swallows a couple of times. Is God really willing to bless a nation that has caused so many problems in the lives of his people? And yet, it is written that He does not want anyone to perish. Suddenly, he thinks of Paul. *He was a dangerous Jewish extremist, and yet, Jesus personally revealed himself to him. If God was willing to extend his grace to the one who tried to kill the Christians, He must also be concerned about today's Jews and desire to save them.*

When Youssef tells Noura what he is thinking, she cries out, "Amen!" She feels a glowing warmth flow through her body. *How my cousin has grown in his faith!* Barely able to contain her excitement, she says with a smile on her face, "Do you remember when I spoke to you about Tass Saada? He is the Palestinian man who, when he was a Muslim, tried to kill the Jews but now he is telling them about God's love."

Youssef thinks back to the website he had found. "Isn't that the man whose aim it is to reconcile both Arabs and Jews to God?"

"Yes! What do you think of that now?"

"Yeah, that is actually pretty amazing." While Youssef is still speaking, a flood of love and compassion comes over him. Suddenly, he can no longer see the Jews as his enemies but rather as a lost people, a flock of sheep without a shepherd.

"Let us pray together for Tass," Youssef suggests. Without waiting for Noura's reply, he pours out his heart to God. "Thank you, Heavenly Father, for your grace in our lives. Thank you, Lord Jesus for loving the Muslims. You died for them all, even for the most violent extremists. You alone can change the hearts of men. Please, reveal yourself to those who are blind and use our brother Tass to bless your people…" For a moment, Youssef's voice falters. *Am I really going to pray for the Jews as God's people?* The thought of Ishmael and Isaac as half-brothers helps him overcome his hesitation. "… to bless and love your people, Israel. Use us, Lord Jesus, to make them jealous according to your heavenly plan. Amen."

Noura wipes her face with a tissue. She has been deeply moved by her cousin's words. She then prays, "Thank you, dear heavenly Father, for your Word through which we can know your will. Thank You, for the work of your Spirit in our hearts, who teaches us all things. Thank You, Lord Jesus, for coming to save sinners. Please, bless our brother Tass and protect him. Bless our people and use us for your glory. Make us a blessing to the Jews that they may be saved too. In Jesus' precious name. Amen."

In this part of the book, we have met several people whose opinions represent points of view regarding Israel and the Arabs. We followed Ahmed, a Muslim man in his sincere search for God. When Jesus Christ revealed himself to him, Ahmed believed, and he found peace. We also met Youssef, the Palestinian Christian, who tried his best to love the Muslims. Then, we encountered Noura, Youssef's praying cousin, who made some incredible discoveries during her studies in the US, which in turn caused her to revise her ideas about the problems in the Middle East. Finally, we crossed paths with Pastor Majed, who at first held on to the traditional notions of Arab Christians, but then took a bold step against these convictions.

Which one of these characters would you identify with the most? Are you like Ahmed, trying to obey the things you read in the Bible? Or do you think like Youssef, who wants to do God's will, but somehow can't fully understand why his grace extends to all people. Perhaps you feel more of a kinship with Noura, who is open to exploring new ideas, away from the church traditions. Or maybe you prefer Majed, who holds to certain evangelical doctrines, which offer a degree of security in life. Perhaps you recognize something in yourself from all four of them?

Please take the time to re-read the Scripture verses mentioned in this section of the book without any pre-conceived ideas and ask the Lord to give you clarity and insight. The apostle Paul wrote, "Faith comes from hearing."[183] Our faith, as well as our expectations for the future, come by hearing God's Word, not by strictly adhering to our Christian traditions.

Perhaps you did not recognize yourself in any of these characters. Perhaps you were even a little annoyed with the pro-Palestinian tone of this last part of the book. This is understandable, as the story has been written from a Palestinian perspective; hence, the image of reality presented appears to be somewhat skewed. Truth be told, there is wrongdoing on both sides of the Israeli-Palestinian conflict. The Palestinian people suffer under corrupted regimes that do not honor God or his commandments. But this also applies to the Jews, of whom 20% claim to be completely secular, and only 25% view themselves as orthodox or ultra-orthodox.[184] The current state of Israel was founded on secular principles, and it is the secular intellectuals who control the political climate. In short, they do not seek God's will for their nation nor for their lives.

Let us review some of the Bible passages we came across.

Romans 10:19-21 speaks of God's intention to make the Jews envious of the Gentiles. It describes people who have not become a nation. Usually, this is seen as a reference to the followers of Christ from all nations of the world. In a spiritual sense, they are identified as God's people. However, the passage also speaks of a "foolish nation". This points to a specific people, in contrast to those who are "not a nation."

Could this refer to the Arabic nomads who cross national borders with their flocks without carrying passports and who are not a nation, while at the same time being descendants of the Ishmaelite tribes? Or is this about the Palestinians, many of whom originate from the Ishmaelites, and today live across several Middle Eastern nations. The description, "not a nation" can equally be applied to both groups. Also, historically the Ishmaelites have not been known as a nation, even though they were a distinct people group.

Furthermore, we read that God would reveal himself to those who did not specifically ask for him. The words in Isaiah 65:1b perfectly fit with this notion. It says, "I said, 'Here I am, here I am,' to a nation that did not call upon my name." Alternative translations may say, "a nation that was not called by my name." This, too, speaks of a specific people, a people who did not call on the Name of the Lord (Yahweh), or was not called after him. The descendants of Jacob were called the people of God, while the descendants of Ishmael and Esau were not. God did not, however, forget about them. He promised to look after them as well.

Romans 11:11 states that salvation has come to the Gentiles to make Israel jealous. This begs the question as to which Gentiles or non-Jews are most likely to make the Jews jealous? Wouldn't that be their nearest relatives – notably the descendants of their half-brother Ishmael? If the descendants of Ishmael came to faith in Jesus Christ, would the Jews not want to follow as well? Could it be God's plan to firstly save many Muslim Arabs to arouse the jealousy of the relatives of their ancestor's half-brother Isaac? Could it be that the Arabs are called to prepare the way for the Jews to come to Christ, in that when they see God's plan of salvation at work in the lives of their half-brothers, they will no longer be able to deny that Jesus of Nazareth is indeed the Messiah?

Perhaps you are wondering, "What about God's judgment on all the nations during the end times who turned against the Israelites?" There are after all, many clear Scripture references about this.

This is true. Judgment is coming and many Muslims do not seek peace for Israel. According to Islamic eschatology, Jesus will even return to earth to destroy all the Jews.[185] On that basis, one may easily conclude from the Bible that God will judge many Arabs. Yet, an in-depth search of the Bible brings to light other interesting facts. For example, in Isaiah 66:14-18 one finds a description of the events unfolding on Judgment Day. Many Gentiles will be slain by the Lord. In verse 17 they are described as people who eat mice and pork! Furthermore, who are the people who will worship God in Jerusalem, according to Isaiah 60:6-7? Indeed, they are the descendants of Ishmael, together with the Midianites and the people from Sheba. All this points to a special role God has reserved for the Arabs in the end times.

What about the Christians? Does God not want to use them especially to arouse the jealousy of the Jews? As a matter of fact, God wants to use each one of his children across the whole world; every follower of Jesus Christ can and should serve as God's instrument. Unfortunately, we must admit that the church of Christ has done a rather poor job of making Israel jealous over the past 2,000 years. During a large part of that time the church has even laid claim to many of the promises meant solely for Israel.* Only after the Jews proclaimed the State of Israel in 1948 did many Christians begin to view God's chosen people in a new light. Over the past 60 years, people have become more and more aware of God's plan for the Jews, the descendants of Abraham, Isaac, and Jacob. Many Christians believe that the Anti-Christ will come out from among the Muslims, descendants of Abraham's son, Ishmael. They refer to the hatred Muslims display towards the Jews, and to the fact that some would like to wipe the nation of Israel off the map. There is, however, no indication in the Bible that supports the claim that Ishmael's offspring wish to kill and destroy the descendants of their half-brother. Even the passage in Galatians 4 does not offer any clear proof to support that notion. Therefore, we can safely conclude that God wants to and will use Arabic Christians, and that in his sovereign will He will draw many Muslims to himself, in order that his greatness might be shown to the Jews.

What about the hatred directed at the Jews in the Middle East? The Bible speaks of another people, who hated the Jews from the very beginning. It all started with their ancestor, Esau, who wanted to kill his brother. God protected Jacob and eventually, Esau changed his mind, but throughout the history of the Old Testament, we notice that the Edomites, the descendants of Esau, have been very envious of their twin brother. Not only did they attack him regularly, but they also had no compassion for Israel when they were taken into exile. On the contrary, they were very eager to take the Isra-

---

* This began in the second century and became a generally accepted theology after Constantine the Great made Christianity the state religion. See also
www.godlovesishmael.com/replacement.

elites' land for themselves. They set themselves up against God's plan and He opposed them, judging them severely.*

Nowadays, one can distinguish between Arabs who have the spirit of Ishmael and those who have the spirit of Esau. The Arab Christians are peace-loving people who worship Jesus as Lord, just like some of their forefathers - the wise men from the East – once did shortly after his birth. Many Arab Muslims are peace-loving people as well, to one another and to non-Arabs. Whoever travels to the Middle East, whether to Jordan or to Yemen, will immediately be moved by the heart-warming hospitality of the Arabs.

The spirit of Esau is rampant in some of the smaller groups of Muslims who have no respect for life, who are willing not only to sacrifice themselves but also many innocent lives, in order to cause as much death and destruction as possible. Though they think they serve God in doing so, nothing could be further from the truth.

What then is God's plan for the descendants of Ishmael? In the next, and also last part of this book we will arrive at a conclusion. Read on to catch a glimpse of God's great grace and his sovereign plan.

---

* See for instance Ezekiel 35 and Obadiah. For a more detailed study, please go to www.godlovesishmael.com/edomites.

Part 6

Everything at a Glance

A Summarizing Overview,
A Preview, and
A Personal Application

1 *Rejected*

What went through the mind of thirteen-year old Ishmael when he heard the news of a baby brother? And not just any brother! God had told his father that Sarah would have a son. Surely, Ishmael reacted in much the same way his father had done, "Impossible!" Then, when Sarah became pregnant despite her advanced age, he must have been astonished but probably not very worried. Only when Sarah made it clear that Isaac would be the son of the promise did Ishmael understand the reality of God's plan and what that meant for him. The birthright due the eldest son was no longer his; he lost the honor of becoming the patriarch of the next generation. Finally, he could no longer lay claim to God's promise of becoming a blessing for all nations.

Ishmael had been rejected. He was not the son of promise. God's people would not come forth from him. Neither would his offspring produce the Savior God had promised to Eve while she was still in the Garden of Eden.[186] Contrary to what he had believed, he was not the fulfillment of God's promises. Ishmael's world suddenly collapsed. To make matters worse, his father sent him away, straight into the desert. And this happened at the command of God himself!

Many centuries later, an Arab man arose, claiming to have received messages from God. He gave his people, the Arabs, hope and an identity. Many began to believe he was the promised prophet, of whom God had spoken to Moses. When they first spread the teachings of their prophet, they greatly succeeded. Within several decades, they conquered the entire Arabian Peninsula, subjecting everyone to what they believed were the true teachings of God. Less than a century later, their influence extended from Spain all the way to India. To them, their military successes meant that God was on their side.

Yet, the rapid expansion finally came to an end; they were unsuccessful in their efforts to subjugate the whole world to their teachings. Over the past two centuries, their followers suffered many defeats and they even saw the colonization of large parts of their territory by Western nations. The roles seemed to have been reversed. The ones whose mission it was to conquer the whole world for their religion, were now dominated by governments of – in their eyes – infidels. They had failed.

This in turn raised a question that still rings today. Where is God in all of this? Has He rejected the Arabs, just like He rejected their forefather Ishmael?

2 Beloved

Many years before the birth of Ishmael, God told Abraham that all nations of the earth would be blessed through his offspring. Later, God made a covenant with him and promised him large areas of land, land where, at that time, other people were living. Years after the birth of Ishmael, Abraham learned that God was going to give him another son, a son by Sarah. God renewed his covenant with Isaac, the son of the promise, and not with Ishmael, Abraham's first-born son. This raises the question: What about the earlier promise that through Abraham's offspring all nations would be blessed? Does this promise apply only to the descendants of Isaac or could it apply to Ishmael and his offspring as well?

To answer this question, let us take another look at the life of Ishmael. In the review of part one, several unique occurrences and blessings were highlighted. Some of the key ones are expounded below:

1) The Meeting With the Angel of the Lord

When Hagar fled, God sent his Heavenly Messenger – the Lord Jesus – to her. It is remarkable that today, Jesus reveals himself to many descendants of Ishmael, not only to his direct descendants in Jordan and Saudi Arabia, but also to his spiritual descendants: Muslims worldwide. Many of them have dreams and visions in which they meet Jesus, the Eternal Word of God.
See also: www.godlovesishmael.com/angel

2) A Large Offspring

God promised to make Ishmael into a great people (Genesis 16:10, 17:20), in the same way He had previously promised Abraham (Genesis 15:5). After that, only Isaac received the same promise (Genesis 17:6,16). Abraham's children by Keturah received no share in this blessing. In the next generation, God distinguished again between two sons, whereby Jacob became the recipient of the blessing, instead of the firstborn Esau (Genesis 28:4,14).

It is amazing to see that God has truly kept his promises. Both the descendants of Ishmael and those of Isaac, through Jacob, have grown into great nations. It is estimated that there are about 14 million Jews worldwide, while approximate calculations deem the number of Ishmaelite Arabs to be roughly 18 million.

This, in and of itself, is quite remarkable, considering the harsh environment in which Ishmael's offspring lived. The desert does not provide for livable conditions and yet this is exactly the place where Ishmael and his descendants dwelled all of their lives. The children of Israel survived 40 years in the wilderness, only because God cared for them in a special way (Deuteronomy 8:2-4, 29:5-6, 32:10-11). Likewise, God looked after Hagar and Ishmael when they wandered about in the wilderness together. While Ishmael lay dying, God miraculously provided water for Hagar and her son. Later, Ishmael became the father of twelve healthy sons. It is a miracle that the Ishmaelites survived in the desert. To even grow into a great nation in their dire circumstances can only mean that God richly blessed them. Thanks to his protection against disease, danger, and starvation, the Arabs have been able to carve out a life for themselves and multiply. In the same way God watched over Ishmael (Genesis 21:20), He also remained faithful to his offspring.

God had promised that the descendants of Abraham, Isaac and Jacob would become a great nation. He deliberately blessed them so that they would serve him and make his name known among all the peoples of the earth (Deuteronomy 4:6, 28:10, Psalm 67, 96:3, Isaiah 56:7b, Jeremiah 33:9). Being blessed to be a blessing to others is a recurring theme in Scripture. Logically this principle would also be true for Ishmael and his offspring. Therefore, we conclude that God blessed Ishmael with many descendants that they might also bless others. He wants to use the Arabs to make his love and grace known.

3) The Name 'Ishmael'

Only four times in the history of mankind did God make the name of a child known before it was born. The two most well-known of these are John the Baptist and Jesus (Luke 1:13, 31). The other two are Ishmael and his half-brother, Isaac (Genesis 17:19). God honored Ishmael in the same way He honored his own Son. This shows his love for Ishmael. Since God had a unique plan for the three others, it is most likely that He also had and has a special purpose for Ishmael, a plan that would extend not only until the birth of Christ, but also long afterwards. Even as God's purposes for the descendants of Isaac will come full circle in the end times, so also will Ishmael's offspring play an important role before Jesus returns to this earth. This view is supported by several prophecies about Nebaioth and Kedar, Ishmael's sons - prophecies that are yet to be fulfilled.

Furthermore, the name Ishmael has a prophetic meaning. Through this name, God is telling Ishmael's descendants that He hears them. He is the God who hears prayer. One day, many centuries ago, the descendants of Ishmael began to follow the teachings of an Arab man, who ordered them to pray five times a day. He told them that God is too great and too mighty for man to have a direct and intimate relationship with him. In this, he seems to have followed his Jewish contemporaries who did not dare call God by his name. Through Moses, God had invited the children of Israel to call him by his personal name, Yahweh* (Exodus 3:13-14); however, a couple of centuries before the birth of Christ, the religious leaders decided that God was too exalted for anyone to call him by his name. Instead, they started to call him *Adonai*, which means "Lord" or "Master", to signify a deferential distance between man and God, the Creator of heaven and earth.

God, however, loves us so much that he wants to have an intimate relationship with us, just like He had with Moses and Abraham. He showed us this through Jesus Christ, who said, "Whoever has seen Me, has seen the Father."[187] God also made known to us through Jesus Christ that He hears and answers our prayers. Jesus emphatically told his followers, "Truly, truly, I say to you, whatever you ask of the Father in my name, He will give it to you."[188]

Many Arabs kneel down, prostrating themselves on the ground several times a day, praying, "Guide us to the straight path."[189] Would God not answer every prayer that comes from a sincere heart? Considering the meaning of the name of Ishmael – *God hears* – it is fascinating to see that God gives many Arabs dreams and visions, in which Jesus appears. In this way, God shows that He still watches over the Hagars and Ishmaels today.

4) A Wild Donkey of a Man

This divine prediction perhaps best expresses the epitome of God's love for Ishmael. This tremendous promise assured Hagar that neither her son, nor his offspring would ever live under the yoke of slavery again. God had said that they would live in freedom, just like the wild donkeys, in contrast to the domesticated ones who were yoked to a plough. Later, God mentioned to Job the freedom the wild donkeys enjoy as they roam in the wilderness (Job 39:5-8). In the same way, Ishmael and his descendants would live in the desert, freely and independently.

The following example perfectly illustrates the beauty of gaining freedom from slavery. Even today, slavery is an issue in the Middle East. There are entire groups of people descending from slaves. Even those who have attained high education are not permitted to hold certain government positions. Their family name betrays their heritage and it is virtually impossible for them to remove themselves from it. It takes a miracle to free them from their identity.

---

* The Hebrew Yahweh means 'I am who I am'.

This is exactly the miracle God promised to Hagar, which became a reality the very moment she and Ishmael were sent away. On the one hand, they were rejected, but on the other hand they were freed from slavery. From that moment on, they were able to go where they pleased. Even today, we can observe the literal fulfillment of this promise. The wild donkeys of the United Arab Emirates and Oman migrate in groups from one oasis to the next. In the same way, nomadic Bedouins travel freely between the nations of the Arabian Peninsula without any passport or visa!

Yet, most Arabs lack inner freedom. Spiritually speaking, they have not yet entered their destiny. They suffer the yoke of faithfully observing many religious laws and rules by which they were raised. At the same time, they are plagued with uncertainty, not ever knowing whether their good deeds are good enough. Consequently, they live in constant fear of God's judgment. Furthermore, the temptation to fulfill the fleshly desires, as well as the pressure to gain excessive wealth, has caused many to become entangled in webs of lies and corruption. Finally, the need to constantly guard not only their own honor, but also the honor of their family, their tribe, their land, and their religion, paralyzes their soul and hinders them from fulfilling their God-given purpose.

Some are proud of their name, such as Abdullah or Abdel Rahman, which mean "slave of God" and "slave of the Merciful"; claiming they are enslaved to no one. Still, many are addicted to a craving for more wealth and riches, to smoking or drinking or to eating lots of good food, or to intimate physical relationships outside of marriage. Without realizing it, they are like the Jews during Jesus' time, who declared, "We are offspring of Abraham and have never been enslaved to anyone." Jesus explained how God sees them, by stating, "Everyone who practices sin is a slave to sin."[190]

Although millions of Arabs are caught in a life of slavery to sin, there is hope for deliverance. Jesus said, "The slave does not remain in the house forever; the son remains forever. So if the Son sets you free, you will be free indeed"[191] Jesus' invitation to be delivered from the slavery of sin goes out to every human being. How much more to the descendants of Ishmael who were destined to be free according to the prophetic word in Genesis 16:12.

5) Ishmael's Circumcision

Why did God give Abraham the order to circumcise every male in his household before sending Ishmael away and not after? Why did God not say, "Only circumcise yourself and your son Isaac." Would that not have avoided a lot of confusion? We do not know the answer to that question. All we know is that in his sovereignty, God did not exclude Ishmael from this sign of the covenant. He must have had his own good reason. Strangely enough, all Muslim males worldwide are being circumcised today, even though the Qur'an does not dictate this. This custom then, goes back all the way to God's command to Abraham when He made his covenant with him.

6) *Twelve Sons*

True to his promise that twelve tribes would come from Ishmael, God blessed him with twelve sons. Even today, people in many cultures view having many sons as a blessing from God. This is in stark contrast to Ishmael's half-brother, Isaac, who had only two children. It was only Isaac's son, Jacob, who received twelve sons from the Lord, each of whom also became a tribal leader.

In the end then, we can safely conclude that Ishmael was not completely rejected by God, even if it seemed so when he was sent away. Although he was not the son of promise, he was not rejected as a son. The same goes for his offspring. God's love for the Arabs did not cease after Ishmael, but rather extended to his descendants and holds true to this present day. They have not been rejected; on the contrary, God loves them and is concerned about them.

It was God's will that through Isaac and his offspring, all nations would be blessed. What then is his will for Ishmael's descendants?

3 God's Plan

What does the future hold for the Arabs? Some Christians believe there is enough evidence to conclude that the anti-Christ will come out of Islam. This position, however, ignores the fact that there is great diversity among the Muslims. While it is true that, based on the Qur'an and Hadith, some of them have made it their goal to destroy Israel, the majority desire to live in peace and quiet with their neighbors. God is patient, for He is "not wishing that any should perish, but that all should reach repentance"[192] If this is true for Animists in Africa, Buddhists in China, and Hindus in India, wouldn't it also be true for the 1.8 billion Muslims worldwide? Wouldn't God desire to set them free from the slavery of sin as well?

More than that, if God has promised that the whole of Israel will come to faith (Romans 11:26-32), would He not extend his plan of salvation to Isaac's half-brother? The prophecies in Isaiah 42 and 60 point to Ishmael's descendants willingly bowing down before King Jesus. They will follow in the footsteps of the wise men from the East who came to worship Jesus shortly after his birth in Bethlehem. In addition to his willingness to free all of Ishmael's offspring, God wants to use them in a very special way.

Ishmaelites a Blessing to Other People

God has blessed Ishmael in several unique ways. Ishmael was not required to do any good works to obtain these blessings; he received them unconditionally, through God's grace. As it is a Biblical principle to pass on what you have received[193], it was God's plan from the start that Ishmael and his descendants would, in turn, bless others. They indeed became a blessing throughout the centuries.

The first indication is in Ishmael's willingness to subject himself to God's plan. He did not oppose his father when he sent him away, neither did he harbor any envy or bitterness against his father or his half-brother. On the contrary, he reconciled with his father and continued to maintain an amicable relationship with Isaac. As such, he is a prime example for anyone who finds himself in a humiliating situation.

About a century later, God used Ishmael's descendants in a crucial moment in the life of Joseph. Joseph's life was spared by the appearance of the Ishmaelite traders, and so Jacob and his descendants eventually escaped death from starvation. This, in turn, also saved the Egyptians and other surrounding nations from the same fate.

Job, who most likely was a descendant of Ishmael, offers us a powerful example of patient suffering as an innocent man. He has become a tremendous blessing to all generations after him and countless believers worldwide.

In the centuries following these events, the Ishmaelites were generally on good terms with the Israelites. Though there were occasional skirmishes between them, they cannot be compared to the many conflicts between Israel and other neighboring people, namely the Philistines, the Moabites, the Ammonites, and the Edomites.*

During that time, God gave Israel and her neighbors many prophetic messages. Many of them focus on judgment, but there were also great promises.**

Isaiah, for instance, prophesied boldly about the day that the descendants of Nebaioth and Kedar would come freely to worship God in Jerusalem. We have had a foretaste of this fulfillment in the visit by the wise men from the East, who worshiped young Jesus by bringing him precious gifts and bowing down to him.

Are the Arabs to Bless Other People?

We have been able to see how the Ishmaelites were a blessing in several ways but what about the Arabs of today?

The prophet Isaiah predicted that one day Egypt and Assyria would worship the Lord, and that they, together with Israel would become a blessing in the midst of the earth (Isaiah 19:18-25). In the days of Isaiah, the Assyrian Empire covered large parts of Southeastern Turkey, Northeastern Syria, Northern Iraq, and Northwestern Iran. The prophet also spoke of Sheba, whose queen had visited King Solomon a few centuries earlier. In the Gospel of Matthew, Jesus says that on the last day, she will judge the unbelievers (Matthew 12:42), thus declaring her to be a believer. Isaiah prophesied about the people of Sheba, which is modern-day Yemen, that they would honor God in Jerusalem (Psalm 72:15, Isaiah 45:14, 60:6).

Since history gives us no indication to suggest these things have already occurred on a large scale, it is reasonable to assume that these promises point to a future fulfillment. Although most inhabitants of Egypt, Iraq,

---

* For an overview, please consult www.godlovesishmael.com/conflicts.

** For an overview, please consult www.godlovesishmael.com/prophecies.

and Yemen are not direct descendants of Ishmael, most consider themselves Arabs. It is simply astounding that it was foretold thousands of years ago, that these Arab nations would one day seek and worship the God of Israel whole-heartedly.

In the light of this, we know that we can expect a large-scale revival in the Middle East. God indeed desires that all should come to faith (2 Peter 3:9).

The Fullness of the Non-Jews

We arrive then at the culmination of world history, a climactic event still ahead of us. Led by God's Holy Spirit, Paul proclaimed that the Jews will come to faith in the Messiah on a large-scale (Romans 11:26). This will happen after the full number of the Gentiles are saved (Romans 11:25).

Today, many Gentiles (non-Jews) have come to know Jesus Christ, the Son of God, crucified and resurrected for the forgiveness of their sins. Through faith in him, they have entered into the rest God gives to both the Jew and the non-Jew. By putting their trust in the completed work of Jesus Christ, they have found rest from trying to earn their way to heaven through good works. They have been set free from the fear of not knowing whether these works were good enough or not (Hebrews 4:10).

There are, however, also large numbers of Gentiles who believe that Jesus was only a prophet. Among them are many Arabs, as well as non-Arabs, who hold this view. They believe that their prophet is a descendant of Ishmael and see Abraham as their spiritual ancestor, just like the Christians and the Jews. They may be considered the spiritual offspring of Ishmael. How can we speak of the fullness of the Gentiles if they all remain under God's judgment?

God promised that Ishmael would be 'a wild donkey of a man' – living in freedom. The prophecies have shown us that this promise is not limited to Ishmael himself but has been given to all his descendants. The prophecies also name some other people groups who are considered Arabs today, such as Egyptians, Iraqis, and Yemenis. God wants to bless them with freedom as well. Wouldn't God bless all spiritual descendants of Ishmael, wherever they are in the world, in the same way?

Paul wrote that God has allowed the Israelites to be disobedient, in order that He might show them his mercy (Romans 11:31-32). In the same way, many Arabs and other Gentile nations have been walking in disobedience, but God has compassion on them as well. The fullness of the Gentiles cannot be accomplished until many millions of Muslims worldwide bow down to the Lord Jesus, following the example of the Wise Men from the East.

It is striking to note that the Muslims are so close to the truth. They confess that there is only One God, the Creator of heaven and earth. They recognize the prophets whom God sent to his people in the past and they expect God will judge every person on earth. Many of their actions can be traced back to the Laws of Moses*, and thus Muslims believe and often practice Biblical principles much more than, for instance, the Hindus, Buddhists, Animists, and atheists. What they lack is a personal experience with God's fatherly love and a revelation that Jesus Christ is who he says he is.

God wants to use us, followers of Jesus, to pray for them, love them, and show them the light of Christ.

The Role of the Arabs during the End Times

Paul describes how God will touch the hearts of the disobedient Israelites: they will become jealous of the Gentiles (Romans 10:19, 11:11). This raises the question as to which Gentiles are most likely to arouse the jealousy of the Jews. Over the past 2,000 years, the non-Jews from the West and other parts of the world have only been partially successful. Could it be God's plan to reach the Jews through the Arabs? If many of the descendants of their half-brother Ishmael come to faith in Jesus, the Messiah, what will the response of the Jews be? Will they not envy them? Will they not want to receive God's grace as well? Will they not desire the supernatural peace the Palestinians, Jordanians, Saudis, and all the other nations around them experience through faith in Jesus as Lord and Savior?

Humanly speaking, this seems impossible. Peter, one of Jesus' followers, was confronted with a similar impossibility. When Jesus said that it was easier for a camel to go through the eye of a needle than for a rich person to enter the kingdom of God, Peter asked him, "Who can be saved, then?" Jesus responded, "What is impossible with man, is possible with God."[194] God wants to save all the Arabs and in the end use them to draw the Israelites unto himself.

It is fascinating to see that God has already begun his redemptive work among them. These days, more and more Arabs are coming to faith in the Middle East and in other areas, and some of them, such as Tass Saada, are already working tirelessly to bring reconciliation between them and the Jews.

Once the Arabs begin to experience God's loving-kindness and his gracious compassion deep in their souls and they are delivered from the burden of sin, they will find the courage to live their lives in radical obedience to him. Only when Hagar was touched by the love of God, was she able to freely

---

* For a comparison between Islam and Jewish laws and customs, please consult www.godlovesishmael.com/koran-thora.

submit to Sarah. In the same way, the Arabs will no longer resist the Jews, but instead they will accept Sarah's descendants as God's chosen people and serve them by leading them to Jesus.

The Desert Will Begin to Bloom.

Finally, in Isaiah 32 and 35, we witness a remarkable transformation that will take place in the desert. When we read these passages through the eyes of an Arab, we can understand it differently. Then we realize that God is not simply talking about the wilderness of Judah, but that He, in fact, will cause even the deserts of Jordan and the Arabian Peninsula, to bloom like a rose.

This seems impossible and it raises the question as to whether these prophecies should be interpreted literally or figuratively. Could it be that the sandy desert plains of the Middle East will be transformed into an earthly paradise or will God cause the hearts of the inhabitants to flourish?

Perhaps God envisions both. Worldwide, we can observe many examples of how these two scenarios fit together. Whenever people start to serve God wholeheartedly, they also begin to improve the way they treat their environment. Invariably, they begin to utilize their natural resources better, consequently reaping much bigger harvests.[195]

When the Arabs begin to obey God's commandments, the landscape of the Middle East is bound to change from a barren wasteland into fertile soil dotted with pools of water.

For a documentary about a present-day example, please refer to: www.godlovesishmael.com/desert.

The Timing

A popular interpretation of the verses and promises mentioned above is that these things shall take place during the 1,000-year reign of peace. God's timing with regards to the fulfillment of his promises has been a matter of debate among scholars and theologians for centuries. Perhaps, God did not see the need to give us any further details.

However, there is one thing we can be sure of: God has given us ample evidence within his Word for us to conclude that the Ishmaelites have a special place in his heart, as well as in his plan for this world. Yes, God will use them indeed in his own time and for his own glory!

4. What Next?

Congratulations! You made it to the end of the book! What will you do now? Perhaps, you will put the book aside, thinking, "Interesting, but not for me." You could also think about the question, "What does the message of God's love for the Arab people mean to me personally?" I challenge you to consider the latter.

When I started writing this book, several people asked me, "Who is your target audience?" Initially I thought about those Christians that have difficulty accepting Muslims. Then I considered the multitudes of Muslims who live in fear of the Day of Judgment. Some-time later, someone told me that the book is also relevant to the Jews. And finally, I came to the conclusion from my conversations with those that claim no adherence to any religion that even they might benefit from reading this book. That is why would like to close with a few personal thoughts to each one from these four groups. But before I do, I want to share a general principle with all of you.

Desire to Bless

God said to Abraham, "I will bless those who bless you, and him who dishonors you, I will curse"[196] The message is clear. God wants us to desire the welfare of all the descendants of Abraham, both the Jews *and* the Arabs.

If we only support the Jews and they come to faith, Palestinians and other Arabs will likely make the Jews' lives miserable. And if we only help the Palestinians, the Jews will likely respond negatively, as the guiding principle of both these peoples is "an eye for an eye and a tooth for a tooth."

Only the love of Jesus can reconcile the two half-brothers. If you were to picture these two people groups as the two rails of a railroad, the ties would represent the love of Christ, which allow the "train of peace" to travel back and forth.

God linked a promise to his message: whoever blesses Abraham will be blessed. Ishmael, Esau, and Jacob are all part of his offspring. I encourage you to seek the good for both the Jewish people and the Arab nations that surround them. As a result, you will be blessed yourself.

If you are a Christian reading this, I would like to ask you to seriously put into practice God's commandment of loving your neighbor. God wants to use you to help the Muslims around you to find freedom. Perhaps you fear them because they behave differently or because they speak a different language. Perhaps you consider them your enemy, because you have seen acts of violence reported in the media. However, when you start loving your Muslim neighbors, colleagues, and classmates, you will find that they are very friendly and hospitable. And even if there are some who react with hostility to your kindness, they usually have a good reason. Perhaps they have experienced rejection in their new country. Or perhaps their hostility comes because of centuries of rejection.

For a detailed study on Muslims' feeling of rejection, please visit: www.godlovesishmael.com/rejected. The website also provides useful tips on how to love the Muslims you meet in simple ways.
See www.godlovesishmael.com/6tips.

Let us continue to prayerfully look forward to the fulfillment of God's plan and let us love the Arabs in the same way God loves them. May the name of God be glorified.

If you are a Muslim reading this, I encourage you to open your heart to the things God is saying to you. God wants a personal relationship with you, in the same way He related to the prophets Abraham and Moses. This has been made possible by the coming of Jesus the Messiah, who, through his death on the cross, reversed the consequences of the sin of Adam and Eve. Because of Jesus, you are no longer a slave to sin, but you can become a son or daughter of your heavenly Father. This is God's plan for you. Accept the truth about who Jesus really is and allow him to free you from your burdens. God loves you. He does not reject anyone who comes to him. Jesus said, "Truly, truly, I say to you, everyone who practices sin is a slave to sin. The slave does not remain in the house forever; the son remains forever. So if the Son sets you free, you will be free indeed."[197]

Maybe you can only see obstacles that prevent you from putting your trust in Jesus the Messiah. Ask God to reveal himself to you. He will do this and give you the courage to believe the good news that the Messiah already took the punishment for your sins and bore the shame. Then you will experience the freedom from needing to perform all kinds of religious duties and rituals and you will find rest for your soul (see Hebrews 4:1-11). God will fill you with his Holy Spirit, who will give you strength and lead you into his way.

If you are Jewish and reading this, please be assured that God still considers you as his chosen people. The Jewish apostle Paul is very clear when he states that the believers worldwide have not taken your place in God's heart. On the contrary, he compared very explicitly the non-Jews to the branches of the wild olive tree, while he equaled the Jews as the branches of a cultivated olive tree. If you are separated from God, He desires to bring you home and graft you onto the cultivated olive tree. He has compassion for you (see Romans 11:13-36).

God does not *only* love *you*. He also loves your distant relatives. There is a special place in the heart of Yahweh for the Arabs. You are related to them and there is nothing you can do to change that. Now is the time to make peace and settle the family quarrels. John says, "If anyone says, 'I love God,' and hates his brother, he is a liar; for he who does not love his brother whom he has seen cannot love God whom he has not seen."[198] If you have been touched by the love of God and if you have found peace with him, it is time to make peace with your family as well. By human standards, this is an impossible task. God knows this and that is why He will help you by putting his love for others in your heart. Jesus, through his death on the cross, has broken down the walls between the Jew and the non-Jew. Because of him, you now have free access to God, the Father. Because of him, you have been reconciled to God. Go now and become reconciled with your neighbor as well. No man, and indeed no nation, is inherently better than the others. We are all offspring of Adam and Eve. If you bless the other peoples, God will bless you too.

If you do not consider yourself part of any of the groups mentioned above, you are perhaps still fascinated, but not personally touched by these stories. Or maybe you believe religion is the cause of all troubles in the world.

I would like to encourage you to think about what Jesus taught. He has given us answers to life's most important questions. His commandments to forgive one another and to love our enemies are universal truths. Only then can we have real peace on earth. God knows that you do not have the strength or the love within yourself to forgive others, but He wants to help you. If you believe there is a God and that He rewards those who sincerely seek him, you will experience this. Then you will know in your heart that God is who He says He is and that He loves you.

Whichever group you fall into, it is my prayer that you will have peace with God and with the people around you. Be a blessing and you will be blessed.

How Prophecies Are Fulfilled.

After God made Adam and Eve from the dust of the earth and had blown the breath of life into them, He gave them the authority to reign over all the earth. Very quickly, something went wrong and those first two people gave away their authority to the enemy of God: Satan. God's charge to man, however, did not change. He continued to deal with man in the same way, respecting the authority He had given to them. This means that, while God used his prophets to make his will known, the people He created still played a vital role in the fulfillment of his promises. God did not breach the order He himself had established. There are many examples of prophecies in Scripture that were fulfilled only after the people petitioned God to remember his promises. Famines began, then ended after prayer, and the exiles returned from Babylon in answer to the intercessory prayers of the believers. God has given mankind authority on the earth and He is waiting for them to use it. I am convinced that the prophecies concerning the Arabs will only be fulfilled when God's children plead with him and obey him in love. Although it is certain that God will fulfill his promises, we play a role in the timing.

Throughout the centuries, God has drawn different people to these prophecies, and it seems that in these last few decades, their number has increased. I would like to end this book with examples from the 19th century and more recently.

Lord, bring the millions unto yourself.

Isaac Da Costa

In 1847, the Dutch Jewish poet Isaac Da Costa wrote a beautiful poem about Ishmael and his descendants. Below is an excerpt in English. Notice the progression from the past to the future in the last stanza.

"Mother of Ishmael!

The word that GOD hath spoken
Never hath failed the least, nor was His promise broken.
Whether in judgment threatened or as blessing given;
Whether for time and earth or for eternal heaven,
To Esau or to Jacob . . .
The patriarch prayed to GOD, while bowing in the dust:
'Oh that before thee Ishmael might live!' - His prayer, his trust.
Nor was that prayer despised, that promise left alone.
Without fulfillment. For the days shall come
When Ishmael shall bow his haughty, chieftain head
Before that Greatest Chief of Isaac's royal seed.
Thou, favored Solomon, hast first fulfillment seen
Of Hagar's promise, when came suppliant Sheba's queen.
Next, Arabia the blest brought Bethlehem's newborn King,
Her myrrh and spices, gold and offering.
Again at Pentecost they came, first-fruits of harvest vast;
When, to adore the name of JESUS, at the last
To Zion's glorious hill the nation's joy to share
The scattered flocks of Kedar all are gathered there,
Nebaioth, Ephah, Midian . . .

Then Israel shall know Whose heart their hardness broke,
Whose side they pierced, Whose curse they dared invoke.
And then, while at His feet they mourn His bitter death,
Receive His pardon . . .
Before Whose same white throne Gentile and Jew shall meet
With Parthian, Roman, Greek, the far North and the South,
From Mississippi's source to Ganges' giant mouth,
And every tongue and tribe shall join in one new song,
Redemption! Peace on earth and good-will unto men . . .
The purpose of all ages unto all ages sure. Amen.

Glory unto the Father! Glory the Lamb, once slain,
Spotless for human guilt, exalted now to reign!
And to the Holy Ghost, life-giver, whose refreshing
Makes all earth's deserts bloom with living showers of blessing!

"Mother of Ishmael!

I see thee yet once more,
Thee, under burning skies and on a wave-less shore!
Thou comfortless, soul storm-tossed, tempest-shaken,
Heart full of anguish and of hope forsaken,
Thou, too, didst find at last GOD's glory all thy stay!
He came. He spoke to thee. He made thy night His day.
As then, so now. Return to Sarah's tent
And Abraham's GOD, and better covenant,
And sing with Mary, through her Saviour free,
'GOD of my life, Thou hast looked down on me.'"[199]

Da Costa viewed Hagar's return to Sarah as a precursor for Ishmael's return to the God of Abraham. Almost two centuries ago, he expressed the hope and expectation that one day many Muslims will turn to Jesus. The message of this book is not new.

The rest of the English translation of the Dutch poem can be found at www.godlovesishmael.com/poem.

Samuel Zwemer

The American Samuel Zwemer, also nicknamed the Apostle to Islam,[200] worked in various places in the Middle East from 1890 till 1929. Zwemer wrote many books about Islam from a Christian perspective. In his book, *The Cross above the Crescent*, he wrote, "The Holy Spirit spoke by the prophets. In the Old Testament Scriptures the promises of God to Ishmael and his descendants and the spread of the Messiah's kingdom across the Arabian Peninsula have been too long neglected. Professor J. A. Montgomery calls attention in his book, *Arabia and the Bible*, to the prominence of the Arab in the Old Testament. An index of all the scriptural references to Arabia and the Arabian Bedouin life includes twenty-five books of the Old Testament and five of the New. The Messianic promises in the Psalms and in Isaiah group themselves around seven names which have from of old been identified with Arabia: Ishmael, Kedar, Nebaioth, Sheba, Seba, Midian and Ephah."[201]

Zwemer is also the one who translated the Dutch poem of Da Costa into English.

Besides the two people already mentioned in this book, Tony Maalouf and Tass Saada, the Pakistani Faisal Malick frequently refers to the prophecies in his book *The Destiny of Islam in the End times*.

Recommended Reading

For more information about God's love for the Arabs and His plan with them in the end time I warmly recommend the following books:

Maalouf, Tony. *Arabs in the Shadow of Israel: The Unfolding of God's Prophetic Plan for Ishmael's Line.* Kregel Publications, Grand Rapids MI, USA, 2006.

Malick, Faisal. *The Destiny of Islam in the End times: Understanding God's heart for the Muslim people.* Destiny Image Publishers, INC, Shippensburg, PA, USA, 2007.

Saada, Tass. *Once an Arafat Man: the true story of how a PLO sniper found a new life / Tass Saada with Dean Merrill.* Tyndale House Publishers, Inc. Illinois, USA, 2008.

Copyright Information

Unless otherwise indicated, all Scripture quotations are from The Holy Bible, English Standard Version® (ESV®), copyright © 2001 by Crossway, a publishing ministry of Good News Publishers. Used by permission. All rights reserved.

The Scripture quotation marked with GNB is from the Good News Bible © 1994 published by the Bible Societies/HarperCollins Publishers Ltd UK, Good News Bible© American Bible Society 1966, 1971, 1976, 1992. Used with permission.

The Scripture quotation marked with GW is from GOD'S WORD®, © 1995 God's Word to the Nations. Used by permission of Baker Publishing Group.

The Scripture quotation marked with KJV is from The Authorized (King James) Version. Rights in the Authorized Version in the United Kingdom are vested in the Crown. Reproduced by permission of the Crown's patentee, Cambridge University Press.

The Scripture quotations marked with NIV are from THE HOLY BIBLE, NEW INTERNATIONAL VERSION®, NIV® Copyright © 1973, 1978, 1984, 2011 by Biblica, Inc.® Used by permission. All rights reserved worldwide.

The quotation from the Qur'an marked Asad is from *The Message of the Qur'an*, Muhammad Asad, Dar al-Andalus Limited, 1980.

The quotations from the Qur'an marked Saheeh International are from Saheeh International, *The Qur'an: English Meanings and Notes*, Riyadh: Al-Muntada Al-Islami Trust, 2001-2011; Jeddah: Dar Abul-Qasim 1997-2001.

The quotation from the Qur'an marked Yusuf Ali is from *The Holy Qur'an*, translation by Abdullah Yusuf Ali, 1938, copyrighted by The Islamic Computing Centre, London, UK.

The original map of the illustrations 1, 6 and 9 has been used with permission of Eric Gaba – Wikimedia Commons user: Sting (http://commons.wikimedia.org/wiki/User:Sting).

The original map of the illustrations 2, 3, 5 and 8 is from
http://upload.wikimedia.org/wikipedia/commons/d/d1/Relief_Map_
of_Middle_East.jpg

The original map of the illustrations 4, 7 and 10 is from © ILumina, ©2002
Tyndale House Publisher

Endnotes

1   Translated from MESSIAANSE JODEN. VERGETEN EERSTELINGEN, Serie: Monografieën van Messiasbelijdende Joden. ISAAC DA COSTA, Dr. J. Haitsma Uitgeverij J.J. Groen en Zoon, Leiden, 1993
2   Genesis 16:8
3   Genesis 16:9
4   Genesis 16:10
5   Genesis 16:11a
6   Genesis 16:11b
7   Genesis 16:12
8   Genesis 15:5 NIV
9   Genesis 15:13 NIV
10   Genesis 17:20
11   Genesis 18:14
12   Genesis 21:17
13   Genesis 21:18
14   Genesis 20:17
15   Genesis 22:12
16   Genesis 25:32
17   The word 'angel' is derived from the Greek *angellos*, which means 'messenger.'
18   See for example the NIV, "He will be a wild donkey of a man; his hand will be against everyone and everyone's hand against him, and *he will live in hostility towards all his brothers.*" (italics added) *New International Version*, 1973
19   Maalouf 2006:67
20   Matthew 28:20
21   Based on Job 1:21
22   Job 39:5-8
23   The word "LORD" in capitals stands for Yahweh in Hebrew
24   Deuteronomy 6:4-5
25   Numbers 6:24-26
26   Psalm 72:9
27   Psalm 72:11
28   Psalm 72:1-2
29   Psalm 72:7-11
30   Psalm 72:12-14
31   Psalm 72:15-19
32   See Proverbs 9:10
33   Proverbs 8:17
34   Based on Exodus 3:14-15
35   1 Kings 8:41, 42b-43a
36   1 Kings 9:3
37   Genesis 12:2-3
38   Psalm 22:25-26
39   Psalm 22:27-28
40   Psalm 72:10b, 15a
41   1 Kings 10:8-9
42   Psalm 72:18-19
43   1 Kings 11:11-12
44   2 Chronicles 20:6
45   2 Chronicles 20:7

46 2 Chronicles 20:10-11
47 2 Chronicles 20:12
48 2 Chronicles 20:15
49 2 Chronicles 20:16-17
50 Psalm 114 GNB
51 Exodus 14:13
52 2 Chronicles 20:21
53 Psalm 83
54 Psalm 83:11-12
55 Psalm 83:5-8
56 We find the following people named Ishmael in the Bible: one of the six sons of Azel, a descendant of king Saul (1 Chronicles 8:38), a member of the royal family at the time of Jeremiah (2 Kings 25:25), the father of a top judge at the time of king Jehoshaphat (2 Chronicles 19:11), an army official of king Joash (2 Chronicles 23:1) and a priest during the time of the exile (Ezra 10:22). This shows that the name Ishmael was common among the Israelites
57 Maalouf 2006: 136-144
58 Syrians, Sidonians, Moabites, Ammonites and Philistines: Judges 10:6, 16:23; 1 Kings 11:5,33 and Edomite: 2 Chronicles 25:14,20
59 See for instance Judges 3:12-14, 10:8-9, 11:12-15; Jeremiah 49:1; Amos 1:13; Zephaniah 2:8 (Ammon), Judges 3:12-14; Zephaniah 2:8 (Moab), Ezekiel 36:10,11 (Edom) and 2 Chronicles 20:1-23 (all three)
60 This is true for all Arab Muslims and for many Arab Christians
61 Ezekiel 27:21
62 Ezekiel 25:1-4
63 Ezekiel 25:5
64 Ezekiel 25:9-11
65 Isaiah 2:2-4
66 Ezekiel 35:3-15
67 Proverbs 5:1
68 Isaiah 42:11a ESV, Isaiah 42:11b KJV
69 Isaiah 42:1-4
70 Isaiah 42:5-9
71 Isaiah 42:10
72 Isaiah 60:1-3
73 Isaiah 60:4-7
74 Isaiah 62:1-2
75 Isaiah 62:3-4
76 Isaiah 49:5-6
77 Isaiah 21:13-17 NIV
78 Isaiah 9:2-6
79 Jeremiah 49:28-32
80 Isaiah 35:1-2 NIV
81 Isaiah 35:6b-7 NIV
82 Isaiah 35:8-10 NIV
83 Isaiah 35:3-6 NIV
84 Isaiah 32:15-17 NIV
85 Isaiah 32:18 NIV
86 Isaiah 32:1-4 NIV
87 from Isaiah 42:1-11
88 Isaiah 9:2
89 Isaiah 9:6-7
90 Numbers 24:17
91 Hosea 2:14
92 Hosea 2:18b
93 Hosea 2:19-20

94   Hosea 2:21-23a
95   Hosea 2:23b
96   Micah 5:2
97   Isaiah 16:5
98   Isaiah 9:7
99   Isaiah 9:2
100   Isaiah 9:6b
101   Matthew 2:13
102   Proverbs 3:5-6
103   Habakkuk 2:4
104   Exodus 34:6
105   Micah 5:2-4
106   Numbers 23:19
107   Luke 3:11
108   Luke 3:14
109   John 1:23
110   Isaiah 35:1a/8a
111   See John 1:26-27, 30
112   Luke 3:22b
113   See Luke 3:16
114   Matthew 5:43-48
115   Matthew 5:38-39
116   Luke 19:38a
117   Based on Luke 1:50-55, 68-70 and Galatians 1:3-5
118   Acts 2:14-21
119   Based on Acts 2:22-24
120   Acts 2:25b-28
121   Based on Acts 2:29-32
122   Based on Acts 2:33-35
123   Acts 2:36
124   Based on Acts 2:38-39
125   Based on Isaiah 42:1-4
126   Isaiah 52:13-15
127   Isaiah 53:4-9
128   Isaiah 53:10-12
129   Acts 9:3-6
130   Isaiah 53:5
131   Isaiah 9:6-7
132   Isaiah 60:5-7
133   Isaiah 42:11a ESV, Isaiah 42:11b KJV
134   Isaiah 42:1-4
135   Matthew 9:12 NIV
136   Isaiah 32:15-17
137   See Matthew 16:16-17
138   Surah 3:55 Asad
139   "None can alter the words of Allah." Surah 6:34 Saheeh International. See also
       Surah 6:114-115, 10:64 and 18:27
140   Surah 5:82 Saheeh International
141   See for instance Surah 4:157
142   Surah 1:5-6 Saheeh International
143   Ibid 7
144   Lamentations 3:22
145   Lamentations 3:25-26
146   John 1:16-17
147   Surah 10:94, Saheeh International
148   John 1:1

149   Surah 4:171, Yusuf Ali
150   Job 39:5-8
151   Romans 9:25-26
152   Romans 10:19-21
153   Romans 11:11
154   Romans 11:25b
155   Romans 11:26
156   Romans 10:20
157   Romans 11:25 GW
158   hopeforishmael.org/about-us/accessed on December 31, 2020
159   Galatians 4:29
160   scriptoriumdaily.com/calling-ishmael-tony-maalouf-at-biola /Accessed on December 31, 2020
161   ibid
162   ibid
163   ibid
164   Matthew 5:43-48
165   Ezekiel 35:10-11
166   Matthew 5:43-48
167   In the Qur'an Surah 5:45, in the Bible Exodus 21:24, Leviticus 24:20, Deuteronomy 19:21
168   Philippians 1:6
169   Well-known Arabic hymn based on Psalm 103
170   Isaiah 35:1-2 NIV
171   Isaiah 35:3-4 NIV
172   Isaiah 35:5-6a NIV
173   Isaiah 35: 6b-7 NIV
174   Isaiah 35:8-10 NIV
175   John 14:9
176   Isaiah 19:23-25
177   Translated from Arabic from the *Holy Bible Old Testament Commentary*, Father Tadros Yacoub Malaty on Isaiah 19:18-25 and Isaiah 32:15-18, accessed at st-takla.org
178   part of Surah 4:171, Yusuf Ali
179   Acts 2:17-18 NIV
180   2 Corinthians 13:14
181   John 10:10
182   2 Peter 3:9b NIV
183   Romans 10:17
184   en.wikipedia.org/wiki/Secularism_in_Israel   and   jcpa.org/dje/articles2/howrelisr.htm
185   See for instance the hadiths Saheeh Muslim *Book 041, #6985*, Abu Dawud Book 37, #4310 and Saheeh Bukhari Volume 3, Book 43, #656
186   See Genesis 3:15
187   John 14:9
188   John 16:23
189   Surah 1:6 Saheeh International
190   John 8:33-34
191   John 8:35-36
192   2 Peter 3:9
193   See for instance Matthew 10:8 and Luke 12:48
194   Luke 18:25-27
195   A modern example of restoration of nature through good care based upon Biblical principles (where the initiator may or may not have been inspired by the Bible) is the *Löss-plaşteau* in China. (Environmental Education Media Project led by John D. Liu.) youtu.be/UAmai36XJDk

196   Genesis 12:3a
197   John 8:33-36
198   1 John 4:20
199   Zwemer, Samuel M. *The Cross above the Crescent*. Grand Rapids: Zondervan Publishing House, 1916. p280-281
200   en.wikipedia.org/wiki/Samuel_Marinus_Zwemer
201   Zwemer p275-276

Timeline of Abraham and his descendants
1900 B.C.
1850 B.C.
1800 B.C.
1750 B.C.
1700 B.C.
Sarah
† 1859
127
Abraham
† 1821
175
Ishmael
Isaac
† 1773
137
Jacob
† 1716
180
Joseph
† 1689
147
1921 Abraham to Canaan
1910 birth of Ishmael
1897 birth of Isaac foretold + circumcision
1896 birth of Isaac
1893 Hagar and Ishmael sent away
1856 Isaac marries Rebekah
1836 birth of Jacob and Esau
1796 Esau marries 2 Canaanites
1759 Jacob to Haran
Esau marries Basemath
1752 Jacob marries Leah en Rachel
1745 birth of Joseph
1739 Jacob returns to Canaan
1728 Joseph sold
1715 Joseph in command of Egypt
1708 beginning of 7 years of drought
1706 Jacob moves to Egypt
Legend:
175   age reached
† 1821   year of death

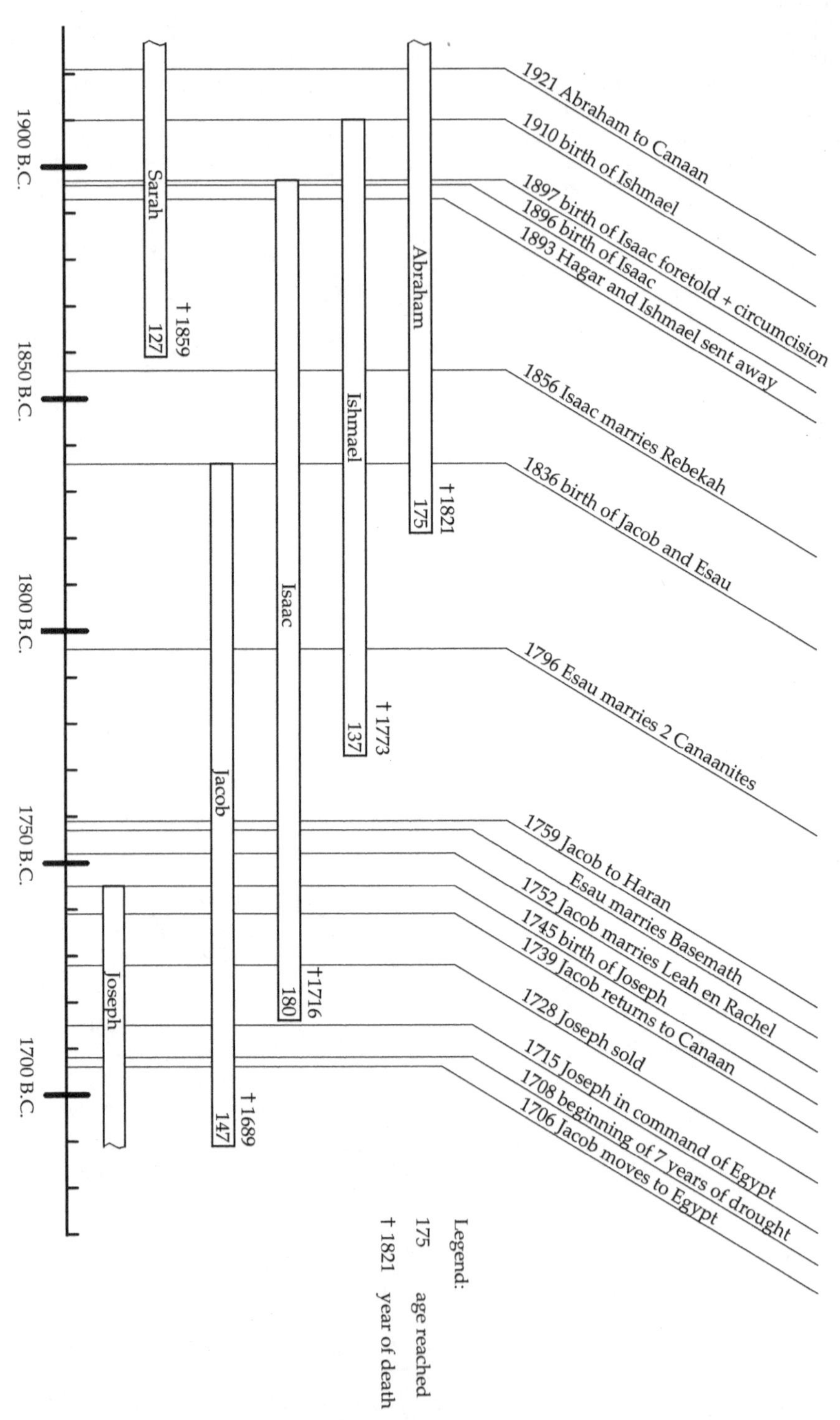

380

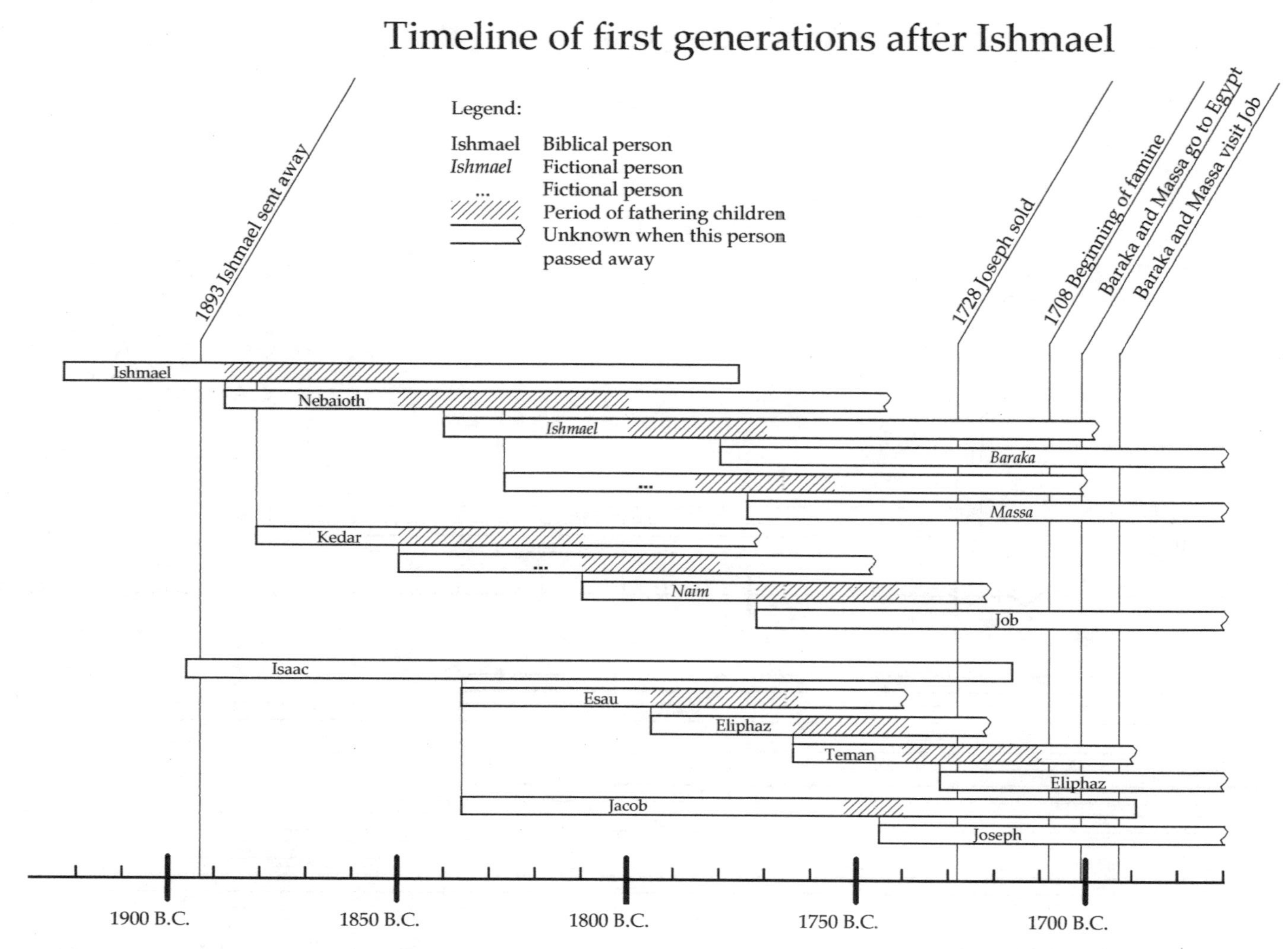

Timeline of first generations after Ishmael

Timeline of Jesus and Arabs

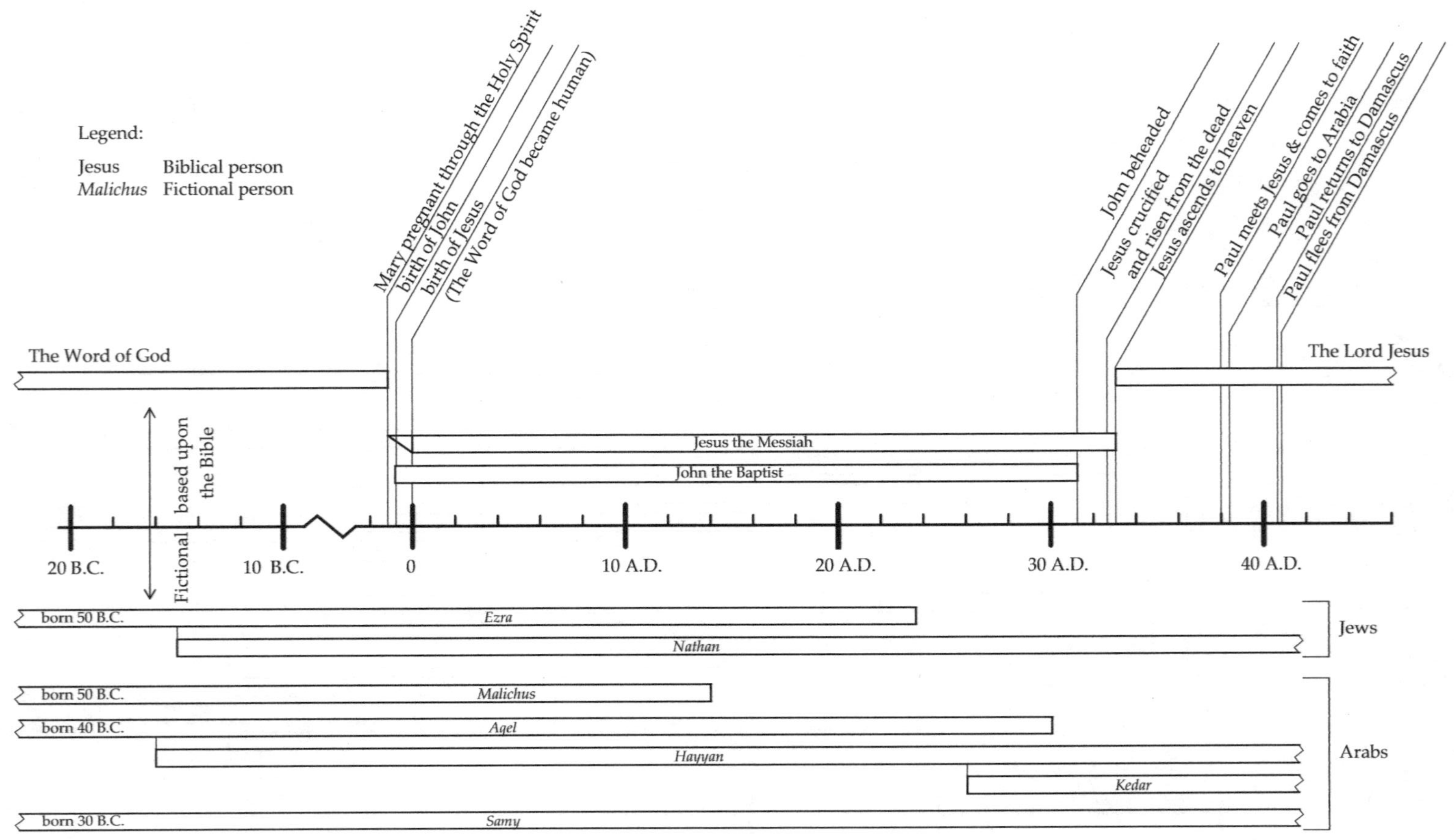